National bestselling author David McCaleb delivers a thriller like none other, opening our eyes to a realm ever present, but thinly veiled.

A World Not His Own...

Michael is suddenly drawn back in time by the spirit of his dead sister to the age when Vikings ventured to North America. He finds himself in the body of a Norseman and a member of a raiding party tasked with rescuing their chieftain's kidnapped daughter. He soon discovers a chilling link between her and his own world. In his journey back to the present, he battles warring natives, shapeshifting demons, and the insecurities of his past.

A World Torn Apart...

Kiona, the daughter of a powerful Mi'kmaq shaman, struggles against her deceitful mother whose actions threaten the peace between her tribe, their Abenaki neighbors, and the newly arrived Vikings. Will she choose to remain loyal to her tribe, or instead to help Michael free his Viking sister?

Vestmen's Gale is a story of sacrifice, redemption, and purpose.

Novels by National Bestselling Author David McCaleb

RED OPS Thriller Series

RECALL

RELOAD

RECON

Vestmen's Gale

Son of Blackbeard (coming soon)

Vestmen's Gale

DAVID McCALEB

Sonia,

Thank you for your interest and support. Congratulations on the win. All the best!

— David McCaleb

Vestmen's Gale is a work of historical fiction. Places and incidents are inspired from historical context. Names, characters, and events are all products of the author's imagination. Any resemblance to actual persons, living or dead, or actual events is purely coincidental.

Published by Sunset Point Publishing

ISBN 978-1-7362857-1-8

Cover design by Abigail McCaleb, www.abbygallery.com
Cover photo of Viking ship *Islendingur* by Antonio Otto Rabasca

Dedication

To my wonderful daughter, Abigail. Who would think that the brainstorming sessions with your creative writing class would spark the plot for this work? I will always cherish how we developed the characters and outline together. When it was time for my next book, I couldn't get this story out of my head; it had to be written. Thank you for your unwavering belief in and continual support of this novel. I love you!

Every novel has at least two stories. The first is what is happening on the page, whereas the next, though unwritten, is what the book is truly about. If I have done my job well, you will enjoy both.

- David McCaleb

Contents

Chapter 1 – Gabby's Call

Cape Elizabeth, Maine

I snapped around at the sound of my dead sister's laugh. I searched the waving stalks of grass atop the sand dune, from where her voice had come. Gabby had been gone five years now, almost to the day. But sometimes I still caught her excited shout in a throng on a soccer field, or even in a gaggle of geese flying overhead. Or, as just now, her high-pitched laugh in...what? There was nothing there.

This time it had been clear, as real as terror when waking from a nightmare. Gripping. I jumped from the deck of our family's vacation bungalow and sprinted up the sand dune. Tall stalks of grass sliced my bare shins and knees as I ran to the top and peered over at a thick forest of oaks and maples. My calf cramped. I grimaced and pushed the ball of my foot against a rock to stretch it out. As a cross-country runner, I'd averaged five miles a day during school. But now, three weeks into summer, I hadn't been keeping up and my body enjoyed reminding me.

Her name had been Tabitha. Most had called her Tabby. But because of her incessant chatter, I'd christened her Gabby.

"Whatcha doin', Michael?" Nikki, my other sister, asked. The one still alive. The one I could hug and harass and irritate. She was younger. Fourteen. A little older than Gabby had been when she'd disappeared. And just as talkative. Hadn't noticed her standing up here.

She slid next to me, head barely past my waist. That thick mop of hair even looked like Gabby's, wavy as a current washed sand bar at low tide. Though hers had been fiery copper red, while Nikki's hung coal black and shiny. Like mine. And my mane would be just as unruly, if I ever let it grow out. Funny how Nikki looked more like me than Gabby had, my fraternal twin. *Huh...* Gabby would've been nineteen in a couple of weeks.

Nikki tore off a chunk from a slice of bread and tossed it into the sky. A pair of circling seagulls dove, colliding in midair. The loser gave a harsh cry. That must've been what I'd heard before. But it had sounded just like Gabby's high-pitched cackle.

1

I wrapped an arm around Nikki's shoulder. "Look at all those gulls. You attract those flying bums the same way you do boys? A little tease?"

She kicked my shin, but it was only a halfhearted tap. "I'm *not* a tease!"

"Come on." I balled a fist and tagged her shoulder. "You're the biggest flirt in the Outer Banks. Admit it. How many boyfriends you go through last school year?"

"Pfft." Her eyes rolled away, as if she suddenly found the forest fascinating.

"Seriously! You don't even know, do you? Bet you've kissed every guy in your class."

Her eyebrows arched, and she punched my stomach. Not a bad swing. "Someone's gotta make up for you. Last time you kissed a girl you were twelve."

I huffed. The comment hurt more than her fist. If only I possessed half her spirit. She never cared what anyone thought. Self-confident, just like Gabby had been. Here I was about to head off to Duke and I hadn't had a date for years. Not that I hadn't tried. Girls just thought I was a creep. All I'd done was joke with a couple of them like I did with Nikki...and Gabby. They'd always understood it was out of fondness. But word had spread through school I was a cocky jerk and it stuck. That was that.

Another laugh, this time behind me. It was echoed by a distant rumble that rolled up the dune. I turned to see a towering thunderhead dividing the northern sky. Morning rays illuminated its brilliant white peak that stretched till it seemed to lean over us, tall enough to churn hailstones. Flashes of lightning streaked from the beast's dark underbelly, sliced away by the string-tight line of the water's horizon. One flash seemed to leave a distant white dot below it, suspended by the brush strokes of dark rain. A sail, boaters probably enjoying the last few minutes of calm before being overtaken by the squall. Hard to tell from this distance, but they were headed our way. Directly on the Atlantic coast, our dock at the bottom of the dune was the only pier for a good distance in either direction. The nearest harbor at least two miles south. I squinted at the tiniest speck of orange atop the sail. A distress flag? No kidding. They'd never make it to shore in time. No choice, now.

Make fast and ride it through.

I pointed my chin toward the water. "I'm going to head down to the dock. We've got time before the storm gets here. Gonna get a better look at that boat."

Nikki shielded her eyes with a flat hand. "They're about to be swallowed."

I hiked down the path toward our blue clapboard house that faced east, toward the rising sun. Nikki shadowed me, slipping over rocks. She trailed a growing avian fan club, like her boyfriends back home. Their tails were tipped in black, as if dipped afresh in an inkwell each morning. Their songs sounded so much like Gabby's laugh, not like the gulls back home in North Carolina. Were the ones up here in Maine a different breed? They were cleaner, even. Feathers neat and in place.

Maybe life could be better in a different location. A new start. At Duke, maybe?

Nah...no escaping myself. The birds endured harsh winters up here. More likely they died before reaching the haggard beach-bum stage of the ones back home.

I turned the corner around the house's wide deck, distant sail and orange banner still in view, and continued down toward the shoreline. Maine beaches were the very definition of lame. Mostly just a bunch of boulders and stones piled with dank seaweed. Why'd we drive every year all the way from Hatteras to vacation here? Though I considered the hill we'd just hiked over a *sand dune*, in reality the berm was no more than packed dirt and gravel. Nothing like the clean, sandy stretches of the Outer Banks. Yesterday when Dad had tossed me the keys to the pickup and we were on the way to Barne's Pizzeria, we'd passed a metal warehouse with *Courter's Curling Club* on the side. Curling? How to know you live too far north—your club sport involves sliding pumpkin-sized granite rocks on slabs of ice. Then again, they'd made it into an Olympic sport...

The sail seemed to wink, as if obscured by tall waves.

"You should ask Alice out when we get home," my social coordinator persisted. "You run with her brother and she—"

"Thinks I'm a creep." I stopped and held up hands in surrender. "Remember? She was the one standing near me after the race where we won state." I'd just finished, and the manager had given me a huge cup of ice water. I'd raised it to my lips when her brother ran across the line and crashed into me. It dumped down the front of Alice's white T-shirt, making it instantly transparent. And the frigid water had a sudden effect. I was still out of breath, delirious with oxygen deprivation, and my first reaction was to brush the cascading liquid off her. The gesture had been captured by our school photographer in a shot that, even I had to admit, made it look as if I was molesting her. The paper never printed it, but the photo leaked and went viral online.

Nikki snorted. "Yeah. I'd forgotten about that one. Maybe she has too."

"Nah. Girls like that don't forget being embarrassed." I rubbed my cheek, remembering where her slap had landed. I'd done everything to apologize, but she wouldn't hear it.

Below us, at the bottom of the hill, a rising tide lapped at the rocks. We picked our way between sea grass clumps and brambles, then gazed over a flashing trail of silver water that led to a low, burnt-yellow sun. Amazing how early light over the ocean always bathed the landscape in golden tones. A cool breeze chilled the sweat beading on my arms, and I shivered. The sail barely maintained distance from the monster storm, and still seemed to be headed our direction. However, the squall stood distant enough that it'd be a little time before arriving. The cars were already in the garage, so nothing more in preparation could be done.

Nikki pointed to it, a slice of bread still in her grasp. "That looks pure evil. See how dark it is beneath it?"

We skidded onto the gray weathered wooden dock that stretched across wet black boulders. Nikki's light, sand-scratching footfalls scurried behind me to catch up. What a socialite. Couldn't stand being alone. This was the same pier where Gabby had disappeared five years ago. Her body had never been found. Detectives presumed she'd fallen off and drowned in an outgoing tide. But she'd been much too strong a swimmer. I had been with her that entire morning, paddling around in sea kayaks. I'd only run up to the cottage to use the bathroom, but returned to an empty dock. She'd always been so protective of me even though I was her older brother...by fifteen minutes. And the one time she needed me, I'd been absent. Ever since then, nothing in life seemed complete.

I drew a breath. The dank seaweed musk here was less pungent than the sulfur marsh scent endured at home around Albemarle Sound. I stopped before a long aluminum gangway, the ramp leading down to a floating dock that rose and fell with the tide. Such a contraption wasn't needed in Hatteras, with its four-foot swing. Here, jagged granite boulders formed a breakwater a distance out, protecting the structure, placed by some megarich playwright a couple of decades ago. Mom claimed the screenplay for *Jaws* had been penned here, in our family cottage.

A wave crashed nearby and someone giggled. Fifty yards distant, a flash of red jumped from the bank onto the rocky beach. Not Gabby. But Christine! From Ontario.

Nikki shoved my shoulder. "Your girlfriend," she teased.

"As if," I mumbled.

However, since we were ten, our vacations had always overlapped. She'd been bright and happy no matter when I saw her. I'd fostered an attraction to her ever since I could remember, though we'd never spoken beyond casual greetings. Two years ago, I'd finally worked up the courage to introduce myself. Christine had smiled and talked a bit, but never hinted at any real interest. Turns out she was a runner too. But like a coward, I hadn't approached her again that entire summer. Why couldn't I be more outgoing like Gabby? Or even Nikki?

Wait. I slapped the handrail. No more of that! It was a new summer, and I'd be on my own soon. The old me was dying. I could be *anyone* I wanted in this place, starting now. Working oyster cages on the water with Dad the last few years, I'd finally started filling out. The muscles on my arms and back were wiry and taut. Though Mom had said girls really didn't care about stuff like that. "At least no girls *you* should be interested in." Just what the mother of a gawky cross-country geek would say.

I forced my gaze back up the beach. Christine turned to face the bank and *wow!* She'd filled out even more than I had. Was that even her? The spaghetti straps of a fire-red bikini top stretched to their limit. *Don't stare!* But oh, my goodness, it was hard not to notice. Why did girls think it's OK to walk around in view of everyone while wearing less-than-underwear?

Christine raised her arms, and a kid in pink jumped from the grass into them. Her little sister, in a life jacket. I laughed, recalling the child's playful spirit. How last summer she'd tossed rocks into piles, trying to make a Maine sandcastle.

Christine glanced over, set her sister down, and waved. I looked behind us, but no one else was on the beach. *She's waving to me!* Like a dork, I lifted my hand slower than when answering a question in world history. By then the two had their heads down, already stepping over rocks, making their way toward the water.

Nikki turned on one heel and sauntered back up the dock. With a toss of her head and a flip of one hand, she said, "Handled that like a pro, big brother. You could jump into a barrel full of boobs and still come up sucking your own thumb."

"Watch your mouth!" I called after her.

She turned her head and rolled her eyes.

I sighed. *Pity Mom and Dad next year when that girl gets into high school.* She was trying to grow up entirely too fast, and she hadn't a clue. I twisted again to the approaching squall, sailboat still barely outrunning it, distress flag blown straight as a board. *Maybe I should go tell Christine about the storm.*

Hey! Great to see you again. You may want to head inside. There's a storm coming.

Oh, you mean that huge thunderhead with lightning streaming below it? Hadn't noticed.

No. That wouldn't work. I'd wait a little longer. Then if they didn't go in, I'd wander over and mention...something. But what? How should I—

A flash of light and *boom!*

More flickers popped from the advancing threat, blazing dock poles like camera flashes. The snarl of thunder wheeled across the water in a constant stream. The storm was closer than I thought. I should've followed Nikki back to the cottage, but I still had a few minutes, and wanted to catch another glance at Christine. I stepped down the gangway, willing myself to be casual, to not crane my neck her direction. Instead, my eyes caught the boat. It was moving quickly, and still toward us.

The floating dock rose and sank on gathering waves, sides screeching against thick wooden guide pilings as I passed them. How did the contractor ever sink those huge logs into the earth with all the rocks down there? At the end, I sat in a lone Adirondack bolted to the deck, my back to Christine's house, and studied the approaching vessel.

It was close enough now to see that the sail billowed fatly, like in old seafaring movies. Except I'd seen local vessels like that before: *Elizabeth II* down on Roanoke Island and others at the tall ship festival at Wilmington. This one was smaller. Long and skinny, with the sail set low, the bottom of it just over the gunwales. An old tender vessel? Maybe some antique boat show was nearby. And the flag wasn't a distress signal, but a red-orange square with black figures.

A cold drop of rain splashed my face. *Crack!* Another struck my arm like a hot needle and I gasped. "Ouch." Bits of ice slurry ran from the red mark on my skin. Sleet, really? And the wind was picking up. If this storm *were* bringing hail, I'd better get inside. I turned to the beach and Christine was out of sight. Smart girl. I trotted toward the gangway, the sections of the floating dock already whipping like a rope. This storm was going to bring waves worse than the nor'easter Dad and I had weathered last summer on the sound, working our oyster cages. I'd saved every penny Dad had paid me and put it into my own equipment and seed. Double-lashing the floats to an anchor line that afternoon, I'd determined nature wasn't going to destroy my investment.

I stood still, deck bucking below my body. The ship was less than a quarter mile away now. Were they just making a beeline for land and going to run it ashore? Maybe old-fashioned vessels like that couldn't be steered well in strong winds. But wouldn't a replica have a backup motor, to help it out of trouble?

A wave broke a few feet away. Or maybe a striped bass or school of mackerel were hunting, stirring up littler prey. A drop in the barometer often meant feeding frenzies.

Smack!

Ice shards blasted my legs. A golf ball–sized hailstone had crashed on the dock, scattering crystals in a cone. Red dots like measles began to welt on my shins. One of those things could knock me out! But still, the boat. It could be in trouble. If it wrecked on the rocks, I could help the crew to land, get them inside till this thing passed. I couldn't just leave them.

Across white-crested surf, long sticks jutted from the sides of the vessel. Waving, like the wings of a stingray. Oars rowing! There must've been a dozen on each side between round, brightly colored shields mounted so high they obscured the view of the deck. A replica Viking ship. *Must be thirty people on that thing!*

Crack! A hailstone struck my big toe like a framing hammer.

"Ahh!" I knelt, squeezed it in my palm, and blood and ice ran between my fingers. Between gritted teeth, I growled, "Gonna lose that nail for certain."

A roar rose as if from a jet about to take off. Several hundred yards out, behind the approaching ship, the water was aboil. *Oh no.* I stood and limped toward the gangway.

The boat headed straight for the end of the dock, probably hoping to tie off. They really had no other choice.

And neither did I.

I turned back and hustled to the end of the T. Rifle shots of thunder cracked every few seconds. The deck screeched against the pilings like the call of a ghost. This storm was altogether violent. I knelt to maintain balance. Who was steering that thing? No crew stuck their head over the shields to navigate. No one stood to toss a bowline to me as the ship closed in. I snatched up a coil of dock rope and twisted a honda knot, forming a lasso. The other end was already fast to a large cleat. *Should hold.* The oars lifted straight up like a line of wharf pilings and thunked down as the rowers shipped them.

"Lower that sail or it's going to tear loose!" I yelled.

The boat jerked to a halt at the edge of the dock, bobbing two feet away in its berth. *Pilot must've dropped an anchor.* An approach precise as a drill team. The oily scent of some rancid, spoiled meat blasted my chest. No cleats on the vessel's gunwales, so I tossed the loop over the ship's tall stempost, which curved along the leading edge of the bow like a swan's neck. A spiral decoration in light-colored wood crowned it, gouges from a drawl knife or scooped chisel littering its surface. But the long, flat strakes that shaped the boat's sides were dark with a preserving oil. Gouges revealed light, fresh timber, though, as if it had recently been run aground. The owner must've really wanted an authentic look.

The unrelenting churn of hail marched toward us.

I ran down the starboard side and beat on round shields. Some metal, others wooden, each painted in mismatched colors with heads of wolves or wings of a hawk. "Let's go! Get out!" I pointed up the hill toward the cottage. "Inside!"

No one stirred. Were they all sick? Too weak to move? They'd better figure out how or the hail was going to chew them up.

A seagull's cry sounded from somewhere within the vessel. Amazing I could even hear it over the roar of the wall of ice grinding toward us. It called again, but this time no seagull. Gabby's laugh.

What? My chest tightened. Maybe I was dreaming, fallen asleep in the Adirondack. My ears must be hearing seagulls, my brain thinking it was—

Smack!

Pain seared my shoulder. "Ahh!" Ice spray blew into my eyes. I gripped the spot where the stone had struck me. The pain was real, for certain. I wasn't sleeping through this. And Gabby's laugh had been as clear as life.

A huge hailstone crashed against a shield and knocked it into the boat, permitting a glimpse behind. I gripped a greasy gunwale and hoisted myself up. Balancing on my stomach, I leaned in and stared at sparse deck boards lashed to rough-hewn beams. The entire ship's skeleton was laid bare to sight. The rancid stink of the wood's oily coating filled my lungs. From stem to stern, she was empty.

Chapter 2 – Vestmen's Gale

I rolled head over heels into the boat, falling between deck boards and splashing into bilge water pooled about the keel. Must've lost my balance, though it had seemed cold fingers had gripped my skin. The vessel surged forward. I shoved myself up. Grabbing a beam, I braced myself upright. Another surge, this time with groans of wood against wood, like pine trunks during a windstorm. The cicada moan of rope stretching. And men. The grunts of jocks pushing a football sled. The sweaty stench of a locker room mixed with...wet wool.

Rowers lined each side of the ship. They sat on rough-hewn planks, bracing their feet against the legs of the bench ahead of them. They must've just...appeared. *No way I could've missed them before.* I stared, unable to comprehend the sight. Linen and leather wrapped their waists. Loose, coarsely woven black and brown trousers covered their legs. Bare, suntanned backs and sinewy arms strained against oars in unison, their growls blending into a coxswain's rhythm. Muscles bulged against their load in synchrony, as if the entire ship were a behemoth preparing to plunge below the surface.

Must be a professional team from a Norsemen's museum headed to a boat show. That's how the tall ship festival had been, folks dressed in period garb. But these guys were built like athletes, and each sported a beard, longer ones braided or bound below the chin with a thong of leather.

The navigator was a huge gym rat with a dappled gray-and-white wolfskin draped over his shoulders. He stood astern leaning against an oar lashed to the gunwale as a tiller. White hair tufted straight up from his scalp in a topknot, like a ponytailed child pretending to be a unicorn. The sun was sinking low behind him in the west. But that was crazy—it was morning. Had they turned around? No, we were still headed away from the storm.

Topknot narrowed his eyes, then stomped toward me down a gangplank lashed between the rows of men. He grabbed me by the hair and lifted me from the bilge with one arm. My scalp seared, like it was about to tear loose. Vertebrae in my neck popped as I hung like a doll.

9

I pointed toward the rocks. "You guys need to—"

Crack! I gazed over the shields at an empty beach. But I hadn't turned my head. Needles stung my jaw, and my nose throbbed. *He'd hit me!*

The huge man tossed me onto one plank and lifted a long oar like a mere stick. I raised my arms to deflect the coming blow. He'd crack me like a twig. Instead, he shoved the grip into my chest. "Put your back into it, witch-boy!" His voice was gruff and hoarse. "Pitch another wave with your paddle and I'll cut your corpse into chum."

The words came to my ears as gibberish, a foreign language, like a squall of German and Old English. Still, I somehow understood their meaning.

I hadn't done anything wrong. All I'd tried to do was help these guys ashore, but one of them must've pulled me into the boat. Must've had ice in my eyes. Yeah, that's why I hadn't seen them. I stood, several inches taller than him, bent my neck till our noses almost touched, and yelled, "You can't just—"

Crack!

This time, I'd seen the fist coming but had only managed to close my eyes before it struck the other side of my face. Red dots floated in the air, as if projected upon the sail. My chest warmed in anger, but another swing and I'd be knocked out. Mind numb, I fumbled with the oar. Didn't he tell me to row? Anything to stop the beating.

Topknot gripped a thick twist of rope, turned his back, and stretched a long arm toward the blackness behind us. "Row! All you dogs. Your life depends on it." He drew a short bronze-colored sword from a sheath of leather, its leading edge gouged deeply. "If the storm catches us and spares your life, make certain I won't!" Wind blasted his beard and ponytail, whipping them like flags in a gale. "Thor sends his blessing to speed us down the coast. Now prove yourself men! But know he'd rather chew you up for dinner." He jumped back to the small deck astern, sheathed his sword, and gripped the tiller again.

The butt of an oar jammed into my back. "Get rowing, Matok! Halfdan wants a reason to kill you. Don't give him one." I peered over my shoulder at a tall, pale man with shiny skin and a thick, curly black beard. He was tugging on the oar behind mine. One of his little fingers was completely missing. Lightning flashed, reflected in his eyes. His broad smile was absent several teeth. On the return stroke he jabbed the oar into me again. "Row! We need you." His arms were thick, but flabbier than those of the rest of the crew. A paunch hung over pants sewn of brown deerskin, bound around his waist with a rope of flax.

I glanced at the long handle he gripped. How was it even possible to manage one of those things? Must be twenty feet long—and solid wood. Dad had always maintained the motors well. I'd never had to use an oar on a boat. But if it kept me from being beat unconscious...

I turned, and lightning flashed behind Halfdan as he strained against the tiller. That's the name Little Finger had called him. Thunder boomed, reverberating through my chest, never so loud as then, the shock wave a blast of heat. The line of boiling water still churned a few hundred yards behind us. There was no escape. If I jumped overboard, the passing hail would knock me out. I'd drown in the rough seas. Maybe we could stay ahead long enough for it to die out.

Make fast and ride it through.

Kidnapped or otherwise, I had no choice. I shoved the pole across the gunwale in front of a hook-shaped oar stop till it hovered over the water the same distance as the others. Its weight less than I'd expected. Leaning forward, I tried to match my rhythm to the bobbing, sweat-streaked back of the man before me and the growls of the others. I dropped the end into the water and pulled back. Far too easy. Must not have lowered the paddle enough. Peering between shields, I dipped the oar, pulled back, and a miniature whirlpool formed at the tip. Just like everyone else. I was rowing, all right.

I adjusted my grip and—*Wow!* These couldn't be my hands. They were huge. Thick calluses bridged my palms and ran down my fingers, skin dense as a leathery turtle shell. My arms were long and wiry. Lumpy biceps coiled on each stroke. A cold breeze blasted my chest, bare and sun splotched. I glanced down. My stomach tensed flat as a board, skin ridged tight across it. *What?* My belly button was an outie!

I stood and glanced at my own foreign body. Another blow sent me sprawling forward, this one to the back of my thigh. Little Finger again. "Keep rowing. If not for your own hide, then for ours."

I spun and held up a clenched fist. "I swear I'll break your oar in two and bludgeon your fat ass with it if you hit me again!" I clamped a hand over my mouth. *Where'd that come from?*

Little Finger smirked. "The way you're rowing now, my sister could pull better. Get with us."

I glanced at Halfdan, who was scowling back at me. I sat and coordinated my strokes. In a couple of minutes, my back burned across my shoulders and down my arms. A pain as intense as when my gut cramped last year at a cross-country meet. But I was already used to this new sensation. A familiar heat. This body—whatever it was, whoever I was—enjoyed the rhythm. I could keep this up all day.

I inhaled, and my lungs swelled larger than bellows. The bow crashed into a wave, and salt water peppered my back, stinging like beach sand in a gale. With every breath my body recharged, as if the air were rich with oxygen, forcing itself into my blood. With each stroke, the ship lunged forward, almost breaking out on plane. Was I dreaming? No. I'd never been more alive than at this moment. I was certain of it.

Gabby's laugh floated to me as if upon a lapping wave, from the direction of the shoreline. A flash from her copper red hair zipped between the trunks of soaring pines atop the berm. But wait. What happened to the hardwoods? And no houses. *Where am I?* The trees grew all the way up to the water's edge, massive, brown, and tall as radio towers. Like the stories in American history class, how many coastal virgin forests had looked before being cleared. No underbrush sprouted beneath, so I gazed deep into the forest, following the distant bounce of her red hair as she turned inland and disappeared.

Had the spirit of my dead sister called me to this place? We'd always enjoyed a close bond, not the typical siblings-are-evil relationship my friends complained about. When we'd been ten, she'd told me to quit being a wimp when I'd hooked a four-foot mako. Even grabbed the rod and finished reeling it in. She was my twin, her bright red hair matched only by her fiery personality. My curls, black and dull as my own.

Had her spirit escaped to another world? Then found a way to bring me here?

Our boat veered toward land. Halfdan aimed two fingers at a spot on the shore where the rocks were smaller. "We'll beach. Pull ashore. Wait out the storm beneath shields."

The jagged stones appeared only slightly less hostile than the crags that rose on either side. As if this were a new land, still with rough, sharp edges. What if a gust blew us off the mark? We could survive under shields, but the vessel would lose rigging and sail at a minimum.

I craned my neck around and—Froggy Rock! A huge boulder cracked in two that resembled a squatting amphibian. Only a half mile down the beach from our vacation home. I'd taken Nikki exploring there just yesterday—she was the one who'd named it. Only now, it was missing its slimy greenish-brown coat. *I'm still in the same place. But a different time?* The huge trees. Sharper rocks. Were these real Vikings? If so, I could be a millennia in the past. Either way, in another mile we'd hit Prouts Neck, with its towering southerly cliffs that dropped straight into the water. A much better harbor than a small patch of rocky beach.

My shout was hoarse. The words I bellowed out sounded like muddled nonsense, in the same accent as Little Finger's and Halfdan's. Still, my mind knew their meaning. "Another mile and there's a high bluff to the leeward side of this storm. Anchor close enough, and it could shield us from the hail."

Halfdan scowled. Had he even understood what I said? "Shut up, witch-boy!" Still, he stretched on tiptoes to peer over the tossing bow.

I turned my head as well, but the storm's haze had overtaken us. No way he could see that far.

Little Finger's oar handle slammed into my back again. "Ow!"

He glared at me, cheeks flushed, breathing twice as labored as my own. "What's wrong with you? You have no idea what's down there."

"I do! I've been there. I...I can't explain." I turned back to Halfdan and shouted. "There're three sides, all steep. The southern is tallest, with deep water. As long as you keep us off the cliff, it'll be safe harbor."

Halfdan frowned and maintained his course to the rocky beach. "Idiot. We've never sailed this far south."

I glanced at Froggy Rock, now behind us. No way could I have mistaken it. What had Dad yelled at me as I tried in vain to throw a simple loop of line over a dock piling during that gale last summer? "You're useless as tits on a boar!" I yelled. Both lines of rowers turned their heads and peered back at me, frosted breath streaming from their mouths, disbelief stitched into contorted faces.

Halfdan leaned hard on the tiller and the vessel turned away from the shore. "Better not be wrong, witch-boy!" Long, white hairs of his moustache curled up in a wicked sneer, as if he hoped I was.

We screamed by the coastline thirty feet away. Must've been making fifteen, even twenty knots with the wind. A few minutes later, he peered over the side and steered us farther from the beach. Prouts Neck stuck into the water, a miniature peninsula.

Massive, dense pines grew across the land bridge and filled the overlook, as if the forest were marching in war out against the white-capped ocean. As the boat shot past the eastern wall, their green tops swayed like ruffled grass stalks. Halfdan leaned hard on the oar and turned inland. Two lanky men, one with an empty eye socket, sprang up and gathered in the sail. We heaved on the oars and pulled along the massive blue granite wall. Once we were in the lee and protected behind the natural windbreak, the waves calmed. The plateau loomed forty feet above, higher than I recalled. The trees atop it, though not as impressive as the giants on the other shore, rose at least another five stories and caught the slanted sleet and rain, spraying the vessel with thick, cold mist. I propped my oar tip against the rocks along with the rest of the rowers on the starboard, maintaining our vessel's distance. The ones on the port stroked gently to ensure we didn't drift out of the protective covering.

A low grumble rose, like a hundred bulldozers chewing up the trees above us. The shotgun blast of snapping limbs. A wall of hail marched past the edge of the cliff only fifty feet away. In seconds, the murky brown of a boulder's north face was blasted a clean, bone white. The sea spewed salt spray in a thick haze. Hailstones the size of baseballs screamed overhead, thick as a hundred flocks of snow geese, carried by the wind, splashing into the water beside us. Lightning flashed somewhere beyond that crystal curtain, blazing the boat in prism colors. The wild crack of a cannon and a half-trunk plunged into the water at our stern. Shards of hail pelted us, but the pines and bluff had absorbed most of their fury.

Only minutes, and the attack rolled slowly down the coast, ending as abruptly as it had begun. Cold rain showered and pine needles fell like green snow until they coated the ship an inch thick, perfuming the air in a sharp phenolic scent. I snatched a clump from the breeze as it drifted down, stuffed a wad into one cheek, and chewed on the resinous mash. But I'd never done that before. As if this body had belonged to someone else and remnants of their memory and habits remained. The same way rowing had been familiar, despite the fact I'd never crewed a longboat. And if so, what else was I now capable of?

A red berry the size of a small grape bobbed on the water. It could be poisonous, but I snatched it up and popped it in my mouth, trusting my newfound instincts. After all, this body must've been here longer than I. I flinched at my reflection in the water. When the ripples calmed, I stared down at a man with long neck, hard jaw, and young, light skin. The same age as I, but somehow the tan of this new face betrayed a depth of experience I'd only seen in the oldest watermen. Young, but already full of stories. A short, dark beard grew from my cheeks and chin, bound with a tie of white wool. My hair hung to my shoulders, wild and raven black, tight curls tied behind my neck in an unruly ponytail. Like Gabby's. My eyes glinted green as emeralds.

I bit down on the hard berry and it popped open. A bitterness even more intense than the pine needles shocked me from self-absorption. Cranberry. I'd always hated tart candies before, but now I savored this fruit and swallowed the skin. What other tastes was I to expect? *And how do I get home?*

Why was I called *witch-boy?*

Sun glimmered over the forest above, warming my face. I turned to it and glimpsed a flash of Gabby's copper hair as she disappeared atop the cliff.

Chapter 3 – Oyster Rocks

Deck boards rattled as Halfdan pounded toward the front of the ship. Toward me. He smiled, but his gait was even heavier than Dad's when he'd picked me out of the back of Sheriff Jacobs's cruiser after he'd clocked me thirty miles per hour over the limit. This gorilla-sized man stopped in front of me, one foot on a plank, the other against the gunwale. His fist flew in an uppercut that caught me below my sternum and lifted me from my feet. My legs slipped between boards, and I dropped onto an oak plank at the end of my bench. I'd tensed my stomach at the last second, but now it cramped and I struggled to draw a breath. Couldn't this guy say anything without hitting me first?

"That's for calling me useless as tits on a boar!" he shouted.

I hunched, arms crossed over my belly, trying to inhale. He lifted me by the hair, just as he had before. *That's it. I'm shaving my head.* He plopped me next to him and I braced for another blow. Both his arms wrapped around my back and he raised me in a bear hug, squeezing until my spine popped. "And that's for saving our boat."

Each of the crew raised an arm. "Fram!" they shouted. *Forward!*

He dropped me to my feet, and the cramp in my gut subsided. I wheezed and the sound of the wind filled my ears again, as if I'd been deaf. The head of the gray wolfskin that draped over Halfdan's shoulders stretched down an arm. The dark skin of his biceps peeked through the animal's vacant sockets. He gripped my chin and put his nose to mine, staring into my eyes as if trying to peer through them. His breath was earth and oak. "How'd you know of this cliff, witch-boy?" He rapped a knuckle on my scalp. "Your mother's spirits rattling around in that skull?"

I must be this feral ape's beating toy. Was I going to have to endure this till I found a way out of this body and woke from this nightmare? But now his insults held an edge. Personal. My stomach soured with anger despite that I didn't even know this body's mother.

My mother! Only an hour ago, I'd sat on a barstool as she leaned over a hickory cutting board, dicing onions and chopping

16

tomatoes for her seafood paella that she made every year up here. Scents of paprika, thyme, and steaming shrimp had filled the cottage. The welcome aroma of her cooking transforming the vacation cottage into our home, though hundreds of miles distant.

Dad had stood at the sink, one gloved hand gripping an oyster, another a shucking knife, grumbling how Mom had forced him to pay four times the price up here than we got at home.

He'd raised the short, blunted blade in the air, to emphasize his point. "And look! Their meat is lean! Like they've been raised in some back bay."

Mother had pursed her lips into a twisted smile. She'd tucked a straight brown strand of hair behind her ear and pushed a red pepper slice into Dad's mouth. "But they're worth the price tonight," she'd said, patting his belt buckle. I'd laughed then, though it was always disgusting when they flirted.

Now, since I was here, I'd be missing from my own world, wouldn't I? If I were gone long, she'd worry, scared to death thinking she'd lost yet another child. Gabby's death had been such a blow. I *had* to get back quickly. But how?

Halfdan flicked his thumb against my forehead. "No witchy mother to protect you out here, Matok."

My fingers balled into a fist. But I couldn't fight this man. He was strong as a bull shark, and I'd never hit anyone in my life. Not only did I need to keep myself in check, but the urgings of this new body as well. As if pieces of the prior owner's personality remained. This monster staring into my eyes could crush me. And Little Finger had said he was looking for a reason to kill me.

I clenched my teeth, willing myself to remain silent.

He turned to the crew and pointed up the Nonesuch River. "We've outrun the Mi'kmaq. We'll head inland and make camp. Cut the little savages off." He pounded toward the stern. Heavy steps must've been a Viking virtue.

Most summers up here, we'd borrowed a friend's twenty-six-foot Sea Fox, moored in the Nonesuch, and gone fishing after pollock. That waterway quickly broke into several smaller tributaries that didn't really go anywhere.

"We should sail south a little farther." The words left my lips before I'd realized my mistake. I'd addressed the guy that threw punches just to clear his throat. I was always saying stupid things, speaking without thinking. Seems some of my faults had followed me.

Halfdan ducked below the boom and froze. His eyes narrowed, as if considering the thought.

Maybe I should smooth it over. Explain. "My father and I'd go fishing from—"

At the mention of *father*, Halfdan's lip curled into a sneer. He shouted, "You've got no *father*, witch-boy!" He stretched his arm toward the river. "That's as big as any stream we've seen."

I tapped the side of the cliff with my oar. "I got us here. Trust me. A couple more miles and we'll be at the Saco."

"You named it!" He tugged on his beard, as if the gesture were an insult. "Now I know you're crazy. You caught that wave with your paddle and your oar knocked your senses loose. You thought you were talking to Freyja in Fólkvangr when I picked you out of the bilge. We're heading up *that* river."

I opened my mouth but held my breath. Mom would always clear her throat before I further incriminated myself, and I imagined her doing so now. I pursed my lips and tapped the blue granite cliff with my oar once again.

Halfdan turned with a jerk and hopped atop his perch. We all sat and readied our oars. Halfdan nodded to the two rowers closest him, and they made a preliminary exaggerated stroke. The rest of the boat followed their lead and we pulled away.

"You OK?" Little Finger asked.

My neck was cramping from craning backward to speak with him. "Yeah. Thanks."

"You sure? Halfdan's killed men punching them like that."

I glanced at my belly. A red welt the size of a saucer swelled below my rib cage. "Killed?"

"You know. Their heart stopped."

I shook my head. "That's the problem. I don't know."

"You took a nasty blow when your paddle caught that wave."

"What does that mean, *caught a wave*?"

Little Finger breathed deeply for a few strokes, as if an asthmatic, though our pace was much more relaxed now. "You know, your oar digs into the water on the return stroke. Launches the grip straight at your head. You haven't paddled a wave since you were a kid. A bad omen."

We passed by the mouth of the Nonesuch. *I guess Halfdan isn't completely close minded.* The wide opening was clogged with piles of rocks protruding from opposite shores like fingers, knitted together until only a narrow waterway remained that zigzagged between the banks. At Halfdan's nod, One-Eye and his skinny companion jumped up and hoisted the sail. It billowed out in the stiff breeze, shaking a mist from the damp fabric that drifted across my face and chest. The scent of wet wool filled the boat again, and strokes came easier. I shivered. A tan rough-woven bag, like a burlap sack, was strapped to the leg of my bench.

I caught Little Finger's gaze and pointed to it. "That mine?"

He smirked. "Yes, that's yours. Either by oar or by Halfdan's fists, your memory's been beaten from you."

Rowing with one arm, I reached in with the other and pulled out a collarless linen shirt, embroidered with red and turquoise beads on the chest. A brown cross ran down the back. I shrugged it on and fiddled with string loops over pewter-colored buttons carved with swirls and dots. The stiff, rough fabric cut the wind. I'd anticipated it would itch, but it didn't. Bow spray beaded upon its surface and ran down the seams in streaks, as if the fabric had been oiled.

Oil. *That* was the stench I'd been smelling. The wood of the boat had been rubbed with a greasy substance, probably for waterproofing. Even when I'd gripped the gunwale it had been slick under my palms. What would a Viking use? Seal fat? If so, no wonder the vessel stank like a slaughterhouse.

The rocks piled on the beach as we passed were smaller and less hostile than the ones earlier. I studied the forest, anticipating a flash of Gabby's red hair, or hearing her laugh over the splash of the bow. But the next few miles passed without such evidence. The woodland grew darker as we continued. Still, the sky was bright, though the sun sank lower. In her absence I sensed another spirit, unfamiliar, that chilled my skin. Maybe this was why they called me witch-boy. Was I now some sort of shaman who could sense such things? When I'd glimpsed her red hair, my body had been light and arms strong. Now, though our pace had slowed, the oar was dead in my grasp, as if a darkness had pushed her aside. Was I losing my mind? *I'm not asleep,* I reasoned. Not dreaming. I was physically in another man's body, same place, different time, ruled by a fist-happy, white-haired Neanderthal. Or had my old life been a dream? I startled at the thought.

I scanned the coast again, but no Gabby. The bow plowed through a wave, its spray chilling my neck and stinging my ears. All my senses seemed twice as intense. But none were bothersome. Reassuring, in fact, that I was alive. As if for the first time. Pain seemed an ordinary part of me. Like the last mile in a cross-country race, maybe I needed to push through the wall.

Make fast and ride it through.

Halfdan pulled on the tiller and steered toward the mouth of the Saco. Now that we were headed across wind, the sail was dropped again. Slack tide had passed and the rising current carried us toward the mouth of the river, as if to swallow us whole. The boat accelerated the closer we traveled, drawn like a hooked fish. We barely had to paddle, though I wouldn't have had the strength, so oppressive came the shadows. Once inside the channel, we were a slave to its powerful flow. The current carried us so swiftly no amount of struggle would've gained our release.

Just like the Nonesuch, the entrance was constricted by low rock shoals. We slipped between them at what must have been fifteen knots. Approaching the first cutback, Halfdan shouted, "Reverse!" Each man leaned against his oar as if doing a pushup. I locked my feet beneath the bench in front of me and mimed the strokes of the others on my side. We slowed, but our momentum carried us zipping past the cutback toward the rocky shore. Like a tugboat easing a barge to a standstill, our rowing slowed forward progress and we stopped mere feet from slimy granite boulders. The current pulled us along once more, carrying us backward in the opposite direction.

If I'd been navigator, I'd have tried to steer the vessel around the sharp turns. That would've just blasted us onto the bank. I'd worked on the water since I was six, but still would've wrecked trying to navigate this channel myself. I needed a guide. Gabby...

Is that why she had called me here? Was I to learn something from this world? If so, what? And from whom? Hopefully not the white gorilla.

We passed one shoal close enough for my oar to touch. The rocks stood upright and sharp, like blunt arrowheads the size of dinner plates. "Oysters," I whispered. I never knew they could grow so huge! These were the oyster rocks the old-timers talked about. Except these monsters were bigger than even Granddad's wildest tales.

The sun began to paint the sky in strokes of orange as it disappeared behind the towering pine forest. Something shimmied in the river, and I leaned my head over the gunwale. The water was clear as a crystal, but waves distorted my view. The bottom snaked only feet below us in iridescent silver and black stripes, as if the mud were a leviathan shaking its scales. I struggled to understand. Then I gasped. *We're floating atop a school of striped bass.* Must've been thousands of them, many a yard long. They writhed and slithered just beneath the surface, as one. I squinted, amazed, as an oval opened in the glimmering mass. The fish parted around what appeared to be a floating boulder. My chest froze as it waved a knife blade tail. A gigantic great white, or maybe a bull shark, at least twelve feet long, lollygagged in the water. Its pointed snout was gouged with brown scars.

"Want to take a swim?" It was Little Finger, sticking his head between the shields and staring down along with me.

"You first."

"*An omen*, your mother would say."

My mother. "You know her?"

He flashed a grin, his pale face glowing orange in the setting light. "The shark, or your mom? Oh, same thing." He laughed.

"Reverse!" Halfdan yelled.

We sat upright and pulled a stroke. I glanced ahead. The moon was already up and many more cutbacks remained before we'd break into open, navigable waters.

My stomach growled. I'd never been so hungry. "When did we last eat?"

Little Finger grimaced as he pulled on his oar. "I don't know about you, but I haven't eaten all day. You already finish your fish? You packed a dozen."

I stuck a hand into the sack below my bench. I wriggled fingers past fur and leather, linen with metal buttons, and finally brushed against a solid mass. I pulled out a tan bag with a drawstring and spread open the top. Several foot-long filets of a white-fleshed fish were stacked inside.

Little Finger's eyes cut to the food. His tongue pressed against his upper lip. "Enough to share?"

Why not? I peeled off a stiff layer, like days-old pages of a book after being left in the rain. The meat was light. Dried, I suspected. No smoky odor. The skin was gray with rusty spots. Cod. I passed it back over my shoulder, and a maggot dropped onto the deck board. Little Finger curled up the meat like a burrito and shoved half of it into his mouth. Chewing, he puckered and pulled out needles of bone. I copied him, though no maggots dropped from mine. It would've made no difference, though. If it had been packed in horse manure, I was so hungry I'd have brushed it off and still gobbled it down. Only a hint of fishy taste came from the fat layer between the skin and meat.

I cinched the pouch and stuffed it away. No telling how long I was going to be aboard. Where was Gabby? Why'd she seem to only allow a peek before she shot away? *She's got to be the key for me being here. Find her, and I'll figure this thing out.*

Though I was still famished, my body no longer felt heavy and cold. Had the evil presence from earlier simply been hunger pains? No, there had been much more to that darkness. It had been alive.

Curious, but with sinister intent. Like a search party, probing for weakness.

The remaining cutbacks took a half hour to traverse. The sky was pink and fuchsia when we broke free from the oyster maze. Trees grew even taller as we rowed farther inland. Buoyed by the incoming tide, we stroked another mile before Halfdan steered us toward a clearing where the shoreline scooped away from the river, forming a pool. As soon as the keel touched, Little Finger leapt from the bow with a line in his grasp. One-Eye did the same from the stern and splashed into waist-deep water. The two lashed the lines to trunks, stringing the vessel such that it bobbed out of danger of striking rocks.

Halfdan stomped down the deck and gripped my arm. I covered by stomach with my free one as he took a breath. He pointed to Little Finger. "You and Tryfing scout a half mile each direction, then take first watch."

Tryfing must've been Little Finger's real name.

Men shipped oars and pulled on coarsely woven shirts similar to my own. Lines were strung and the boom was turned to support the sail so it draped across the boat like a tent. Gripping the gunwale with one hand, I jumped over and planted my feet on the side of the vessel, hanging like a monkey from a branch. My fingers never threatened to slip. I leapt onto a near boulder and drew a long knife with elk horn handle from a sheath strapped to my waist. I hadn't noticed it was lashed there, but my hand was somehow familiar with it, just as my body knew how to move in this world. I stabbed at several huge oysters at the base of the rock. One popped off, and I thrust the blade between its halves and twisted, wedging the creature open. A quick slice of its muscle and it floated freely in its juices. I cut it into quarters, lifted the shell to my mouth, and slurped the pieces. Briny liquid ran down my beard and wet my throat. *Great. Now I'm thirsty.* But the heavy meat tasted just like the ones I raised, though less salty. Most importantly, it sated my hunger.

I popped open another and passed it up to Halfdan. His scowl faded, he raised it to his lips and tipped his head back. A lock of copper-red hair dangling from his neck beneath his beard on a string of leather trembled in the breeze.

Chapter 4 – The Witch

I pushed a thin, chest-high pine branch out of my way as I walked beside a tall sapling. One of the few young trees that had found purchase beneath the shadow of the virgin forest. Thin flakes of bark stuck to my palm. Little Finger, or Tryfing as Halfdan had called him, followed a few yards behind, head pivoting, scanning the forest. His pale skin glowed ghostly in the moonlight. The air was cool, curiously absent the hum of mosquitos. I passed below a silver maple and noted its leaves were pale green, only two inches long. Must be spring, and too early for most bugs.

I gripped the handle of a battle-axe. At least that's what Tryfing had said it was. Looked more like a hatchet with a narrow head and long wooden handle. "Why don't I have a sword?" I asked.

"Because you haven't bought one," he muttered, grinning. He wore a vest of brown deerskin over a long-sleeved linen shirt. A sword hung from his belt in a leather sheath. "You value women over weapons."

We slid away from the boat, scouting the immediate area as Halfdan had ordered. I'd expected Tryfing to lead, but he'd just stood there, like I was supposed to go first. So I did, setting out along the riverbank.

I raised the axe and chopped a low branch from our way. What were we looking for? Then again, why did I care? I needed to get home. And with every hour, the memories of that world, of Nikki's free spirit, of Mom's harebrained inspirations and Dad's unfailing encouragements, of North Carolina and Maine—of Christine and possibilities—they all were fading as if I were waking from a dream. Why had Gabby brought me here? Or were we both prisoners of the same evil, snatched from that world against our will? Gabby's body had never been found. The police had presumed she'd been drawn out to sea in her kayak, capsized, and drowned. But she had been much too strong for that.

I'd been gone only a half day, I assured myself. Still, they'd all be worried senseless. Mom to a fever, for certain.

I glanced back at Tryfing, incessantly searching the forest. What was he scared of?

"Ask your question," Tryfing said.

I snorted. "Which one?"

"I don't know. You keep looking back at me, not where you're headed. It's not like you.."

I swung the axe and dropped another limb. The iron twanged a high note, like a tuning fork. Its weight and balance similar to the twenty-five-ounce framing hammer I'd swung countless times building wooden docks and bulkheads. I could drive a sixteen-penny nail in two swats. But now my shoulders slumped. "What are we doing here?"

He peered below thick black eyebrows. "Scouting."

"No. I mean, why'd we come here? On the boat."

Tryfing stopped and braced a palm against a trunk. His breathing was heavy. Deep, but quiet. He stepped toward me, his cross-laced leather boots silent on the pine needle blanket. The moon glinting off wide black pupils. His bushy eyebrows cinched together as if yanked by a drawstring. "You've taken beatings before, but never lost memory. You really don't know what we're doing here?"

I sighed and shook my head.

"What's my name?" he asked, suddenly frowning. "Say it."

I wanted to say Little Finger but thought better of it. "Uh...Tryfing."

A distant screech sounded through the forest and his eyebrows bundled even closer. Though it seemed my answer, not the shriek, was the reason for his concern. "No. What *you* call me. Not the others."

Why not? "Little Finger."

He drew back. "Little Finger?" He held up his hand and curled its four digits into a fist. "You making fun?"

OK. Guess that's not what I usually call him. "No."

He grabbed my shoulder, turning me to face him. "It's happened again, hasn't it?" His eyes widened. "You're not Matok."

What did he mean by *again*? "I..."

His hands moved up to my shoulders. He stared into my eyes, as if in a panic. He shoved me away, turned, and beat the air with his fists. "*Curse* that mother of yours!" He spun back around, gripped my shoulders again, but closer to my neck, as if wanting to choke me. "No wonder you're stomping around the forest like you don't care who hears. Who are you?" He shook me, his face reddening. "Tell me!"

I grabbed his wrists and squeezed, my fingers tightening down like screw clamps, strengthened by what must have been a lifetime of gripping an oar. His mouth stretched wide and he released me. I backed him into a tree trunk. "What do you mean *again*? Has this happened before?"

No answer, so I squeezed harder.

He winced. "Yes. Once."

I let go and stepped back. "Tell me."

He rubbed his bruised wrists and stared at the ground, as if no longer concerned about the forest. "Come on," he said, and turned to lead me along the river. As we walked, he explained how we'd been friends since childhood. "We were eight, playing in a stream. Suddenly you stood up, glanced around, and screamed. I'd thought you'd cut your foot on a shell or been struck by a viper. I carried you to the bank and you calmed after an hour. Except you told me your name was Troy, not Matok. That you'd been out fishing next to your tent, and suddenly the whole camp was gone. You said a bunch of other stuff that made no sense. And I knew then, just like I know now, you weren't my friend inside that body."

Tryfing turned from the water and we began a long, slow arc inland. He periodically glanced at the stars and adjusted our line of travel. We would eventually make it back to the river if we kept our slow turn.

"How long did it last?"

Another distant screech. This one closer. An owl, maybe. The moon seemed to darken a shade, and once again the same evil I'd experienced on the boat chilled my skin.

"Half a month, I'd say. Till Matok returned."

"How'd that happen?"

He stepped around a towering pine trunk. "I don't know. One day, you were just...back. You didn't remember anything. From the weeks you were was gone, nor from the time Troy was in your body."

No wonder they called me witch-boy. People must've thought I was possessed. "Does everyone know about it?"

Tryfing whipped around to glare at me. "No! Only your mother. She hid you away." He reached to grab me, but I stepped aside. Still, his soft face betrayed no anger. It was as if he was pleading. "She told me not to tell anyone, to swear my silence, or she'd kill me." He snorted. "Me, eight years old, bound by an oath to your bloody mother. You know how scared I was? Well, I still am. I never told you—never told *Matok*—because he'd think I was crazy. And he didn't remember it anyway." He wrapped his arms around me. "I was just glad to have you back." Then he pushed away, as if suddenly remembering I wasn't his friend. "And we can't tell

25

anyone on the boat. They won't believe you or they'll think you're mad. And your mother...she'll know I betrayed her."

If this grown man feared my mother, she had to be a powerful woman. Who could she be, to wield such effect? "I can't just pretend to be a Vestman. They'll figure out I'm not, just like you did. I don't even know what I'm here for. Or how long. Maybe one of the others can help, if I ask."

He gripped my shoulders again. "No! I'll help you. I'll...I'll explain how things work, so others don't figure it out. Make up excuses for your mistakes. You took a beating, anyway. Just till you're Matok again."

This made no sense. "But I don't care if others figure it out. I want them to. I don't belong here. And why are you so scared of my—I mean *his* mother. Who is she?"

The glint of moonlight faded from his eyes. "She's our witch," he said, shoulders sagging hopelessly. "Odin himself would never trust her."

Chapter 5 – Stryker

Stryker slowed his pace to a trot and leapt over a thick, fallen bough. His wide paws silenced his landing on the mat of dry pine needles. He panted from the heat of his exertion, having run for two days, almost without pause. Of all the forms a demon could inhabit, this one, the black panther, was his favorite. Thick, leathery muscles and glossy black coat. An apex predator in these coastal woodlands. But such a large cat was built for explosive bursts—not the two-day marathon he'd been running. Cracks in the pads of his paws burned, still bleeding from crossing a briared meadow a mile wide yesterday. One fat thorn still stuck through the flap of his torn ear. But now was no time to stop and dig it out.

A clear, chill spring night blanketed the pine forest around him. Green peaks of white pines speared the sky, their trunks towering a hundred, even two hundred feet in the air. The dense virgin woodland stood tightly packed; the only means for trees to grow toward the sun was straight up. No branches graced the tall, rough pillars for the first half of their height, as if they'd been pruned away by giants. Any twigs that sprouted there, starved of light, eventually died and fell to the ground. To decay...

Stryker's stomach growled with hunger, though he'd snapped the neck of a tawny rabbit that had sprinted across his path only a few hours ago. All fur, meat, and bone. No fat. Rabbits were plentiful but never could satisfy this body's cravings. Its warm blood had only served to excite his hunger. But oh, the succulent taste of blood! That meaty, luscious liquid was what made inhabiting any bodily form so pleasing. Exquisite, no matter how small the kill.

He slowed as he topped each ridge, hoping to surprise a flock of turkey. Their gamey flesh was enough to push aside hunger for a couple of days. But hunting such wary birds meant waiting in ambush from low-lying limbs. No time for such patient schemes. His orders from Ernick, his captain, had been clear. *Overtake the Mi'kmaq, migrating to their summer camp. Ensure the way ahead of them is clear of the enemy.*

The Mi'kmaq. Putrid indigenous humans. No problem trailing bipeds. Their path stank like maggot-filled piles of feces. Their offspring were the worst, crapping and pissing all over themselves. But their flesh was savory. He'd caught one alone last month near the river, stupid baby hadn't even known who Stryker was. She'd not been afraid. How disappointing. He'd snatched her from the bank, careful not to puncture that tender flesh as he sprinted away. A mile distant, he'd dropped her on the moist dirt near the river. The child had grabbed his neck, wanting to play. So he did. He'd batted her about till she was coated in her own bloody juices. But she'd only become angry and screamed. Annoying. Fear was always the best seasoning. Even so, the little one had proven a delicious treat.

He'd caught up with the Mi'kmaq yesterday and now was so far ahead of them it'd take three or four days for the fetid humans to catch up. Why had Stryker been sent to ensure clear passage for them? He'd never been ordered to such lowly labor.

In fact, Ernick had always seemed to find no greater pleasure than tormenting the pitiful creatures. But then pink-skinned men with sun-golden hair, *Vestmen* they call themselves, arrived on our shores in longboats, and Ernick catered to their every whim. Well, only *one* of them. But that witch made supplication for the entire Vestmen village. Humiliating, for such a high-ranking demon such as Ernick. What pleasure could he take in the Vestmen that he could not already have with the Mi'kmaq? *Let them kill each other!* How wonderful that would be. A banquet of blood and hate. A little encouragement was all that would be needed to get them there. Yet Ernick protected the Vestmen because their witch was loyal to him, which meant Stryker couldn't lay a paw upon them. But maybe now he could create an opportunity for them to kill each other...

No, Ernick must have a plan. He was shrewd. Always played both sides. And usually against each other, to his own profit. That's how he'd earned the rule of his day region—the area a captain could circumnavigate in the time of a single winter's night. No request from a human was granted without payment. Whatever deal the Vestmen's witch had struck with Ernick, in the end it would cost her more than she'd ever want to pay. Still, clearing the enemy from the path of the Mi'kmaq? Stryker had never stooped to such a thing.

He slowed to an amble, approaching the clear top of another ridge. The moon shone bright as daylight, another reason he loved the black panther. He could see prey, but his dark fur proved invisible to them. As he peered down, a long, wide stream stretched as far west as a big cat's eyes could see. He snorted in disgust and shivered in anticipation of the icy water. He'd only recently dried from a swim across another river a few miles back.

He lifted his nose to the breeze and, for a second, caught the woolen scent of Vestmen. *No.* They couldn't have traveled this far south already. Their ships were fast, but not as quick as Stryker.

He took a step, and a pinecone pierced one shredded pad. With a shriek, he batted it away.

"Let me take the form of a bald eagle for such a long journey," he'd asked Ernick. "It will serve you better."

"No," the demon had bellowed, lifting a jade hand tipped with the most beautiful blades of black obsidian. Lips of liquid ruby curled into a luscious grin. "For this mission, you must be ready to kill." His voice had vibrated the ground, as if he were speaking into the earth. There was no changing his mind then.

A shadow flew across his path and Stryker glanced up. A buzzard, soaring on a lingering updraft. Slaughter? No. *That* captain would never humiliate himself to assume a scavenger's form. Stryker had left Ernick's day region yesterday and was now deep within Slaughter's, the reason for his angst. Getting caught here would be devastating, considering Stryker's low rank—his ransom would be too high for Ernick to pay. Stryker had served his captain well, but expected no mercy. Another reason the panther had been a good choice, he assured himself. Invisible to everyone.

As Stryker trotted down the hill, sparks flew in the distance, near the river's shoreline. His silky pelt quivered at the sight. *Stupid cat! It's just a campfire.* This beast's primal instincts were difficult to control at times. But it was the other primitive drives that made this form so pleasurable. The ecstasy of a kill and the taste of blood on his tongue as his prey bled out.

Still, flames had always chilled his spirit, no matter what animal's form he took.

He sprinted toward the fire's glow. Then, belly to the ground, stalked closer. The blaze was burning bright and large in the center of a meadow, tall as a sacrificial pyre. He stepped into the clearing, the heat burning his nose so hot was the inferno. No one in sight.

The thick fur of his neck rose. Fear, but not of the flames. His instincts warning him of impending battle. *The enemy is near.* A low growl rumbled deep within his rib cage, but with gritted teeth he silenced its sound. He couldn't warn his prey.

A chill breeze brushed the flower of a shriveling dandelion before his nose and carried the woolen stink of—*Vestmen!* So, it *had* been them. How'd they get this far south so quickly? And this was one of their watch fires. But what evil was Stryker sensing? Vestmen weren't the enemy.

Stryker slunk back behind a stand of grass. Had an enemy spirit discovered a means to hide among them?

The enemy was sly, taking the form of innocent doves, or innocuous rabbits, all to conceal their true spirit that dripped with violence and lust. The most powerful, he'd heard, could even take human form, though he'd never seen such himself. Encounters with enemy spirits were rare...though a few had occurred since the arrival of the Vestmen. Stryker stared at the fire as that thought struck him. His last encounter with an enemy had caught him off guard. He'd been in his panther's form then as well, ordered to patrol the dense forest north of the Vestmen's new camp when he'd heard the laugh of a young girl. A peculiar sound, high and rolling, almost like the call of a seagull, down near a creek bank flooded by the rising sun. Curious, and intensely hungry, he'd been stalking nearer the sound when a raven lighted upon a pawpaw branch ahead of him, flapped its wings, and transformed into a stag large as a moose and with legs thick as oak branches. Veins bulged down its neck like vines choking a tree as it thrashed its huge rack in threat. It was protecting whatever human had made the sound. Stryker had retreated and finished his patrol, but he never mentioned the encounter to Ernick. There would've been no profit in that.

A bear-sized man wearing a vest of deer hide stumbled from the forest into the firelight. From behind a veil of tall grass, Stryker purred his approval at the choice of garb—the human's only endearing quality. How wonderful it must be to *wear* your prey.

Another man, tall and slender, with ruddy, muscular arms and raven-black hair, braided and tied behind his neck with a leather thong, followed behind the fat one. Glimpsing him, the fur along Stryker's spine stood on end. Cold pressed upon his chest, hard as frozen earth. Every muscle tensed, ready to spring, fight instincts pumping furiously. The sensation unmistakable. Certain.

This man, the tall Vestman, was no ordinary human. He was an enemy.

Chapter 6 – Pyre

I dragged dry pine logs near the fire and propped them together, making a low bench. Tryfing plopped down next to me. The blaze warmed my cheeks. White moths the size of Monarch butterflies circled in the smoke, drawn by the light. Two aqua-blue dots like eyes, one on the underside of each wing, winked in the firelight. Caught in the updraft, the insects rose high as the trees, fluttered out, and drifted down toward the fire again. There were so many, it must've resembled the pillar of fire and cloud from Exodus. Now here I sat, a stranger in my own land. Yet with no promise of deliverance.

I straightened my back and pointed at Tryfing. "So, let me get this straight. My great-great-grandfather was banished from Norway to Iceland because of manslaughter. My great-grandfather was banished from Iceland to Greenland for murder."

Tryfing drew his sword and laid it across his thighs, rubbing fingers down its centerline. He nodded.

Nice family tree. How bad did a man need to screw up to be banished by Vikings? "But then my grandfather discovered this land, *Vinland* you called it, because it had grapes."

He stuck a hand into a leather bag dangling from his belt and drew out a round stone with score marks across it. "That's right."

I held out another finger. "So, we live in Vinland now. We call ourselves Vestmen, because that means *western men*. My father's name is Thorkell, but he's not really my father because he hasn't married my mother."

"She's a frilla."

"But, she *lives* with my father, along with his real wife? My mother is some sort of witch, you say, but many of the village are Christian?"

Tryfing drew the stone across the blade. It clicked across shallow notches in the sword's edge. Another nod.

Some of my earliest memories were Mom kicking Dad's shins beneath the table when his eyes lingered too long on a young waitress. She wouldn't stand second to anyone. If the village were Christian, that'd explain the cross on the back of my shirt. But the beads on the front? "How does that work? Women living in the same house?"

Firelight glinted off Tryfing's teeth as he smiled. "In Thorkell's case, not well. But, it makes good gossip around the village. And what's wrong with a man having a frilla? If I were chieftain, I'd have twenty."

I waited for a smile or any other sign that he was being sarcastic. None. "Tell me about my mother, then. The witch."

The skin across Tryfing's knuckles stretched as the grip on the hilt of his sword tightened. "She's the most powerful woman in the village. Even more than your father, some might say. It's why Thorkell took her as a frilla." He grinned and held up a hand as if cupping a breast. "That, and her..." His eyes searched the fire. "She has other strengths besides witchery."

"She's a witch. But you said the village is Christian. Wouldn't they hate her? Or burn her at the stake, or something?"

"Why? She protects us. Just because she's a witch doesn't mean she lacks followers. Many are Christians. And since she's so popular, your father having her in his house ensures no one will challenge him as chieftain."

"But why are you scared of her? Of some promise you made as a kid."

He laid his sword back upon his lap and rolled his shoulders, as if warding off unpleasant thoughts. Gabby used to do the same thing when she was hiding something. "She's a powerful woman."

"You've said that. Tell me what you mean."

He drew a breath and closed his eyes. "Only last month I was asleep on my bench in my house. The sheep were down. My children asleep next to the fire. A breeze chilled my feet, and I woke. I figured it was morning and my wife had gone for wood and left the door open. But the fire was still high, so I couldn't have been asleep long. Light reflected from fresh snow outside and blazed through the open door like daylight. I was about to get up to shut the opening when the entire world went dark. Even the fire dimmed till only the faintest orange glow of coals remained.

"It snorted next to my ear." Tryfing shivered, though sweat was beading on his forehead. "Normally I would've thought it was Sattick, our horse, loose from her tie again, trying warm herself. It wouldn't be the first time she had wandered into our home. Except I couldn't breathe." His face seemed to shrink, and he placed his hands on his stomach. "And I couldn't move. I lay on my side, terrified. Its breath was hot, whatever *it* was. Hot as if I'd fallen into the fire. Yet my body was ice. I couldn't see because of the darkness. And I was paralyzed. But I remember four legs, and huge hooves, shaped like a goat. And the smell of..."

"What? What did it smell like?"

He kept his face toward the fire but cut his eyes to me. "The sweetest scent I've ever enjoyed. Sweeter than a turning apple. But terrifying. It burned my throat and choked me. I wanted this four-legged demon to leave, but it pressed upon my chest. Drool dripped into my ear and it said, 'Never tell. Never tell.' I knew it meant the story about how you'd become Troy for a time as a child. It had been years since I'd thought of it, but somehow I knew."

"But...you did. You told me."

Tryfing turned to me and stared, as if realizing what he'd done. "You won't always be here." He faced the fire again. "Matok will return." He clenched a fist. "He will."

"So, what happened? You woke up? The beast was just a dream."

"No dream. I was dying. Drowning, like someone had lashed me to a boulder and thrown me overboard. But it turned on its hooves and fled, fast and straight, as if an arrow shot by a bow. The door slammed after it so loud that my wife startled awake. The fire blazed high again. I gasped for air and coughed on the smoke.

"Then the baby started to cry. The door wedged open and I thought the demon might be returning. I scrambled to grab my sword from beneath my bench." Tryfing stood and held his blade toward the blaze. "If a draugr could take a fleshly form, then its flesh could bleed. But..." He turned toward me and sheathed his weapon. "It was your little sister, Astrid. She often helped with the baby. For never being a mother, she was the most patient child alive. She was the daughter of your father and his wife. Your half sister." He shook his head. "But she often couldn't sleep. She'd been walking, heard the door slam, the baby's cry. So, she slipped in, lifted him into her arms, and the chubby worm calmed down. He loved to grab her red hair, curl it into his fist, and suck his thumb."

That couldn't be a coincidence. "I have a sister? With red hair? But, you were talking about her in past tense. Is she still alive?"

His stare was blank. "That's up to us. She's the reason we're here. A few days ago, she was taken by the Mi'kmaq."

Leaves crunched behind a distant line of tall grass that danced in the faint fire light near the edge of the meadow. A few tall stalks shuddered, as if an animal were creeping among them. Or was it only the licking flames that gave it the appearance of movement?

I shivered despite the heat. "You feel that chill?"

Chapter 7 – Slaughter

Back beneath the dark concealment of the forest, Stryker slunk away from the watch fire. How humiliating to retreat. Yet, he had to think. Formulate a plan. Ernick's orders had been clear, with no room for interpretation...at least at the time. *Clear the way of the enemy ahead of the Mi'kmaq.* That's all he had to do. To go before the Indians and make sure no enemy was near their path. What price had they paid to Ernick, he wondered, to warrant such protection? A blood sacrifice, no doubt.

Yet Stryker couldn't touch the Vikings. Ernick himself handled all dealings with those men, and directly with their witch. So Stryker had been told.

But now...one of the Vestmen was an enemy. No mistaking it. Stryker's blood had almost been aboil when the tall, lanky one stepped from the forest. But that was impossible. How could a mere human pose such a threat? A member of the cursed species. Stryker had been tempted to launch himself upon the mortal right there, next to the fire. And why shouldn't he? Ernick had no eyes in this region, and Stryker could lie better than anyone. Yet, could he fool Ernick? Of course. Ernick was beautiful, but a hollow shell. Not cunning, like Stryker. However, the fat Vestman had held a sword, even while sitting. Vigilant, as if anticipating battle. The enemy, on the other hand, had sat oblivious and unaware of anything except the fire's heat. Stryker would've killed him if alone, without the pudgy man nearby.

Stryker's neck tensed as if with a chill. He couldn't fail. Failure meant exile to the Abyss. The memory of that punishing dungeon was the cause of his unease. The absence of light, sound, and all feeling except the pain of unbearable, enduring heat. It's where Stryker had been imprisoned when Ernick purchased him, and why he was enslaved to his clown of a captain.

He raced on. *Patience,* he thought. Another opportunity to kill the lanky one would arise. But Stryker had little time. The Mi'kmaq would be here in days, and the enemy needed to be gone. Yet he couldn't touch the Vestmen. He had to use other means to drive them away. But how? Fear? Hunger? Lust? Hate? What would motivate the tall Vestman to turn around and go away?

Leaves slapped his fur as he bounded through the forest, staying abreast of the stream. The Mi'kmaq's summer quarters lay only eight miles away. He could ensure those were clear of other threats, continue to their hunting grounds to do the same, then return here to deal with the lanky human who was now an enemy. The cursed among a cursed species. *What to do about him? Don't overcomplicate it.* Ernick would never learn the truth. If the enemy had become a mortal maggot, *squash it! Death solves every trouble.*

Stryker leapt over a knot of bramble and a thorn tore through the fur of his belly. He stopped just long enough to lap the blood till it stopped. As he did, he pondered a question he'd never understood. Why was it that Ernick obsessed over the mortals and gaining their worship? All the captains were the same. Arrogant and shortsighted fools, the whole lot. The real battle with the enemy was here, in the flesh, not in the flattering babblings of humans in their dim, meaningless religions. It was Ernick's keenest weakness. He adored its flattery. Which was why, Stryker suspected, he'd been ordered to not harm the Vestmen. Well, too bad. The putrid walking beasts stopped to pee everywhere. That would be an easy time to tear out his throat and slip away before anyone spotted Stryker. *Death solves every trouble.*

The reflection of stars twinkled on the water as he bounded down the riverside trail. The air was still and the surface glass. He leapt from boulder to boulder and slid to a halt. The hair on his neck rose, his back arched, and his mouth tasted of gall.

Again? Another enemy?

He glanced around but heard only the trickle of water, the hum of dragonfly wings, and the hoot of an owl. He sniffed. Pinesap, field mouse, and week-old skunk. No reason to be alarmed. Yet the chill, the pressure in his chest, just like back at the fire. *An enemy is near.*

He leapt to the blistered trunk of a loblolly near the river and sank his claws into its bark. In three powerful strides he rested high atop a thick branch, camouflaged by night. Invisible. A large clearing lay fifty feet ahead, the ground a huge dome-shaped boulder. As if the earth were giving birth to granite and this were its head, crowning. A crack ran down its center and a single pine sapling sprouted from the middle. All around, trees towered over the spot, stretching limbs into the space, fighting for light. A breeze stirred their tops and branches creaked.

A bald eagle glided in a circle, swooped lower among the towering tips, and dove through a hole where the longest branches couldn't reach. Cupping its wings, it slowed and landed next to the sapling. Its long talons scraped the granite as it slid to a halt.

Was that Slaughter? *Could be.* No reason an eagle would swoop so low unless hunting. Had Slaughter seen him? No. An eagle's eyes were perfection, but not at night. And Stryker had been careful to watch the sky. It was a skill every ranger practiced.

But what Stryker had sensed was not Slaughter's presence, the captain of this day region. No, an enemy, and a powerful one.

The eagle ruffled its feathers as if shaking off a chill, then unfolded its wings and lowered them, like it was bowing in worship. Its feathers melted and tightened into glowing cobalt-blue scales. The beast began to grow, its wings rippling into arms planted on the granite, back arching skyward, tall as a horse. Spear-tipped talons extended from its legs till they covered the creature's calves like quills of a porcupine, thick as a panther's tail and ebony black, wet and dripping with sulfur-yellow venom. It stood upright, like...a man. Hair hung in cords of braided rope, leathery green and purple. Its face glowed like burnished bronze, and flashed, as if reflecting fire. Silver knives tipped each arm like fingers.

It was the most glorious demon Stryker had ever seen. The richness of his appearance was far beyond Ernick's. He'd never met such wealth. Stryker gazed, drawn as with a sensual desire. But no! His legs quivered. He couldn't be caught here, trespassing in another captain's day region. He lowered his head to the limb. Mustn't be noticed.

The glow of the demon's scales dimmed, and the creature opened his mouth. His voice boomed but quickly trailed off as his body vanished into darkness. "Don't you know who I am? Why would you—"

The creature disappeared from Stryker's view as it left this fleshly realm and slid into that of the spirit. How wealthy was this beast? Enough to change physical form without a thought. And to slide into spirit at will. Both of those required unimaginable riches, and only captains held such currency. Stryker could try and follow him into the spirit realm, to spy on what was happening there, but because he lacked affluence, he'd risk losing his panther's form. And the black panther was his only tool to succeed on this mission.

No gain without risk. Stryker closed his eyes and concentrated on the enemy, the evil presence that had caused him to stop in the first place. It slipped him out of the flesh and closer to the spiritual realm, as if allowing his soul to be carried along by a rising tide.

The trick was to be drawn only a short distance, to not get swept away, or he'd lose grasp on his panther's form. He left the big cat's body on the limb and fell comfortably into the bulk of his demon's stature. In spirit, Stryker resembled a panther's form as well, but larger, with a broad head and thick black plates of scaly armor instead of a silky pelt.

He stalked up behind a tree next the dome-shaped boulder. With every step, his grasp on the big cat weakened. This was as far as he could go. Any more, and he might never be able to make it back into its flesh.

The clearing blazed as if from a fire. The blue glow of the wonderful, towering creature came back into focus, now that Stryker was gazing through his spirit's eye. But the brilliant light...he couldn't see where it was coming from. Somewhere behind the demon.

Stryker strained to slip further into spirit, as if pushing off into the river's channel where the current ran swift. The image before his hazy eyes sharpened, focusing on a thick, tall sword, but not that of the demon. This one glowed as if just pulled from a hearth of blazing embers. Its tip rested atop the granite slab behind the sapling. The blue creature towered over its owner, blocking a clear view.

"Putrid, stinking, cowardly fool!" the demon yelled. "I dare you to take form. Any of them!" His scales flickered, flashing blue to green and back again, ruffling like feathers. "You think you can come into *my* day region? It's not my time yet. Take form and I'll bend you over a rock and pleasure myself upon your corpse."

The venom of his talons sizzled and dripped, forming pools, but none flowed near the sapling. It was as if the crack in the boulder were a cliff, beyond which nothing could pass. The creature had claimed this was *his* day region, so he was Slaughter after all. But who could be standing against such wealth?

Slaughter stepped aside and Stryker's breath caught. His shoulders tensed, chest froze, and mind thrashed, as if drowning. *An enemy.* The one he'd sensed. But only a hideous, small, red-haired girl. She held the hilt of the sword, the weapon as tall as she. Its light seared his eyes and anger surged hot in his chest, but fear cooled his impulse to lash out.

Fear? From this girl? No, Stryker was no weakling. The dread rising in his throat was from his keen instincts, to stay hidden from Slaughter.

That demon flattened his palm, forming the blades of his fingers into a fan. He swung, and they passed over the girl's head, her copper curls shaking with the wind. She didn't flinch. Like a statue.

The demon slashed at her again, knives flashing before her face, but still she didn't move. He bent down to her, braided cords falling over tiny ears the size of acorns. Fat lips drew into a tight sneer. "Coward," he whispered. "I'll have my way. I'll have *you*." He jerked his head violently and snapped into the flesh of an eagle again. Spreading his claws, he flew through her spirit, circled the boulder, climbed through the trees, and shot away.

The girl's eyes twitched. The first movement Stryker had seen. She stared at him through the tree he hid behind, then disappeared. She'd known he was there!

Stryker turned and strained back toward the panther upon the limb, but any movement was as if swimming against a current. The enemy had weakened him somehow. The tree was farther away now, was it not?

The Abyss. If he failed now, that's where Ernick would toss him. The terror of that heat drove his legs. He hoisted himself up the trunk that he'd so easily scaled in the flesh just moments earlier. When he finally reached the branch and entered his fleshly form, the panther's body lay limp, heavy, and exhausted, though it hadn't moved.

He lay his muzzle upon the flaky loblolly bark. A red ant crawled upon his nose and bit down, but he remained still. Who was the girl? How had she seen him, though he'd been hidden? And why had she not alerted Slaughter to his presence? Even more, why couldn't Slaughter touch her? If such a glorious demon couldn't kill the girl, an enemy, how was Stryker supposed to?

Ernick must've knowingly assigned him an impossible mission, trying to get rid of Stryker. He was threatened by Stryker's skill. Yes, that was it, Stryker reasoned. His captain was shrewd, but painfully predictable. He'd do anything if it proved to his benefit.

But Stryker was cunning. He'd figure a way to succeed in the mission, despite his captain's too obvious "hidden" motivation. And in doing so, victorious over such a powerful enemy, Stryker would demand the attention of Malsumis, lord of all the captains. He'd notice Stryker as worthy and promote him to captain himself. Give him his own day region to reign. Maybe even replace Ernick, that hollow shell of a demon. Stryker would figure out a means to succeed...

Another ant bit his nose. He breathed slowly, willing sleep to overtake his body. But the image of the girl stared back at him whenever he closed his eyes. His mouth soured at the sight of such a pitiful, insignificant spirit standing as if it owned the region. Such pride! It would be her downfall.

The tear in the skin of his belly burned. Sleep was no option. And he hadn't yet reached the Mi'kmaq camp. His legs quivered as he struggled to his paws and leapt to the earth.

Chapter 8 – Félagi

I drew the head of the hatchet across the pine log upon which I'd been sitting, peeling off bark in brown cakes. The fresh wood below lay a Celtic maze of a boring beetle's long, twisted passages.

Tryfing had ambled away to rouse our relief watch. Now he stepped back into the glow of the fire. A minute later and a tall, slender, pale-skinned man wearing a tan linen vest stumbled into the clearing, picking burrs from the knees of his trousers. In this ancient forest, brush and grass could only grow near the edge of clearings. He stopped and dug at one prickly ball, then tossed it into the fire. One-Eye followed, with long, wild, white hair brushed back from his face, like a winking Einstein facing a stiff wind.

Tryfing tapped my arm and started back toward the boat. We stepped out of the fire's cast and the dark swallowed us. I flinched at the scratch of an invisible twig on my cheek. A few more steps and the huge black columns of tree trunks appeared as my eyes adjusted to night. The pine needle bed below sprung against my feet like a taut mattress. And silent, as if standing in the nave of Duke's towering limestone chapel. For a time, the forest stilled in an eerie moment of remembrance.

Once out of earshot from the others, I asked, "How do we know my sister's still alive?"

Tryfing's arms swung like thick cords of wet hawser. "We don't. I'm thinking she's dead." He jerked to a halt and glanced back with an openmouthed smile of shock and horror. Then, as if remembering I wasn't Matok, he resumed his slow, loping stride.

"Looks like Matok and his sister were close, then?"

Tryfing's neck stooped a notch. "What do you care? You just want to get back to whatever world you came from."

True. "But I had a twin sister, once. We were close. She was young when she disappeared. If I can help save Matok from that, I'll do what I can while I'm here."

"What you can do is keep your voice down and not wake the crew." He turned and shoved a fat finger in my chest. "Look, your mom's a witch, your father's the chieftain, and Halfdan wants you dead to ensure he becomes lord when your father dies. You're also the village donkey, screwing any jenny in heat. And I don't mean slaves. Men's wives. Half the crew hates you for it. But Matok's the only friend I've got." He held the finger before my nose now. It quivered. "You need to be like smoke. Fade into the forest. Don't draw attention. Maybe soon enough you'll be gone, and Matok will be back." He turned and stomped away.

"But you said Matok was the son of a frilla. I've got...I mean, he's got no claim to be lord."

"No," Tryfing hissed back.

"So why would Halfdan be trying to kill him?"

He turned. "Matok could be chieftain if he desired. Only half the men hate you. The other half admire you. And most women..."

"But Halfdan is five times the man I am."

Tryfing gripped my neck and pinned me to the trunk of a pine, lifting my feet from the forest floor. I clawed at his grip, but it only clamped tighter. He growled, "Halfdan may be five of *you*, but Matok is twenty of him. Vestmen choose our own chieftain. We serve no tyrant. Our village would prosper a hundred times better under Matok than Halfdan." He dropped me to the pine shatters as quickly as he'd snatched me up, then turned again toward the boat. "In the meantime, we've got a toad of a man who doesn't even know how to row."

I rubbed my throat and passed a bayberry bush, its heavy fir and balsam scent reminding me of a hot Saturday as a child on the sand dunes harvesting tiny blue bayberries with Dad and Gabby. We had boiled them down and skimmed off the wax to cast candles. Gabby had tired of the chore, stripped naked, and run into the water, only to be stung by a swarm of sea nettles. Dad had consoled her, but it had been a family joke for years.

A few leathery leaves from last season still clung to this bush's thin stalks. Past it, the boat rocked in its berth forty feet away, strung between the same two trees, but five feet higher upon the tide than before. A patch of white seafoam spotlighted by the moonlight twisted in the creek's channel, rushing past like a fish escaping a hawk.

The sail draped over the boom, forming the peak of a tent. The oars, sticking straight up and lining each side of the vessel, shaped the walls. A dim glow spilled from one end. Halfdan lay upon a rower's bench, head below the gunwale, legs sticking into the aisle, the same color and thickness of the log I'd been skinning.

We walked by a freshly dug waist-high pile of dirt and rocks. Tryfing grabbed a copper mug from atop the mound, knelt, and dipped it into the hole next to it. Water had filled the shallow well and he dipped the cup several times. He pushed it into my palm and whispered, "You got it?"

I took that to mean *Don't drop it or you'll wake the crew.* "Yeah. This OK to drink?"

He gripped his beard and wrung out a few drops. "No. It'll kill you."

I smiled at the sarcasm. Comforting. It was a good sign he didn't think I was a complete screwup. It takes effort to be sarcastic.

"It's fine," he muttered. "Just dig a hole next to a creek and it'll fill with water. No raccoon piss in it, so won't give you the runs."

I knelt. The water's surface had calmed, and I flinched at my reflection. The chiseled, sharp jawline seemed so confident and proud. So not me. Still, somehow I'd known this body my entire life. My fingers wrapped the cup and I bowed, reaching in and drawing water out.

Dampness pressed through the knees of my trousers. I stared at the mug and remembered how I'd knelt and prayed five years ago, next to a similar beach, for us to find Gabby alive. As the days wore on, my prayers had changed to simply that we would find her body. Neither had been answered. A senseless suffering. Meaningless.

"Drink," Tryfing whispered.

I brought the cup to my lips. Maybe this was God's way of answering that prayer. If so, He was more sarcastic than I'd given Him credit for. *I* was the one who'd last seen her, who'd left her on the dock by herself, though only for a minute. I'd run up and down that shoreline, searching all afternoon. I'd even borrowed our friend's skiff and combed the water till the Coast Guard told me to go home. Maybe I was being given another chance. Maybe this was how I'd return to my world. To what was left of it. Mom, Dad, and Nikki. To Christine, maybe...

I drank. The water proved bitter and metallic, but cooled my throat and quenched my thirst. We crawled up the gangway, a plank lashed to the gunwale and sloped to the shore. The tent was high enough that I needn't duck. The sail had dried, but still the scent of moist wool filled the air. I felt a belonging, as if I was home. One of Halfdan's eyes cracked open but rolled up and closed again. His massive chest, still bare except for the wolfskin draped across his shoulders, swelled with a deep breath. The shock of red hair tied to a necklace lay centered on his sternum.

Smoky light glowed from a clay lamp lashed to the mast with a flame rising on either side. The crew sprawled atop their benches like drunks at a keg party: one on his back with feet planted on the deck to keep from rolling, another sideways with his head atop a bag or wooden block, and one even on his stomach with neck atilt and legs and arms drooping loosely, resembling how I might have imagined a corpse in a crime scene photo. My body grew heavy when I glanced my own sturdy plank. Never thought a piece of rough oak could look so welcoming. It was difficult to avoid kicking anyone, but Tryfing even bumped a man's arm with his knee and didn't rouse him. As I lay down, the seat, gouged with an adze, polished with wear, fit my shoulders perfectly. Tryfing lay on his back as well, long arms flopping to the deck on either side.

I turned my head to face him. "Why does Halfdan have the lock of red hair?"

One eye opened. He pinched his nose and scratched it, then dropped his arm again. "It's your sister's. Enough for one night. We'll talk about Halfdan in the morning. He's a *félagi*."

I scowled. It was all I had strength to do. "Félagi?"

His eye closed and his nose dipped in the slightest of nods. "A warrior. A bondservant to our military. Your uncle by marriage."

Chapter 9 – Tuurngat

Tuurngat opened her eyes to thin smoke from a smoldering fire rising in a stream, pooling near the top of her wetuom before it slipped out a half-opened flap. The tight vertical branches that formed the shallow walls curved upward toward the opening, woven like crooked fingers knitted together, ready to crush whatever it held. Soft soot blackened the limbs near the apex, and the sweaty foot stink of the charred sacred mushrooms still clung to the air. Her spirits had warned her an evil was approaching, and as the shaman of the Abenaki, her duty was to protect the tribe. Smoking such plants allowed clear communication with her spirits. She needed to discover from which direction the evil would appear.

Her mattress of dried reeds covered by moose skin warmed her, tempting her back to sleep. She'd woken from a recurring dream where she'd been seated on a white beach that stretched as far as she could see. Before her had lain an immense lake of crystal water. No waves disturbed its glassy surface, yet silent flashes of the brightest light blazed beneath it, like a noiseless lightning storm, as if the water itself were a living creature. Across the lake's expanse had sat the Great Enemy, the one her spirits always warned her about, the overlord who demanded worship of all his followers. What a haughty taskmaster! She'd observed him many times before, but always from a distance. He was the reason for all suffering, her spirits assured her. This time, his subjects had knelt in defeat before him, enslaved to his service. Thousands of men, women, and children, even millions, offered a constant stream of compulsory praise. Still, the lake had flashed flax-flower blue and emerald green at their song, the most peaceful harmony she'd ever heard.

A temptation. Must've been. The dream had been a test. Had she passed?

"Two are coming," came the hissed whisper of a spirit in her ear. Her eyes blinked open again to the smoky air. The voice had woken her the first time as well. She sat up and rubbed her eyes with her palms and shooed a mouse skittering near her feet. She stroked the necklace of finger bones her mother had bequeathed to her at age eight, a means to control the voices of the spirits in her head. Still, those advisors seemed to chatter and shout incessantly, never sleeping.

The voice that had woken her had been Healer's. So many years ago, when she'd found him deep in the forest, she'd been fasting for a week and smoking the sacred mushrooms then as well. He'd worn a coat of purest white egret feathers and brushed her cheek with a plume, like a lover wooing her to bed. "I'll heal everyone in your village," he'd promised. "You'll be the most powerful shaman ever."

She'd invited him in.

Yet, like most of her lovers, he'd provided little benefit. Any help she had to coax through chants, petting his insatiable ego before he'd even look at a single suffering child. And now his cures seemed to harm more than heal. Yet this was a shaman's way for the tribe. To serve and restore. To protect and love. She'd devoted her entire life to the Three Truths, the foundation of their whole society, and the guarantee of her village's health: *Peace: Is this preserved? Righteousness: Is it moral? Power: Does it preserve the integrity of the tribe?*

Healer was a good spirit, she assured herself. Any problem must be her fault. She needed to work harder to understand him and all the others, for the benefit of the tribe. "Hearing from the spirit world is a blessing," the elders had always said. So, she'd begged the spirits' favor, listened to their wisdom, and even sought out other counselors when necessary. If the wellness of her people meant she lived with a head full of tumultuous chattering, it was worth it.

She dropped her chin to her chest, stretching her neck, fighting the desire for sleep. "Who is coming?" she asked, keeping her voice low to not wake her husband. His massive head rested upon a rolled deerskin across a bed of coals smoldering between them. Dim orange light danced on his rough cheeks and long, noble nose. He'd never disappointed her. Even encouraged her to work harder to learn from her spirits, despite frequent setbacks. To fail would be to shame him. She couldn't bear that thought.

"Two are coming. One by water. One by foot. The one by foot is waiting for you now, in the woods behind the wigwam."

"Who?"

A whiff of oak filled her nose. She pinched it to keep from sneezing. The clamor of the other spirits calmed as Healer gave his answer. A rare quiet she wished could last a lifetime. "A black spirit. A ranger."

Not a person? But she'd always had to seek spirits on her own. A smile spread across her lips. Was her power finally turning? She tried a self-assured tone. "What does it want?"

"We will guide you. Speak to him. Discover his desires."

She winced as a shout rose from the throng in her head. "Do not fear him. We will protect you!"

* * * *

Stryker slowed to a walk, then crept from the shadow of the towering forest, across mossy granite, and stalked to the edge of a rivulet. He'd been running for a half hour since witnessing the engagement between Slaughter and the bizarre girl. Searching the surroundings, he lapped at the gentle water and it cooled his throat. Relief. It was one of the mercies of taking a fleshly form. Otherwise, a demon's spirit was never at rest.

He dipped his tongue once more then bounded ahead, into the cover of the far woods. Within moments, he stood near a clearing along a low riverbank. A few stiff brown clumps of grass stood upright, scattered across the meadow. The rest of the field had been combed down facing east by a winter snow, as if in worship. Only a few green blades had begun to sprout this early in the spring. In the middle of the sprawl stood at least fifty hump-shaped wigwams constructed of sticks and grass, like beaver dams upon the ground. Most were covered in birch bark or grass mats, but branches still poked through their coverings like half-buried bones.

This Abenaki settlement was exactly where Ernick had said it would be. The southern Indian tribe hunted and lived like the Mi'kmaq, their northern counterparts. But the Abenaki were weaker. "Peaceful," Ernick had called them. "Another name for weakness. Use them if you must, but owe them nothing. Their shaman is loyal to demons."

Stryker stalked forward and crouched behind a thick stand of dry grass. A huge mound of sun-bleached oyster shells stood to one side, stinking of rotten shellfish. An ant ran up one nostril and he stifled a sneeze. The bent stalks rustled in a breeze and he peered over them. A woman swung open the door flap of the nearest wigwam and crawled out. She stood only the height of a child. Deer hide clothing, cut in strips and tied at the seams, did little to veil her thin frame. The blouse was decorated with a plate of white tube-shaped beads across the chest. Long black hair hung straight, and a tan-and-red shaman's mask of woven sweetgrass covered her face from the nose up. A black feather hung from each cheek piece. She walked toward him and stopped in front of the grass clump he waited behind.

Had they sent a child to speak with him? Stryker was no amateur. An insult to his status! He spread his toes and his claws dug into the earth. His haunches tensed.

A knife pricked his sternum.

"I wouldn't do that." A woman's voice, rough with age. He stared at her chin, the only visible portion of her face. Wrinkles sprouted from the corners of her mouth.

Stryker closed his eyes and slipped into spirit. Not as deeply as when he'd spied on Slaughter and the girl. But just enough to see the real world through his soul's eye. Below him, a long-hooked claw came into focus, the tip of the arm of the smallest demon he'd ever seen. Like a scorpion with a gleaming black talon instead of pincers. Stryker would've laughed, had he not stood in such a vulnerable position. Despite this demon's small stature, his strength was enormous, able to prick his body without even taking a fleshly form.

"Impressive, isn't he?" the woman asked.

Stryker glanced up at the shaman. She stood wavering, thin and emaciated, smelling of wood, smoke, and dung. There had been many others like her, neglecting themselves, even ingesting poisons, barely alive, just to gain the attention of their spirits. And she had many. A crowd of them surrounded her; dozens of scaly creatures, short and small, a horde of pitifully weak demons missing eyes or limbs. Drooling and dragging half-paralyzed bodies that resembled sickly rats. What a wretched existence, to possess a human, a member of the cursed species. The lowest form of insult. Still, if Stryker had to choose between it and the Abyss...

"Impressive," he muttered. A half lie. The clawed demon seemed to be the single *impressive* spirit of the bunch. A black serpent twisted around the shaman's neck, entwining itself through a necklace of finger bones, and whispered Stryker's reply into her ear. His tail wrapped around a single white egret feather that he brushed against her cheek. That would be her head demon, the leader of this pitiful pack. Whenever multiple spirits took up residence in a single host, fights would inevitably pursue, resulting in a chain of command, of sorts. This serpent spoke for all.

"What do you want?" the woman murmured.

To slice your bowels and tie them around—

The claw dug into his skin. His most pressing question had just been answered. This tiny demon really *could* kill his panther's body. What to do? *Flattery.* Humans loved it. "I need your help."

The serpent whispered his answer to her.

The crowd of devils squirmed. The shaman's wrinkled skin stretched tight as a smile spread across her face. "My help? You're the wealthy one. A black panther? That must've cost a fortune. Where do you come from? Who's your master?"

Not telling you. "I've come because I heard of your power. Are you as skilled as I was told?" Other than the clawed demon, with this gaggle's aid the woman would be lucky to utter a single chant without accidentally cursing herself.

Her chin lifted in defiance. "You lie. You've heard nothing. And I only serve our tribe. You aren't from nearby, so why are you here? What are you unable to accomplish yourself?"

She'd seen through his flattery, and all but refused to aid him. Her concern seemed to be for her people. Such compassion soured his tongue, but he could use that weakness to manipulate her. "I've been sent to warn you. There is one you must slay."

"I protect our village, not kill them!" Her lip curled as she spat the words.

Ha! This woman still thought she was doing *good*. What a fool. This horde was more deceptive than Stryker had given them credit for. Demons disguised themselves as messengers of peace, masquerading as birds or rabbits. If only she could see their true form, she'd realize she'd been lied to by each of them. "No. None of your own. A Vestman. A white warrior. A threat to your village. So, by your own admission, it's your duty."

"A warrior?"

"Yes. And a threat. Many will paddle in by the river and pretend to come with peace. Even brings gifts to trade. But why would they send warriors carrying weapons if not intending to use them on you? A special enemy is among them. A strong, fierce man with raven-black hair. You will notice him when he arrives, taller than all the rest. Kill him."

She looked away, toward the stream. "Kill him yourself. Your master didn't provide your form for no reason. Use it. Or are you a coward?"

He flicked his tail and tensed his haunches to spring upon her. The tiny demon's claw bit through the flesh of his chest, and his heart quivered within him. Sharper than any talon he'd seen. The pain of the cut was only slight, but the threat was clear. With just a flinch, his life could be ended. Though these demons used the shaman for their own pleasure, her death would mean seeking another host. So they'd never allow him to kill her. Human-dwellers were the lowest form of demon.

What to say? He couldn't touch the Vestmen. Orders of Ernick. What else? Stryker had grown too accustomed to working alone, and lying was a skill that needed to be practiced. He blinked as an idea slammed his mind, as if thrown by an outside force. *Use it.* "Not my battle. I've been sent to warn you. You've earned the respect of many kindly spirits. Kill this man, and your village will be safe."

The serpent winked at him, then whispered into her ear while he stroked her cheek with the plume. He seemed to enjoy the game. No wonder he was this horde's leader.

She grabbed a stiff stalk and twisted off a length. "I don't believe you." She walked around the stand of grass and stared down at him. Then stooped low. Her eyes glowed as if afire. He saw her own spirit within them; caged, naked, and up to her chin in her own filth. A prisoner within her own body, and ignorant of the fact her spirits had put her there. She deserved it, the foolish demon-whore.

The skin on her neck throbbed as copper-scented blood pulsed through gorgeous, hot veins just below its surface. Such thick, fat conduits. One on either side of her windpipe. Tasty flesh. It'd been too long. He'd be doing her a favor, killing her. And he would, if it weren't for her guard's talon holding him back. He'd have another chance later, he assured himself. When she least expected it and her demons were otherwise occupied.

Her luscious throat swelled as she spoke. "You've come for help, not to warn me. If I kill this warrior. This Vestman, as you call him. You give me what I want in return."

Owe them nothing, Ernick had said. "What do you desire?"

The fire in her eyes dimmed. "A powerful spirit. One...to control the turmoil of the others within me. To quiet their voices."

Wretched creature. That wasn't the way the world worked.

The crowd of spirits giggled.

"Of course. A Driver." Sounded good. It slipped from his panting tongue. The lies were starting to flow more naturally now. "All practiced shamans own a higher class of spirit, one that brings order to the others. If you agree, I'll bring you a Driver." Such didn't exist. He'd bring her whatever gnawing, groveling, diseased demon he could find, dress it in white plumage, and pump it full of lies. Stupid humans thought anything in white could be trusted.

She stood, twisting the reed between her fingers till it broke, then spat upon the ground. The covenant was sealed.

Chapter 10 – Upstream

Gabby pats wet sand over my toes. "Quit wiggling them! You're ruining it."

We're on the beach at Kitty Hawk, and she has me covered in grit up to my neck. I think of the Apache Gukimazin, who once killed a man by burying him inside an anthill. Last week's storm washed up an entire stretch of tiny, black-spotted shells that crunch beneath her palm as she packs me in tighter. Three girls in two-piece bikinis strut past, the dotted husks crackling beneath their feet brittle as potato chips.

Gabby giggles as she pours water from a pail over the sandy mound and it runs around my neck. We're twelve, and neither of us want to ever grow up.

A wave crashes and foam rushes up, almost to where I'm lying. "I'm going surfing," she announces. Then hops up, grabs a pink bodyboard, turns her sunburned back on me, and runs to the water.

No! Stay away from the water! This is how it always ends. I try to shout, to warn her not to go into the surf, but can't draw a breath. The wet sand is too heavy. Panic scorches my belly as I rock my neck, trying to free my arms. My legs are pinned too, as if trapped beneath a car. A white sand crab crawls up and tears at my left ear. Another scales my chest and pinches my nose. A hundred others move to cover my face as Gabby leaps into the water and paddles out.

* * * *

I woke with a gasp. A prick on my earlobe and I swatted away a fly. Heat suffered my cheeks and bright light burned my eyes. I lay upon an oak bench with my neck craned to one side, rerunning the dream through my mind. I'd often had this same nightmare— Gabby running to the water. She never comes back. But what were the crabs all about? Those were new.

Another pinch, this one on the side of my nose. Instinctively, my hand slapped it and squished a plump mosquito. I lifted my head and my neck cramped from resting in its twisted position.

The bench across from mine stood empty, though the rest of the crew still lay snoring at their various stations. *Waked from one nightmare, but trapped in another.* Still on a Viking longboat. I dropped my head in despair and my skull bounced on the plank with a hollow *smack!* Ouch! Forgot I didn't have a pillow in this world.

I sat up, shading my eyes from a rising sun, only half over the horizon, yet its hot rays already blaring into the open end of the tent. The bow faced east and the cutbacks of oyster rocks we'd navigated the previous day jutted like finger bones across the shimmering water. I stood, grasping the air, reaching for the edge of the sail to steady myself. I stepped up onto a narrow platform just behind the curve of the bow. Leaning upon the stempost, I studied the carved spiral decoration clutching its crown. A whirlpool of wood. A spinning fury that either gave birth to, or signaled the doom of, this vessel.

A thin white fog boiled through the trees and spilled down the riverbank, as if flowing from a bubbling caldron. The heat of the rising sun fell upon the sail and steam rose from the moist material, disappearing into the cool morning. I stretched my lungs, filling them with the humid air, and was suddenly fully awake.

Sulfur and salt water. The two scents of a waterman. They had greeted me every morning of the summer at 4:00 a.m., loading the skiff, trolling slowly out of Jeezer's Marina to avoid creating a wake, then opening the throttle and skimming across glassy blackness as if it were ice, skating between miles of charcoal marsh lined with yellow-green seagrass, till the creek spilled into Albemarle Sound. Funny, how smells can arouse memories so vividly. Or connect worlds. Sulfur and salt water.

Copper glinted on the bank above. *Gabby!* Maybe. The light was striking her hair, but the witch's mist half concealed her body. My fists clenched and I filled my lungs again to call, but remembered the slumbering crew and thought better of it. She pointed a finger away from the light, up the creek, into thick fog.

I glanced down the length of the boat. Several of the crew began to stir. Halfdan's tree-trunk legs rose from the deck as he stretched them. No getting past him to meet with Gabby, or whoever it was.

I turned toward her, lifted my arms, and shrugged. She puffed her cheeks and, with both hands this time, pointed fingers and swung her arms emphatically, toward the west. It was Gabby, all right. She'd made the same gesture one hazy morning standing on the bow of Dad's skiff, acting as a spotter, pointing us toward our oyster cages.

I cupped my hands around my mouth and whispered, "What?" As if she could hear me from this distance.

She pressed flat-bladed fingers against her lips, blew me a kiss, and disappeared. Whether she vanished as a ghostly apparition or simply turned and walked into the fog, I couldn't tell.

"Love the calm of first light," came Tryfing's groggy voice next to me.

I flinched at the sound. "Didn't hear you wake."

His eyelids drooped pink and puffy, but his expression seemed bright. And he didn't squint at the sun. He chuckled. "That's a funny saying. Waking doesn't make noise. Sleep does." He grabbed the knot of my beard and gently turned my face toward him. "Anticipating trouble? Looks like you started your war stripes."

I pulled my head back. "No. Just swatted a couple mosquitos."

"Huh. That's your battle face. Red paint on the side of your nose and across one ear."

Low thuds of boots on wood came from inside the tent. Halfdan stepped along the deck boards and kicked the feet of those still asleep. Tryfing stepped aside and Halfdan hopped onto the small deck next to me, almost spilling me into the water. The boat shook under his weight. He untied the rope of his trousers, they fell to his ankles, and he relieved himself over the side of the boat. A swollen ribbon of scar tissue crossed the backs of his thighs. He spoke to the river. "I've changed my mind. As soon as the tide swings, we head east, back into the ocean. There's a chance we aren't far enough south yet. We need to be certain to cut off the Mi'kmaq and not have to chase them on foot."

But Gabby had pointed inland. "I think we should head upstream," I said.

Tryfing turned quickly and busied himself helping One-Eye roll up the sail tent and secure it to the yard. Halfdan tied his trousers and squared to me. His gaze was hot, as if his anger had been revived by a good night's sleep. "You may own a share of this boat, but you don't say where she goes on this quest."

Own a share? I'd have to ask Tryfing about that. I stepped down from the platform. "I'll row where you tell me, but my sister's up this river."

"Your *half* sister," said Halfdan, almost yelling. His eyes cut to the tall, thick forest. The first rays cast gold light onto a landscape of tall brown trunks behind him, silhouetting his wide frame. "You knew of those cliffs where we waited out the hail. So...when you say she's up this river, is that Matok speaking, or the voice of your witchy mother?"

"What difference?"

"Difference? Because if it's your witchy mother, I'm inclined to believe her. But *you* are a fool."

I pointed upstream, to a spot where the fog had burned off and the water gleamed black and slick. "I can't say. I just know what I'm looking for, and it's up there."

A brown branch with thick green clumps of pine needles rushed past on the incoming tide. Probably torn down by yesterday's storm. Halfdan stared as it shot past, then reached to his head and cinched his upturned knot of hair, the same way Gabby had adjusted her ponytail. "Incoming tide just started. We'll travel inland until it slackens, only that long. If we don't find anything, we turn around and ride the current as the moon calls out the water."

That only gave us about four hours to paddle inland.

Halfdan spat over the side of the boat and galloped to the stern. Within minutes the deck was cleared. The two remaining lookouts trotted up the gangplank as half of us put our backs into the oars. Five strokes and we were in the middle of the wide creek, racing silently inland, with the tide. Halfdan steered us between fallen trees, barely visible through the fog, roots still anchored in the black earthen bank, green limbs stretching skyward through the brackish water like arms reaching from a grave.

We rowed at a fraction of the pace we'd kept in the heated panic of outrunning the ice storm yesterday. My body reveled in its use, shoulders loosening from sleep, tingling and pinching all the way to my fingernails. No one shouted a rhythm, yet we rowed as one man. My body knew the pace, sensing when I pulled too hard or dipped the oar too quickly. For a half hour we continued our leisurely strokes. Silence on the boat, but we all seemed to listen to the forest noises creeping upon the mist. In one spot, a chorus of frogs croaked so loudly pain throbbed between my temples. As our boat passed near, they fell silent, but the clamor picked up again behind us.

Dip, pull, finish, and recover. Dip, pull, finish, and recover. We rowed as if our oars were tied together. I was a part of a crew. I'd never played team sports. Cross-country was only a team with regard to scorekeeping. But this body had been born among these men, grown up under their eyes. I studied my enormous fingers gripping the handle. Matok belonged. Maybe I'd always been this person, or had been him in a previous life. And was once again.

"On the bank!" One-Eye hollered. With his wild, brushed-back hair, he looked to be in a perpetual state of surprise. He pointed past the bow. "A man, I think. He was on that limb over the water."

Halfdan steadied his gaze in that direction then spat into the water. "You couldn't see your fat cow of a woman if she stripped naked and danced in daylight." The boat erupted in nervous laughter.

One-Eye pointed again. "You see him now! Running on the bank. Faster than a wolf."

Everyone raised oars and the boat coasted in silence. Quick footfalls upon wet earth cut through the mist. I glimpsed a dark body flash between tree trunks. If it was a man, he was at a full sprint. Halfdan called for a rapid pace. Within a few strokes, we were shooting along the creek. I steadied my gaze upon the bank and we gained on the runner, though gradually. He ducked below vines and vaulted limbs like an athlete running hurdles. As he passed between shadows, his skin was light, though darker than that of the Vestmen. He was bare chested, with only a flap of leather around his waist. No taller than a boy, but his legs carried him so quickly they were a blur. As we pulled abreast, he was carrying a short pole, maybe a spear. His head was shaven on the sides, and his hair drew into a single braid that flapped behind him like a whip. A native.

Halfdan leaned on the tiller and we rounded a shallow bend. "He's Abenaki, not Mi'kmaq. Marr, tell him to stop. That we're peaceful. We want to trade."

I glanced at the brightly colored shields stowed on the gunwale and the sword hanging from Halfdan's side. The runner was an Indian, not an idiot. My breathing was starting to come harder now, and the entire ship sounded a chorus of grunts as we strained to keep pace. With each stroke, oars creaked against their keepers and the bow lifted. My arms and back began to ache, but they didn't tire.

A shout echoed from back near the stern. A man I'd noticed earlier, with high cheekbones and brown eyes. I'd figured him to be a slave due to his features, though he dressed like the Vestmen in rough wool and fur. His shouts were in a different language than that of the others. The words were smooth, less guttural, sounding of many vowels.

The runner turned his head toward us, but leapt over a branch and increased his already astounding pace.

Halfdan stretched an arm toward the shore. "We need him to show us where the Mi'kmaq are. Tell him we just want to trade. We'll pay him to talk."

Before Marr could shout again, the runner dropped his spear on the ground and shot off. Marr called after him, but he'd disappeared into the forest on a trail that led inland. Halfdan raised an arm and we all ceased rowing. I glanced back. Tryfing's face was red as the brightest shield. He craned his head back, straightened his windpipe, and drew air in loud, wheezing gulps. A wisp of fog drifted over us, and only then did I notice most of the mist had burned off. We coasted along, carried by the tide, around another shallow bend, and into full view of the village where the runner had been charging.

Chapter 11 – Caged

Stryker raced across the matted brown meadow surrounding the Abenaki village, leaving their tiny shaman to ponder how she'd kill the tall Vestman. Her problem now. But it was never wise to trust humans too much, not for matters of such importance.

At the edge, he shot between a stand of thistle weed and a thick knot of blackberry vines. Briars scraped his cheek as he pondered the unusual woman. Most humans trembled at the sight of a black panther. Even shamans, despite often speaking with local demons who assumed all variety of animal forms. But she hadn't exhibited the slightest fear. Why? It was as if she counted herself already dead.

He slowed and trotted along the stream bank, headed west toward the Mi'kmaq camp. After several hours on the trail, the moon's calming glow faded as the sun's piercing brilliance overtook the night. Now a tangle of vines and green leaves hung like a curtain ahead of him. It signaled a clearing, around the edge of which smaller trees and shrubs grew. Meadows like this were the only place the virgin forest couldn't choke out smaller plants. The enemy always camouflaged itself with light.

He tore through the green mesh and stepped out among tall grass and scrub. Hundreds of large wigwams stood near the center of an expansive field with smaller dwellings scattered at the edges. Dirt trails radiated from the settlement like the lines of a spider's web, disappearing at the edge of the woods. The clearing ran all the way down to the creek where large boulders had been uncovered by the wash of centuries. This was the summer village of the Mi'kmaq, much larger than that of the pitiful Abenaki. Why didn't the Mi'kmaq just kill their rivals and be done with the nuisance tribe? Every summer a few Indian scouts would be waylaid, from one village or the other. Still, after the confrontation their chiefs would meet, smoke a pipe, then leave each other alone. The Mi'kmaq, though warlike and strong in number, like every other group of humans, were still weak at heart.

He stalked down one of the paths and eased his belly to the ground outside the first house, ears turning fore and aft. Eyes darting ahead, then skyward. It was too risky, exposing himself during the day. If Slaughter or one of his scouts spotted him, there would be no escape. He had witnessed the disembowelment of three of Slaughter's demons, coyotes, that had wandered into Ernick's day region. But the pain and shame of death was welcome when compared to the burning torment of the Abyss. And no captain would ransom a disgraced demon from that pit when there were so many others from whom to choose.

The breeze rose around him, hissing through the grass. The bark wigwams shifted and groaned. A thin rat waddled out from below a broken bark shingle upon the ground, stopped in the middle of the path and glanced at Stryker, then shot into the neighboring hut. Stryker considered nabbing it for breakfast but didn't want to risk drawing attention. Each summer, the Mi'kmaq would migrate down from the north and repair their dilapidated village. Within days, the entire place would stink like a mass grave. Because that's what it was. Full of putrid, mortal humans. All they did was eat, sleep, and die. Of what use was a mortal, except with which to pleasure oneself?

He lifted his nose and sniffed. A light breeze had blown from the north for the last few hours and carried a tinge of their scent. With hundreds traveling together, he could smell them a day out. They could arrive as early as tomorrow morning.

Stryker trotted between the dwellings, pausing to glance in each one. Ernick had said to clear the way before the Mi'kmaq, to ensure no enemy was waiting in ambush. A family of raccoons and a host of rats were the only occupants. No wolves. He licked his nose in disappointment. Sometimes they adopted a hut as their den, and canine flesh was almost as delicious as human. He could certainly stand his ground against any lone eastern wolf, though never a pack.

The huts were arranged in concentric circles, radiating outward from a large dirt-packed arena. That was where the natives complained to their chiefs about how one man had stolen another's wife, or how he'd been cheated in trade. Even their leaders were weak!

The more he considered the Mi'kmaq's imminent arrival, the deeper his claws dug into the earth. How dare those squalid humans walk upon this ground as if they owned it! And cross from one day region to another without a care? None should be allowed to strut about as if they belonged to a place they could only occupy for a single lifetime.

In one of the dome-shaped homes a woven mat of salt grass lay in the corner. It was the size the Indians used for their babies.

Infants stank worse than the grown ones. Stryker lifted the pad in his mouth and ran to the edge of the forest where poison ivy grew in a thick clump. He placed the bed roll upon it and pushed it down, grinding it back and forth upon the leaves with his claws. He flipped it over and did the same to the other side, then placed it back into the wigwam. He licked his nose at the thought of the suffering it would bring to the child of the hut's unsuspecting inhabitants. He'd been instructed to clear the way, but no restriction on entertainment had been given.

The fields and hunting grounds still needed to be searched. Too little time. At the last wigwam, he heard the rustle of feathers above and slipped inside. Only a flock of blackbirds. But the enemy was deceptive. Always changing form. How had it become a human, a Vestman? To dwell within a human like the gaggle of demons inside that tiny shaman was below Stryker's status. But to take a human's physical form—could there be any worse fate? Why would any demon stoop so low? And who was the spirit of the girl he'd seen Slaughter threatening? The enemy was plotting something, but Stryker was cunning and would figure it out. Tricking the shaman to kill the Vestman had been brilliant. That woman held the heart of her entire tribe. She could turn them against the Vestmen with a word, a glance. And she was so eager to believe Stryker's lie. "I'll bring you a Driver," he'd said. What a joke! So easily malleable, she deserved whatever homeless, diseased demon he found her.

His stomach burned with growing hunger. Rabbit would be plentiful at the hunting grounds. But it would take hours to scout the area and the sun was full in the sky already. He would need to climb a tree and wait out the day on a high branch. He glanced over his shoulder to the arena in the middle of the village, raised his tail, and marked the hut with his scent. A plan was forming. One cunning and steeped in deception. Stryker might even gain his own day region. He sprinted down one of the paths to the edge of the creek and continued west, away from the sun.

* * * *

Tuurngat lifted a wooden peg and opened a cage barely long enough for the skinny, naked, adolescent boy lying upon the ground within it. Thin oak saplings and willow boughs formed the walls and ceiling. The child could have escaped if he had wanted at first, but he'd been brave then. Now, halfway through the two-week ritual, her child was so weak he couldn't stand. And deranged to the point he couldn't remember his name. Or his mother's.

Healer, her medicine spirit, rustled his feathers anxiously. "Shove it in his mouth! Give him the potion!"

The other spirits chattered away excitedly as well, and she winced. Her head could barely contain the noise. How was it no one else could hear such turmoil?

"Freehap, sit. You must eat," she said. Her son's eyes were red as strawberries, but dull and dry. His breathing was shallow, like a dog's panting. She placed her hand upon his chest. His heart raced. She scooped his neck in a palm and pulled him upright, though his rigid body resisted. Leaning him back upon the wall, she lifted a gourd of water to his white, cracked lips, but most of it ran down his neck. "You need to drink, Freehap."

"Leave it for him," said a plump man squatting outside the cage. He leaned upon a spear with a split tip for gigging frogs. "Just because he's your son doesn't mean he gets easy treatment." The chief had sent the warrior to ensure just that. Their leader needed to appear impartial but had assigned a different watcher each day, allowing her an unspoken degree of leniency. She could lie to one and not be caught by the other. And calling this one a warrior was to insult the real men of the tribe. Crouching on his haunches, his belly stretched over his loincloth like one of his frogs that he so relished. Even his wide lips resembled the amphibian. But he was a loyal guard, she reminded herself.

She quickly lifted the water to her son's lips again. "He has not drunk for three days."

He had.

She dipped her fingers into her mortar and pinched a small glob of fibrous green datura. The potent medicine was force-fed the entire duration of the ritual. It drew a boy to the spirits who then erased memories, graciously allowing him to begin life anew as a man. If any of them still remembered his childhood after the first two weeks, he was sent back for another treatment.

"Quick! Shove it in!" Healer shouted, as if a sexual experience for him.

Freehap was already unaware of his surroundings, and now the real peril was that his spirit might not return. She'd led many boys through this same ritual, and knew when one's spirit could no longer sustain him. She had secretly weakened this mixture by cutting it with grass, but her fingers still quivered as she cupped his neck and brought it to his mouth. The clamor in her head rose to a frenzy, as if a thousand clay pots were being shattered.

"To the river! Thirty fighters approach, by canoe," a runner shouted as he raced past, footfalls stirring dust.

Squatting Frog glanced toward the water and Tuurngat flicked away the datura into a bush. The chief had deployed the scouts days earlier because the Mi'kmaq returned this time each year. He'd doubled their count yesterday when she'd warned him an enemy would approach by the water. Squatting Frog growled at Tuurngat as she wiped her son's lips, as if she'd given him the medicine. But he turned and sprinted away.

The spirits calmed till none spoke. Feet thudded on packed dirt, racing toward the stream. A mockingbird chirped atop the adjoining wigwam, no longer drowned out by the noise within her head. She touched her finger bone necklace. Was its magic finally working? Why was the world suddenly silent?

Healer's voice was a whisper now. "The enemy is here. We must go. We'll be back when he is gone."

"Which one is the enemy? Why are you leaving?"

"We must go!"

She probed under the green goo in her mortar where she'd hidden a slice of venison, mashed to a pudding. She scooped it up and shoved it inside her son's mouth, then pressed the cup to his lips. He gagged and swallowed, but his eyes remained dry, gaze unfocused. She propped him in the corner and kissed his cheek. "Even if you remember me, deny it."

She placed the mortar and cup upon the floor of her wigwam, grabbed a flint-bladed knife, and continued down the rocky path to the creek. If there were thirty of them, how would she know which was the enemy? Her spirits had left and the panther had only described him as tall, ruddy, and with black hair. She shouldn't be near the water. If an enemy approached, a battle was certain. But the panther had told her *she* must kill the enemy. Was it necessary that she pierce his heart, or would a warrior suffice? "Power comes from the spirits you choose," her mother had taught. She slipped the dagger beneath her belt and rubbed her bone necklace as she trotted toward the creek.

The grass hissed in the breeze like the whisper of one of her spirits, but the wind stilled and the noise ceased. The click and crackle of hundreds of dragonfly wings sounded above her as the insects shot about after gnats and mosquitos. Noises she hadn't heard since a child. Such silence of her spirits seemed to carry a sense of dread, yet she reveled in her newfound freedom. As she neared the bank, the air cooled and the early morning sun blazed upon the faces of a battle line of the tribe's warriors gripping spears, bows, and clubs. The chief stood behind them in the middle, gripping his own spear, his body aged but straight and proud, wearing his vest of white and copper beads. An expensive display. His cheeks drooped, but his eyes were sharp and his forehead raised. He tried to shoulder his way between two warriors, but the men only tightened their ranks, protecting him. Still, nothing stirred upon the water. Only a pine branch with short limbs of wet needles floated past.

The men straightened as she stepped around their line and descended to the water's edge. Their eyes darted to her, then away, scared to look upon her masked face. "Don't let them stare at you," Healer had always said. "They know nothing of our ways." Yet now he was absent. And their gazes arrows flying through her body. Did they know that her spirits had left? If a spiritual enemy approached, its death fell upon her shoulders, the shaman's. That's why the panther had said *she* must kill him! This was her calling. Her time to prove herself. Her fingers rubbed the bulge of her knife beneath her belt.

A silver trout rested in the still water between two rocks. The silence in her mind was the most peace she'd experienced since that bitter cold night as a child when a spirit had first spoken to her. Her ear for their words was acknowledged by all to be a gift to the tribe. Yet now, it was as if her own spirit had been finally set free.

But, she'd never been caged, she assured herself.

The image of her son jolted her mind. Propped up. Drugged. Unaware. Had she been deceived? She was a shaman's daughter, a shaman herself. She must protect her tribe. And if she did, the panther would bring a more powerful spirit to control all her others.

A whiff of burnt oak stung her nose and a forgotten image came into focus. It had been winter and her uncle had been lying ill for weeks next to the fire in their hut. Spirits had only recently started to speak to her then. Still, she had chanted incessantly and smoked the sacred flowers, warding away evil spirits, wooing good ones.

She hadn't been strong enough then.

As her uncle's breathing had become laborious, he'd mumbled a hundred meaningless phrases. Then, with supreme effort, he'd spoken his last hollow words. "Panthers lie."

Chapter 12 – Kiona

Kiona climbed upon a stump-sized boulder in the middle of the stream and sat. She dangled her legs into the rushing, frigid water. She had inherited the build of her mother, tall with ropey muscles and the long legs of a gifted runner. Last year she had even been stationed as a lookout when a fever had restricted many warriors to their wigwams. An honor reserved for only the fastest scouts, and never a girl.

The icy liquid still carried the bite of snowmelt from far inland, numbing her skin. The last few families of her tribe, the Mi'kmaq, passed by on either side. Six days into the migration to their summer quarters, some of the older members had begun to lag. They picked their way across the streambed carefully, children or young braves on either side to steady them. On this year's journey their tribe numbered at least a thousand, and Kiona's job was to follow and ensure none became lost.

She slipped off her moccasins and the icy liquid swirled about her toes. She reached down and plucked three thorns from her skin where she'd pushed through a briar patch leading down to the stream. A short brave with shocks of white in his ponytail ambled by, cupped a drink to his mouth, then jerked his head in a *let's go*. He was the last of the group and trotted up the opposite bank.

Kiona stood, raging water up to her thighs, and started toward the forest. Mother appeared beneath a tree, as if from nowhere. The entire tribe called her Mother as well, a term of respect and endearment as the tribe's shaman, though Kiona and stubby little Nabid were her only true children. Mother stepped into the stream and waded toward her. Her brown face shimmered, as if she'd recently washed it. And she was smiling. *Good.* Maybe she'd come to apologize for their earlier argument. The woman simply wouldn't stop talking about Achak, the chief's son, and why Kiona should marry him. It had been weeks she'd been pressuring her. Achak was pleasant enough, but Kiona wouldn't be manipulated into anything. Mother's insistence was just another power play. For her, everything was about control.

But Kiona's rebelliousness was as well. She didn't want to marry Achak simply because Mother wanted her to. She sighed at the newfound realization. Still, Mother hid her power lusts behind the disguise of her shaman's mask, and Kiona would never stoop to be her puppet.

Kiona marveled at the irony of her mother's beauty as she neared. Eyes as dark as onyx, hair black and shiny, movement graceful. How could such a gorgeous woman be so—

Mother's face twisted into a wicked snarl. Her lip curled and she bared teeth like a cat. She screamed as if in pain, bitten by a serpent, spittle flying.

Kiona stopped. It was the expression Mother bore only when her most powerful spirits visited. Usually such malevolence was hidden beneath her shaman's mask.

Mother splashed toward her. Kiona broke toward the shore, but Mother grabbed her by the throat and, with the strength of two braves, dunked her beneath the water. The frigid stream washed over her body, leeching her strength. Her head smacked a rounded boulder on the shallow bottom and light flashed in her eyes. She cracked an eye and peered up toward the shimmering surface only an arm's length away. The river's strong current tugged her, but Mother's grip pinned her firmly to the bottom.

Mother stared back, her face just above the flashing churn, coal-black eyes glaring down at her, the whites shining clear and wide through tangles of Kiona's hair swaying like strands of kelp. Mother was shouting, but the water drowned her words. It numbed everything.

Yet, she wouldn't kill Kiona. She wouldn't dare. It went against every one of the Three Truths, and then the tribe would lose faith in her. Mother's power would suffer. But if she couldn't control her daughter, what kind of shaman would they think her to be? A weak one. And weakness was not one of Mother's faults.

But Kiona could hold her breath longer than any of the other girls, and most of the boys. It was a game they'd play in the hot summer to cool down. All the unmarried would grab a rock and sink to the bottom of the cool stream. The last to surface didn't have to carry water for the evening meal.

Kiona rarely carried water.

She imagined herself now holding a rock instead of smacking painfully into them, air slowly bubbling from her nose, keeping her lungs' craving at bay. Except her throat was clamped shut by Mother's thumb. She'd shoved her under a river before. Those times Kiona had tricked her into letting go by thrashing about, then going limp. Pretending to be completely out of air and on the verge of death. It had worked well before.

It wouldn't again.

Her lungs ached, then burned as they clamored to open. She gripped the wrist that held her down and twisted. Mother plunged her face below the surface and shouted, black irises now rimmed in blood red, bubbles streaming from her lips as she screamed indecipherably, the water muffling her magical curses. The nub of her other arm struck Kiona's cheek. Mother had lost that hand to a panther when Kiona was only a child.

Maybe Mother really did mean to kill this time. She'd completely lost her temper. Fits of rage like this usually lasted only a few minutes. Other times, hours.

Kiona dug the sharpened nails of her thumbs into Mother's wrist. The grip loosened, but now the nub of arm pressed upon Kiona's forehead, slamming her skull back against the rock. She gulped for air, no longer able to resist the urge, and inhaled water.

Panic shot through her body like a thunderclap. She pressed against a boulder with both feet, gave a mighty push, and twisted free. She hoisted herself up, gagging, coughing, gasping, and wielding her nails like a badger baring its claws.

Her mother gripped her throat from behind. "You *will* marry him!" she shouted.

Not while I still have breath. Kiona ducked, twisted out of the hold, then grabbed a melon-sized boulder and hurled it at her mother with both hands. The rock caught her in the belly and knocked her into the stream.

"Stop it!" screamed Nabid, Kiona's tiny younger brother, a green stripe painted across his fat quivering cheeks. He jumped between them, panting, winded from running. He faced Mother, who was standing in openmouthed surprise. Several families had gathered on the far bank. Noticing them, Mother beamed a broad smile and casually flicked water from her deerskin dress, like she'd only meant to wash it. But a snake has only one face. Blood dripped from Mother's wrist into the current. "Oh, thank you for coming back to help. But Kiona is pleasant. I saved her from the current."

Did Mother really think the tribe would believe that? Probably. And it would work. No one dared to speak a word against their shaman. Even if Mother *had* killed Kiona, all the family leaders would still sing her praises that evening. Because she was the one who told them whenever a brave from another tribe was within a half day's run from their camp. And where the most favorable hunting could be found. She'd even healed young Shada when the girl had fallen from a tree and her shinbone had stuck out from her skin like a dry white twig. Anyone who disapproved of her eventually died of a wasting disease, or simply vanished. She was the most powerful shaman ever to protect the Mi'kmaq. The chief feared her as well. Almost as much as he lusted after her.

Thick-chested Huritt stood in the shallows, mouth agape, heaving from a run, but out of Mother's reach. That boy would be a great warrior one day. He feared nothing. But even he respected the shaman's power.

Mother smiled again and sauntered back to the shore. One of the older men held out a hand and gripped her nub to steady her as she stepped out of the water. Scene already forgotten. One of the women mumbled something about how ungrateful girls were until they had their own children. The small crowd turned and headed into the woods.

Huritt splashed over. "You pleasant?" He panted, concern filling his eyes. He must've run back when he'd heard the commotion. He wore his hair cropped above his shoulders, shorter than most Mi'kmaq braves. His arms were thick as oak branches. Though at eighteen, he might fill out even more considering the muscular heft of his father, Great Scout.

Kiona spat white froth into the stream and gazed after it until the patch disappeared into the foam-churned water. The rumble and splash of the current over rocks filled her ears now, as if she'd been deaf to it before. She cleared her throat, trying to steady her voice. "I'm pleasant. Mother got in one of her evil-spirit moods." She kept her gaze downstream, not wanting to meet his eyes. A kindhearted warrior, but compassion wasn't what she needed right now.

Little Nabid leaned against her and hugged her waist. "What'd you do this time to rash her skin?"

She coughed to keep from laughing and patted his head. "Don't talk about her that way, or you may be the next to rouse her anger."

But he wouldn't. Nabid was Mother's only son, the favorite, and the youngest. The boy could murder the chief and Mother would still smile on him. Plus, she had plans. He was to be chief one day, though she never said it aloud. And if he succeeded, she'd try to manipulate him into becoming her puppet as well.

Nabid pulled away and gazed up at her. "She talked to you about Achak, didn't she? She still wants you to marry him."

Huritt glanced toward the shore and rubbed his neck, as if embarrassed. Kiona smiled and held a hand out to Nabid. "Of course. And I was the compliant daughter."

Now it was Huritt's turn to cough.

Nabid grabbed Kiona's fingers, and the three started to shore. "What does compliant mean?"

Her legs shook with cold, or maybe anger. She stumbled, and Huritt gripped her other arm with a massive, rough hand, steadying her. "It means you do what you're told," she answered.

Nabid frowned as they picked their way over the slippery rocks. "You aren't compliant." He squinted back, sun glinting upon a broad smile. Then widened his eyes, as if fearing he'd offended her. "But I like you that way, I mean. You do what Mother says...sometimes. You just don't want to marry Rat Nose." The young boy giggled at his clever insult. Truthfully, half the tribe secretly called the chief's son by the same name. The man did have a long, thin nose, smallish mouth, and pinched expression much like a rodent's.

Still, she couldn't let her brother be disrespectful. It broke one of the Three Truths by disrupting the tribe's peace. "You shouldn't call him Rat Nose, Nabid. Even if some family leaders call him that in jest, those words are not for a child to say. Know your place, and don't let anyone else hear you say it. Pleasant?"

Huritt nodded in agreement, staring at Nabid with sternness. Huritt would make a strong family leader one day. He'd been like an older brother to her and Nabid their entire lives.

At the shoreline, Kiona gathered her long hair and wrung it out. She brushed the water from her dress, though it clung to her body. The drops were tinted red and blue, bleeding paint from the leather. They rolled down the muddy bank and mixed with the stream, the current diluting, then erasing their vibrant hues. Just like such a marriage would do to her.

Huritt tucked two fingers beneath her chin and lifted it. "Your neck is bleeding a little. Can you breathe well?"

Kiona inhaled the clean musk of damp leaves and fresh grass. The cold air stung her throat. "It hurts. But will go away." She patted the tender skin there. A bruise would form, for certain. Still, the tribe would believe all of Mother's lies. She had only been trying to help her daughter across the river. How? By beating her head against the bottom of it, of course.

Large boulders lined the top edge of the bank. A thin layer of black earth spilled over them, crowned with lush grass and tall pines. A wide, muddy brown swath stained the rocks here from the feet of a thousand Mi'kmaq who had climbed back up to the migration trail, smearing the green slime that coated smaller stones near the water's edge. The front half of a wet footprint darkened a slab of granite. Mother's unmistakable track. She always walked on the balls of her feet.

Huritt pointed toward the trees. "We'd better catch up."

Kiona propped her hands on her hips. "And what's the big hurry?" No one was going to rush her into anything.

He smiled uncertainly. "She's babbling something the others can't understand. They need you to interpret."

"Who's babbling? That toothless old woman again? I love her as much as everyone else, but not even I can understand her anymore. She hasn't made sense for years."

Huritt wrung out his own hair now. When he let it go, it remained gathered straight down the back of his neck like a shaft of pine needles. As if he were a married brave, entitled to that style.

It wagged like wet rope as he shook his head. "No, not her. The girl. The fire-haired Vestman."

Chapter 13 – Evil Spirits

I studied the line of warriors as our boat coasted upstream. The current crept along, nearing slack tide. They stood shoulder to shoulder, most of them naked. Though a few wore leather blouses or trousers, tied at seams with strips dangling. All gripped spears, clubs, or bows. They were still a distance away and remained motionless, void of expression. Neither angry nor scared.

The Vestmen stared at the shore and Halfdan gripped his beard. "Quiet. We aren't here to battle these little savages, but will if we need to. They've gathered their warriors as a welcome. Let us repay their hospitality. Ready yourselves."

We stowed oars in brackets, pointing them straight up as we had the night before. Reaching beneath their benches, crew pushed aside deck boards and from beneath lifted gray metal swords the length of a crowbar. I pushed aside a plank below my feet. Under it, suspended in a wooden box, lay a thick leather belt rolled around three small-headed axes identical to the one I'd been carrying. A palm-sized sharpening stone stained with rust sat at the bottom. I turned to Tryfing. "Do I get a sword now?"

Over his head he lowered a vest sewn of several layers of deer hide. Its tan fur down the backbone stuck up like the hair of an angry dog. Armor, of sorts. "I told you, you never bought a sword."

Searching my sack, I pulled out a similar vest constructed of a single layer of heavy brown skin. No other armor or clothing. At least thick woolen trousers covered my legs. Matok mustn't go into battle completely naked. I glanced across my arms and legs. No large scars to note. That could be a good sign. Or bad. "Have I been in battle before?"

Tryfing searched about, but the others were too preoccupied to notice our conversation. He inserted a small peg into a hole in his belt and began to pull his sword from the sheath, glanced toward Halfdan, then slid it back. "Don't worry. Abenaki greet this way. They live near the Mi'kmaq, so it's their custom. Unless Halfdan says something stupid, no fight will erupt."

I slid on the vest and wrapped the belt around my waist, threading its end through a slot and buckling it as Tryfing had. The axes hung from belt loops. I'd spent many a weekend splitting logs for my grandfather's cottage. The old man had grown up on wood heat and had refused to modernize. So, Dad and I would help him chainsaw fallen oaks and maples, then split and stack them for drying. But the tools around my waist were mere hatchets with long handles. I'd always pictured a Viking's battle-axe as something huge and imposing.

I pulled one out and laid its grip in my palm. The wood was smooth, but substantial. I stroked its neck. The grain stood close, like ash. I tried to dig a fingernail into it but barely left a mark. The head proved small and light. My hand knew its weight and balance the same way it knew those of my fingers. I slid the blade across the bench and a shaving curled from the edge as if by a hand plane. I slipped it into its loop and arranged the heads backward, away from my swinging arms.

Tryfing leaned close. "Matok with a throwing axe is worth two with a sword. Try to look like you know what you're doing."

Halfdan steered the boat near shore, and we dropped an anchor in shallow water. Once the vessel settled, Marr, the Indian slave, and Tryfing lowered a gangplank.

Halfdan pointed to my side of the boat. "You men, with me." He rested a hand upon the shoulder of a stout crewman with short blond hair, whose station had been astern, close to Halfdan's perch. The fur of his vest was dappled with white. His beard short, also tipped with white. "Push off when we're ashore," Halfdan said. "Don't let the tide go out from below you. We may need a quick retreat. Protect the boat."

White-Tip pushed out his chin, lifted a boot upon his bench, and rested his hand upon the pommel of his sword.

Tryfing untied a knot, gripped both sides of the shield fixed near his bench, and yanked up. It took several tries, but with the squeak of wet wood, it broke free from a mounting post. The shield was painted yellow and black with a dark metal hub in the center, around which silver spikes radiated, like the spokes of a sundial. My own came free with less effort. Despite this armor, I pictured myself naked as the Indians. Chalky, dark blue paint covered my shield, red about the rim, and silver spikes the same as Tryfing's. *Great. I'm the Viking Captain America.*

I slid my forearm beneath a strap and gripped a wooden handle. The leather rested against a dark band of my skin, calloused and thick, near the crook of my elbow. Apparently, I had wielded this shield many times before.

As we ambled toward the gangplank, I whispered, "How does this work? I'm supposed to use this little axe against someone with a long spear?"

His hand rested upon the grip of his own weapon. "Only if you've failed to kill him already." He raised an arm and stretched his fingers flat, then lowered it in a chopping motion. "You throw it. Your enemies fall three paces before you." He flicked his wrist down. "You've tried to teach me how you hurl those things without spinning. Your axe flies straight. No one else does it like you."

He jumped upon the gangplank and trotted down into knee-deep water, light upon his feet despite his heavy appearance. Like an offensive tackle might in a ballet. I followed, balancing with the move and bob of the vessel under me. Though I'd been awkward on land my entire life, boats and salt water had always suited me.

We lined up beside the stream across from them, forming a single rank. The rocks here were the size of baseballs and coconuts, so I chose my steps carefully. Only fifteen of us, including Halfdan who had stepped out ahead. Marr stood at his side.

The Indian warriors were shorter than we, though no Vestmen were tall. I glanced down our rank and only then realized I stood a full head above the rest.

A flash of brown in the sky and I glanced up. A bald eagle circled and had just dove low over the Abenaki. A short, thin woman walked beside Halfdan, her frame covered in a blackened buckskin dress that hung to her knees and cinched around her waist with a wide belt. Stitched across her chest were white beads in diamond patterns. A braid of black hair fell upon each shoulder. A necklace of several loops of small bones draped around her neck. The upper half of her face was covered with a mask woven from grass, like the baskets sold to tourists in downtown Charleston. Or *would be* sold, I reassured myself. Current time was uncertain, but most likely a thousand years earlier than when I had left. Before Columbus. Possibly even before trappers had made it to this continent. These pale Indians held no iron knives, and their spear points were stone or wood blackened by fire to harden them. I could perceive no signs of European trade. But I couldn't rule out being in a different world altogether, as crazy as it seemed. Maybe in this one there would be no trappers. No Columbus. No me.

And how did I get home? It'd been over a day since I'd left. For Mom and Dad's sake, I needed to figure this out. My mouth tasted of vinegar as I considered them mourning the disappearance of another child. And Nikki...she'd be lost. I needed to get back.

Make fast and ride it through.

I stared at the line, struggling to grasp anything with certainty. My gaze fell upon Gabby, standing motionless on a dusty path leading down from the village. She was clothed in a buckskin dress similar to the masked woman. Had she been there all along? Another flurry of movement and the eagle dove toward her. Halfway into its dive, it abandoned the attack but continued to circle. A young warrior trotted behind Gabby and joined their line, paying her no attention.

Staring at her, I spoke out of the side of my mouth. "Tryfing, you see anyone on that trail leading up the bank?"

His head turned in that direction. "Just that new warrior. Think they're setting an ambush?"

"So, you don't see a red-haired girl?"

He squinted. "No time for games, Matok."

She stood still enough to be a statue, and in plain sight. But she'd pointed up this river earlier. She'd lured me onto that boat at the end of our pier. Either that, or I was mad. Yet, gripping my axe, I felt more alive than any deception of madness. *I've simply been drawn back in time, placed inside the body of a Viking, and am being led by the spirit of my dead twin sister, on a mission to rescue my Viking sister.*

There, clear as day.

My windpipe stiffened at the realization of how stupid I'd been. Gabby had fiery-red hair. The lock around Halfdan's neck was the same color, from my Viking sister. My mission, the reason I was here, might not be to save my Viking sibling at all, but Gabby. Maybe she wasn't dead, but alive in this world! At the least, the two were connected. And now, so was I.

The short woman danced around Halfdan, looking him up and down, shaking a stick with cords and feathers, mumbling.

Somewhere down the line one of our men shouted, "Looks like your mother, Matok. But with smaller breasts." Half the men chuckled and grinned. The others glanced nervously in my direction.

"Their witch," Tryfing said. "Every Indian village has one. She checks us out, then tells the tribe whether she finds any evil spirits among us."

Going down their line, I counted over thirty, with more arriving by the minute. "Do they ever find evil among us?"

The corners of Tryfing's black beard twisted in a smile. "Once. But that was in Vinland, and we had met the Mi'kmaq. Your mother somehow made it right. We've never been this far south. Never seen this village."

"How do you know these are Abenaki and not Mi'kmaq?"

"They look similar, but Abenaki grow their hair longer. The married ones shave the side with the rest in a single braid. They have lots of villages. Lots of chiefs. But don't give us problems unless we take too many slaves."

"Marr, is he a slave?"

Tryfing nodded.

"And Halfdan uses him as an interpreter?"

Tryfing rubbed his forehead. "Too many questions. We never trust slaves. But sometimes have no choice."

The witch circled Halfdan and Marr, chanting. They stood motionless, arms crossed.

"Has she found me to be an evil spirit?" Halfdan asked, loud enough for our line to hear.

"If she hasn't, she's not worth a damn," shouted One-Eye. All the men laughed. But I studied the warriors. No expression creased their faces. How could our men be so relaxed, outnumbered two to one, while their line continued to grow?

"Tell her why we're here, to rescue our chieftain's daughter. We need directions to the summer village of the Mi'kmaq." Marr turned to the witch and spoke. Upon the word *Mi'kmaq*, the line of warriors stirred and leveled spears in our direction. The Vestmen raised shields, and I overlapped my own with Tryfing's.

The witch turned to her people and waved her stick, which seemed to settle them. She looked over her shoulder in my direction. Though her mask concealed most of her face, she seemed to stare at me. She lowered her scepter and stepped across the rocky shore till she stood directly in front of me. Her scent was smoke and sweat, absent the sweet scent of anger. *What a crazy thought. Anger doesn't smell.* Yet somehow, I knew it did.

Gabby smiled at me, blew another kiss, and then vanished like smoke.

The witch locked her eyes with me and I lowered my shield. If this situation was going to make any sense, I had to follow it through.

"Maintain the wall," called Tryfing.

"Matok just stepped ashore and he's already got a woman wanting to bed him," One-Eye hollered.

The laugh from the men died as she stepped closer. She pushed her scepter into her belt and slid a hand between the flaps of my vest, placing it upon my chest. Her skin was cold and greasy. Her fingers scaled with dirt, nails long, blackened, and sharpened to a point. Gazing upon my face, she dropped her hand to my belly. A chill passed into my stomach. It turned around there, as if icing my guts, then rose into my lungs. She was trying to communicate, but I didn't know how to respond.

Tryfing raised his sword between us. "Don't trust their witch."

But Gabby did. I pushed his weapon away, then slid my axe into my belt. Her eyelids quivered and her pupils were large, as if she were the one scared. She dropped her hand to my crotch and gripped tightly. I grunted a whimper. My eyes bulged and watered.

Tryfing's weapon came between us again. "This is all kinds of a bad idea. This witch will rot your walnuts and curse your sword."

Her eyes quivered, and she closed them. Her other hand moved to a lump beneath her belt. The chill in my lungs rose through my throat and pressed against my teeth. As if it wished to speak. Suddenly, she released me and the chill vanished. I gasped at the relief.

She turned to her line of warriors. They had separated and an old man in vest of white and copper beads stood between them now, brown and gray feathers woven into his braid, gripping his own spear. She spoke quickly and pointed her stick in his direction, then at Halfdan, then to me.

Marr interpreted. "She said, 'We must speak with these men.' She says many of us are veiled in darkness. That we are protected by a powerful shaman. She cannot find any evil spirits. But she says Halfdan is cunning and not to be trusted."

"I'm half-blind and can see that," One-Eye called.

Halfdan smiled at the remark and pinned his shoulders back, as if receiving a compliment.

Marr continued. "She pointed at Matok and said, 'This one is veiled in light. He speaks truth, but is ignorant of the spirits within him.'"

Chapter 14 – Vision

We sat on the floor in the chief's longhouse, an extended hut in the middle of the village. We lined one side, Abenaki the other. A low fire separated us. Steam rose from my wet trousers and leather boots. My hips had never allowed me to sit cross-legged, but now my legs hinged at the knees and slid neatly beneath me like the blade of a jackknife. Only Marr, Halfdan, Tryfing, and I had been invited. The rest stood on the shore or maintained watch on the boat, at least till the chief determined our motives and a deal could be made. These Indians enjoyed barter.

Tryfing had meant to stand with the others upon the shore, but the witch had pointed to him and spoken to Marr. "She thinks Matok a jarl and Tryfing his servant." Marr had argued the matter, but the woman paid no attention. I was relieved at Tryfing's company; his humor made this world seem less weighty.

The chief's house stretched as long as our boat and twice as wide. The skeleton of the walls and ceiling were knit from sapling-sized poles and rafters. These supports had been sunk into the ground and bent together in the middle where they were lashed around a center beam, tied in place with long blades of grass. Or possibly hemp. A teacher once had told me how Indians wove that plant into strong cord. Rafters were mounted horizontally between the poles and supported coverings of birch bark and grass. From inside, it mimicked the structure of our vessel turned upside down over us, though the craftsmanship was simpler.

The chief sat across from Halfdan with two warriors flanking him. The guards had traded spears near the entrance for ones with shorter shafts, such that when the butt rested upon the ground the point reached only to the men's neck. The smaller weapons allowed them to maneuver in the tighter space, I presumed.

The witch danced in bare feet upon the dusty floor near the triangular opening we'd used as an entrance, then settled next to her chief. When he spoke, his voice was loud, as if he was hard of hearing. The peremptory tone contrasted with his noble meekness.

"He asks us why we are here," Marr interpreted.

Halfdan brushed dust from the knees of his trousers. "We already answered. This old man losing his memory?"

Tryfing chuckled. I made no reaction, as stoicism seemed the way of these people.

Halfdan tucked his chin and lifted the leather thong that bound a lock of red hair over his neck. "Tell him again. Our chieftain's daughter was kidnapped by the Mi'kmaq. We come to get her. This is the color of her hair. She'd be hard to mistake, living among them."

Marr said only a few words. The chief waited in silence, then spoke, all the time gazing at Halfdan. It seemed Marr often spoke too few or too many words. I wondered if he was getting across the meaning necessary, or adding to it.

"The chief asked if the Mi'kmaq have demanded ransom."

Halfdan brushed dust from his shoulders. "Tell him *no*."

Though the fire was small, smoke built and swirled about the rafters near the ceiling, like low clouds among trees. I began to sweat in the stuffy closeness of the room.

"He says if they haven't demanded ransom, then they haven't kidnapped, but stolen her. He asks us if it is the white devil's custom to steal people."

Tryfing heaved a sigh. Halfdan gave Marr an accusatory scowl. "No. We take what we need from those who are weak. We give them a chance to become great."

More words, the chief's voice rising louder, his lip vibrating with each carefully pronounced syllable. Marr listened closely and said, "He asks if we think his village is weak."

Halfdan pushed a hand toward the fire. "What does this have to do with Astrid?"

The two argued back and forth, the chief pausing at length each time before he spoke. Halfdan blurted out whatever came to his mind, like an adolescent boy. Twice Marr glanced uneasily at the chief's bodyguards. Halfdan was a warrior and no diplomat. He'd get someone killed before the sun set.

The witch's frail body swayed, as if to music. Her eyes, behind the wide holes of the shaman's mask, seemed a portrait whose gaze fell upon me no matter which way her head turned. Rocking back and forth, she began to hum. The ice returned to my belly, though not as coldly as before. And this time it didn't frighten me. But familiarity has a way of lowering one's defenses. The chill crawled up my throat, like an ice spider with sharp claws. I coughed several times, but nothing came up. My mouth filled with a chill, like one gets from eating snow. My ears crackled and popped, as if the air in the room had changed pressure. As her hum rose and fell, my eyelids grew heavy and I began to sway as well. The voices of Marr, Halfdan, and the chief faded into a gentle wind.

I was running through the woods, dreamlike. My booted feet raced across clear forest. The tree trunks were unimaginably huge, even larger than those venerable giants we'd already seen, and spaced well apart. I neither tired nor slowed as I shot up steep hills and across wide gullies, speeding faster than a wolf at full sprint. I ran so quickly, the water only rippled beneath my feet as I raced across a narrow creek. The axes at my side made no sound, though the handles slapped my thighs. I leapt over fallen trees, clearing them as if low hurdles. I was headed northwest, judging by the rising sun, following no trail but my route straight as a taut fishing line. Coming over a low ridge, I skidded to a halt. Two bare-chested Indians trotted up the opposite side toward me, gripping long spears. They carried several more of the sharp weapons over a shoulder, as if balancing a quiver of javelins. They sweated little, though the day by now was warm, and they breathed easily, though the hill they'd just climbed was tall. Their long black hair was pulled back into a single braid, but the sides of their heads were not shaven. They seemed taller than the Abenaki. They paid me no attention, though I had run directly between them. They paused at the top of the ridge and glanced down, searching in all directions. They studied each tree, as if expecting it to come alive and swallow them like a dragon. One had an eye socket painted blue. He spoke to the other who wore a small feather, also blue, in the knot of his braid. The language sounded almost the same as the Abenaki.

I raced down the ridge in the direction from which they'd come, though not from fear. A primitive urgency filled my lungs, like a pearl diver straining to reach the surface. I shot across another narrow gully and sprinted up the opposite hill. Laughter and the crunch of footfalls surrounded me. I stopped at the base of an immense chestnut tree. Its deep green spearhead-shaped leaves studded branches that hung almost to the ground. The ghostly cry of a baby sounded behind me. It moved toward the two scouts. From every direction came laughing, yelling, and idle chatter. Though steps trudged past me, no one was visible. A scraping noise slid by, like a branch being dragged.

Was an enormous ghost tribe moving through the woods? A rustling in a nearby bush, then a *crunch* like when Granddad opened pecans, and a child's giggle. I spun, searching for signs of life. My breath caught in my throat. Gabby was standing next to the huge tree's trunk.

Her hair was longer now, past her shoulders, wild and unkempt. She wore a menacing grin on her lips and the same Indian tunic I'd seen about her near the river's shore. Leather moccasins with tiny red beads around the seams covered her feet. And she was...taller. Her figure had filled out, obvious despite the unflattering attire. As if she'd continued to grow even after her death. I stepped closer, until at last I wrapped my arms about her frame. She felt solid. Real. I buried my face in her hair, warm and scented of smoke.

She returned a quick squeeze then pushed me away, saying nothing. She just stood with that grin on her face, as if half of her was playing a game, and the other half scared for me.

"Are you real?" I asked.

She raised her eyebrows but said nothing.

"What the hell is going on?"

Her reply was sharp. "You shouldn't curse, brother."

"I'll say whatever I want! In the last two days, I've been yanked out of my world, imprisoned in the body of a Viking—"

She shook her head. "A *Vestman*."

"Who cares what I call them?"

"You need to be accurate. Words have power. Don't misuse them."

"Whatever. I'm stuck in the body of a *Vestman*. Beaten by a sadistic taskman. Rowed to outrun a hailstorm threatening to pulverize our boat. And have no clue why I'm here."

"Must there be a meaning to everything?"

"A meaning? Yes! God would have to be pretty sadistic to put me through this for no reason."

She smiled as invisible children giggled and chattered past. "So, you think this life has meaning. What about the last?"

"Why are you so full of riddles now?"

She propped fists on hips. "Brother, all life has meaning. It is we who deem it insignificant. And if life has meaning, so must death. Did my death have meaning?"

I took her hands in my own. "Gabby, you were my world. With you, life always had meaning. When you...left, there was only a chill like a fire that had burned out. And for what? Your death was senseless."

She pulled her hands free. "So, you've given up."

"Given up? On what?"

She pointed to a gnarly pine trunk, from where a voice echoed, high pitched and young, as if from a girl. The invisible Indian spoke for a minute as she walked past, interrupted only by an occasional answer in baritone. "Two out of every three of these people die before the age of ten. If infection, disease, or famine doesn't get them, then war is to fear. It would be rare for any brother among them, at your age, to not have lost two sisters. Every life has meaning. As does death."

"Why are you telling me this? And did you get here the same way as me? Did you actually die, or were you sucked away while sitting on the end of the dock that day?" My neck chilled at the thought. "Wait! I disappeared from the same place as you. Is it a magic pier that transports you back in time?"

She covered her mouth and giggled. The red beads on the chest of her dress shimmered in a light beam. "Magic pier? That's a good one, brother. There is no such foolishness as magic. Yes, I died in that world...unlike you. But death is only a chestnut burr from which grows a new tree. Don't get hung up on what world you find yourself in. I've been sent to help you."

I closed my eyes and rubbed my forehead. An ache had begun to grow between my temples. "Sent by who? Help with what?"

"We all serve a master. You need to choose yours. Don't get distracted trying to figure out stupid stuff like magic piers. Instead, ask yourself *who* brought you here."

I held up my hands. She was making no sense. If she weren't already dead, I'd be tempted to kill her myself. "I thought *you* brought me here!"

"Me?" She placed palms across the red beads. "Any power I have comes from the One who sent me. There is a battle raging, its fury worse than the hailstorm your ship escaped. Choose a side. There are only two, so even you should be able to figure it out."

"Why are you telling me this? What does any of this have to do with me?"

She raised an eyebrow, and I couldn't help but smile back. She was so beautiful. So pure. Always happy. She slapped my chest. "Exactly, brother!"

"Stop with the riddles! Exactly what? What do you mean?"

"Life isn't about *you*, Michael." She shoved me with both hands. "Maybe none of this is about *you* at all."

The wind gusted, carrying the distant hum of the witch. The beam of light that had once sparkled upon Gabby's red beads now shone through her body, as if she were vanishing. I reached to hug her again, but my efforts were a grasping at mist. A breeze rose and tugged her hair. She lifted her eyebrows as if in surprise. She blurted, "Quit trying to figure everything out. Your way is already clear. I'll always be near you." Her waving curls flattened into autumn leaves lifted by a gust and were carried back toward the hill from which I'd come. The rest of her form had already disappeared, and I was alone beneath the chestnut.

I stared up at low clouds that scudded over branches. They morphed into thin smoke that swirled instead among the blackened rafters of the chief's wigwam. Now the fire sat before me again, warming my legs. I found myself leaning forward, arms stretched over it, reaching toward the witch, who was still swaying and humming. I glanced around. Halfdan's mouth was agape. Marr regarded me with an amused grin. The chief sat straight-backed, eyes still on Halfdan.

Tryfing smacked the back of my skull. "Out! Out of him, devil!" He clutched a wooden crucifix hanging from a leather thong about his neck.

The witch admonished Tryfing with a thump on his head with her rod. She pointed the stick at me and spoke a sentence or two.

"She asks what you saw."

I lowered my arms and rubbed my knees. "I...I just fell asleep. Please tell her I'm sorry."

Marr grunted, but spoke to the woman. She cackled a laugh so sharp I flinched. She hopped to her feet then came over to sit in front of me, almost in the fire. Her few remaining teeth were yellow, but her breath was sweet. A whiff of fresh-cut oak filled my nose. She reached up and slowly lifted her mask. One of the guards shivered nervously and turned his gaze away. The whites of her eyes were yellowed. The irises black, framed by creased pouches of skin. Still, she somehow seemed younger than her looks suggested. She brushed my cheek with black-stained fingers, and from the corner of one eye I caught Tryfing gripping the handle of a dagger on his belt. The witch spoke to me, and the chief nodded.

Marr's gaze stayed upon the witch. "She said you weren't asleep. She said a vision is a gift and is to be shared."

I argued, but the witch wouldn't relent. I struggled to relay the dream, being careful to call Gabby *my sister* without further explanation. I knew everyone would think I meant my Viking sister, the chieftain's daughter. By now the two were getting confused even in my own mind. And Halfdan would just think I was a crazy witch-boy, no matter what I said.

The old woman asked many questions regarding the details of where my vision had taken me. "How many creeks did you cross?" asked Marr. She thought my soul had traveled to the Mi'kmaq and the spirits were showing us they were still some distance away, headed toward their own camp, not here. The chief seemed relieved at her interpretation. Apparently, I'd closed my eyes and everyone thought I was simply enjoying the fire, till I started babbling incoherently. Tryfing had appointed himself my personal exorcist and had smacked me on the neck and ears till the witch told him to stop.

Now she touched my cheek, turned my face to hers, and spoke again. The chief said something to Halfdan, and Marr moved to sit between us so he could interpret both conversations. Evidently, my trance hadn't broken any social taboos. In fact, it had convinced the chief we came in peace, though Halfdan still stared at me, distracted.

"Why couldn't I see the Mi'kmaq in the vision?" I asked the witch. She only stared with those yellowed eyes and hummed. Finally, she spoke.

"She says the Mi'kmaq are protected by a powerful shaman," Marr relayed. "Her spirits blinded you."

She hummed and stared till my skin felt as if ants were crawling up my back. I tried to stand, but she pulled me down, leaned to Marr's ear, and whispered. His eyes narrowed. They spoke further in hushed tones.

Tryfing and I exchanged glances. His hand was still upon his dagger's handle.

"What'd she say?" I asked.

Marr shuddered, as if shaking off bad thoughts. He glanced at the chief who was patiently listening to Halfdan, though he surely couldn't understand a word. Then he turned back to us and whispered, "I don't know how to interpret it. She cannot *see* you. No, your spirit. As if you are protected as well. But she believes you to be a great shaman, and wants to pay for your blessing."

A loud clatter of metal on wood rose outside. Furious shouts from Vestmen mixed with angry whoops and calls of Abenaki warriors.

Chapter 15 – Astrid

Kiona stepped over a thick maple branch, half-buried in leaves, one end ragged and sharp where it had torn from the trunk. Lichen the same blue green of a horned caterpillar covered the bark that sloughed off its rotting hardwood core. The forest had turned from dense pine near the stream to towering hickory, oak, pecan, and the sacred chestnut. Their high branches knit together so tightly, like the roof of a wetuom, only a few shafts of light penetrated from a bright midday sun. Down the hill before her zigzagged a ragged, churned trail, pounded flat by the soles of a thousand pair of moccasins over the last few hours. Scarred in twin ruts by almost as many sled poles, dragged by men transporting food stores and the elderly.

Halfway down the slope shuffled the tribe's prisoner, Astrid, her friend, a leather collar and leash about her neck, like a wayward dog that hadn't learned its home. Wrists bound with a braided strap. Eyes as blue as lapis lazuli. Her hair the brilliant color of maple leaves in the fall. It had been bright, wild, and untamed two weeks ago when four braves of the chief's personal bodyguard dragged her into the village. Now, it hung unkempt, snagged and matted with leaves. The hem of her dress almost dragged the ground, fabric woven of the coarse hair of their animals, dyed a pale green. Curious, Astrid's tribe was. The blue-eyed, pink-skinned Vestmen. How they raised sheep the same way the Mi'kmaq planted corn and squash.

When the Vestmen had arrived on their shores, Kiona had been the first to discover them. She'd glimpsed Astrid across a meadow and originally thought her to be the spirit of Sacred Fire, visiting her in a vision. But she'd been real, and Kiona had spent several weeks among her tribe, at the urging of the chief...and Mother. They thought Kiona, being a young woman, would seem less threatening. If she could learn the language of *the invaders*, as the leaders referred to them, they'd suggested she might overhear their true intentions. Mother had been too suspicious. The Vestmen had made no threats.

On the next half-moon, more had arrived in a fleet of their huge canoes, several packed with the stinking, bleating sheep. Kiona had watched how the men used sharp knives, stronger than flint, to slice off the hair, called *wool*. Their young women washed it over and over, then combed it for hours and twisted it into yarn. Finally, the married women wove this into dresses and tunics, even sails for their boats. They seemed to use the oily animal hair for everything. It must be a part of their religious worship, she'd originally thought. Because why else waste so much time on it, when in a single afternoon a deer could be killed, carried to camp, and the carcass produce enough skin for a pair of winter trousers and meat for several families?

Huritt laid a hand upon her shoulder. "You'd better talk to her. The family leaders think she's chanting vile curses."

Kiona huffed, then jogged down the slope. The family leaders were suspicious of everything, but even more so of Vestmen. All because of an old prophecy that a light-skinned people would invade their shores. If it were up to the tribe, they'd have driven the Vestmen back into their boats as soon as they'd landed. But Mother had convinced them otherwise, after she'd visited the newcomers' village. Kiona had led the introductions, having earned the trust of the strangers and learned some of their language.

In the time she'd spent with them, though, she hadn't been able to figure out their religion, which is why the chief had then sent Mother. She'd worn a shaman's mask the entire time, searching for evil spirits among them, but had found none. The Vestmen had two shamans of their own, with such different practices it perplexed her. One was a gray-haired man with blond beard, a wealthy belly that hung over his trousers, and a shiny amulet in the shape of a cross hanging from a thong about his neck. The other shaman had been a pale, squinty-eyed woman with breasts large enough to nurse a bear. Their men had backed away nervously when that witch had approached Mother. The two women had stood there, in the center of the village, studying each other, heads tilting this way and that, both remaining silent. Still, something unseen had passed between them. They'd exchanged an eerie smile; then the pale shaman had taken Mother by the hand and led her into a long, dark wetuom covered in earth.

The gray-bearded shaman had stood at a distance during the exchange, back with the other men. He'd circled the two women, hands clasped, chanting in their rude tongue, likely seeking a spirit's blessing upon the meeting. Once the women escaped into the earthen wetuom, he'd approached Kiona with his warm smile, the fire-haired Astrid beside him. She'd always been at his heels.

And he'd always seemed happy. Surely a man who ate as much as he should be content. But Gray Beard had not been the only one who'd brightened when Astrid approached. She and Kiona had become close friends, the red-haired girl seemingly adopting her as a sister.

Now, Kiona caught up with Astrid and matched her pace. The young prisoner's gaze remained upon the ground before her feet. She shuffled to a halt beneath an ancient, venerable chestnut with branches that scraped the ground. The blue of her eyes was pale as a summer sky. Her lips were dry and cracked. Had her minder not allowed her to drink when they'd crossed the stream? The crooked-eyed guard gripped the end of Astrid's leash. He was skilled with a spear, but beat his children when he sank into foul moods. A cruel man, he'd probably dragged her across the water by the hair.

Kiona mimed cupping her hands and bringing them to her mouth. In the Vestmen's tongue, she said, "Pleasant? A drink?" Their language had proven difficult, but Kiona had gathered most of their words and, after several months in their company, spoke freely. However, the Vestmen hadn't seemed able to learn the Mi'kmaq's language. Or perhaps were disinterested, as if they felt no need of it.

Astrid gave her a faint smile.

Kiona glanced back at Huritt. "Water." The solid young man nodded and ran off.

Astrid gazed at Kiona's neck. The prisoner lifted both bound hands to her own and stroked near her collar. Kiona flushed, realizing she'd noticed the bruise from Mother's grip. It must've grown purple and yellow.

Astrid stepped closer. "How did that happen? Does it hurt?"

Kiona pointed at Huritt trotting away and, with her arm, mimicked a branch whipping back and hitting her neck. "Clumsy," she muttered. The man wouldn't care if she blamed him. He was a friend, but he *was* clumsy at times and even Astrid must've known he could've absentmindedly let a branch smack Kiona if she'd been following too close.

Instead, Astrid's eyes narrowed. She pursed her lips then glanced ahead, to a family near the bottom of the hill, Mother walking among them.

Kiona picked up the prickly ball of an unopened chestnut, pretending not to understand her friend's insinuation. She wedged her fingers between the sharp petals of shell and peeled them back. Three shiny brown pebbles dropped into her palm. "Have I told you the story of the chestnut?" She glanced at Astrid, then continued without waiting for an answer. "One day, Malsumis attacked Gluskabe and pelted him with rocks of fire stolen from beneath the earth. But Gluskabe made himself big as a mountain and blew on them as they fell. They chilled into ice that smacked upon the ground. The next spring, tiny saplings with leaves the shape of spearheads grew from the earth where they'd fallen. The braves thought them a gift, that the shape of the leaves meant they should make weapons from the wood. But the wood grew slowly, and it split too easily. After many years of trying, they gave up. Then, the next fall, the young trees dropped these." Kiona scooped another prickly ball from the ground. "All the children cried when they stepped on them. Their fathers burned with anger and began to chop at the trunks shouting, 'Gluskabe gave these as a blessing, but the curse of Malsumis's fire still lies within.'"

Astrid stood still, eyes locked with hers.

"But an old woman who'd birthed twenty-one braves stepped forward. 'Don't cut them down. Gather the needle-rocks into a pile. Clear other trees, but not these. Bring water from the river, so they'll grow strong. Wait one more year and see if, with that care, they give us real fruit.' The men grumbled, but did as she ordered, for she was highly esteemed.

"That winter was the hardest ever. The tribe ate all their dried fish and corn. No deer or bison could be found. The pecan harvest had been poor, and families began to starve. The tribe's children cried with hunger. While searching for firewood, a young brave came upon the mounds of needle-rocks and threw some angrily into his fire. 'I will use the curse of Malsumis to keep us warm,' he said. But soon, *pop!* Then again, *crack! Pop!*" Kiona snapped her fingers to mimic the sound.

Crooked-Eye gave her an irritated glace, but Astrid raised her eyebrows and bounced with excitement. "The pops were the chestnuts!"

Kiona reached out and tucked a lock of Astrid's hair behind one ear. "Yes. Soon, all the wigwams were filled with the sweet scent of their roasting. No animals had eaten the chestnuts because of the spiky petals. The hard shells inside had preserved the tender meat. The tribe survived on them for three months, until the snow melted."

Astrid shrugged. "So, what does it mean?"

Kiona smirked. The Vestmen, like the Mi'kmaq, held a passion for stories. The foreigners even had a man who did nothing but tell fables of gods and wars and heroes. But Astrid's excitement suggested she'd learned from the Mi'kmaq traditions while living among them. All tales hid a moral. Kiona continued, "It means you can take what one intends to be a curse, and turn it into a blessing. Just like Gluskabe with the fire from Malsumis." She held out one of the prickly balls in her fingers, and Astrid gingerly accepted it. Kiona whispered, "And to be patient. That sometimes even curses are blessings in disguise. You may feel a prisoner today. But *somehow* your life is being preserved."

Kiona popped a shiny brown nut between her molars and bit down, cracking the shell. She picked out the meat and placed it carefully in Astrid's bound hands. Its scent, lightly sweet, always reminded her of maple sap.

Huritt ran back up the hill, cradling a tan waterskin made from a deer's stomach. Astrid stared, as if in admiration, as the young warrior stepped back into their company. He passed her the pouch.

She gave a slight bow. "Thank you," in the Mi'kmaq tongue. Astrid had managed to learn a few words as well.

Huritt smiled, but for only a second. Then his face flushed. "Uh...Father needs me." He trotted back down the hill. But his father, Great Scout, was at least three hours away. That man was a strong warrior, one of the best runners of the tribe, who stayed many miles ahead to ensure no dangers surprised them. Huritt could not have spoken with him today. Thus, what to make of his uncomfortable expression? Huritt must be attracted to Astrid.

Kiona studied the fire-haired young woman. Despite being fed poorly since her capture, and enduring days of constant travel, she stood straight. Her skin was perpetually pale, though, as if her body were sickly. But that was the way all Vestmen appeared. Her arms were curved with muscle, and her hips branched wider than most Mi'kmaq girls. She would easily bear children, a most appealing quality in a young woman.

Astrid's gaze followed Huritt as he ran down the hill. Yes, the attraction appeared to be mutual. When had it started? Kiona glanced at Crooked-Eye, peeling the thorny skin from a chestnut, talking to his skinny son next to him. Huritt had served as Astrid's guard every fourth day. That must be it!

Suddenly, fear stung Kiona's belly. Mother couldn't know. "Don't look at him," she snapped, hoping she'd chosen the right words. That her friend would understand the correct meaning.

Astrid's head drooped, as if suddenly ashamed. "Oh. I'm sorry."

Kiona searched her memory frantically for the right Vestmen saying. Their language had come easily after spending so much time in their company, but now swallows seemed to pluck the words from her lips. "Not with other tribesmen near." She nodded toward Crooked-Eye.

Astrid drew in a breath of recognition; then a smile spread across her lips. She chewed the chestnut, then lifted the waterskin to her mouth and drank greedily.

Crooked-Eye tugged on her collar. His voice was hoarse and raspy. Malevolent. "Get moving."

Kiona followed, hand on Astrid's shoulder. "What were you chanting? Some said you were cursing the tribe." She wasn't certain of the word *curse*, but she'd heard their large-breasted shaman use it a few times in Mother's presence.

Astrid's brow furrowed, but then her smile returned. "Oh, that! I was singing." She cleared her throat, spat upon the ground, and began a beautiful melody. One that would make a mockingbird jealous. Strong, high, and clear, it echoed from the trees. The hills beyond caught the lively tune and threw it back, to be enjoyed again. A family of three on the trail below turned and stared, the man's face etched with worry. Crooked-Eye sped up, yanking the cord, as if moving quicker would keep the girl quiet.

Kiona had heard the song before but understood little of it. Words in a Vestmen's tune were more difficult to figure out. But she gathered that Astrid sang of Hvítakristr. It was name of her God. Kiona had sat next to Astrid many days as Gray Beard, their fat shaman, had rambled on about this White Christ. His lectures bored her, but they'd been a good way to learn the Vestmen words.

So, the family leaders had nothing to fear. Astrid was only singing about her religion, and Kiona knew from Gray Beard it forbade her to curse anyone. Strange customs, this foreign religion. But Mother would be happy to learn this too. No chants to decipher. No spells to cancel. No magic to counteract. Maybe she wouldn't pressure Kiona to marry Achak for a few days.

Astrid's song ended and she trotted to keep up with Crooked-Eye, who tugged at her leash. Even with bound hands, she still moved gracefully. "How much farther?" she asked.

Kiona jogged to keep up as well. "Another day."

"What's your mother going to do to me?"

Kiona glanced at Crooked-Eye, then remembered he couldn't understand a word. "I don't know. But don't worry. I have a plan to help you. But it won't work while we're traveling." She was lying. She hadn't formulated a means of escape, though she'd been trying desperately. None of the chief's bodyguards ever allowed

Astrid out of their sight, even to relieve herself. And if she could escape, trackers would run her down within minutes.

Was there a reason to fear for the girl's life? The chief was indeed worried about the prophecy and the Vestmen's weapons. He'd seen their sharp knives of metal, long as a man's arm. And how they'd carried slaves from other tribes in their longboats. Astrid had been kidnapped, a hostage, to ensure the safety of the Mi'kmaq. All parties would remain at peace, Mother reasoned, as long as the Vestmen didn't attempt to rescue her.

Kiona pulled a leaf from Astrid's hair as she jogged beside her.

The prisoner glanced at Crooked-Eye, his jaw clenched. "I'm worried about your tribe," she said. "All of you. Even this warrior, because of his family. But especially you and your little brother, Nabid. My father *will* send for me, soon. And the man he sends never leaves an enemy alive. That's his way. Promise me, when they come, that you'll run. And take Nabid with you." Then she started her song again, but slower this time, panting a bit at their pace.

Kiona stared at the girl, singing boisterously to the trees, leash about her neck, pulled along like an animal. Yet her concern was not for herself. Not a good sign. Mother denied it, but keeping an innocent person as prisoner broke two of the Three Truths. Even if there was a hidden evil among the Vestmen, as Mother claimed, it wasn't to be found in Astrid. The spirits protecting the Mi'kmaq couldn't approve of this. Could they? The Three Truths ensured the strength of not only their tribe, but the Abenaki and so many others. All peoples were connected in the spirit realm. Mother herself had taught Kiona that. These three beliefs maintained peace among their society. But imprisoning a pure, innocent soul such as Astrid weakened that foundation.

Nothing good could come of it.

A brave jumped over a log at the bottom of the hill, running toward them. Though still distant, Huritt's stocky, hitched stride was unmistakable. *Huritt...*if he was attracted to Astrid, he might be convinced to aid her escape during his day as guard!

He skidded to a halt, spear shaft in his grasp.

"I thought your father needed you," Kiona jabbed.

He'd run quickly, for his breathing was like a winded deer. "Your...brother," he panted. "Mother needs you...to tend to him."

"What? The boy can take care of himself. He needs no older sister watching him like a—"

"No." Huritt waved a hand, still trying to catch his breath. "An enemy approaches. The spirits...they visited your mother. She

89

passed into one of her screaming fits. The worst I've ever seen. Worse than back at the river."

So, the evil spirits hadn't left Mother after all. They'd just been quiet for a few hours. They only visited her in such force when bringing the tribe a warning of attack. Why did they torture her, though, if they were supposedly trying to help? Kiona was glad no spirits ever spoke to her. If they ever did, she'd ignore them. "Where do they come from?"

"The ocean. Up Wandering River."

"Abenaki, then? But they haven't given us trouble for years."

"No. Not Abenaki." He glanced at Astrid and his hard brown gaze softened. "Vestmen come."

Chapter 16 – Substitute

The Abenaki chief rose at the sound of the angry brawl outside. His warriors leveled their spears at Halfdan, who hopped to his feet, raised his shield, and drew a short sword. His movements were quick, fluid, and compact. He hunched his back like an angry cat, full of fury and spit. The warriors shouted, but Halfdan beat his shield with the hilt of his weapon and roared back, all the while smiling as if this were a great game.

The witch stood, squinted toward the door, then stepped between the facing parties and stared at Halfdan. Then at her warriors. Halfdan closed his mouth and the Indians cast their gaze aside, trying to not look at her face while keeping watch on the angry Vestman. She raised her mask, placed it over her head, and stepped out into the daylight. The chief and his guard followed. Halfdan glanced at us and jerked his head toward the opening. "Ready yourselves."

The sun was blinding as I stepped into the arena at the center of the village. Whoops and yelps swelled from the riverbank. A small group of warriors trotted toward us. The two ranks near the boat still stood apart, so no fight had erupted. Maybe the commotion had only been bravado.

The troop spilled into the arena. At the head of the pack, they carried a brave by the arms and legs. The body hung limp, a huge gash in one shoulder near his collarbone. The witch placed her fingers on his eyes and lifted his lids, then put an ear to his mouth. She spoke and pointed to the longhouse and they continued past us, carrying the wounded man. The chief trotted behind him, paying us no attention, a glimmer of wetness in his eyes. An angry shout rose around us and we were surrounded by warriors with spears, taunting from curled lips, scooping dust from the ground and throwing it on their chests. Women and even children thronged among them, some with arrows strung and bows drawn. The four of us stood with our backs together, shields raised. As close as we could press, yet still their edges did not overlap. An axe was in my fist, though I didn't remember drawing it.

"Marr, what happened?" Halfdan shouted above the noise.

A child loosed his arrow. I flinched, and it thumped into my shield. He drew back another. Women waved stout rods over their heads. More warriors trotted toward us from a side path. Behind them, near the edge of the village, a boy stood inside a tiger cage woven from branches. He gripped the bars, shouted, and shook the door. A flurry of brown feathers streaked overhead as an eagle's talons swept past my ear.

"I don't know," screamed Marr. "They're just yelling. Threatening to kill us."

I stole a glance toward the boat. Both ranks of warriors were still separated. We could expect no help from our side. Halfdan had warned them not to engage, and they'd have a mean fight on their hands before they could reach us anyway.

A brave stepped forward with a spear held in a cocked arm. A trill sounded behind him, like the call of a boisterous pine warbler.

The crowd fell silent. The brave lowered his weapon. The circle of angry villagers broke open to reveal the chief standing before the door of his wigwam. One of his guards had his hands cupped over his mouth, the source of the shrill whistle. The chief stepped into the arena, gripping his spear as a walking stick, gaze to the earth, but with tense jaw and straight back. He stopped before Halfdan, who stared over the rim of his shield, glancing between him and strung bows. The chief looked up and stood in silence, then moved around our defensive position and stopped before me. The same ice churned in my stomach as he glared. Anger burned red in his narrowed eyes, but he did not move to strike me. My grip on the axe eased and a peace washed over me, the same feeling as when I'd glimpsed Gabby on the riverbank. I dropped my shield and slung my weapon from a loop on my belt.

Halfdan jabbed his elbow into my ribs. "Don't break the wall!"

I flinched, but the chief stood erect, pointed to me, then turned and headed for the riverbank. I followed, Tryfing trotting after me. Halfdan yelled for our return but then stormed behind us. The circle parted before their chief and we followed through the gauntlet, like the great white shark I'd seen yesterday lumbering through a school of striped bass. Spear tips hovered inches from my face, but no harm came. Loud shouting and clanging of metal rose from the riverbank, thundering against the simmering silence of the crowd we'd just escaped. But even that stilled as the chief and Halfdan approached.

White-Tip stood on the shoreline with our men now, his sword in his grasp, blood dripping from the blade. Halfdan pushed his way forward and scowled down at him. "What have you done?"

White-Tip pointed the weapon at two warriors at the end of the Indian's rank, then slashed it toward three skin canoes on the shore. "Those little savages wanted aboard. Came next to us. I stepped on their fingers as they scaled the sides, but they kept coming so I figured I'd let them satisfy their curiosity. They danced across the ship like a scurry of rabid squirrels. One shot up the mast and hung from the lines, then dropped and studied the wool of the sail. He rubbed it like a dog's belly. I didn't care what he did, till he pushed a flint knife through the fabric and smiled." White-Tip stuck out his jaw. "Then I drew my sword. Fate ruled from there."

Halfdan turned to Marr. His voice a growl. "They will want a blood payment, but they threatened our boat. None is owed."

Tryfing stood next to me and raised his shield. "This will not end well. Had the savage put the blade through Halfdan's wife, he would've counted it a lesser offense."

Marr turned slowly to face the chief, who was speaking with the two warriors toward which White-Tip had aimed his sword. They spoke, then Marr turned back, gripping his own weapon. He explained the injured warrior was a son of the chief. Halfdan scowled. Apparently the chief had acknowledged his son's foolishness, but blood had been drawn by the white devils, and now it was owed.

"We had a deal," Halfdan said.

I glanced at Tryfing. "A trade was set while you were possessed by the demon," he explained.

Marr bowed his head. "The chief will not relent. A blood payment is their...oh, I don't have a word for it. It's their law."

Halfdan raised his sword over his head and shouted, "They want blood? We'll shed it. The river will swell with their own!" Our rank erupted in a battle cry that shook my chest. It rose from the rocks of the stream, through the souls of my feet.

When the racket subsided, Marr turned to Halfdan, scowling. It seemed he'd found courage somewhere. "Let it be me," he said, patting his chest.

Halfdan sneered. "No. You're my property. And valuable."

Marr swept an arm to indicate the long line of warriors. "There are two, even three to every one of us. We might slaughter them, but for what? What treasure? They have no gold. No silver. Slaves? They will only slow us down, keep us from our mission. Sport, then? To slake your own bloodlust? Even so, surely a few of our own will perish. But if you let me go, only one will die, and the law will be satisfied. No enmity will remain between you."

Halfdan's chest swelled. He gazed at Marr in surprise. "You would do this?"

Marr spat onto the rocks between them. "Not for you, dog. You slaughtered my family and stole my life when I was only a boy." He pointed to the chief. "I do it for them. For *their* lives." His eyes narrowed to slits. "If yours is spared in the process, that is a pain I will bear."

Halfdan reached for him.

"Kill me, and the law is not fulfilled."

He gripped Marr's tunic and pointed his sword at his belly.

"But if the Abenaki kill me, all will be settled," Marr said calmly. "I belong to you. I am your substitute. But if you plunge that sword through me, you'll not know the location of the Mi'kmaq's village. What will happen to your family, félagi, if you return without the chieftain's daughter?"

Halfdan's arm shook. The sword inched forward. He released his slave, then stepped back and spat in his face. "I will take pleasure in watching you die. There is no seat in the great hall of Valhalla for men whose lives are taken without a fight."

"Your pagan mind is a heap of dung, blind to the true battle." Marr turned away and approached the chief. He spoke three words then grunted as a bloody spear tip suddenly jutted from between his shoulder blades. He dropped to his knees and the chief yanked the weapon free as the body fell back. The corpse's fingers twitched. The strike appeared to have been merciful, though, through his heart.

Halfdan ordered forty seal pelts and five axes brought from the ship. White-Tip and several men laid them at the feet of the chief, next to Marr's body. Village women carried down armloads of salmon. The fish had been headed and gutted, splayed open and spread flat, some almost as large as rugs. Judging from their blackened underside, they'd been smoked. Other Indians piled a large mound of moose antlers as well. One of the bodyguards produced a skin that the chief unrolled atop the seal pelts. It stretched the length of a man's leg. Beginning at one end with a piece of charcoal, he sketched the ocean's shoreline and the river, pointing to what appeared to be fingers of oyster rocks, as if to ensure that Halfdan was oriented. He drew the waterway's meanderings, then tapped one of its bends next to which he'd traced an arch, which I took to be a wigwam. Our current location. The river wandered until, halfway through the length of the skin, it was interrupted by other arches. Lots of them. The village of the

Mi'kmaq? The chief pointed to a boulder, his arm undulating like the course of a running stream.

Halfdan turned to White-Tip. "Fast water, or a waterfall. We'll travel on foot from there."

The river continued almost to the end of the skin, where a branch forked north. In its crook, the chief drew two humps, tapped them, pointed his bloody spear toward Halfdan, then spat on the ground.

"Clear enough," Halfdan mumbled. The Vestman raised his arm to the sun, then swept an arc to the west, upstream. He tapped our location, then that of the Mi'kmaq. "How many days?" he said slowly, as if that would help the Indian understand.

The chief picked up two palm-sized stones and placed them in Halfdan's grasp. The Viking's fingers were short, as if missing their final digits, thick and crooked as gnarled tree roots. I had failed to notice his abnormal mitts when he been beating me earlier.

White-Tip picked them out of the man's hand. "Two days. One rock for each. It's how the Abenaki up north talk as well."

Halfdan rolled up the skin and slipped it under his belt. He dropped the two rocks into a vest pocket. We carried the dried fish and antlers up the gangplank and stowed them in bags beneath the platform in the prow. Tryfing explained that the antlers were used to make knife handles, tools, combs, and buckles. I filled my arms with fish and trotted up the gangplank again. They were much lighter than I had expected, and my mouth watered at their smoky scent.

I passed the stores to One-Eye. A breeze from the east blew his hair back, accentuating his look of perpetual surprise. I swung from the gunwale and dropped into the water.

"Your witch comes to bed you," he called after me. The witch stepped carefully down the bank and picked her way across the flat to the edge of the water. Was she really waiting for me?

"Go on, then," Halfdan gruffed.

Did they seriously think this witch wanted to seduce me? Was it some sort of sadistic ritual? A part of the bargain? She seemed one of the most powerful people in the village, though. How could I politely decline without giving offense and risking some warrior trying to skewer me? I was no saint, but I certainly didn't want to have sex with an emaciated, wrinkled woman as old as my mother. Not even while in someone else's body.

The village rose behind her on its gently sloping meadow. Next to a distant hut, I again glimpsed the boy in the tiger cage. Now he was leaning on one barred wall, unmoving. As I approached the witch, Tryfing splashed through water to my side. "What are you doing? Leave this woman to her own wretchedness."

She stepped upon a basket-sized boulder and held out one arm to me, as if afraid of water and asking for help. I stepped closer, and she laid a palm upon my stomach as before. I tensed, ready to jump back in case she reached for my crotch again. The chill in my belly rose, a familiar sensation now. The ice spider crawled up my throat. I blew out a short pant, expecting to see frost in the air. The witch leaned her face close to mine, closed her eyes, and inhaled deeply. She held her breath for nearly a minute; then her eyes popped open, pupils dilated despite the strong sun.

"I have blessed you. Now, give me yours." Her speech sounded as it had earlier, the same as the chiefs and other Abenaki. But now, just like I understood the Vestmen, I grasped her words as well. As if she'd somehow opened my ears to them.

"I am not a shaman," I explained. "I have no blessing to give." My words echoed the tones of her language. My own speech must have changed.

She touched my shoulder and I glanced nervously at those grimy, sharpened nails. She pressed one against the black tattoo of a mallet, or a hammer, upon my skin, then raked it across my chest, beneath my throat, her face so close to mine I expected her to either bite my neck or pull me into an embrace. Her breath was sweet, like fear. Again that thought jolted me, how I sensed sweetness in terror. Her nails scraped to my other shoulder and stopped upon another tattoo, this one a cross. I hadn't seen them earlier. "Your blessing," she said.

Thor's hammer. The cross of Christ. And my mother a witch. Matok was as mixed up as a gill net knotted by a school of skates.

She pulled me close and whispered into my ear. "The Mi'kmaq have known white devils will come. When I was a girl, their shaman said that to rid the land of them, they must enslave their red-haired girl. The fate of their village depends upon it."

One-Eye shouted from the boat. "Stop stalling and do your duty!"

I pulled free of her grasp. "How do you know this?"

She made a fist and placed it on her opposite palm. "Their shaman was my mother."

The caged boy screamed in the distance. I flinched. "You're a Mi'kmaq? Then how do you live among Abenaki?"

The witch glanced over her shoulder toward the cries. Eyes glittered with tears. Her fingers straightened flat as a blade. "Your true red-haired sister visited me this morning. She convinced me not to kill you." She pulled me toward her again. "My mother did not tell the Mi'kmaq her entire vision. Only the part they wished to hear. The rest, she spoke to me."

Her fingernails pricked the skin on my belly. "What else did she tell you?" I whispered.

Her smile spread nearly as wide as the mask on her head. "You are much feared among the spirits, but that is not for you to know. Still, if you wish your love to live"—she glanced at Marr's corpse— "someone else must die. It is the law."

Chapter 17 – New Master

Stryker stalked through dense, high grass. The wide pads of his feet fell silently upon the ground. He bent his neck low until his whiskers brushed the earth where prey traveled. The cumin scent of rabbit was everywhere. It rose in such a thick herbal aroma, he couldn't follow an individual trail. He nosed through a dense clump of blades and scented a game trail, a narrow tunnel. The stalks formed a green canopy overhead, an anthill of hallways, shielding prey from the predatory gaze of eagles and hawks. But these passageways weren't large enough for a panther to travel.

A crow cawed in a distant tree. The drone of cicadas ebbed and flowed. The rustle of leaves came from a side corridor.

Stryker stepped back into cover and crouched upon his belly, ears pricked toward the muffled approach of padded feet. His nostrils flared at the subtle earthen scent of unspilt blood. A snowshoe hare whose coat still retained streaks of white hopped past on enormous tufted feet. Stryker unsheathed his claws, reached into the alleyway, and swatted it to the ground. The hare shrieked. Stryker jerked his head upright at a flurry of footfalls thumping away in all directions, like a covey of quail taking flight. The long-eared little beasts were fast, for certain.

His prey struggled to its feet, but Stryker slashed it down again, sending it tumbling back toward his other mitt. Its screams were shrill, like a stabbed child's. The terrified animal leapt straight up and nearly disappeared in the grass, but Stryker followed and soon had him again, rolling and shrieking, batted from paw to paw. Until its cheeks became matted in blood, an eyeball fell from its socket, its efforts to flee slowed to a pained crawl, and Stryker grew bored of the game. The little beasts had large adrenal glands, and this one's were now empty. Fear was always the best seasoning.

The animal shuddered as he lifted it in his jaws. Its paws twitched and claws scratched Stryker's nose. He clamped down, snapped its neck, and dropped the corpse to the ground where it lay for several minutes. Fleas and ticks fled from a cooling body like a cat from running water.

He lifted his snack and scrabbled up the coarse gray bark of a locust tree, then stretched out on a thick limb. The sun was almost directly overhead. He'd napped most of the morning despite intense hunger, hidden on the same branch, intending to wait for nightfall. But his growling belly had jolted him awake. So, he'd crept a few feet into the grasses along the meadow near the Mi'kmaq village to score this rabbit, but the risk had been worth it. It still had a thin layer of greasy fat beneath its thick coat.

He raised his nose to inhale the faint scent of blood. Not the rabbit's, but a different species. The wind had shifted to blow from the east, the direction of the Abenaki village. More could be distilled from scent than one could ever determine with the naked eye. He'd often taken the form of a gray wolf on his patrols. Nothing compared to the sexual ecstasy of the smell of your prey's emotions. Fear was sweeter than fresh honeycomb, hate bitter as goldenseal root. But this scent had been coppery human blood. He was several hours distant from the Abenaki. Two days' travel for those putrid, weak men.

Stryker licked his nose to cleanse his palate. He opened his mouth to study the fragrance. This blood had been drawn in anger, with acidic iron tones harshly staining the air, thick as revenge in a tribal feud. The Abenaki shaman must've killed the enemy! Another whiff. Slick fish oil, the sweat of men, and wet wool. Woolen scents were persistent, heavy. They stuck close to the ground and carried long distances. He'd caught that same aroma earlier this morning. The Vestmen's sail, no doubt. But the sweat of men, though prone to linger, was not nearly as persistent. Which meant the Vestmen were getting closer, driving inland. He cared not where they wandered, as long as the taller one was dead. He needed to confirm.

He nuzzled between the hare's front legs and sank his teeth into its chest. What were Vestmen doing this far south, anyway? It could be no coincidence that Ernick had sent him on a seemingly otherwise simple tasking while the Vestmen, those rancid, walking corpses, had shown up with an enemy among them. And Stryker under orders not to touch them? Ernick's instructions conflicted: to clear the way of the Mi'kmaq of all enemy, yet not to harm those among whom the enemy had found harbor. And if Stryker failed, Ernick would still hold him accountable.

He must be plotting against me. Yes, that makes sense. Ernick sees me as a threat and is looking for an excuse to exile me.

But a ranger was used to working alone. He depended upon no one's mercy. He'd survived much larger challenges. Now he'd slaughtered the pagan Vestman and nothing tied him to the act.

He finished off the rabbit's hindquarters, crunching bone between molars, sucking out the rich red marrow, then backed down the tree. His legs were heavy as he started to lope. He needed to hunt beaver, anything with more fat. But that would have to wait. He slunk east along the narrow river, following the game trail that formed on all riverbanks, tracking the woolen scent, pausing only to cool his tongue with a drink from the stream, clear and gentle so far inland.

After two hours he passed a section of the river that splashed over shallow rocks and churned to a frothing white boil. A black bear was planted in the middle of the rumble and glared expectantly at the water before him. Too early for the salmon run. A waste of time.

The woolen scent grew thicker, disappearing for only a few minutes before suddenly drifting back upon the path, proffering new clues. The stench of rancid seal fat. Vestmen rubbed it on their ships to preserve the wood. Another of their endearing practices: to hunt and kill prey, liquefy their blubber, then smear it all over their boats—the same vessels used to hunt yet more seals. He chuckled to himself. Maybe these Vestmen weren't as bad as he'd thought.

His muscles burned, but he quickened his pace. After another hour the Vestmen's square sail came into view upon the river through thick brown columns of loblolly pine that sprouted from the bank. He slowed to a trot, sliding beneath the concealing shadows of tree trunks. He climbed a lone oak and crept along a thick branch that stretched over the water. He dropped to his belly and panted. The boat's sail billowed softly, the wind behind it. Wet, narrow-bladed oars flashed in the sunlight. The craft sailed westward, high in the water, its draft shallow enough to float through even low marshes. With her shields affixed to the gunwales, she was outfitted for war and would be carrying little cargo, to encourage her light stance and agility.

A breeze picked up and the sail billowed, flashing a huge black cross on its chest. Stryker's belly tensed and he rose to a crouch. The heathen symbol was flanked by the heads of two wolves. The boat passed almost directly beneath his perch, oars creaking against their keepers, leather boots squeaking against chocks, and breath hissing through teeth. The wake of the bow leaving a mere ripple.

The men bent naked backs to the noonday sun as they pulled. Stryker's gaze ran down the port side and a growl rumbled in his chest at the sight of the enemy, the tall Vestman leaning into his work, like a pagan bowing before his god. *The witch failed.* Coward! He snorted in disgust. He'd have to kill the dog himself. Word might get back to Ernick that a black panther had slaughtered a Vestman, but Stryker would simply deny involvement. Ernick had no eyes to spy for him here.

The panther crouched and stalked down the branch, digging his claws into the bark, tensing for a leap. The enemy gripped an axe along the length of the oar handle. Those long, thick fingers wrapped around both, as if choking them. As the boat passed below the tip of the branch, the enemy's oar stilled. His green eyes searched the bank suspiciously. This was no ordinary prey. He was a hunter, and sensed a trap had been set. Stryker couldn't take him now. Just who was this man, an assassin sent by Ernick?

As the boat slipped upriver, the enemy again dipped his oar in unison with the others. Stryker would have to trail him now. Humans were always poorly vigilant. His guard would tire eventually. He'd catch the fool taking a drink, or watering the ivy, or just as his eyes grew weary with slumber.

Stryker leapt to the dirt. A rustle of feathers came from behind him. A low growl rumbled, "A long way from your master's region, aren't you?"

Stryker spun as an enormous, short-faced she-bear lumbered up the path, long legs swinging with the same rocking motion as a camel. The beast towered over him, tall as a horse, a great brown boulder for a head, paws the span of tree stumps. Fear swelled his chest. He backed away. Not that he couldn't outrun her. But the last short-faced bear had died out centuries earlier. This was no ordinary animal.

The monster's voice was a low growl that vibrated along the path, traveling up through the pads of Stryker's feet. "Don't look so surprised, ranger." Her lip curled, revealing long canines in an amused grin.

Instantly, Stryker was yanked into the realm of spirit. The transition had always been under his own control. Not this time. And now, so sudden and violent was the change, he struggled to gain his bearings. The world was a blur. He blinked, and shimmering blue scales came into focus.

Slaughter!

He twisted to free himself, then noticed a silver blade at his throat, brilliant as a mirror, reflecting his own fearful expression.

More blades curled around his neck like snakes. One flinch, and he'd find himself in the Abyss.

Slaughter's fat lips puckered. His bronze face creased with delight. He clucked his tongue. "Your master will be so embarrassed. So angry. One of his rangers, in *my* day region?" He shook his head. Green and purple dreadlocks swayed over well-muscled shoulders. "He'll be indebted to me, you see. It's the law. He won't kill you, of course. What fun would that be? Instead, he'll just slice off your feet and let you lie crippled till you're so hungry you'll inhabit any filthy, fleshly beast that comes along. Just to satisfy your craving."

The grip around Stryker's neck eased. He drew a shaky breath, but remained silent. Anything he might say would only worsen his fate.

Slaughter glanced over him, at the disappearing ship. "Nothing to say? No lies for me?"

Stryker bowed as low as he dared, his breath frosting the shiny blade. "Many lies, my lord. But none for you."

Slaughter's face glowed, but gave off no heat. His snout was flat like a bull, with eyes so deeply inset his sockets appeared empty. "Disappointing. But wise." He dropped Stryker to the ground and studied him. In spirit, Stryker was no black panther, but a creature of similar proportion, twice the size, with thick, gray-scaled armor that resembled the hide of a rhinoceros. His weapons were built for close quarters combat...knives for claws and a mouth full of daggers.

Slaughter paced as he spoke. "It would be wrong of me not to pay you a compliment." The thick talons surrounding his calves rose like the hair on a dog's back as the monster lumbered past, pointing toward Stryker's face. "You snuck into the heart of my day region undetected—that will cost the command of my northern guard his life—and I caught you preparing to kill a Vestman, in defiance of your master's orders."

How did Slaughter know Ernick's orders, his rival? He forced the question from his mind.

"Who aided you?"

Stryker sneered, "I am a ranger, my lord. We are given no aid."

Slaughter snatched him from the ground and plunged the sword of his index finger through Stryker's belly, neatly between scales of armor, such that the blade stuck out between his shoulders. Pain seared from his crotch to his eyes. Every joint in his body locked. His legs thrust straight out as if pulled by chains.

His claws jutted so violently they threatened to snap off. His mouth locked agape, and pain seared each shallow breath.

Slaughter's gaze drifted across Stryker's impaled body like a cat studying a skewered rabbit. The blue scales of his belly flashed green as he laughed, curling fingers as if playing an instrument. "No lies, remember?"

Stryker tried to speak, but air only gurgled around the blood channel in the sword.

Slaughter grinned and plucked its crimson-smeared tip, its metallic note the music of war. "What? Can't talk with a sword through your diaphragm?" With a flick of his wrist the weapon pointed to the earth and Stryker slid from it.

He gagged and coughed, but produced no blood. He patted his belly where the sword had pierced, but no wound festered. The pain had been real enough. His lip curled, revealing two gleaming daggers. "No aid," he gasped.

Slaughter resumed his pacing. "Always need to be sure. No captain can tolerate a traitor." He spun and planted his fingers into the earth like roots of a tree. He leaned forward, face hovering above Stryker's bowed head. His breath was hot, but sweet as a rotting apple. No, that must've been wrong. Why would such a beast be afraid of anything? What could Slaughter possibly fear?

"Then how did you slip through my defenses?"

Who did this demon think he was? No guard could keep him out. Though the captain's swords were sharp, apparently his mind was not. Stryker spoke slowly, trying desperately not to sound condescending. "I am a ranger, my lord. And as vicious as I am silent." He bowed his head lower. "Though I am not clever enough to elude your eye."

A grunt, then the monstrous demon stood and turned. The ground shook beneath each step, though he left no footprints. Stryker chanced a glance up when his back was turned. The scales across his shoulders rippled and turned a blazing red. "Your captain is a fool!" Slaughter shouted. The swords of his fingers flashed in the glaring sun like the wet oars of the ship. "He protects the Vestmen, though the enemy is among them. He puts all hope in a human. Their witch! That she might win back their allegiance. His fate placed in the hands of a single spirit-whore!" He spun and plunged his fingers through Stryker's shoulders before he had the chance to flinch. He knitted them together through his chest, threatening to slice his body in two. The pain more intense than anything Stryker could imagine. Spittle flew from the captain's wet lips as he yelled, "No one can turn an enemy! Death is the only way to deal with them."

One of Stryker's eyes spasmed and the demon started at it, then withdrew his fingers. Stryker gasped as the pain subsided. The cobalt scales on Slaughter's chest flashed like fire as he chuckled. "That is their weakness. Death. Filthy mortals. Yet, we can't just kill them all."

Stryker squinted. What did he mean by that?

Slaughter fanned fingers before his face, as if to cool himself with a breeze. His tone was patronizing. "Don't look surprised. You're a *ranger*. But your ignorance doesn't shock me. Ernick is secretive. I'll give him that. Yes, mortals are a joy to kill, but their allegiance is currency." He spread arms, their heft as substantial as tree trunks. "And I am quite rich."

His fingers swelled as he spoke, and broad lips spread into a grin. "Every mortal within my region is firmly under *my* power. Their loyalty, unwavering." He pointed a fat sword up the river, where the Vestman's boat was disappearing around a bend. Once more the sweet aroma of rotten apples filled Stryker's nose as Slaughter spoke. "But now that fool Ernick's problem has become my own. An infection." His gaze heated the base of Stryker's skull.

"Yes, my lord."

Slaughter planted his fingers into the earth once again. His lip curled, and the talons about his ankles dripped yellow venom into hissing, steaming pools. "You belong to me now, ranger. I don't care how you do it. But you will kill that Vestman!"

A blinding flash of light and Stryker found himself in the panther's form once again, leaning upon a tree trunk, legs shaking as from a violent cold. A brown feather dropped from the wing of a huge bald eagle as it flew northward, rising in the air over a gully, a gash in the earth among the brown pillars of the forest.

Chapter 18 – Duck Hunt

The afternoon sun warmed my shoulders as I bent to heave upon the handle of my oar. The vessel lurched forward, and each stroke gained us less ground as the creek upon which we navigated turned into inland river, its current working contrary to our efforts. Throughout the remainder of the morning, and now, well into afternoon, the water had turned brackish, the salt scent disappearing completely. The farther we traveled this direction, the stronger the current, and the stream flowed more clearly. Splashes were ice upon my skin, the water most likely fed by snowmelt from mountains further inland.

We navigated close to shoreline, but not so near to endanger the boat by shallow rocks and stumps. In this manner, we also avoided the river's strongest current. Along the handle of my oar, I gripped an axe, my long fingers wrapping around both with ease. I considered returning the weapon to its loop upon my belt but glanced at the shoreline instead.

It had been several hours since we'd passed yet another bitter, oppressive darkness. It had been late morning, not long after leaving the Abenaki village, and the same cold anticipation of simmering malevolence had weighed upon me heavy as a wool sweater drenched in rain. My arms had trembled with a terrifying chill. I'd scanned the shoreline then but had seen nothing upon the riverside trail. It was a sensation of being watched, and had peaked when we'd passed a lone oak tree among a stand of pine. Something sinister, I knew, among its boughs. A bald eagle had circled above the scene, probably scouting for fish. But the evil had passed, and my body had warmed again. Still, I refused to return the axe to my belt.

Rowers grunted with each pull, though the pace was slow, one I could maintain all day. Our music proved a cadence of hypnotic rhythm, no doubt sung by slaves upon countless Greek and Roman warships. And now I was a captive chained to this vessel. Caught in an inescapable, cruel maze. A labyrinth, like the myth of Theseus and the Minotaur that my European history teacher had told. Yet, unlike that hero, I hadn't volunteered for this task. I'd been waylaid. Shanghaied by the spirit of my dead sister. Or, according to her, her "master" had brought me—whoever that was. The both of us were somehow caught in this same insane story.

I tucked my chin and spoke quietly over my shoulder to Tryfing who was grunting behind me. "That witch, did you understand what she said?"

He was silent through a couple of strokes. "She didn't speak our tongue. Marr interpreted."

I scowled. "No. After that, just before we left. She was standing on that rock and asked me for a blessing."

He sat upright and wheezed as if he'd been sprinting. "I don't know what she said. She spoke in her own tongue. And you answered in gibberish. I figured you were mocking her."

I considered that as my shoulders warmed to their work. Maybe language worked the same way in this world for everyone, just as I could understand Tryfing now. Could that be right? I hadn't understood her or the Abenaki chief earlier, not without Marr interpreting. What had changed?

A breeze chilled my bare stomach. I recalled the icy spider crawling up my windpipe and the witch's dilated eyes, like she was high on drugs. Or possessed. *I have blessed you*, she'd said. Maybe she'd cast some sort of language spell, just to ask for my blessing in return. Too bad for her I had none to give.

Halfdan yelled at Tryfing and he began rowing again. I timed my questions with the rhythm of the oarsmen's grunts. "How is it that I own a share of the boat?"

Tryfing did the same. His answers came in short bursts. "Nothing to explain... You own one-third... Halfdan two-thirds." Then he lowered his voice until I could barely hear. "That's one reason you need to be careful. Halfdan wants your share too, but you've never sold it. If you die, it falls to your father, and he will sell."

"One reason. What's the other?"

Tryfing's breath became raspy again. "Probably many... He wants to be chieftain... Remember? The village prefers you... But if he rescues Astrid..."

"What would happen?"

An exaggerated groan, but he kept his voice low. "Are all men so stupid in the land you come from? The only person more beloved than Matok is the fire-haired Astrid. She possesses a temper to match. Halfdan aims to marry her. Your father would not refuse, for he's just as much a scoundrel. They'd make a bargain. Halfdan is his brother, but only by marriage, so no blood relation exists between Halfdan and Astrid. But if he becomes our next chieftain the village would starve because he doesn't have the sense to wipe his own ass. All he knows is to drink, piss, and swing a sword."

So, why was I here? I'd assumed it was to free Astrid. It'd be as if I'd saved Gabby, like I'd always wished I had. But whether at the hands of the Mi'kmaq or her own people, Astrid would be enslaved. How was I to help?

We rounded a bend in the river where fresh black earth spilled over large boulders, as if from a mudslide. The tinny wash of white water swelled to a roaring grumble. Just ahead a tall waterfall spilled from a rim of charcoal-colored boulders. Two enormous maples stretched over the site, one from each side, our boat drifting into the long shadow of their leafy boughs. Halfdan steered toward the bank. We tied the bow to a rock two oars' lengths from the shore, allowing for a quick retreat. The sail came down and I joined several others to fold the heavy cloth atop the boom, securing it with slick ropes that looked like tanned intestines. Halfdan ordered twenty of us to shore. I trotted down the gangplank and waded into frigid, waist-deep water. Behind us, White-Tip raised the plank and shouted, "Lookouts! To the bow and astern."

Tryfing splashed through the water behind me, holding his sword and shield overhead with one hand, cupping water to his mouth with the other. I drank as well, till my belly swelled, my beard was drenched, and my shoulders ached in a shiver.

Halfdan spoke with One-Eye as I trudged up the stony bank to the narrow path that followed the creek. Over me, gnarled limbs of tall maples, oaks, and chestnuts twisted together, weaving a thick lime-green canopy of young leaf growth. A rabbit with huge white feet stood frozen on the trail, its chest pulsing with rapid breaths. It bounded behind a bush. I flinched at a slurping sound just ahead and cocked my arm, ready to loose an axe. Then a squish of mud, as if someone were raking for clams on marsh flats. A deer and its spotted fawn picked their way carefully along the muddy trail. Unlike yesterday's coastline, the ground here was a mixture of rich earth and boulder, deposited by ancient glaciers. The black path upon which I stood appeared to have been churned by an entire herd.

I glanced behind me toward the bend in the river. Indeed, there had been a mudslide. A thick wall of tumbled dirt, trees, and rock buried the eastern passage. Not a single animal track crossed it. The damage must've been from yesterday's soaker. Yet heavy foliage remained, so the hail had been limited to the coast.

Halfdan joined me upon the trail. He sat on a boulder and lifted each leg, emptying his boots of water. He stood and took off at a trot. The other Vestmen followed. My shoulders slumped. It had been a long day. Did this man never rest? Tryfing shoved my shoulder and pointed after him.

Halfdan's pace was fast, but fortunately not near what I was used to maintaining in cross-country practice. Most of the men ahead lumbered in a two-legged gallop, feet and knees pointing every direction except straight ahead. Yet they never tired, despite their poor form. Even Tryfing, though he wheezed like an asthmatic. I slung my shield across my back. My axe handles slapped my legs just as they had in my vision, so I carried them by their necks, two in each hand.

Mud squelched beneath my boots. We bounded over fallen trunks. Several trees had already been pushed to either side of the trail. This path had been maintained, though not recently. Just as in rowing, I settled into a loping rhythm. The rim of the shield cut into my back and I shrugged it into a different position. My belly growled at the thought of the dried cod stashed in the sack slung about my waist.

Tryfing and I formed the tail of our troop. But after an hour he began to lag. I slowed as well, enough to keep an eye on the runner ahead, and Tryfing behind. My legs burned and sweat stung my back where the shield rubbed it raw.

Gabby's high-pitched laugh sounded behind me. "Speed up, Michael." She sprinted, passing me, white legs flashing beneath her short, fringed leather dress, moccasined feet caked with mud, hair pinned back in the wind.

I glanced at Tryfing, but he betrayed no sign of seeing the pale red-haired ghost running effortlessly next to me. Or maybe he was too preoccupied with necessities such as breathing.

"I can go faster," I told her, "but I'm keeping an eye on the dying guy behind me."

She quickened her pace. "He's the least of your worries."

So I matched her, and Tryfing disappeared as we began to catch up with the rest of the group. A shadow passed over the trail, and branches shook in a cold gust. "It sounds like I'm supposed to rescue my sister from a pack of Mi'kmaq Indians. I'm hoping that will end this nightmare."

She glared. "*I'm* your sister. And I'm the one doing the rescuing."

I clenched my fists. "I swear, could you be any more confusing? You called me here—or your *master*, whatever that means—and now I'm—"

She curled her lip. "Don't you get it? Can't you smell that? It's right in front of you, plain as the sun."

There she went again with her riddles. "Smell what?"

As soon as the words left my mouth, a memory slammed into my mind. Duck hunting with Granddad, sitting in a plywood blind, a Winchester 12 gauge side-by-side across my knees. This image was almost as vivid as my vision, as if I'd just stepped from that day. Peering over the fresh-cut cedar boughs tacked to the outside, the air had been heavy with their resinous fragrance. Before us, golden morning rays sliced across miles of rye-brown marsh grass.

Granddad had gripped the tip of his shooting glove in his teeth and yanked it off. He pointed an age-spotted finger toward the distant Atlantic where whitecaps frothed. A cold wind carried their grumble against the shore. A small flock of ducks had just banked hard, dropping into the open slot of marsh that ran before us, slipping low over the narrow creek. Their wings beat fast as wasps', flashing black and white.

"Bufflehead," he'd said, grinning like a child. "A whole squadron of fighters, lining to strafe our beach."

Now Gabby elbowed my ribs. "What do you smell, there, when the ducks set their wings?"

Her touch jolted me. I'd only been able to feel her in the vision earlier. And how'd she known what I'd been thinking about? "You in my head now?"

"*Pffft*. Not like I have to fight for room."

Had she brought that hunt back to memory? No, she hadn't been with us that day. "Who cares what I smelled."

Her eyes widened, face flushed with anger. "*Think*, brother."

She ran beside me as we splashed through mud and crossed a tight gulley, still gaining on the other Vestmen. A cold wind whipped down as I reached back again to that time on the marsh with Granddad. Remembrance came with surprising clarity. We'd set the decoys in a half-moon across the thin channel, anticipating the wind would drive waterfowl inland, toward us. The shape provided the most appealing landing spot just in front of our blind. Granddad had crouched and raised his Browning Double Automatic. The ducks were screaming-fast, wind up their tail feathers, shooting toward us. One in the lead cupped its wings and began a descending glide. It dropped webbed feet and skated across the surface like a water-skier.

"There," Gabby said. "What do you smell?"

My legs were beginning to tire. I gave a frustrated huff. "Cedar. We'd camo'd the blind with it."

"No, silly. That's not the kind of smell I mean. Remember," she said, pointing toward the line of lumbering Vestmen ahead of us. "Their lives depend on it. And yours upon theirs."

The lead duck's momentum had bled off. He'd dropped into the brown water, shaking tail feathers, the tall marsh grass barricading the kill zone from wind. The rest of the flock, about two dozen, had followed and settled next to him. Granddad winked and we jumped up, leveled our guns and...*maple sap*. Not the heavy sweetness like the syrup, but a light, wooden fragrance with a hint of sugar. I knew it from helping Granddad collect it in winter for boiling down. The distinctive, honey scent of a maple tree's blood had wafted through the blind, from nowhere.

Why had I never remembered this before?

Gabby shoved my shoulder and I stumbled, thumping to a stop into a trunk of scaly brown pine bark. "*That's* the scent." She stepped close and brushed my beard with the back of her hand. Staring at me, her searching gaze switching from eye to eye. Concern creased her face. "You have so much to learn, brother. But there's no more time."

Halfdan raised his arms high over his head and the column before me came to a halt.

I stood at the bottom of a short hill and turned, but Tryfing would still be a couple of minutes catching up. "Then teach me. What do I need to learn?" I asked. But she was gone. The only remnant a trace aroma of maple sap. Though it seemed more than a scent. It clung to my body like sweat, running down my back in drops, between my shoulder blades. I shivered as the cold, pressing malevolence from the prior day returned to my shoulders. The maple fragrance increased in strength, as if coming from up the trail. Yet, Gabby had left. So, why was the smell...*oh no!*

I gripped an axe by the end of the handle and sprinted toward the men. "Shields!" I shouted. They stood motionless as I passed them. "Shields!" I yelled again, fumbling with my own, lifting it from my back, carrying it in front such that my knees slammed its rim as I pumped up the incline. Still, they stared with hands resting on belts, or leaning on their knees while catching their breath. Halfdan glared down at me from the head of the line, his face screwed into a knot. One-Eye pointed and laughed; then an arrow sliced through the cheeks of his opened mouth and sunk into the ribboned bark of a chestnut.

Chapter 19 – Great Scout

Kiona stomped her foot at Nabid standing next to her in knee-high cotton grass. A narrow slice of sun blazed upon it through a tear in the forest canopy where a tree had blown over. Last season's soft tufted heads slapped her shin, and the fresh perfume of mint bloomed as strong as allspice bush. She tugged on her little brother's elbow, but the child yanked free. He grew stronger with each day. She raised her arms in frustration. "You can't go with the warriors!"

The boy turned and sprinted into the woods, his bow in one hand, a fistful of arrows in the other. Not old enough to make his own heads yet, he'd sharpened the tips of birch shoots and hardened them slowly over a fire. He often dipped them in one of Mother's poisons, though she chastened him not to, in case he accidentally poked himself.

Kiona ran after him and caught up in a few strides, but didn't grab. She'd let him run until his energy was spent. He was stone headed, but only a boy. His short legs flashed like the beating wings of a duck, but he began to slow as the path angled up a long hill. She trotted easily.

He stopped and bent, hands on knees, wheezing. "How can you run so fast?" he huffed.

Kiona gripped his shoulder, turned him around, and shoved him back toward the migration trail. "My legs are twice as long as yours. If you take after Mother, you'll be a fast runner someday too. If you can't outrun me, how will you outrun an enemy warrior?"

His shoulders slumped.

Good. Maybe he was finally admitting defeat.

"Why can't I go with the rest of the braves?"

Soon after Kiona had finished explaining to the chief how Astrid was only singing a song and not chanting a curse, he'd ordered the warriors to grab spears and run toward the tribe's eastern lookout. A few had sprinted ahead on the migration trail to gather the families there. Members traveled at their own pace, and the tribe had been spread out. The eastern lookout was a bluff cleared of trees, overlooking the riverside trail, upstream of the waterfall by a couple hours' run. Mother's spirits had said the Vestmen would come by water, but unless they stopped to carry their long canoe up a forty-foot incline, they'd have to proceed past the waterfall on foot.

"We're still a day's journey from summer camp," Kiona explained. "The lookout is even farther than that. If you could keep running, it would take you almost until sunset to make it. Do you think you can do that?"

A pair of squirrels chased each up and around a tree, spiraling till out of sight. The boy stared at his legs, as if asking their opinion. He puffed his cheeks. "I could." He shuffled ahead, but wandered in a curve. Did he think Kiona was blind? That she couldn't see the position of the sun? She shoved him west again, back toward the trail. "Maybe you could, but you aren't a brave yet."

"Not a brave! I trained with them all winter! Great Scout taught us the Vestmen's weaknesses. How to attack."

Great Scout was a skilled hunter, warrior, and trained the braves for battle. He assigned the tribe's guard. Nabid had only observed the other Indians on warmer days as they practiced attacking fences woven of willow, other men sentried behind it, mimicking how they'd seen the Vestmen warriors practicing with shields and swords. Great Scout had only allowed Nabid to watch, and that because he was Mother's son. No other youth had been present.

"You may have trained with them"—she didn't want to bruise her little brother's fragile pride—"but these are fierce men, with long swords, and merciless, even toward boys." She put her arm around his shoulder, almost up to her belly. Hadn't he only been up to her hip back in the stream? He seemed to be taller by the hour. One day, he'd be a warrior and under Great Scout's care as well. "You will have your time. Be patient. Finish growing."

Nabid slid an arm around her waist and gave a quick hug. Then he turned and sprinted off again.

"Ugh!" Kiona shouted. She started after him. What did the boy not understand? Was she this obstinate when she'd been his age? She would waste no more words. She trailed him a few paces, waiting till he tired again. Shouldn't be far. Then she'd drag him back by the hair if he resisted. Put him in a collar like Astrid.

But her brother didn't seem to slow so quickly this time. Had he been pretending? He was passing between two huge trunks when a wooden shaft, straight and hard, swung from behind one like a whipping branch. It caught the boy square in the chest and sent him sprawling back on pine needles. A shiny red welt stretched across his thin skin.

A huge warrior stepped from behind the tree, spear gripped in one thick hand, tomahawk tied about his waist. In his other he grasped a narrow club of ash wood. Turquoise-blue clay adorned his eyes. It was Great Scout. What was he still doing here? His warriors had all run ahead.

He stood over the boy, who scrambled away like a crab, eyes welling in pain. "Go back to the others, little brave. Don't disobey your sister again."

Nabid jumped to his feet and hid behind Kiona like a scared dog. The man didn't need to beat her brother! Kiona squinted. She wanted to lash out, to wrestle his club away and make him feel its blows. But that would be foolish with such a brave. Uncertain how to respond, she dropped her gaze. "Let's go, brother." Neither Kiona nor Nabid had known their father. Only that he'd died protecting Mother from a black panther. The same one to which she'd lost her hand.

Nabid seemed to find his courage and stood his ground. He stroked the green stripe across his cheeks and stuck out his chest, red band across it.

The scout laughed. "You are a brave little one, aren't you?" He tossed his club in the air and caught it by its end, then held the handle out to the boy. "Take it. Your arrows will do little good. You need to protect your sister and Astrid. That's your job now."

Astrid? What did he care about the prisoner? She lifted her gaze and studied the man. He wasn't Great Scout after all, but stood with a familiar bulky posture, thick arms holding out the weapon. The sides of his head were unshaven. It was Huritt! His face had been disguised by his family's war color. Great Scout was Huritt's father, and their similar appearance had confused her. Plus, she'd never seen Huritt in war paint.

But now her chest grew hot. She stomped over and slapped him, smearing blue across his nose. "Don't you dare hit my little brother again or I will beat you till you're talking to the spirits!"

A red handprint grew across Huritt's cheek. He clenched his fist, then glanced away. "He isn't your little brother anymore. He's a young brave, and his job is to protect your family. You would do well to recognize that." He turned and began to walk into the shadow of the towering trunks where he'd been hiding.

"Where are you going?"

"I'm guarding our trail. The others have gone ahead. I'm a scout, like my father, and will join them before nightfall."

113

Huritt? With his father? Fighting the Vestmen? "But you're too young. You've never fought in battle. You can't attack Vestmen. They have swords."

The brave spun and hurled the spear toward her. Before she could flinch, the shaft sank into the ground between her feet. "I'm a warrior, Kiona! Seasons pass, no matter how you wish them to cease. This is my honor."

She ran to him and gently placed her palm on the welt where she'd slapped him. "I'm sorry."

His eyes softened. "You're more like your mother than you'd like to admit."

She stood on her toes and leaned her forehead to his. He pulled away, confusion spreading across his face. "Not for me," she said. "But for Astrid."

Nabid gripped his new club and swung it at a trunk, his white teeth bared, beaming, unaware of their conversation.

Huritt froze, his gaze distant, nostrils swelling like those of a startled buck. "You know of us."

She smiled, trying to convey calm. "It was hard to miss. But the Vestmen...they come for her. To bring her home. What will you do?"

He strode to the spear, thick arms swaying, and yanked it from the earth. His expression hardened back into his father's. "My duty."

Crack! Nabid's club smacked a tree, like a frozen branch breaking under the weight of snow. A deer startled, tawny hide camouflaged against the forest floor, and bounded away, white tail flitting.

Chapter 20 – The Accuser

I was sprinting up the muddy hill, picking stones for footing. One-Eye pressed both palms to his cheeks. Blood dripped down his wrists. As I passed him, he drew his sword and another arrow thudded into his shield. I was halfway up the incline and the darts flew from between densely packed trunks of pine and oak. A stretch of new growth among the otherwise virgin forest. There the woods seemed to slope upward, though I could see only a few feet into it. Blackened, charred bark climbed the trunks of a few scattered old-growth trees that towered over the rest like giants among mortals. The perfect spot for an ambush.

"Shield wall!" Halfdan yelled.

We formed into a rank and faced the forest. I stood near the middle. The river protected our rear, but made retreat impossible. Halfdan stood at the highest point of the trail. Beyond that it dropped out of sight. The enemy could be gathering there for an attack. In the other direction, at the bottom of the hill, the path curved, disappearing around a bend. The sun had started to set, and nothing but a packed stand of gray-and-brown trunks stood before us. We were blind. A perfect kill zone.

Another arrow thumped into a shield next to mine. Its shaft was narrow, straight as a reed, fletched with black feathers. The Vestman beside me had blond hair thick and curly as sheep's wool. His eyes narrowed with surprise, cheeks tensed in anger. "Where are they? Did you see them?"

"No."

"Then how'd you know this was a trap?"

Because my dead sister's spirit that was just running next to us reminded me how I'd once smelled maple sap in a duck blind back when I was a kid in a different world. The truth sounded insane. "I...I don't know."

"Over there!" another yelled, pointing a long arm wrapped in deer hide toward the jungle of trees. I followed his gaze but saw only saplings leaning in the wind. An arrow struck my own shield's metal band, shattering shards of flint against my forehead. The only movement came from leaves stirred by the wind. Just as in

115

my vision, we were blind to whoever was shooting. *The Mi'kmaq are protected by a powerful shaman*, the witch had said.

A Vestman beside Halfdan cursed as an arrow sank into his calf. He reached down, broke off the shaft, and flung it back toward the forest. It twisted, caught in the wind, then lifted and sailed over our heads into the water behind us.

The warrior beat the rim of his shield with the hilt of his sword. "Cowards!"

A growl rose along our line. Metal rang against wood as we shouted insults at the invisible enemy, daring them to give up their cover, to meet us in battle like men. It would be foolish to wade into the thick wood before us. *Never bet at another man's game*, my father would say. Our shields would be useless, even an impediment in the brush. And it seemed to be what the Indians were tempting us to do.

Without taking my gaze from the tree line, I tapped the edge of my shield against that of the men next to me, ensuring an overlap. I don't know if nerves or instinct prompted my action, but it seemed the right thing to do. The fighters on either side did the same, and a clatter repeated down the line. I held an axe over my shoulder at the ready and hoped Tryfing was right, that Matok was skilled with the weapon. And that somehow, I could channel his reflexes.

I'd never fought anyone. Not even scraps at school. Could I do this? Swing an axe to harm another man? Or even kill him? My thoughts flashed back to that same hunting trip with Granddad. When his curly tan Chesapeake retriever laid two more bufflehead at my feet. I had lifted a drake in my palm and stroked the dark iridescent green and purple around its eye, amazed at how the colors morphed into black depending on the angle of the light hitting it. Such a beautiful creature. Granddad had sipped coffee from a thermos, slapped my back, and said, "*Now* look at who's the hunter!"

My grip tightened on the axe handle. A bitterness filled my mouth, coating my tongue. I hunched my shoulders and a snarl rose from my belly. Anger filled my chest and stiffened my spine. A raw, primal hate warmed my legs, a feeling I'd never experienced before. As if a spirit—or demon even—stood behind me, clutching my forearms, urging me to do its bidding. All fear died away. I was light, as if just released from a burden. In that instant, I knew with certainty how to wield axe and shield. In fact, I'd done so many times before. In a past life, maybe this one. Or one yet to come.

A gust carried another sweet, resinous whiff of maple sap.

How dare these men think of me as a victim! *I* was the hunter, the predator to the prey. This world was no longer my prison. Here I had purpose. This world held freedom. The freedom to fight. Freedom from fear.

Suddenly, the forest exploded. Green leaves thrashed and shot toward us, as if blown in a squall. Ashen-skinned warriors leapt onto the trail, reaching back like a baseball pitcher winding up, gripping short spears whose blackened points hovered just beside their faces, sighting down their shafts. Naked except for loincloths, the Indians had coated themselves with a gloppy gray paint, or maybe mud, the exact color of maple tree bark. But faces were colored in dull hues of blue and green. Even purple. War paint.

They charged in pairs, one directly behind the other.

Time seemed to slow.

The first warriors struck low, thrusting their weapons beneath our shields. I lowered mine to deflect the attack and threw my axe at the same time. A spear splintered one of my shield boards. I stumbled backward beneath the shuddering blow, but my axe caught the attacker's partner behind him in the throat. He doubled over and convulsed. Vomit and blood spilled through the gash in his neck as he collapsed to his knees.

Our entire line had dropped shields as well. But a second wave of warriors' spears flew immediately after the first, the entire rank synchronized, quick and precise as a drill team. Only I had managed to take out the second attacker. The forest echoed with the thuds of lances piercing leather and striking bone, the pained screams of our wounded, and the gurgle of air sucking through gashed chests. Vestmen fell and our line opened like cracks in a splintered hull. In seconds they would overrun us completely.

But now came the cleavered hack of steel upon skulls, the wet thud of swords into flesh. The same noise a butcher's knife makes deheading trout. Curly still stood next to me unharmed, but a short Indian leaned upon the thick shaft impaling his shield, straining to expose him to the attack of his partner. Curly slashed his sword at a downward angle. The air filled with the stench of excrement as the Indian's bowels spilled onto mud.

The one in front of me abandoned his spear stuck in my shield and reached down to yank the axe from his partner's body. A mistake. I drew another from my belt and hacked off the back of his skull like pruning a tree with a hatchet.

Downhill, half our number writhed upon the ground or leaned gasping and bleeding against rocks. One-Eye thrust a sword through the gray belly of a warrior with one blue-ringed eye socket, the same as in my vision. Two others turned toward One-Eye, rushing at his blind side. I hurled my axe and it flew straight into the spine of one. He screamed as he fell, and One-Eye turned in time to deflect the spear-point of the other. A strong slash across his attacker's forearm sent the Indian stumbling back into the woods. One-Eye glanced at the hatchet in the fallen Indian's back, grinned, and winked his empty eye socket at me. Even with death all around, the gesture still raised the hair on my neck.

For a second the world seemed to fall silent again, except for the rush of air through leaves and the wind of my own breathing. As if no battle had just taken place. A dozen of us remained on our feet, while twenty or thirty gray corpses splattered in crimson, stained with mud, lay scattered upon the earth. But their attack had been sudden and precise, with a practiced coordination. Obviously not the first time they'd studied Vestman defenses.

The forest rumbled like a stampede of cattle. "Shield wall!" Halfdan yelled. We closed ranks, standing upon bodies piled like rocks. As I found footing, a scream gurgled beneath my boots, but I dared not risk even a fleeting glance to see whether it was one of our own.

The edge of forest erupted again. More soot-gray warriors charged, wielding black-tipped javelins, stone-headed tomahawks, and drawn bows. The archers stood back near the trees while the others charged forward. A warrior gripping a club in one hand and spear in the other, glared at me, howled like a tomcat, and rushed. I hurled a hatchet, but he batted it away. I drew another, my last. But he was already upon me, hammering my shield. He raised the spear and jabbed it over its rim. I ducked, but the point sliced down my back. I hacked at his ankle and he toppled into the warrior attacking Curly.

My thigh seared, as if stung by a giant hornet. A short-shafted arrow stuck out above my knee. When did I get hit? A child-sized brave with a small bow, a green stripe across his cheeks, smiled, turned away, and sprinted back into the woods. More Indians stepped between the remaining archers, waiting to join the battle. How many could there be? A whole village?

A stocky warrior, his face also adorned with blue paint, attacked at the next onslaught. I braced my shoulder against my shield and batted away club and spear, my long, powerful arms breaking his grip upon his weapons. But he was quick; I drew no blood. The ends of our rank began to curl inward as the Indians tried to flank us. Halfdan wedged the unprotected edge of his shield against a chestnut tree on the riverbank. But the downhill end of our dwindling line had no such buttress.

A shrill, warbling whistle sounded, and the warriors shifted their attack to this vulnerable side.

One-Eye held that position. He swung his head wildly, as if to ensure nothing escaped his sight. Warriors with spears stood two and three deep before him. One raised a weapon just as a bloodied sword sliced through his throat. It was Tryfing! He'd finally caught up and came at the warriors from behind. He stood red faced, white eyed, crimson splattered, swinging quick as a dog snaps teeth. He seemed to swarm, as if he were many. A half dozen enemy fell before they knew what was happening.

Halfdan screamed, his words unintelligible over the hack of blades and the cries of battle. Our fighters broke the line and lunged forward. Then another shrill whistle sounded, ending in a low note.

* * * *

Kiona sprinted down a hill through the open forest, passing through sun and shadow, heat and cold flashing upon her face, arms, and legs. Dashing across a narrow rocky gash, she didn't pause for a drink, though the impressions of a hundred pair of knees remained in the soft clay bank where a trickle of water flowed. She followed the fresh trail of the Mi'kmaq warriors, evident upon the forest floor by disturbed pine needles, though she could make her way without it. She headed straight for the eastern lookout, knowing that portion of the forest well.

Her breathing came hard, but she pressed through a swath of bramble and briar. Her dress was hiked around her hips so she could run unimpeded. It made no difference if she happened upon some brave who glimpsed her nakedness. She'd be happy, in fact, because she could ask him if they'd seen Nabid. The stupid boy had run off after Huritt, who had given him that club!

She'd spoken with blue-faced Huritt only briefly before he turned and jogged toward the eastern lookout to join the rest of the warriors. Little Nabid had run back toward the migration trail as Kiona instructed him. He'd waved his club over his head and shouted, "I'm going to show Mother!" He'd been so distractedly proud of his new weapon, she hadn't suspected he'd try to trick her again and follow the tribe's troop of braves. She'd returned to the migration trail, pondering all the while how she might help Astrid escape and get her to the Vestmen. It would save the lives of their warriors if the Vestmen returned home.

Back at the migration trail, she'd watched as their tribe had gathered to a halt. They would wait until they heard from Great Scout it was safe to continue. Kiona had hoped then, with the distraction of the approaching enemy, an opportunity for Astrid's escape might present itself. She didn't know how long she'd been pondering this when she'd suddenly realized she hadn't seen Nabid for a time. The little brave must've tricked her and headed to the eastern lookout!

She sprinted upon a narrow, rocky trail between another clump of briar. A stray twig scraped her ankle. She was nearing the end of her run's third hour, chasing after Nabid. Maybe she'd passed him. He'd probably heard her thrashing through the forest and hidden. Or, with such a head start, he could have made it all the way to the eastern lookout, despite his short legs.

She passed a lone locust tree among the tall pines. She must be nearing the lookout now. Some cone-bearing trees grew on the riverbank, but the hardwoods dominated that section of the forest. She ducked below an oak's drooping branch and pushed forward. Perhaps only a few more minutes.

Between thick trunks, she spied the Blow. A section of forest where the earth funneled and intensified the breeze. A soft wind would become a gust. And a gust could morph into full gale. The trees never grew tall there. They stood short and dense as grass in a meadow. The eastern lookout was just on the other side of the thicket.

A flash of gray to her side and, there he was! Broad smile beaming below green-striped cheeks. His body was coated in fire ash, his hair even the chalky resemblance of an old man. He stood at the base of a pine. She ran over and gripped his arm. It was slick with grease, used to adhere the soot. Warriors camouflaged themselves with the powder when hiding among light-colored tree trunks.

She was out of breath but still managed a shout. "Don't you ever do that again!"

The boy's eyes grew wide and flashed back and forth, searching. His smile wasn't from joy, but fear. Though the child was trying to hide it.

"What's wrong?"

He strung an arrow with quivering fingers. The club was nowhere to be seen. He glanced toward the impenetrable growth of the Blow. "I shot one."

"One what?"

"One of the Vestmen."

They'd arrived? Already? She glanced about, searching the forest as far as trees would allow her, the glint of steel in sunlight flashing through her imagination. She'd often observed their men practice fighting, swinging their swords, back during the months she'd lived among them. A few times, the aggression had been in anger against each other. At first, she thought it all a show, trying to scare her. But after several weeks, she'd learned they fought because...they were Vestmen. They wielded weapons so skillfully, swords seemed another arm.

The breeze quieted, and sounds of battle carried through the dense trees of the Blow. Distant shouts of men, cries of pain, clanging of metal and wood, as if all the elements had come alive and were enthralled in battle. Then a shrill whistle, like the warning call of a cardinal.

* * * *

The Indians suddenly turned and fled into the woods. I stepped upon the back of one who'd slipped in his haste and sank my axe into his neck. Pausing next to an earlier victim, I retrieved my weapon from the corpse. Two axes. *That'll have to do.*

My leg seared as I charged forward, but it only bled in a trickle. I slipped between the trees, no path to follow, unable to see more than a few feet ahead. Low branches whipped my cheeks. I glanced at each trunk, as much as my pace would allow, thinking any of them could be a warrior with a waiting spear. My shield was useless in such confines. But instead of dropping it, I held it flat against my side. I chased the rapid, light crunch of fleeing footfalls. These men hadn't yet paid an adequate price. Still, I couldn't close the gap. I broke into a full sprint, limbs slapping my shoulders. But the sounds of retreat faded, hushed by the choking gag of the forest. As if it had swallowed them.

Screams of rage sounded behind me, along with the tramp of leather boots and snaps of branches. But I charged on, fueled by the same driving hunger as in my vision. A primitive instinct that compelled me through this thicket.

I emerged into an open forest of large, widely spaced pines. At least a dozen warriors were sprinting ahead of me now, their gray bodies highlighting their movement across the rust-brown mat of pine needles, the crunch and slap of their feet once again easy to hear. But no Vestmen. I must've been the first one. I glanced back and only Halfdan stumbled from the thicket.

As I hurdled a fallen log, a short warrior stepped from behind an ancient pine, bow drawn, green stripe across his cheeks. The same who'd struck my thigh. I swung my shield up. The arrow bounced off the bronze hub. I was upon him now, towering like Gulliver over a Lilliputian, slicing my axe with all my strength at his skull. But I halted the blow. He was a child, wide brown eyes filled with terror.

Halfdan lifted his sword over his head and charged up next to me, slicing the weapon down in a kill stroke. I raised my shield over the kid and Halfdan's weapon glanced off, skinning a chunk of pine bark the size of an oar blade from the tree. Rapid as a snake strike, the kid loosed another arrow which sunk into Halfdan's thigh. He screamed in rage.

I raised my axe. "Run, kid! Get out of here." He wouldn't understand me, but then my words sounded like the Abenaki, all vowels.

A brown arm reached from behind the tree and grabbed his neck. The child's mouth fell open. A girl with shiny black hair in two braids pushed the boy ahead of her. "Run!" she shouted, and they sprinted away.

How was it I understood even this Indian's words? The witch's spell must've—

Halfdan's sword sliced down again, this time at my own head. I barely managed to turn and catch the blow on the edge of my shield. The weapon rang on the metal rim. Halfdan drew back for another strike.

I turned and ran.

"Traitor!" he shouted. The sword flew by me and stuck into the base of a pine. I skidded to a halt. Halfdan limped over, but froze when I raised an axe. The wind twisted the tip of his white beard, streaked in blood, as if he'd eaten one of his victims.

Your life depends upon theirs, Gabby had said.

The light footfalls of fleeing moccasins faded into the rush and rattle of leaves. Curly trotted up to Halfdan, one arm hanging limply, a trickle of crusted red down his biceps, a neat hole punched through the shoulder of his mail coat. His lips stretched in a pained grimace. Others broke from the thicket now and ran toward us.

Blood flowed down Halfdan's calf. "Fool! What did that witch pay you to betray us?"

I stepped back. "*You* led us into their trap. I was the one who warned you."

He pointed a stubby finger at me. "You knew where they were waiting. They knew we were coming. And how to fight us." He pointed in the direction the kid had run. "And you protected that savage whelp!" He curled his lip as he reached down and slowly pulled the arrow shaft from his thigh. It, like mine, had no head. He snapped the shank. "You're one of them!"

There was no reasoning with this man.

He turned to the others and spread his arms. "He spoke their language!"

Curly gripped his injured shoulder, his expression a pained half smile, as if uncertain of what to believe. One-Eye's lips twisted in a snarl, cheeks still bleeding, though I thought his empty socket winked. Tryfing was nowhere in sight.

Halfdan yanked a dagger from his belt and charged me. I couldn't fight this man. I broke into a sprint again. He stopped at the tree with his sword sticking from it and yanked it free. "Run, coward! Back to your witch-whore. I'll cut out your heart and slurp it like an oyster when next I see you!"

I headed uphill, away from both Vestmen and Mi'kmaq. But to where I didn't know. Though I was fleeing Halfdan, instinct urged me onward, goading me just as it had to pursue the Mi'kmaq through the thick woods. A salmon scenting the river of its birth. The battle was over, no one pursued me, yet a resolve compelled me onward. North, as best I could tell by the setting sun. I imagined myself sprinting as effortlessly as in my vision, but the pain from the arrow grew and climbed my leg, as if someone had sliced open my quad. Though the gouge down my back from the spearhead must've been a more serious injury.

But if I could do anything well, it was run.

I crossed a shallow ridge. The aroma of maple sap dissipated behind me in a cold breeze whipping through the trunks, stirring pine shatters. But the gust also carried a new scent. Heavier. Sweeter. Like apples on the verge of turning rotten. I glanced around for the fruit tree, though I knew well there'd be none in this pine forest. The scent of fear?

Towering loblollies covered this side of the hill. High in one I glimpsed a black shadow upon a branch, unmoving, the size of a buzzard with spread wings. The dark form, though indistinguishable from this distance, I somehow knew, studied me.

Chapter 21 – The Ward

Stryker could barely breathe, so astonishing was the sight below him. He lay upon a thick pine branch, high above the forest floor, glaring down at the fleeing Vestman. The enemy moved at a blistering clip, albeit now with a limp. And that after rowing all morning, running most of the afternoon, and the exertion of battle. What gave this rotting sack of flesh such strength? His wounds were an arrow in the leg from a defiant child. And a gash furrowing his back, the errant thrust of a spear.

Stryker had stalked the enemy all afternoon, trotting after him on the streamside trail, waiting for an opportunity to attack. His quarry had begun to slow, separating himself from the rest of the Vestmen. Stryker had sprinted through the woods ahead of him and pressed himself flat to the ground, hiding near a section of the forest where the trees grew thick, as if the earth itself were trying to conceal a secret within its foliage.

He'd risen to a crouch as the Vestmen neared and waited for the enemy to come to him, just like the snowshoe hare, to tear out the enemy's neck before he could even swing an arm in defense. But instead, the line of Vestmen had stopped. And the ruddy, tall enemy had called for arms. Then the thick patch of forest exploded with Mi'kmaq warriors, and a banquet of glorious carnage had spread on the trail before him.

Even Stryker hadn't suspected the natives were waiting in ambush. They'd sprung a skillfully laid trap, pristine in its execution. The air filled with magnificent gut-split screams, shouts of anger, groans of pain—the meaty gravy of war. The breeze had been stained thick with blood and bile and churned earth, arousing that exquisite lustful ache in his belly that only flesh can enjoy.

Now he rose to all fours upon the large branch and, sinking sharp claws into the thick brown skin of the trunk, descended. Silent. Invisible.

Who'd told the Mi'kmaq the Vestmen were approaching? One familiar with the tactics of war, for certain. It could've been Slaughter himself. He'd delegated killing the enemy to Stryker, yet he could have also spoken with the Mi'kmaq's shaman, instructing them how to defeat Vestman defenses.

It all proved Slaughter's arrogance. His foolish self-regard.

Yes, the Mi'kmaq had inflicted heavy casualties, but no rational warrior fights Vestmen in a shield wall. Hunger. Plague. Venereal disease, of course. But to send naked men against a line of Viking shields was insanity. Then again, Slaughter commanded a southern day region. Could it be he'd never seen Vestmen fight before? If so, he'd learned the hard lesson to never challenge one in close quarters combat.

Stryker dropped to the forest floor and landed on a thick pinecone. He stifled a growl as one hard, spiny petal sliced between the pads of a paw. He flopped onto the shatters and gnawed at the thorn, bit down, and yanked it out. Too preoccupied, he hadn't chosen a good landing spot. Too...blind. Could he also be ignorant of other demons in this game? The hair on his chest stiffened at the thought. Someone *had* warned the Vestmen. Stryker hadn't even scented the Mi'kmaq's ambush, yet the tall Vestman had somehow sensed it. So, another force in play. An undefined variable. A rogue demon? A competing captain, trying to weaken Slaughter's grasp on his region? And of the Vestmen that had survived, the enemy was one. That was no coincidence.

Existence is simple. There are only two forces of nature: good and evil. A ranger's calling is to resist evil. To know the enemy. That was the only wisdom he'd ever received from Ernick, his former captain.

No better way to know the enemy than to stalk him. And now his prey was completely alone, separated from the other Vestmen. Wounded. The perfect opportunity. And under Slaughter's authority, Stryker needn't be timid any longer.

He started at a sprint. The iron scent of the enemy's blood bloomed fresh and strong, guiding him straight up a gentle hill between pine trunks, though only a few drops had fallen upon the forest floor.

He bounded over a ridge and his chest squeezed into a fist. A searing pain arced through his sternum, doubling him over, as if skewered again by Slaughter's swords. His legs buckled as he landed, and he slid on one shoulder against a bulging root. The agony was so great, it seemed his heart had burst and frozen at the same time. No threat in sight. He clawed the ground, but couldn't raise himself up. He must've run straight into an enemy ward. But those were mere myths. The enemy knew none of the magic arts.

Despite the agony, he hooked claws on the exposed root and dragged himself an inch, then two more. It was the only thing he could grasp. His tendons cramped tight as iron bars, forearms unyielding. His chest seemed to burn, to blister as he stretched his leg again, dug in, and pulled. Another inch. Death by quartering would've been less painful. But the torture pain gradually diminished with each tug, the farther he carried himself back toward the ridge from where he'd come. After what seemed an hour, his joints began to loosen. He managed to crawl over a boulder and tumble down the opposite side, sliding on shatters and dead leaves, flopping limp as a fresh corpse. He lay still and breathed, allowing the pain to subside. Directly under his nose was a drop of the Vestman's blood. Its scent filled his nostrils and mouth. It putrefied, morphing from iron, to sweat, to rotten flesh. How did—

His gut clenched and he vomited a splash of green bile, covering the small spatter of crimson. As the acid sank through the pine needles, only a shard of a rabbit's rib from this morning's hunt remained atop them.

What had just happened? He closed his eyes and concentrated upon the crest of the hill, where he'd run into the ward. A warm sensation washed against him, like a tepid stream lifting him from his panther's body, a knife-slip into spirit. But so weak already, he could only remain in this state a short time or he'd lose his grasp on his panther's body. He glanced over his own spirit's charcoal-black armor plates, stacked down his ribs and cascading across his chest like scales of a fish. One beneath his neck was missing. A thick one, right in the middle. The exposed rawness oozed blood as black as ink. How had he been wounded?

He glanced up the hill, still in spirit. The boulder at the top was silhouetted by a blazing brilliance. His knee buckled as he stepped toward it. He curled his lips, but his growl shuddered weak and shallow. Whatever he'd hit had affected more than just flesh, and even now debilitated his spirit. But he had to see what he'd struck.

The closer he moved to the ridge, the weaker he became, till he dropped to his belly and crawled the last few feet. The plates on the back of his neck stood upright, though he shivered in cold. Behind the rock, the light glared like a sun, but created no heat, smoke, or sound. He wriggled next to the gray stone, peeked to one side, and his breath froze in shock.

A girl, clothed in brilliant white, not much more than a child, stood with the hilt of a raised sword in her grasp. The same girl Slaughter had confronted on the domed rock earlier. The one who'd spied him as he hid. She held the blade angled away from her body, tip circling gently in rhythm with her calm breathing. The weapon was immense, as long as she was tall. Had she been flesh, she would have toppled from its weight. Red hair in long, thick, curly locks flowed over her shoulders and down her back. Then, she'd refused Slaughter permission to cross a marker, a simple fissure in granite. Denying him access to part of his own day region. Now, she was protecting the trail of the Vestman.

A drop of the enemy's blood lay upon the earth before her sandal, blazing, like a ruby enshrouding an entire sun. Her eyes stared straight ahead, through the trees, though the rock. Through Stryker. He was naked before her. As if no secret could be hidden.

He couldn't skirt around the ward. She'd surely guard the blood trail, wherever it might lead. So, tracking the enemy was out of the question now. *This must be why Slaughter recruited me.* Why such a wealthy demon needed help killing a mere mortal. He'd already tried. And failed.

Stryker slid back down the hill and slipped into his panther's body again. The seductive warmth washed away as he rose on unsteady legs and started off in a shaky trot toward his only remaining solution. He followed the trail of the fleeing Mi'kmaq.

Chapter 22 – Spear-Face

I lay upon the forest floor, mind dreary with sleep, eyes clamped shut, though I sensed enough time had passed it must be morning. I didn't want to wake, to get up. My leg was on fire. Pain seared deep into my thigh, inflaming the bone, down to my calf and up into my hip. Like a tooth with an infected, dying root, it burned hot and throbbed. How could this much agony come from such a small, headless arrow? For a few hours of sleep, though, I'd been able to escape its torture.

My chest was warm as well. Must be a halo from the pain. An artificial sensation, because I'd become chilled after I'd stopped running last night. The forest had been dark as death, blanketed in thick, cold clouds that choked out the stars. I'd barely been able to distinguish the shadows of trunks, towering columns jutting out of an endless, rolling mist.

Whatever primal instinct that had drawn me here, driving me like a madman half the night, had gradually ebbed like the tide. Probably drowned by the rising burn in my leg. I'd finally sat next to a tree and leaned back upon...no, that wasn't right. I'd tried to lean upon a trunk to rest, but bark had pricked the gash down my back. So, I'd lain upon my side instead.

That's right. My last memory was my body locked in a cold, violent shiver. I'd been too tired to continue.

But now, instead of the terpenic scent of pine needles, earth and body odor filled my nose. Must be smelling my own stink.

Snap!

Someone sneaking up on me? I cracked an eyelid and stared at a glowing ember. A small fire of twigs and sticks burned a few feet from my face. Startled, I jolted upright. The scabs down my back crinkled as my skin stretched. I was sitting upon a huge rug of brown fur. Large as a cowhide, but with hair like sheep's wool across the shoulders. An eastern wood bison? I seemed to be inside a domed wigwam, maybe twenty feet across. Tender green vines weaving up from the ground had grown between the sheets of birch bark. Daylight spilled in through the low arched doorway, the shallow angle indicating midday, not morning. The whole space resembled a tall wooden igloo. A woven grass mat with singed edges lay upon the earth opposite me. A mound of tawny fur skins had been tossed against the wall, as if someone had been sleeping beneath them and risen abruptly.

A shadow fell across the floor. Someone stood in the doorway. I reached for an axe, but my belt was empty.

"It lives! I told you such," came an excited voice, rough with age. An Indian with furrowed, pale skin stepped next to the fire. Not albino, but very dusty, as if he'd covered himself with tan chalk. And not the ashen soot of the warriors. His straight black hair was pulled back in a single braid, and the sides of his scalp were shaven. But thick streaks of gray striped the bundle. Spears were tattooed on his cheeks, pointing upward through his eyes, across his forehead, the tips stopping just shy of his hairline. Dark, deep, brown irises stared down at me. I'd seen this man before. Had he been one of the warriors who had attacked? No, I'd have remembered the spears.

He glanced at my thigh and squatted next to me. His movements were nimble, so he couldn't be elderly, though his loose skin looked it. "You told me no such thing... I did!" He reached for my leg and I scooched back.

Spear-Face held up hands, as if in surrender. "Look. You're scaring it... I didn't mean to... Ugly thing, isn't it?... Words have power. Don't say that... Pink skin, like a plucked duck... Check the wound. The poison should be weak now. But don't scare it away." Slowly, he reached for my leg again. I hadn't noticed a bandage covered it, the wrap composed of moss and slime tied with long blades of grass. *Oh no!* This guy was practicing some sort of primitive root medicine. No wonder it burned so badly. Probably mud too, giving me gangrene. *I may need to amputate.*

He tweezed at the grass binding, and it fell away. With skinny, dirty fingers, he peeled up a clump of goo and lifted it off. The hole beneath was red and puffy, but not open or swollen. He patted the surrounding tissue. "Poison still inside, I think... You no medicine man. You don't know... I *am* medicine man. It no hurt, see?" He poked harder with an index finger.

An electric shock ran from my butt to my ankle. I jerked my leg away. "Don't do that!"

Spear-Face's eyes widened. He fell back and crab-walked away, kicking embers across the dirt floor in his haste. "It speaks our tongue!... No, you hear things... You heard it too... I heard nothing. It squealed like a boar. Your ugly face scared it."

A glowing ember that had landed near my knee singed the fur, then sank in a dime-sized hole through the hide as it cooled. The hut filled with the stench of burnt hair. I flicked the cooled ember back into the fire then winced as I swung my leg in front of me for a closer inspection. "I can understand you, you know," I said, gently pressing the wound. Drops of clear fluid, but no pus, welled up. "Whatever you put on my leg makes it burn like this fire."

Spear-Face's expression hardened. He plopped down, folding his legs under him. "It was hit with poison arrow."

I glanced up. "*Poison* arrow?"

"Poison to rabbit or bird. Or maybe young wolf." He shifted, rearranging his legs beneath him. "But not deer or bear. Not to it, either." He pointed in my direction. "How it speak our tongue?"

Great question. Even my best answer would make no sense. Pushing with both hands on the rug beneath me, I slid back toward the wall and leaned upon a post, carefully holding my injured leg to one side. "So, the poison arrow won't kill me?"

His head tilted. One of his eyes squinted. "Not kill. Just pain." He pointed to the glob of toxic waste that had been tied to it. "Medicine. It draws out poison. Hurt bad only short time." His gaze wandered back to the doorway. "You no medicine man. Can no help it... I am healer... You, no. You kill."

Apparently, I was talking to more than one person in that strange body. Was it dangerous to interrupt a conversation he was having with himself? Whatever. I pointed at the ground before the fire. "How did I get here?"

A broad smile revealed yellowed, crooked teeth, but still a full array of them. "We brought it."

OK... "Uh, thank you. Both of you...right?"

He pointed to the door, as if to draw attention to the trees. "Well, there are no more out there! And we strong."

So, I'd narrowed down that I was talking to two Indians, at least, in a way. "Why help? Why bring me here?" I twisted my leg and another electric jolt ran through my thigh.

He lifted his chin. "It was hurt. It needed help... Don't tell him about the spirits... Shut up! He understands you."

My belly growled with hunger. I reached inside my leather pouch, wrapped my fingers around the last dried cod, and plucked it out. The fish jerky was crusted with pine shatters and dirt. Spear-Face must've dragged me here, filling my pouch with most of the forest floor. But I was ravenous, and there was no ten-second rule in this world. I brushed it off with my own dirty fingers and flicked a dried leaf from the body cavity. I brought it to my mouth, then remembered Spear-Face. I broke the fish in two and held out half of it to him over the fire.

He studied the offering. "Look, it bids us eat... Why eat dry fish when we have fresh in the stream?... It's trying to be friendly... We would not bait a trap with such meat!" He frowned, then reached out and snatched it.

I devoured my half like a dog inhaling dinner. There were bones, but I ground them up along with remnants of twig and leaf, then swallowed. One bit stuck halfway down, and I coughed.

The Indian leapt to his feet and ran outside. Returning, absent the fish, he offered what looked like an ancient, yellowed plastic bag filled with water. A water bladder made from animal's innards, I was certain. But I slugged down the liquid and passed back the empty skin, careful to smile.

His face brightened and he blinked, dancing the inked spears upon his forehead. He shot outside again. Each time he moved, I backed another couple of years off his estimated age. He returned quickly with a stitched leather bag the size of a five-gallon bucket and poured brown nuts on the ground before me. They were a little larger than acorns, a deep red brown with tan hats. Some were still trapped inside a stiff cocoon of dry, prickly thorns. I wedged several open, the calluses on my hands foiling the sharp needles. I pressed a nut between forefinger and thumb, but only cracked it with great effort.

Spear-Face stared in wide-eyed amazement. "It can't feed itself. It will starve... It knew how to fish. Maybe it no eat chestnuts?" He picked up a baseball-sized rock and crushed one against a flat stone, then lifted the tan meat from the shards of shell and popped it into his mouth. He passed the two stone implements to me. "Now it do it." He scattered two handfuls near the edge of the fire.

I reached into the sack and soon learned they cracked best by smashing the pointed tips. A furry paper layer needed to be peeled off the nut, and then I could enjoy the pale inner flesh. Not firm as I'd expected, but softer, like a mushroom, the consistency and taste of a potato and mildly sweet. I cast the shards of shell into the fire where they curled, glowed orange, then took on a coating of white soot, almost the hue of Spear-Face's skin.

He studied my progress, his expression bright and soft. "How it know our tongue."

It was the second time he'd asked that question, and I still didn't have an answer. He seemed a friendly man, or men. My stomach was beginning to settle, calmed by the protein. These must've been chestnuts. Granddad, always the historian and spouter of random trivia, had talked about entire civilizations living off such produce.

"I don't know why I can speak your language. Maybe it has to do with an Abenaki shaman down near the stream, closer to the ocean. I think she cast a spell on me." It must've not worked well, because the Indian's words seemed only halfway complete, and he insisted on calling me an *it*. But I'd understood the shaman well enough standing on the riverbank. And the Indian girl yelling at the young boy to run. Maybe the spell didn't work with this man the same way.

Spear-Face had been lifting another nut to his mouth but froze when I mentioned the shaman. He sat, unblinking, unbreathing, till a nut next to the fire exploded like popcorn. I flinched. The charred shell landed on his leg and sizzled. His eyes swelled and he plucked it from his skin, but I couldn't tell if his tears were from the burn or what I'd said. He blew on the fractured nut and peeled it open. "The shaman, we know her. Powerful. She have a son?"

I hadn't seen her with one. Except... "Could be. She kept looking at a boy locked in a cage. Would that be him? I doubt it."

A tear ran down one cheek, a muddy gray drop that left a clean, dark brown track. "The son is man now... *Your* grandson. He won't remember you anymore... He never knew me. It isn't too late... It *is*. She won't let you see him... I never hurt her. She will let me."

These monologue conversations were a dog chasing his tail. "You know this shaman? Tell me."

"Tell it about her... No. We don't even know what it is. It could have an evil spirit... But your daughter gave it the gift..."

I gasped. "She's your daughter?"

Spear-Face lifted his gaze from the fire. "Yes."

That's where I'd recognized him. The high cheekbones and deep-set eyes—he looked like the Abenaki witch. Or rather, she resembled him. No stray bulls in that pasture. But, she'd said her mother was the shaman of the Mi'kmaq. I pointed at him. "Your wife is the shaman of the Mi'kmaq?"

He regarded my finger as if trying to figure out what the gesture meant. "It knows us... She told it... Tell it the truth. She trusts it... The spirits! Don't tell it what they said."

I couldn't stop a smile creasing my face. "You do know, I can hear you when you speak, right? *Both* of you. You've mentioned the spirits twice now. Let me guess, a pretty but annoying girl with bright red, curly hair appeared to you."

He clapped a palm to his nose. "It can hear our thoughts! Don't think anything!"

Even if I had been a telepath, I'd get lost in this guy's mind and never find my way out. "A red-haired young woman...," I repeated.

Spear-Face leaned toward me. "She appears to you too?"

I wheezed a laugh. "You have no idea what she's done to me." Figuring it couldn't hurt, I recounted the last couple of days to the crazy Indian. I got the feeling he didn't understand what I said about being from a different time. But by the end of the conversation, he seemed to firmly comprehend I was from another place. A distant land at the least. I explained how we'd lost Gabby a few years earlier in the water, right near here.

I contemplated that. Yes, we'd lost her up here in Maine, not far from this very creek.

He scattered another handful of chestnuts at the edge of the fire. "Many years ago, a wana-games-ak, a river spirit, rose from the stream. It spoke with my wife." I noted that he'd said, "*My* wife," dropping the plural *we*. "He gave a prophecy, and I spoke it to the tribe. Light-colored men would attack. They would pretend to be friends, even ask for help, but evil would hide among them. An evil that would destroy us, destroy our ways. Their weapons would be more powerful. They would make the Mi'kmaq slaves. The only way to be safe was to steal their chief's daughter, a girl with hair the color of hot coals. War would come, but if we kept the girl, their chieftain would eventually fear us and leave our land. Our tribe has trained for this coming battle ever since."

That would explain how the Mi'kmaq had fought so well. Another chestnut snapped. I snagged it in midair as it fell toward the fire. "Wait. I've heard this story. Your daughter told it to me. But if the river spirit spoke to your wife, why did you tell it to the tribe?"

He poked the fire gingerly with a stick, as if the prod were his finger and he didn't want to burn himself. More likely, he didn't want to answer the question. He appeared to shrink, as if the pale dust covering his body might even conceal him from sight. "My wife was the shaman. She spoke to the spirits. But feared the people. I spoke to them. It is how she desired it. They thought I was the shaman, until she was killed."

"Killed? How?"

He tossed the stick into the fire. "My daughter murdered her."

What? "You mean the Abenaki shaman?"

"No. Our firstborn. Her name Rimlaw. She the shaman of the Mi'kmaq now. The spirits spoke to her as child. Earlier than any other. But the older she grew, the angrier she became. Her spirits tortured her. She killed my wife, my counselor, my agaskw. I had no spirits. The tribe exiled me as a liar. Rimlaw's younger sister fled too." He glanced at me again. "Youngest daughter the shaman of the Abenaki now. She more powerful than Rimlaw, but not know it. Rimlaw think her as enemy."

This family's dysfunction made my own squabbles with Gabby insignificant. Spear-Face was the father of both shamans, the Abenaki and the Mi'kmaq. He'd claimed he had no spirits, but now he whispered toward the door, gesturing with hands upon his chest, then pointing randomly. He glanced at me, then sat stiffly, face turned away from the entry, as if giving a lover the silent treatment. If he'd been alone too long, maybe he'd gone crazy and made up an imaginary friend.

"Thanks for helping me." Though I wasn't sure he might also have given me sepsis. "I need to find the Mi'kmaq. To help the daughter of my chieftain."

He leapt to his feet again and charged for the door, but stopped short. The opening became obscured by dazzling light as the sun blazed upon the dust he'd kicked up. "Your sister's spirit told me to help. She good spirit." He stood in silence, as if contemplating whether to trust the apparition that had appeared to his wife, or Gabby who had spoken with him only recently. Would he be loyal to family and tribe, or to the *good spirit*?

"Why you help chieftain's daughter? You from another place. You not her tribe."

"I...I think she holds the answer to me getting home. I couldn't help my own sister when she died. Maybe if I help this girl, it will somehow...well...make up for it."

"You no fault for sister's death. Why help this girl?"

"I don't know!" The thought confounded me as well. "It's the same as when I knew I needed to run this way last night—though now I'm thinking that may have been delusion from a poison arrow. I've just got this urge to help her that's driving me senseless." It felt as if my survival in this world, and the last one, seemed to hinge upon it. "But I don't know where I am. Or *how* to help. And I can't move until my leg quits burning like a hot poker."

He turned, silhouetted in the opening by the blaze of dusty light, the sun's glare a cape falling to the floor. "You bring a big trouble. The spirit that spoke with wife no wana-games-ak. Even I know that. River spirits only foretell attacks just before. This one foretold attack many years ago. That spirit was metee-kolen-ol."

I curled my lip. "What?"

"An ancient evil-wizard spirit."

My dead sister's spirit was leading me, so I could hardly dismiss his ideas as primitive paranoia. "What difference does it make what spirit it was?"

"If spirit was metee-kolen-ol, it mean a battle has returned. Malsumis sent it."

"Malsumis?" How was I supposed to keep all these weird names straight? And did it even matter?

Spear-Face ducked out the door. "You must go now! If Malsumis is back, an evil greater than any other has returned."

Chapter 23 – The Curse

Stinking, decomposing flesh-bags.

Stryker's head hung as he trotted down a gentle hill speared with endless pine trunks. His belly growled with hunger as he traveled toward the camp of the Mi'kmaq. Fatigue weighted the lids of his eyes. He'd gone much longer without sleep before, but he needed to eat something.

In the east, the dim orange glow of dawn would soon threaten his cover of night. The crisp air carried no scent of other animals stirring recently. Only yesterday's meanderings of rabbit and red fox. A gray owl hooted, announcing morning's imminent arrival.

Wretched humans, he thought, sourly.

Having scouted the Indians' empty summer camp yesterday, he determined they could have only recently arrived. The rest of the tribe might not even be there yet, despite their warriors' attack on the Vestmen. That assault, skillful yet horribly misguided, meant they'd been provided inside information regarding their enemy's location. Facts only Slaughter could've known. If his boss was already working on the Mi'kmaq so they'd kill the enemy hiding among the Vestmen, what could Stryker hope to accomplish? Why was he headed to the Mi'kmaq now, except that he had no other options?

A plan. I must stop reacting and set my own strategy.

But every time he'd tried that, opposing, unforeseen circumstances had arisen. As if an unknown force were overseeing the entire game, manipulating him. His chest still stung from last night's encounter with the red-haired enemy. The ward. What part did she play in this match? A growl began to rise from his chest at the thought of being caught in such a twisted plot. His mission had seemed so simple a few days ago. Now he had a new master, an unknown enemy, and an old one as well. It seemed even the Fates were laughing at him.

Ahead, the forest spilled into a broad meadow. The edge of the Mi'kmaq's hunting grounds. They burned the area every few years to inhibit saplings from sprouting up. They torched the forest floor, removing games' cover, allowing more productive hunting. But the fire didn't damage older trees, only blackened their trunks while consuming vines, bushes, and trees with shallow roots. The field's grasses here had grown tall, though. It must've been several years since the last burn.

He stepped from the forest onto a narrow game trail that wound through the thick pasture. Green-and-brown stalks shot up either side of his shoulders, tall as a human's head. He lowered his nose to the ground and inhaled the scent of rich black earth, ripe honeysuckle, and chipmunk scat. But also the bitter, stinging aroma of a whitetail doe in late estrus. A herd was nearby.

He turned back, dug his claws into the ribbed bark of a gum tree, and climbed. Twenty feet up, he spied sharp white antler tips displayed among brown pods of last season's yellow coneflower. Twelve points, a huge buck. Stryker crept higher for a better view. The thick-necked deer was mostly hidden, but several grazing does and their fawns were visible. The skinny young tottered on gangly legs, hopping and butting each other and playing inside a pasture of matted grass. The wind was still blowing from the east, so Stryker could approach from the opposite side, farthest from the buck. The male would be little threat now that rut was over. That was why the doe still in estrus smelled so desperate. Unable to become pregnant early in the season, her glands must have still been producing an abundance of pheromones in a continued attempt to entice a male. The bellies of two other does swelled as they grazed greedily.

Taking a deer carried much more risk than small prey. They moved in herds, and the animals could outweigh him. The bucks, with bristly racks of antlers sharpened upon rough bark, nonetheless would flee most predators this time of year. Stryker's stomach ached for real meat, something more substantial than the meager servings he'd nabbed the last few days from rabbits. He needed information from the Mi'kmaq, yes—but his body craved food more. Hunting was no distraction, he assured himself. He wouldn't be able to think soundly if he didn't eat first.

He dropped to the ground and sprinted around the meadow to its western border. There, another game trail headed into its heart, this one also thick with the musk of deer. This simple prey was so predictable, always moving along routine paths, as if created solely to be consumed by higher species.

He trotted inward, gazing intently ahead, his pads wet with the night's heavy dew. This trail was wide, the ground churned to mud. He skirted the edge of a long puddle.

Around half the distance in, a hawk cried above him. He stopped and searched the air. One of Slaughter's spies? But only dragonflies and swallows darted and swooped overhead. Merely a thin slice of the sky was visible due to the tall swards that rose on either side.

He resumed his trot, wide pads plodding silently. The confines of the space could prove hazardous, but the wind blew from the direction of the meadow. That was why he'd approached from this side, to hide his scent. Plus, there was no way any threat could ambush him around a meandering bend. He'd smell them early.

A splash sounded behind him. He turned, but the trail there wandered out of view. The hair along his spine stiffened; the primal instincts of his panther host began to awaken. Something was trailing him.

No. *He* was the apex predator. No other creature would dare ambush him. There were, of course, beasts he would not fight, such as bison. Those animals were fiercely protective of their young and impossible to bring down.

A few more steps, then he paused next to a lush stand of green grass. The base was thick with the musk of eastern wolf. A boundary marker. Yes, he would be vulnerable to such a pack for certain. But this scent was at least a week old, and the trail's soft footing held no evidence any had recently passed. He sniffed higher up the stalks and stiffened with fear.

Another panther had marked the spot. The scent contained many layers. It had been sprayed multiple times.

This meant territorial competition. But the big cats were generally timid and easy to scare off. Unless, or course, this was another demon taking the same form he had. A ranger, marking his territory. A rival demon would do anything—*anything*—if it was to his own benefit. Ah, the lovely, predictable selfishness of the underworld. All a captain had to do was to manipulate all his underlings into thinking they were helping themselves by serving him. An easy task, for one as cunning as Stryker. One day soon he'd be a captain too. One more wealthy even than Slaughter. He needed to formulate a plan for that ambition as well.

Another splash. He concealed himself in the long shadow cast by the low rising sun and glanced back. Maybe a bird had landed to steal a drink. But if Stryker *was* being stalked, the prevailing breeze blinded him to any scent from that direction. The heavy fragrance of deer fur blew to him from ahead and his mouth salivated. The clearing should be only a few more paces.

He rounded a bend, and the air became a glorious mosaic of predatory fantasies. Buck marking, doe urine, warm rabbit hide, beaver oil, and...the delicate, sweet scent of fawn. Three of the young were visible now in the pasture, one beneath its grazing mother, head up, suckling. The other two lay in the grass nearby, invisible except for their huge chestnut leaf-shaped ears poking up among the blades. But, where had the dominant buck disappeared to?

A gentle breeze blew a finger of mist to him. He sniffed and confirmed his hopes. The fawns had lost their white spots, but the clean scent of one meant it still hadn't been weaned. Young deer go through a period where they nurse as well as forage. Those were still delicious, but month-old milk-fed fawn was a delicacy. The one still attached to its mother's teat, outstretched throat pulsing as it sucked greedily, was the obvious choice. Oh, how glorious!

Stryker needed to hurry. Though the wind still blew his scent away from the herd, this close the slightest off-vector gust would warn the deer of his presence. He turned and nosed back into thick cover, slipping between tufts of grass and prickly thistle stems, imagining himself a shadow, guided around the edge of the clearing by sound alone: the mother chewing, her fawn sucking, the heavy, sleepy breathing of the other young ones dozing. Coming abreast where he estimated the group to be, he turned and inched in, till the clearing was visible through a woven veil of thin, dry sunflower stalks. From this angle, a pair of does were visible on the far side, along with a spike male. But the buck was still nowhere to be seen.

Stryker shifted his paws beneath him and tensed for a long leap. The fawn's jaw cycled a few times more, then he pulled away from his mother's belly, licking his warm, wet nose. A lookout's snort sounded and all the deer lifted their heads and glanced toward the blast. The air filled with the sharp citrus perfume of warning pheromones.

Too late.

Stryker loosed the taut coils in his legs like an archer releasing a bowstring. He covered half the distance to the fawn in one leap. Another bound. He stretched daggered claws toward the animal and crashed into its neck, piercing tender hide and snagging flesh like the barbs of an arrowhead. The animal toppled, but Stryker gripped tight. The fawn's legs thrashed at the grass and sliced the air as it struggled to regain footing. Its doe jumped back, faltered, then turned and bounded away, toward the trees. Personal survival trumped motherly love in many species of prey.

Stryker stretched the fawn's neck back as the animal's heart raced furiously and legs thrashed in vain. He opened his mouth and bit through the tender hide into the pulsing jugular. Breath hissed through a tear as he pierced its windpipe. Blood filled his mouth, squirting his eye, and he was blinded by its warm beauty. He lapped and gulped the warm, meaty liquid, drawing it out like the fawn suckling its mother. His body warmed and tingled at the mellow, gamey taste.

Another snort nearby, and he stopped.

Stryker licked a paw and wiped the blood from his eye. The massive buck stood at the far end of the clearing and stomped the ground, head lowered and tilted to one side as if about to charge. Except he wasn't facing Stryker.

The fawn's bloody neck slipped from his mouth as another black panther stalked into the clearing. Its head was broad as a grown lion and paws wide as a bear. Muscles bulged thick as tree roots across wide shoulders as the predator placed each step. His lip curled in a snarl, exposing yellow canines as he advanced on Stryker.

The buck grunted and jerked its rack in a clear warning, but the panther continued, as if blind to the dozen thrashing spear tips just paces away. And why wasn't the buck running? His herd had fled. Deer aren't brave—they don't threaten. The panther gazed at Stryker, as if he wanted more than just to steal his kill. Stryker sniffed, trying to sense the other panther's intentions, but it approached from downwind. The hair on Stryker's neck stiffened as it had upon hearing the splash on the game trail. An anger, a deep-seated bitterness, rose in his legs, as if leeching from the Abyss. This other cat wasn't threatening. He was hunting.

The buck charged, slamming into the huge panther and sending it sprawling across the grass. It sprang to its feet, nostrils wide with surprise. It rounded on the buck and hissed a threat so deep it would've sent a grizzly mother into flight.

Stryker clamped his mouth around the dead fawn's neck again. He fled down a side trail to the edge of the forest, carrying it along. He scaled a large oak, dropped the animal into the crotch of the venerable tree, and stepped out onto a limb that stretched back toward the clearing in order to watch the show.

But the meadow was empty.

In the distance, does and the spike male continued their flight, heads breaking the surface of the grass at the peak of each leap, like breeching porpoises. Had the panther killed the buck and dragged him into the high grass? No. Impossible in such a short time. Had it all been a vision, maybe? But that wouldn't explain the feline territory markings.

Stryker crouched low upon the limb to minimize his silhouette. A knurled barb pricked his belly and stung like fear. He scanned the forest floor in case he'd been followed. This place belonged to no ordinary cat. The bitter way he'd locked onto Stryker spoke of an ancient anger. Of vengeance. Retribution. This was another demon for certain, but Stryker hadn't had a chance to slip into spirit, to see who it truly was.

A raccoon led its young across the clearing as if a battle hadn't just taken place. A bad omen of peace. It all made no sense.

Stryker rose and paced back to the trunk. The fawn hung there, delicate head dangling from a long, wilted neck, crimson dripping from the black nub of its nose. He tore back into its belly with ravenous hunger, but the sweet, young meat had soured. Tainted with bitterness. It seemed his appetite would never be sated.

Chapter 24 – No Shaman

I jogged to catch up with Spear-Face, who loped steadily ahead of me on lanky legs through the forest, wielding a long staff like a shepherd's crook. Fast and straight as a black marlin on the hunt. The sun had just risen, and dust devils of gnats spun within long beams of light that blasted through cracks in the forest's tall canopy. Even so, the woodland was dark, a land formed of shadows.

Axe handles slapped my thighs as I caught up with the medicine man, the two I had left after fleeing Halfdan. I'd refused to elaborate on my conversations with Spear-Face's daughter any further till he'd returned my weapons. My wounded leg throbbed where the arrow had struck, but that pain was tolerable compared to its searing burn I'd endured yesterday. The skin had already started to knit, tightening and pulling at times. This crazy Indian was indeed a medicine man, despite what his internal antagonist insisted. And though I tried to keep up, I still lagged his pace. He floated across the ground like a cross-country speed walker. I struggled to come abreast as he plodded along.

"Tell me about the leader of its boat," he asked.

He must be referring to Halfdan. He'd asked so many questions all yesterday afternoon. I'd eventually fallen asleep during the interrogation, up until a few hours ago. "He's huge. Not as tall as me, but arms like—"

Spear-Face waved his staff and stuck out his top lip like a horse asking for food. "Not what he looks like." He pressed his palms to his cheeks. "Tell me about *him*."

I did a skip-step on my wounded leg to keep up. "I don't know about him much. Remember, I'm from somewhere else."

He stopped and stared at me. Black irises, just like his daughter. His breathing wasn't even labored, despite our pace. "It *know* him. Your sister told me."

He'd explained how Gabby had appeared to him, the only spirit he'd ever seen before. She'd told him where to find me in the woods. And instructed him to help me. I was grateful for his aid and tried to answer his many questions as best I could. "But I don't know Halfdan. Just his name. I've barely spoken with him."

Spear-Face stretched out a hand and placed it upon my chest, as his daughter had. "My wife was shaman. She say spirits of men no talk. They speak here." He pushed against me. "You no speak with leader to know him."

I raised empty palms and shrugged, hoping he'd understand the gesture. "I'm not a shaman. I don't know him any other way."

He patted my chest again. "Here. What his spirit *feel* like?"

Maybe he was just asking me what I thought of him. I leaned against a trunk, trying to conceal the ache in my thigh. "He's always angry. When he's not fighting or beating someone, he's wishing he was. He hates me."

A doe behind Spear-Face turned its head, ears pivoting, listening for something. Had it not moved, I would've never seen it. Spear-Face's eyes seemed to dim. "Hate...hate is spirit of murder. Why he lead men to rescue chieftain's daughter?"

I'd already explained this to him last night. How Halfdan wanted to be the next village leader. "The chieftain trusts him."

He flared his nose at my words. "Chieftain send man of vengeance to rescue daughter? No." He glanced at the ground, then back to the deer, though it hadn't made a sound. "Hate man no care for girl. Only himself." His eyes brightened, and he shoved my chest. "*It* must rescue."

That's what I'd been trying to explain to him! And why did he continue to refer to me as *it*? "Like I've said, that's what I'm trying to do. To rescue the chieftain's daughter." My sister, of sorts.

He placed his palm upon my chest again. "It recognize spirit of hate. To rescue sister from Mi'kmaq, it must learn from good spirits."

The deer bolted away, flame of a white tail flicking through woodland shadow. Several others danced and bobbed through the dark forest away from us. "All I know is what I can see. I'm not a shaman."

Spear-Face stared at me. "It from other place. Stepped onto Vestmen's boat."

I nodded. We'd discussed this ad nauseam. Though I hadn't stepped anywhere. I'd fallen into the vessel, though it had certainly felt as if someone had pulled me. I'd rowed only to escape Halfdan's beatings and the massive hailstorm thrashing the water behind us.

"It saw big shark in water among school of bass."

The great white among the stripers. "Yeah, but—"

He waved his rod again, as if to say *Shut up!* "It have vision with my daughter. It guided by spirit of dead sister. It on mission to help sister of the body it inhabits." He touched the butt of the rod to my head, as if knighting me. "I lived with shaman many years. *You a shaman.*" He turned and stepped out again, resuming his long strides. "A stupid shaman, but a shaman it is!"

I stood as he hurried away. I could see why he'd confuse me with a spiritual medium. I *was* talking to the spirit of my dead sister. But only when she randomly decided to grace me with her presence. She was as difficult dead as she was when she was alive.

I jogged after him again. "How much longer till we get to the Mi'kmaq's village?"

"I no take it there whole way. Mi'kmaq may not be in village yet. I bring it to border only." He lifted his head, as if startled, and skidded to a halt. He thumped his walking staff in front of his feet. "This is edge."

Before us a green curtain of lush vines hung from trunks. Through the veil I could make out a meadow of grass almost as tall as I.

Spear-Face aimed his staff toward it. "That start hunting grounds. I go no further."

"Why not?"

He glanced to either side, his playful smile replaced by narrowed eyes and fear. "This border of Mi'kmaq shaman's region. Wife told me so. Rimlaw too. No one enter it without her know it. Mi'kmaq protected by powerful spirits."

It was the same thing his other daughter, the Abenaki shaman, had told me. "How am I supposed to find the village?"

He pointed his staff toward the rising sun, then swung it in an arc to the west. "Follow sunset. By midday—" He glanced at my wounded leg. "By evening you will cross small river. Follow it till it runs back into big one. There is village."

Just like the Abenaki chief had drawn when he'd made the map. "How should I help this girl?"

His shoulders slumped, as if fatigued. "It a stupid shaman. It not know what to do... But fire-hair spirit say to help it... We help it. But it get eaten by wolves before it reach village... We obeyed fire-hair spirit. We guided it. We brought it to Mi'kmaq territory... We should help it more... Who cares what happens to it now?... Daughter believed in it... Rimlaw will kill you. She will know if you take another step. Her spies are everywhere... But if Malsumis has returned, not even Rimlaw safe... You no shaman. You don't know if Malsumis is back..."

I hadn't thought about wolves till he'd mentioned them. Now I scanned the edge of the meadow. The world beyond was cloaked by the veil of hanging foliage. Turkey buzzards pecked and tore at the remains of what appeared to be a small deer below a huge oak tree with thick branches that reached over the grassland. "You mentioned Malsumis yesterday. Who is that?"

Spear-Face took a step back, as if afraid to talk about it. "Tabaldak made all men. Gluskabe and Malsumis sprang from dust in his hand. The brothers could create a good world, but only Gluskabe was good. Malsumis was evil. Gluskabe made all evil spirits small, then turned himself into a rock. Gluskabe said he would return one day. But Malsumis still walks on earth, and seeks evil. Malsumis will rise in power again before Gluskabe returns."

"Why do you think Malsumis is back? What do you see that makes you think he's gaining in power?"

He glanced at the meadow, then turned toward the rising sun. He smiled as he squinted at its brightness. I envied him, always happy. "My wife said it. Malsumis would be one to take fire-haired girl. It made Rimlaw very angry. More furious than ever. She killed wife two days later." He stepped out quickly, heading back uphill.

I called after him. "So, you're just leaving me here? How should I help this girl?"

"You shaman. Ask guiding spirit. Ask sister!"

I stared as the crazy old man trotted away and disappeared among the trunks. He wasn't completely cracked. Gabby had told him to help, and he'd seemed happy to do what he could. It'd be nice to return the favor somehow.

I turned to the meadow and limped toward it, but then froze. A chill crept up my calf, like how the shouts of the Vestmen back on the stream bank had vibrated up through the soles of my feet. My chest tightened, as if asthmatic. Just like when we'd rowed into the mouth of the river.

Spear-Face's voice floated down the hillside. He was arguing with himself again, or maybe singing. His words sounded too distant to understand. I was just being paranoid about the chill in my leg. I was no spiritist. I was simply walking toward a meadow. The patch of forest beneath my feet was no different than the one behind me. Though much of what the crazy Indian had said made sense.

I shook my head and laughed at the audacity of the thought. I was beginning to believe the superstitions of an ancient schizophrenic medicine man. But the more I'd spoken to him about my old world, the further away it had seemed. Like waking from a dream, every second eroding the memory. I couldn't let it slip too far away. How many days had it been now? Two, or three?

Poor Mom. I had to get back. She'd be sick with worry. Dad too. Their marriage had barely survived the loss of Gabby. I longed to sit again on our kitchen barstool, watch her prep whatever recipe she'd printed off the internet, enjoy her soft smile, revel in Dad's sincere interest in whatever I'd done that day, and laugh at Nikki's constant, not-so-subtle obstinations. To see Christine once again, before our vacation was over. I'd been so eager to get out and begin life anew at Duke, but now I just wanted to get home. And my only link to that place was the spirit of my dead sister.

Spear-Face was right about that. She was the one who brought me here. Probably the one that pulled me into the boat, somehow. *I should ask her what to do.* Demand an answer. How long would that take? I couldn't just call her up anytime I wanted.

Because I was no shaman.

Chapter 25 – Malsumis

The soft breeze cooled Stryker's moist nose. He lay upon a low, crooked maple branch in a tree at the edge of the Mi'kmaq village. Distant laughter of children mixed with the hiss of wind through leaves. He cracked an eye and scanned the wigwams upon the riverbank. Two scouts wandered through the trails between the huts, spears in hand, ducking into each abode.

Stryker stood and arched his back, stretching tired legs. The air was crisp, only mildly tainted with sweat and dung from the newly arrived tribe. But within a week, the area would be an unbearable cesspool. He dug claws into the tree's coarse skin and scaled down.

"Pleasant greetings, ranger," sounded a woman's calm voice from behind him.

Stryker spun and hissed. The hair on his neck stood straight.

She was tall and thin, with high cheeks and eyes of darkest jade. Raven-black hair with a single shock of gray fell past her shoulders, not braided in the Mi'kmaq tradition. Long legs, narrow waist, and arms fitted with corded muscle. Her athletic build looked as though it could carry her at an unimpeded sprint for miles. She gripped a long spear in her cocked arm, the point resting upon the nub of her other wrist. It was missing a hand.

Stryker hadn't been alert. She could've killed him if she'd wanted. And she'd spoken to him *in spirit*. The Mi'kmaq's shaman for certain. Not the sallow-skinned complexion with corpse-blue saddles slung beneath the eyes that he associated with most of her type. They always seemed only a few breaths away from becoming a spirit themselves. This one's bright complexion and fit stance appeared...healthy. Young. Alluring, even.

"Why are you here?" she growled.

Stryker considered slipping into spirit just for a second, to see through his soul's eye. To discover what demons she brought with her. Who she really was. A petty shaman with a spear? If so, he didn't need to condescend to her threats.

Her cheek rose as a malevolent smile creased her face. She shook her head. "Don't try it, ranger."

How'd she know what he was thinking?

She stepped closer, light on her feet, as if stalking. "I'll ask again. Why are you here?"

Because I've no other options. "I'm hunting an enemy. An enemy that seeks to hurt your village. I'm here to help."

Her eyes narrowed. "*You* want to hurt us. You smeared a baby's bed mat in venom leaves."

His ears tilted inward as he searched his memory. He'd forgotten about his foul mood when he'd rubbed that grass rug in the poison ivy. The thought cheered him.

"Don't come here and try to pretend—"

A growl rumbled in his throat. He'd had enough of this woman already.

"Don't interrupt me!" she shouted.

Thunder clapped inside his head, slamming his brain against his skull. His eyes watered. Invisible claws dug through his skin into the sides of his chest, holding him fast. Drops of blood fell from the fresh wounds and splattered the earth.

"You're here to help my tribe? You're so inept you couldn't mate if your master made you assume the form of a rabbit. You're here because you *failed*. It's the only time spirits pretend to help. When they need something." She lowered her spear.

Stryker lunged, but the claws, or whatever they were, held fast. Like barbs in his ribs. No thorns dug into his flesh, though bloody gouges sliced into either side of his body. How could this be? A spirit couldn't affect flesh in such a way. But the other shaman— that of the Abenaki—one of her demons had seemed able. *To hell with it.* He cast his gaze through his spirit's eye to view what it was that held his body fast, but nothing. Even more, the shaman seemed to disappear completely. Invisible. How?

An obnoxious thought rang in his mind. To tell the truth. It soured his tongue and burned his nostrils like stomach acid. *No! Lie. Flatter. Promise her whatever she wants.*

What leverage could he use? Unable to see her spirit, he studied her flesh instead. Most Mi'kmaq wore sack-like clothing. But a leather dress stretched tightly across this shaman's body. As if she wanted to assume the form of the animal from which it had been stripped. His mouth watered at the thought of how exotic it would be to wear the skin of his prey. Her skin. Her hips were curvy and enticing. Too much so, for a human.

She sighed. "You test my patience. Tell me why you're here."

"I need to kill a Vestman."

She huffed. "I know your assignment, Stryker. But why are you *here*."

He flinched at the mention of his name. How'd she know it? The claws gripped tighter, sinking between his ribs. He grunted with the pain. "Your tribe attacked the Vestmen, so I assume you wish them dead. I need one among them killed. We can help each other."

She stepped closer and pointed the spear at his face. "You failed, ranger! And *we* paid the price for it. Your orders were simple. Kill a single man. If you'd done your job, there would be no Vestmen remaining."

This woman knew entirely too much. "I'd only been tracking him a single afternoon before the fight erupted. Stalking takes patience. And why would a single enemy among the Vestmen change your battle's outcome? Your tribe's losses are upon your head, not mine."

Her eyes narrowed, and she growled through her teeth. Not the tinny grumble of which most humans are capable, but a low, deep-chested rumble, as from a lion. "Our attack was to be a surprise. And had your quarry been dead, it would've been a slaughter. Your prey, that Vestman, can see in spirit. He knew we were waiting in those woods."

"He's a shaman?"

She began to pace between a thick brown thorn stalk and the rotting trunk of a dead pine sapling. "Hardly. He's an idiot. A fool. A toy in a child's game. But he hears the spirits. Ignorant, but a threat nonetheless."

Drops of Stryker's blood splashed the ground. His tail whipped like rope. "Had I known, we could've worked together. But that's what I am proposing now. I *do* need something. Information. Tell me everything you know about this region. The other demons present, their lusts, and what areas they command. And I need to know how to make it past the wards."

"Wards? There are none here."

None? Ha! "Then you are no shaman."

To her credit, her expression betrayed no anger. Confidence. She glanced behind her into the wood. "Tell me about them. Maybe I'll share what I know."

"I've witnessed two, only a day apart. I ran into one yesterday, and it took me all morning to recover. But it had no effect on my spirit." A lie, but too embarrassing to admit. "The keeper of both wards is a young girl with long red hair past her shoulders. She wields a sword that blazes brighter than fire."

She turned back to him and stared, surprised. A breeze wafted across the meadow and pushed into the forest. It chilled his skin and seemed to cool with every second. Low-hanging maple leaves shuddered in the cold. A rim of white formed at their edges, and veins of glass-like crystal spread across their surface as they hung in what had turned into an unmerciful arctic blast. Frost formed on Stryker's fur, and his feet froze in place. The claws in his sides seemed to release and he strained to bolt away, but now his paws stuck fast to the ground. Even so, the sun blazed upon the meadow only a short distance away as the same breeze stirred warm stalks of grass. He'd never seen such a spell. He tugged and strained, but his feet refused the command.

The cold seemed to have no effect on the shaman. She strolled freely near the frost's edge, weaving into and out of its reach, her booted moccasins crunching frozen pine needles, then padding upon warm leaves. As if taunting, knowing he was unable to attack. Anger burned his throat despite the frigid air. She strutted past like a peacock, then spun and whipped the spear shaft down upon his back. It snapped in two across his shoulders.

Pain shot down his neck. His eyes welled again, though he tried to conceal the sting. If he could free himself, he'd slice open her neck and purr as she bled out.

"That's for rubbing our child's mat with venom leaves!" She pressed a palm to her chest. "I am the protector of this tribe. If you attempt to hurt us again, I will destroy you."

The protector? This witch was as delusional as the last. Her spirits had her blinded, whoever they were. Shaman were slaves, never the other way around. But something was different about this one. He'd never been handled like this, except by Slaughter. And this freeze...

A thick chokeberry bush near the frost line shook, as if from a bear, where the shaman had glanced earlier. Panic began to flutter in his belly. He was defenseless against such an animal. He glanced at his feet, tugging, willing them to move, but something besides the bitter cold held them fast. Another drop of blood dripped from his fur. It froze on its way to the ground, bounced, and rolled upon the earth like a tiny marble, coming to rest in a bright spot of sun where it glittered. Almost how the Vestman's blood had shone so brightly on the ground before the sandal of the keeper of the ward.

A black panther emerged from the quaking bramble. The same enormous one that had stalked him in the meadow. He was even larger than he remembered. A thick forehead jutted over deep-set eyes like armor plating. Claws punctured the forest floor with each step. He ambled toward Stryker till their noses touched. This beast could swallow Stryker's skull in one snap. Scarred lips shook, as if trying to conceal violent intent. He snorted, frosting Stryker's eyes. A weight pressed upon Stryker's chest as distant laughter filled his ears. Though not the earlier sounds of children playing. These were cackles, jeers, and taunts, as from an angry mob.

Beast turned and strolled toward the shaman. He circled her, tail flitting this way and that, then snaking up a thigh, beneath her dress, between her legs, probing her body as he circled. She smiled down at him as he purred, licking his nose. She glanced toward Stryker, a glint of fear in her eyes. Beast rubbed his shoulder against her, spreading his scent, a cat claiming her as his own.

So *here* was the source of her strength. But who was Beast? No panther had ever been as large. To assume a form that had never existed? Such a body meant tremendous wealth. Wealth beyond what he'd ever imagined. Wealth beyond even that of Slaughter.

The shaman's skirt lifted as Beast's tail writhed beneath it, the rise revealing long, furrowing scars down her thighs, some fresh and pink.

"Tell me about this ward of yours, and its keeper," Beast purred. His voice was deep and rough. When he spoke, the laughter subsided.

"She protected the blood trail of the Vestman I'm tracking."

Beast's gaze remained upon the shaman as he continued his circle. "Describe her."

Who was this animal? A competing captain? Stryker dared not ask. He'd noticed Beast's scent in the meadow, some markings being weeks old. Stryker glanced again at the scars on the inside of the shaman's thigh, then to Beast's claws. He was well established in this region. So, under Slaughter's authority? No. Slaughter would never stand for it. A rogue demon, then, hidden within Slaughter's day region, but somehow escaping his notice? A feat Stryker himself hadn't been able to accomplish. This was no ordinary spirit.

"I know only what I've already said. The keeper of the ward appears as a young girl. Red hair, unnaturally so. Like tongues of fire. And a sword that glows just as brightly."

Beast ceased his pacing and stared at him, taking his eyes from the woman for the first time. His tail drooped. "And you witnessed this ward earlier?"

"Yes. Slaughter came against it. I had hidden myself nearby. He was impotent against the girl."

The distant jeers swelled to a roar. Beast began to circle Stryker now, paws crunching frozen, dead leaves. His lip curled, as if he wanted to join the hooting ruckus. "Impotent may be a term worthy of that demon. Yet, he is your captain now, and one of the most powerful servants in my command."

Slaughter, beneath this creature? If true, that would make him...*Malsumis!* His lungs froze at the realization, the bitter air now so frigid he couldn't even cough. And he'd just insulted the shaman, Malsumis's human pet. Obviously, his sex toy. Even worse, he'd failed Slaughter, which meant he'd failed Malsumis as well. No one who'd ever seen this devil had lived to tell of it. Stryker would be banished to the Abyss. Pain shot through Stryker's chest, though the invisible claws no longer gripped him. His legs buckled, but he somehow managed to stay upright.

"That's right. But I chose you, ranger. A loyal demon working for Ernick, your old captain. I knew the Vestmen would arrive upon these shores. Full of ambition and greed, they couldn't refuse the call of this land. But, they'd become infected. The enemy is sly, ranger. Its poison contagious as a venereal disease. Their lies spread lustfully to half their number. Weak-willed pagans. Forsaking the truth of gods who can be seen and held, in exchange for a frail spiritual lie. We know lies, don't we?" He flicked his tail to emphasize his point.

"I chose you, full of talent, polished in the traditions of the black arts. The empire that will soon spread across this land will make every other seem a mist that vanishes with the rising sun. A land of unimaginable opportunity for a demon such as yourself."

Opportunity? The pain in Stryker's chest eased. Why would Malsumis mention that?

"Which is why I chose you. A young, stealthy ranger to slip beneath the enemy's defenses. I instructed Ernick to send you on this quest. And encouraged Slaughter to provide clarity, along with a bit of incentive." He flicked his tail at Stryker's ribs, stinging the spot where Slaughter had skewered him.

"But so focused on the enemy, you ran into the powers that defend him. The keeper of his ward."

Malsumis seemed to avert his gaze. The huge panther had been guilty of the same fault back in the meadow, blind to the charging buck. That memory startled Stryker. *Who was the buck?* Not now. He'd have to consider that later.

Malsumis studied the punctures in Stryker's side, admiring them. He bowed his neck and lapped the blood from the ground, his purr the distant rumble of an avalanche. He lifted his gaze. "You're still headstrong. A ranger must be patient."

But Stryker had stalked the Vestman enemy for such a short time! He'd do it for years if necessary. Patience was not Stryker's issue.

"Not *that* kind of patience, ranger. *Clever* patience. You must wait for him to come to you. As you did the rabbit in the meadow. As you did beside the trail before the attack. Your ambush would have worked, had the Mi'kmaq not been so eager." He glanced at the shaman, and the lips of her smile quivered. "Now, be a ranger once again. Hide where you know he will pass. Kill the tall Vestman, and you will have a place in this new land. I do not accept failure."

"An ambush? Where, my lord?" The acknowledgment of Malsumis's authority tasted of bitter rue.

"The Mi'kmaq have a prisoner. The daughter of a Vestman. The enemy will come for her soon. He can't resist, even though he knows it's a trap. That's when you will kill him." He licked his nose. "But if you hurt even a single Mi'kmaq, I'll let my shaman have her way with you."

He turned and strolled away with the woman next to his shoulder, rubbing his fat neck as if he were the pet. They slipped behind the thick brush from whence he'd emerged. Once they were out of sight, the ground below Stryker began to thaw. His paws stung as feeling crept back. He took a step, choosing his footing, uncertain as to whether his legs would support him.

He peered across the clearing to the village, which was now milling with a few early arrivals, lanky men with packs of stitched deer hide upon their backs. Tonight, he'd search the village to find where the Mi'kmaq guarded their prisoner. He'd hide in ambush and wait. Easy enough. Why did Malsumis need him for such a simple task? He was the all-powerful, was he not? There were no other higher. *He said it himself; he has a plan for me.* Stryker's chest swelled. He ignored the burn of the fresh wounds. Malsumis was grooming him, providing an opportunity to prove his worth. Kill the tall Vestman, and Stryker would become a captain for certain. His ambitions would soon be realized.

Leaves rustled as the breeze switched direction. The acrid scent of buck marking drifted past. Was it the same huge deer from the meadow? Stryker glanced about, but no animals stirred. He opened his mouth, studying the scent, but the message from the pheromones made no sense. Citrus signaled warning, as if alerting its herd they were under attack. But a metallic scent from the same buck spoke of aggression. Stryker had smelled this signal before, used only by prides of lions to coordinate movements when stalking.

But...deer don't hunt.

Chapter 26 – Barred Owl

Kiona lay on her back inside Mother's cramped wigwam, resting upon a stiff black bear skin. Even through the thick pelt, the long chill of winter still clawed at her skin from beneath the earthen floor. She shivered. But the cold's grasp was weakening, as spring had already defeated winter. The strength of Pebon, the powerful ice sorcerer, was ebbing. Another few weeks, and his frozen fingers would no longer reach her at all.

She pointed her toes, stretching tired muscles. Her long legs lay straight, aching from the exhaustion of a weeklong migration, the frantic run after Nabid, and then their flight from the battle. The smoky, bitter scent of the sacred vision plant filled the wigwam. Mother had been burning the herb most of the evening, piling it on the fire, packing her pipe, chanting ceaselessly, dark eyes glazed to milky white.

Kiona squinted, peering at the low, charred bark walls of their summer wetuom. Smoke from a small fire in the center of the floor writhed upon the ceiling, escaping through the many gaps where shingles had blown away in one of Pebon's winter gales. The northern star beamed through one, illuminating a halo about it, large and menacing.

She sat up.

Mother's hunched form sulked across the fire, head bowed, long hair hanging like a veil before her face. Her arms drooped, hands folded in her lap. Her ritual chanting ceased, she breathed deeply and slowly, apparently asleep. The tribe had lost many warriors yesterday, but still managed to kill several Vestmen in return. The braves' deaths were the reason for Mother's late vigil. Assured the enemy had fled, the tribe had continued to their summer campground. Mother had urged the move, claiming her powers were greatest in this region.

Slowly, Kiona stood and stepped toward the door.

"Where you going?" Mother asked, voice hoarse, head still bowed, as if speaking to her own feet. The dim light from the fire played orange and yellow on her black veil, shadows shooting across it like dancing spirits.

"I...can't sleep. Just going to step outside."

"Careful of the braves."

Kiona waited, but Mother fell silent. Her breathing slowed again. She seemed to fade back into whatever suspended state from which she'd roused herself. But her warning was timely. Great Scout had stationed many warriors in the darkness, some close to camp. And after a battle, most would be skittish as a bird, apt to shoot an arrow at any shadow.

She stepped outside, and a breeze from the black night chilled her bare neck. The moon had already set, but the eyes of the Star People filled the sky, casting enough light to distinguish the clearing of the village from the chest-high grass meadow surrounding it. She drew a deep, clear breath and listened. The stream trickled over rocks down at the bank a short walk away. An owl hooted from the hill in the opposite direction, and branches groaned at the edge of the meadow as they rubbed in the wind. The dim glow of small fires flared halfheartedly from the doors of a few wigwams. The homes appeared cage-like, due to unrepaired cracks in their walls and roofs, tired tongues of flame flicking low in their bowels, almost snuffed out.

She stared up at the Star People as they hunted across the sky. A pair of foolish sisters had once married two of them. Surely *they* could see where the Vestmen were at that very moment, if they desired. They knew where the tall, ruddy one was sleeping. Or whether he was, instead, preparing with the others for a new attack.

A brave's moan rasped from a nearby wigwam. Kiona flinched. The man's wound had been a sword thrust into his belly. He'd be dead soon, no matter how much Mother chanted, smoked, or babbled. Kiona closed her eyes and rubbed her cheek with her palm, soothing herself, relieved that Huritt had returned with only a shallow slice in one thigh. He'd escaped the slaughter, a fate better than many had met. He'd fought skillfully, beyond his years, she'd been told. And she'd been able to grab little Nabid and flee with him.

The northern star beamed like a child of the moon, bright and clear, no longer shrouded in the haze of Mother's sacred smoke. Why had that tall Vestman protected Nabid? From his own leader, no less! That madman was their leader, no doubt. The one Astrid had spoken of. The fighter she'd warned her father would send. Kiona had seen him several times during her months among their people. She'd been uncomfortable whenever his gaze had fallen upon her, his searching eyes full of lust. But now they had glowed with the fury of battle, his face hard and cold as river rock, shoulders wider than any brave's. He had the white hair of a devil, beard streaked in blood, frothing at the mouth like a sick animal, babbling in a wild rage. And her foolish little brother had shot him! Then the tall one had covered Nabid with his shield, saving the boy's life, but further angering the White-Haired Devil.

She giggled at the thought. Little Nabid sinking an arrow into the enemy's thigh. How had she and her brother even escaped?

The tall one. He'd saved them both.

Eyes now adjusted to the dark, Kiona paced the perimeter of the camp. Hundreds of wigwams stood grouped by family, the entire settlement in the middle of a large meadow that spilled into the riverbank. The surrounding tall grassland sprang anew each winter, despite snow and frost. But within a few weeks, traffic and clearing fires would beat it down again. Still, anything could be hiding there now. If she stayed close to the dwellings, no warrior would mistake her for an enemy. And they'd heard no wolves in the night.

She rounded a cold, empty hut. Its family's lone brave struck down by an enemy's sword. She shook her head, unable to forget the image of the tall Vestman. Hair black as her own, but curly and wild as Astrid's. His legs strong and straight as the trunk of a young birch, with ropey muscles writhing beneath its bark. As if something otherworldly lay just below his skin.

She'd recognized him as well, from the months spent with the visitors. He was the son of their witch, though Kiona had never spoken to him. He'd seemed different then. Face shallow and void. A skull and skin. Now, he appeared fuller. Healthier. Stronger, even. Back then, he'd spoken harshly to his shaman mother. She'd deserved it, Kiona had thought, the woman talking to a warrior son as if he were still a child in a breechcloth. He'd been the only man who'd dared stand up to her.

Huh. Just like Nabid to Mother.

Kiona was halfway around the camp now, at the end closest the river where many trails wove through the meadow. Leaves crackled behind her and she spun around. A hazy, dim burn glowed from the door of a nearby wigwam. But that hadn't been the snap of a burning log. Another rustling, somewhere in the grass. She dropped to a knee. A warrior, perhaps? So close to camp, he shouldn't be hiding. She patted the belt about her waist until her fingers slid over the reassuring bulk of a leather sheath. She drew a flint knife, gripping its antler handle. It had belonged to her grandfather, and she'd dressed many a deer with the tool.

More movement, approaching the edge of the meadow, possibly traveling down one of the trails. An image of Great Scout patting his stomach came to mind. "Lunge for the belly," he'd said to a gaggle of Mi'kmaq girls he'd gathered for instruction. "Quickly, forward and back again. Always pull back immediately." He chopped one hand like a tomahawk. "You've gutted bison. It takes no time to slice, but jump back before he knows he's been struck. Never go for the neck unless you're close enough to marry him." All the other girls had sniggered at that. An annoying, embarrassed giggle.

Now, she slid her thumb up the shank till it rested on a nub below the stone blade.

Crunch! A rabbit hopped from the tall grass into the clearing. Kiona hissed a sigh and stood. At the movement, it froze. If she had a bow, she'd bag the animal for breakfast. Instead, she waved her arms. It remained, crouching, tense and still as a possum. The wise animal knew while it didn't move it was difficult to spot. She rushed over and it bounded away toward the center of the village, then shot between two wigwams, right past the feet of a stumpy warrior stationed outside the door where Astrid was resting.

She should visit her friend. Astrid was probably awake as well, wondering whether her rescuers would be coming for her again. Kiona started toward the guard, but stopped at a new thought. She leaned against an abandoned wigwam to blend her dark form with it. *If* the Vestmen attempted another rescue, that would be the best time for Astrid to escape, while the tribe was otherwise occupied. The guards had been told to move the prisoner to a hunting camp farther inland if that happened. But, if Huritt was her guard at the time...

A tall clump of lambsquarter shuddered near the edge of the meadow, as if a racoon or fox had brushed past. Then another bunch did the same, this time closer. She stood in the darkness, now still as the rabbit. Staring as other bundles of weeds swayed and parted, each progressively closer. What was snaking through the grass? Should she run? Tell the guard? But what if it was only a fox? Her imagination had already tricked her once tonight. Probably just a warrior had wandered into the grass to relieve himself.

The movement ceased when it reached the edge of the meadow. She stared, straining through the darkness to discern between shadows. Had it seen her?

The screen of grass parted, and a man stepped into the clearing, bent low, long tomahawk in hand.

Her shoulders tensed; her lungs seized. A Mi'kmaq warrior? No. He wouldn't be silently prowling about.

The owl hooted again and the man stopped, turning his head toward the sound. Then he straightened, towering like a rearing bear, hair wild as Astrid's.

This was no brave, but the tall Vestman.

He stalked toward her, long-handled tomahawk ready to slash into her skull. Drums beat in her ears. Did he see her? No. She was invisible where she stood. Her heart pounded so hard, surely he could hear it. She stood rigid, like the young girl in the tribal tale, frozen into a Chenoo while she slept. Like the wise rabbit. He kept to the path that headed for the center of the village and silently passed by, only feet from where she hid.

When his back was finally to her, she gripped her flint knife again, braced her thumb against the nub, and followed.

Lunge for the belly.

* * * *

Stiff, dry seed pods scraped my legs as I wove slowly through the meadow of tall grass surrounding the Mi'kmaq village. It stood exactly where Spear-Face had said, in the crook of land where a small stream meandered into the larger river. The same tributary we'd followed when we'd been attacked. That battle seemed distant now, yet my wounded thigh still ached with each step. Men's pained screams, the tinny ring of metal on wood, the sharp snap of skull bone as my axe cracked through it, the squish of boots in mud. The meaty aroma of eviscerated bowels, the rancid stench of excrement, and the perfume of trampled mint, all in a jumbled fragrance on the chill breeze.

I'd killed men. Only in self-defense, I assured myself. Even so, I'd been *good* at it. I hadn't reacted in a frantic panic, but with the calm assurance of skill, practice, and experience.

Yet, I'd never had any of those. Still, I now possessed them all. My body had known instinctively how to fight. To keep the axe raised just so high, ready for a kill stroke. To swing in tight arcs, to avoid lashing out so far as to throw myself off balance. To strike the unsuspecting warrior attacking the man next to me to keep the enemy's attention divided.

What bothered me most, though, was the pleasure I'd found in it. Not in the pain inflicted, but in the excitement of battle. I'd been abuzz, filled with the glory of bloody victory.

159

Though maybe now, approaching an entire Indian village alone, I'd grown overconfident. Yet the same primitive urgency that had driven me to this point called me now to this place, to do the impossible. To rescue a chieftain's daughter guarded by an entire tribe.

I stepped around a briar thicket. Hard, needlelike barbs scratched my arms. I could've followed any one of the cleared paths, but surely those would be watched.

From my vantage, swimming like an otter through the meadow, the domed roofs of a few taller wigwams floated above waves of salt grass and brush, black tombs against clear night sky. The moon had passed below the horizon, the swelling dark concealing my approach. Above me, the Milky Way burned like the phosphorescent glow of a boat's wake at night.

I knelt just inside the edge of the field, beneath the cover of tall grasses, and peered through their concealing veil. A half dozen huts stood directly before me. The weak flicker of a dim fire glowed from the door of one, a pair of bare feet outlined by its dull radiance. The rest of the huts stood cold and dead, without movement. I listened, but heard only the chirp of crickets, water bubbling over rocks, and the crackle of twigs in the lone fire. A barred owl's soulful song swelled behind me, echoed by its wooer directly across the village. I searched from where it sang, but nothing human stirred.

I parted the veil with axe and arm and stepped into the clearing, damp ground spongy beneath my leather boots. I paused again, allowing my senses to reach what I could not see. Crickets. Barred owl. Rushing water over rocks. Perfume of hardwood smoke mixed with something heavy and acrid, like burnt plastic. I sniffed again. Couldn't be plastic, of course. But equally as pungent, and a bit like herbal tea.

From twenty feet distant, I peered into the wigwam with the low fire. Two bodies lay upon furs spread on either side of it. A black smear ran across the back of the male, lying upon his side, naked to the waist. A gash weeping blood.

They'd keep the chieftain's daughter securely in the center of the village, I suspected. She'd be heavily guarded after the battle, but this was only a scouting run. To get in and out undetected, learn the village's layout, the number of warriors, and where they had imprisoned her.

I tiptoed slowly down a narrow trail toward the far owl's call. A breeze picked up, rustling the tallest grass and flower stalks in the meadow. I took advantage of the sound's cover and made my way past two occupied wigwams.

The bird offered another boisterous chorus, clear and menacing, but the one just behind me refused to echo it. The lonesome call sounded again, washing over the village, as if lulling them to sleep. Still nothing from behind me. Why had the other bird fallen silent?

I turned. A flash of light blasted my eyes, and I fell backward.

Chapter 27 – Turning

I snapped my eyes open and moaned at a throbbing pain in my skull. A trickle of blood dripped from a gash on my forehead. Silky hair brushed my cheek. I searched the surrounding darkness. The face of an Indian girl hovered a foot above my own. Her lips moved, but no sound came to me. The entire world lay silent. My arms tingled, as if they'd been asleep. I balled fists, but they gripped no battle-axe. The distant call of the barred owl sounded as through a tunnel, growing in clarity as the seconds passed. The song was returned by its mate strongly now, as if the other bird was only a few feet away.

"I said *don't move*, or I'll plunge this knife through your belly," the girl hissed in the Vestmen's language. Only then did I feel the cool, sharp blade against my stomach, already piercing skin.

My sight gradually sharpened. We were inside a wigwam. Dim starlight bled through cracks in the ceiling. I searched my memory, but it was murky water. She must've crept up behind and knocked me out. Without moving my head, I tried to glance down. Even so, the throbbing behind my eyes increased.

The girl straddled me, legs locked onto mine. One hand covered my mouth; the other gripped a dagger, its rough blade chipped from flint.

I was completely exposed. She could kill me with a twitch and, having just regained consciousness, I wasn't certain I could move, other than my fingers.

Even with darkness shrouding her face, it appeared familiar. High cheekbones and black eyes. Or maybe it was the smeared painting of a bird and deer painted across the top of her leather dress. I studied her, but my mind couldn't conjure an association.

"Why did you spare my brother?" she asked.

Who was she talking about? I muttered through her clamped fingers. "I don't know him." I'd spoken the same language as when addressing Spear-Face and the Abenaki shaman. My language seemed to change to suit who I was addressing.

Her eyes widened. She pressed the blade harder. "How do you know our tongue?"

162

How could I explain something I didn't understand? "The shaman of the Abenaki gave me her blessing."

Her nostrils flared like a startled deer's. "The *Abenaki* sent you?"

"No. We found them and asked the location of your camp."

"After the battle. You protected my brother from your chieftain, the white-haired warrior. Why?"

Oh. *That's* where I recognized her. The girl who'd yanked the boy with the green stripe on his cheek out of the way and fled, after I'd shielded him from Halfdan's sword.

Her eyes narrowed, but they betrayed doubt. If she were going to kill me, she'd already have done it.

"The white-haired warrior isn't my chieftain," I said. "Killing the boy wouldn't have been right, even though he'd shot me. That's why I protected him. He was only a child."

"He shot at you as well?"

I gave a nod. Pain speared my head, and stars burst before my eyes. Nausea bubbled in my throat, but I swallowed it back. "He was in the tree line during the fight. Hit me above the knee." I shifted that leg, to indicate which one.

Though her hand remained over my mouth, her grip loosed. She twisted the knife, as if to remind me of its delicate location. "Keep your voice low, or I'll kill you. If you attack me, fifty warriors will come running."

"I'll be quiet," I whispered. I had no delusions about escape. If I overpowered her, a single shout and I'd have to run, chased by strong braves familiar with the trails. And I had no idea where she'd dragged me.

She let go of my jaw and sat up, legs still locked around mine, dress hiked about her waist. She was tall for an Indian, her slender arms sewn together with enough wiry muscle she could easily drive that blade through my belly. Gaze still upon my face, she reached around her hips and gripped my thigh.

She growled, "Your leg isn't wounded."

Maybe my words hadn't been clear. "Just above my knee," I whispered.

She touched the spot, probing the tender flesh with hard fingers. She squeezed, and the wound burned hot. I gritted my teeth to stifle a gasp. My leg tensed involuntarily, shifting her weight. For a split second, she was off balance.

I whipped one hand across my belly and gripped her wrist. She stabbed with surprising force, but the knife only sliced my skin as it plunged into the ground next to me. She drew a breath, but I sat up and clamped a hand across her mouth, driving her backward. One second, and our position had been reversed. She screamed, but I squeezed with all my strength. My grip covered her nose and mouth and wrapped halfway around her head.

She kicked and bucked. I pulled the knife from the ground and held it to her throat. Sparkles flashed before my eyes. My head throbbed, and the world spun. But now I locked my legs onto hers. "Calm down. Be quiet," I sneered, pressing the blade against her skin. She held still. "I'm not going to kill you. If you don't move, I won't even hurt you." A drop of blood from the wound on my forehead dripped into her eye. She blinked it away, but terror remained.

I pulled the knife away from her throat, hoping she'd understand the overture as a sign I could be trusted. She squirmed again, but my weight held her down. Her bare thigh rubbed against mine. Dress still hiked, she was naked from the waist down.

"I'm going to move. Pull your dress down, so you're not so...exposed. Understand?"

Her eyes narrowed.

I moved the blade between her breasts, shifted my weight, and rose to my knees, keeping her pinned with her own knife.

She reached down and covered herself.

I glanced about to take stock of my surroundings. My shield lay against one side of the wigwam. Other than that, the hut was empty. No ropes to tie her up. I could use the knife to cut strips of leather from her dress and gag her, but no doubt she'd get a scream out somehow. I could knock her out, *then* tie her up. Probably what she'd planned for me. But what if one blow didn't work? I'd have to try again and probably end up bludgeoning her to death. No, I had to trust.

I pressed my lips close to her ear. "I don't want to hurt anyone. Understand? Just to get my sister, and then leave you all in peace." Venus burned through a crack in the ceiling like a spying eye. The girl's gaze seemed to soften, and she held still. "If I take my hand away, will you stay quiet?"

She clasped her palms together, as if in prayer. I took that as a *yes* and lifted one finger covering her nose. She inhaled deeply. Then another, over her lips. Still no scream. I withdrew my hand, and she lay silent. I lifted the knife and backed away.

She scrambled to her feet and bolted out the door like a flushed quail. *No!* I froze, waiting for her shouts to summon help. Yet, only footfalls. No screams. She must've stopped a few paces away. I should've run too, in case she'd change her mind. But there was a reason she hadn't killed me right away. The same peace that provoked me to lower my guard before the Abenaki chief and the short shaman washed through me now. She wasn't going to rouse any warriors.

After a minute, her shadow darkened the entry. I backed to the far side of the wigwam and sat, hands in my lap, trying to appear less threatening. She ducked through the opening then moved off to one side, as if not wanting any nighttime passerby to see her. She plopped down, legs crossed. A puff of dust floated next to her like a phantom. The room was tight—only eight feet stood between us. A small mound of cold, gray coals from a fire long burnt out separated us. The barred owl still chanted, sounding as if roosting atop the structure.

She whispered, "Aren't you going to run?"

I held up both empty palms. "No."

"Why not?"

I folded hands in my lap again, mimicking her. I had no idea what gestures might seem benevolent or aggressive. "Because if you meant to give me over to your tribe, you would've done so already. You would've stabbed me instead of knocking me out. So...thank you."

Her shoulders lifted an inch, as if she was trying to appear taller. "Only because you protected my brother."

"I don't believe you. There's something else. I saw it in your face when I mentioned my sister. You know her, don't you?"

She sat unflinching, staring at me. "Of course I do. You saw us together many times, back during the time I lived with your tribe."

This was a good sign. I hadn't seen them together, of course, because I wasn't that man. But maybe she'd become friends with my sister. "Then, will you help me?"

The room stood silent for a long minute. The barred owls called lonesomely to each other. At last, she announced, "I will help Astrid."

Astrid. That's right. The name Tryfing had used in his story about the dream with a four-legged monster. "Astrid is my sister." Not a lie, but not the whole truth. "I'll get her home, safely."

She placed her palms together then separated them. An opposite motion than the one I'd taken to be yes. *So, that must mean no.* "Astrid is a prisoner of *your* tribe as well. She does not wish to return."

Says her jailer. "I don't understand."

"She told me her father will give her in marriage to the White-Haired Devil. The one who tried to kill Nabid. Why don't women in your tribe have a choice in marriage?"

Sounded exactly like what Tryfing had said. Halfdan was the Vestman with white hair, and his aim was to be the next chieftain. "Women do have a choice." I wasn't certain, but it was the answer she wanted to hear. "But the White-Haired Devil and my father..." A trickle of blood dripped into my eye, and I wiped it away.

She stood and stepped over the pile of coals. She stared at the knife lying next to me.

I carefully gripped the blade and held the handle out to her. She slipped it into a hidden sheath stitched to the back side of a narrow leather belt, then sat in front of me close enough that our knees touched. She leaned in and gently brushed the wet blood from my eyebrow with her fingertips. She pinched the wound together, studied it with a stern expression, then hopped up and walked out. She returned with a wooden cup of water and a fistful of green stems with narrow, wiry foliage and tiny white flowers. The field had been full of them.

She tore off the leaves, dipped them in the water, then brushed them across the cut. A perfume of rosemary and oregano swelled inside the close space. "Wounds on a forehead are a rushing river. This is yarrow, to stop the bleeding."

If I hadn't seen how Spear-Face's work had kept my leg from infection, I wouldn't have let her touch the cut. The potion stung, but the pain was tolerable. She worked loose caked, gritty dirt, tweezing larger clumps and switching leaves often. It was pleasant to finally be touched by someone who wasn't trying to beat, stab, or kill me. But then, she'd been such an aggressor only a few minutes earlier. I watched her hands, to be sure she didn't reach for her knife. Soon, the water in the cup appeared black as coffee.

"What's your name?" I asked as she stroked more crushed leaves across my forehead.

She drew back, clump of greens pinched between fingers like a painter's brush. The corners of her mouth turned up, so slight as to be almost imperceivable. Then she pursed her lips and returned to her work, albeit with increased intensity. "Kiona," she said. "Yours?"

What *was* my Viking name? I hadn't thought of it for days. "Matok."

"I saw you many times when I was with your tribe. You seem...quieter than I remember."

She probably knew more about Matok than I did. According to what little I'd learned from Tryfing, Matok was a wild man. Best if I stayed clear of discussing him. "Thank you for cleaning my cut." Knocking me out had probably been her only option, other than killing me.

She grabbed a fresh clump, lifted my arm, and began to bathe the slice on my side. "I'm sorry for trying to stab you."

The plant juice stung like rubbing alcohol. I winced as she dabbed. "That's OK. A lot of people have tried to kill me lately."

She paused a beat, as if contemplating my answer, but instead of laughing merely resumed her work. "Your mother is the witch of the Vestmen. Mine is the shaman of our tribe. Do you remember her visiting your village?"

Wait. If Kiona was the daughter of the Mi'kmaq's shaman, that made Spear-Face her grandfather. And the Abenaki shaman her aunt. "No, I don't remember her. But, I've met someone who would. Your grandfather, your mother's father."

She dipped the next clump of leaves into the water, then squeezed so their juices ran onto her fingertips. "You've met no such person. Grandfather is dead."

I told her how Halfdan had tried to kill me after protecting her brother. How I'd fled and Spear-Face had found me, and about his family stories. I left out the part of Kiona's mother murdering his wife, her own mother. Instead I explained that Spear-Face had been exiled from the tribe, and how the old man now desperately wanted to see her again.

She dabbed and wiped, tending my cut the entire time, her expression hardening. She cleaned without a word, till my side was stained dusty green.

"Ouch!" I flinched at a particularly hard pat.

She flicked some green goo into a pile and wiped her fingers. They shook violently, as if she were thoroughly chilled. Slowly, I took her hand in my own, stilling the tremors. "You're angry. I thought you'd be happy he wanted to see you."

She stared at the lumpy pile of used leaves. "My grandfather was killed, Mother told me, along with my grandmother and father. The entire family was attacked by a black panther. Father was the first to die, protecting everyone with his bare hands. But the story never made sense. A panther doesn't attack people unless threatened or starving."

Soft footfalls came from the trail outside. Hushed murmurs. Kiona jumped up. I drew my last axe still looped on my belt. Where was the other? I glanced about. Kiona searched as well. We

167

spotted it at the same time, its light, wooden handle quite visible lying next to the trail outside.

She slipped out and headed for it, but two braves met her and leveled spears. She didn't wait for them to speak. "I am Kiona, daughter of Mother."

I slipped to one side of the doorway, watching from the shadows. The first one spoke with a rasp, like a smoker. "Why are you out so late?"

"I couldn't sleep, so I walked around the village."

The other stepped toward her. "You came from that wigwam. Who were you talking to?"

"No concern of yours."

Another step and his foot struck the axe. Kiona snatched it up from the ground.

"Where'd you find that? A weapon of the enemy. It's worth an entire summer's meat."

"From Huritt. Spoils of battle."

The sentinel glanced at the wigwam, directly at the spot where I stood in darkness. In the moonlight, one of his eyes seemed to aim errantly, crooked. He stepped closer to her.

She held on to the axe, not giving an inch. "I *am* the daughter of Mother," she repeated sternly.

At that, both braves retreated a pace, then continued down the trail. "Best if you went home," the first rasped over one shoulder. They walked in step, as if marching, down one of the trails that led toward the gurgling river. Their bodies swayed in time as they went, gradually blending into one in the distance, their form muddied by darkness until the night swallowed them completely.

Kiona stepped back into the wigwam, gripping the handle of the axe, turning it over in her hands, as if familiar with the weapon. She raised it and touched the head to my nose. Her next words were terse, clipped with determination. "You *will* help me free Astrid, but not to your tribe."

Chapter 28 – Surprise Attack

I turned the smooth handle of one axe in my grip as I hunched and stalked out from beneath the low cover of a Douglas fir, into the darkness blanketing the meadow around the Mi'kmaq village. I gripped one in each hand, turning them over and over, the weight of their iron heads and the grips' long, perfect balance calmed the tightness in my chest. I'd been uneased all day, waiting beneath that tree for nightfall, then for the moon to set.

Kiona had chosen the hiding spot, close to the village but with good cover. Some of their trackers could even smell a man when close enough, she'd claimed, and the tree would conceal me within its tart scent.

Just this evening, she'd wandered down a path that led next to my hiding place. Her gait had been light as a dancer's. She'd walked on the balls of her feet; her chin high, confident. Her long black hair fell straight as a blade past delicate shoulders, her eyes the color and sharpness of onyx. And taller than I'd remembered in the closeness of the wigwam. She'd met my gaze as I sat beneath the tree's cover, and I thought she might have even blushed, despite her olive complexion. But even if so, it made no difference. I wasn't who she saw. Though a girl with a shaman as a mother might be comfortable with a guy from a different time. A different world. Who knows?

Standing on the path, gaze turning away from me, she'd lifted a bare branch from the ground and tossed it in front of the tree, on the side facing the village. Our signal that, tonight, she'd flee with Astrid. Thank goodness! It had only been last night when she'd knocked me out and dragged me into that wigwam. But lying motionless beneath that tree had seemed a week.

I followed a narrow trail through the tall grass. It meandered in the dark and proved difficult to discern, as if only racoon or fox usually traveled it. The sward here was soft and silent against my skin. Thick, short, young growth muffled each footfall. A cool breeze rushed down from the north, further obscuring any sound of my movements.

Footfalls squished in mud only feet away. I froze, straining to hear over the wind rustling the grass. Slowly, I raised myself up to my full height and peered over waving tufts. Still nothing in sight. I thought of Kiona's warning about their trackers and drew in a deep breath. The only smells were damp earth, grass, and the wild mint that grew everywhere.

The waving meadow stilled for a moment. A faint splashing came from the same direction. An animal lapping from a puddle, most likely. Humans would slurp. I was downwind of whatever it was, so my scent hadn't startled it.

Must've been a deer.

I hunched again, turned the axe handles in my grasp, and continued toward the darkened village.

* * * *

Moisture soaked the pads of Stryker's paws as he stalked toward the Mi'kmaq camp. In daylight, he would have to conceal his movements in the tall meadow. But there was no need to be overly cautious. He was invisible at night. A black panther obscured in darkness. He preferred the stealth and agility of this form, perfectly suited for hunting. And his own eyes could see as well as at dawn.

He peered down the path toward the village. A single wigwam stood near the trailhead, cold and dead. The life of no fire flickered within. Much like the one into which the shaman's daughter had dragged the enemy last night. Clearly neither had seen Stryker crouching in the meadow, hidden within its dense foliage. The tall Vestman had emerged downwind of Stryker's own hiding place. The demon had crouched and was about to attack when the girl had suddenly rushed up and bludgeoned the ignorant Vestman with a rock. A fantastic, strong blow! But then, instead of killing him, she'd dragged him into an empty hut. Stryker couldn't move in to finish the job without endangering her, the daughter of the shaman. Malsumis had warned him against injuring any Mi'kmaq. And no one disobeyed Malsumis.

Though it hadn't rained all day, churned mud still covered most of the trail. Crossing a particularly wet section, the thick pads of his paws sank in, making a slurping sound when lifted. He stopped at a deeper puddle and lapped the still water, clear and cold. No one had recently traveled this way to stir it up.

The hair on his back rose and he tensed. A threat was near. He glanced behind. The empty trail disappeared into the forest. He stretched his neck, head high, ears pivoting, listening. Only a slow breeze brushing meadow weeds, the chirping of crickets, and the buzzing of cicadas. What else was he sensing? He sniffed the wind, drawing in deep breaths and panting them out. The savory warm-blood scent of rabbit blended with sour yarrow, sharp thyme, and minty bee balm. His mouth watered at the fragrance of prey. But no sign of threat. Still, he'd sensed a presence. And a dangerous one. Could Malsumis be following him?

No. He'd never stoop to tail a ranger. It had to be the tall Vestman.

Stryker crouched till his belly brushed the water. His claws sank into the mud. His ears flattened against his skull. The enemy wasn't on the trail ahead or behind, and certainly nowhere upwind. He glanced at the dense sward in the opposite direction. Downwind was the only option left.

Stryker's whiskers drew up as he smiled. The Vestman had been silent, displaying more skill than he'd have credited. But no one was cunning enough to trick him. And his enemy would be blind on such a dark night. Stryker could have his way with him. He'd have to disarm him, of course. A deep slash across the forearms would render him incapable of struggle, but keep him alive for play. Then he'd take pleasure in lapping his blood as it gushed in panic. He'd tear out the man's voice box so he couldn't call for help—a surgical procedure using a single claw in a hooked downward slice to avoid severing the jugular. He'd eat through the belly first. A live meal was such a delicacy. Once the Vestman was dead, Stryker would finally have appeased Malsumis too. He would be given a day region, promoted to captain. Malsumis had promised it. In time, he'd be richer even than Slaughter.

A muffled scrape, a dry twig against a leather boot, just inside the dense growth. Stryker nosed between sage and sword grass, then slid into the hunt.

* * * *

Setting one foot carefully before the other, I silently tiptoed toward the village. I'd been on the move for about a half hour, yet was still some distance away. Crouching low, my thighs burned. Moving quietly, even through the meadow, was difficult work. Kiona had pointed out where the Indian guards were stationed around the perimeter, and I was now several hundred yards from the nearest. Maybe here I could be less cautious.

I took another step, suppressing a shiver, chilled by the same oppressive darkness I'd felt back when rowing into the mouth of the creek. And the one encountered after Spear-Face had dropped me off and left. I'd just stepped into enemy territory.

"What are you doing, brother?" Gabby asked suddenly, off to my right.

Startled, I turned and swung an axe toward the sound. She stood just out of reach next to a clump of the white-flowered plants Kiona had used to stop the bleeding of my wounds.

Her lips broke into a grin. "Ha! Missed me," she whispered.

I stared. She appeared the same as in my earlier vision: fair skin, fire-red hair in tight curls, and a leather dress similar to the one Kiona wore. "You startled me," I said.

"But what are you doing?"

I pointed an axe toward the village. "I'm going in there to rescue my sister."

She raised an eyebrow. "Oh?"

"I mean, the chieftain's daughter. A Mi'kmaq will sneak her out tonight. A friend of hers is the guard. I'm going to stay hidden, but close, in case they need help."

She crossed her arms, looking suddenly bored. "And then?"

"I don't know. I'm making this up as I go. It's been a while since you've shown up, you know. And your instructions are never exactly clear."

She tossed her head impatiently. "*Where*, brother. Where will you go if you rescue Astrid?"

Yeah. We should've discussed that. But I wasn't going to let my sister know I hadn't thought that far ahead. "Right now, we're just trying to get her out."

She jerked a thumb over one shoulder, pointing north. "You can't bring her to the Vestmen. She'd be more a prisoner there than she is here. You *know* where to take her. And don't stop until you've found the red sea urchin."

I waved an axe in surrender. "Wait. So, I'm supposed to take her somewhere close to the ocean? You're not making sense again. Red urchins are only on the West Coast. Green ones live out here. And what does any of that have to do with me getting back to *my* world? I don't have time for this right now." I hadn't thought about returning for so long, the idea held only the faintest weight now. Dreamlike. But I couldn't let it slip away. Memories of Mom, Dad, and Nikki. Was this world erasing them?

Her tangled locks swayed as she nodded. "You're right."

"Finally. About what? Which part?"

"That you don't have much time. But even if you did, you might not make it to the village."

172

I twisted the axes in my hands, annoyed, but trying to appear confident. "Why not?"

She tapped a finger on her nose. "What do you smell?"

These riddles would drive me insane! Still, what little guidance she'd given in the past had proven useful. So I closed my eyes and sniffed. "Something...minty. Cold dampness, like a frost is coming. Oh, and..." My shoulders slumped at the faint sweet scent of maple sap. I groaned. "You've got to be kidding me!"

She puckered her lips, blew a kiss, then turned and disappeared into the night. Even as she faded into the dark, something crashed into my chest. A heavy blow that slammed me to the ground.

Chapter 29 – Demon

I tumbled onto my back in the grass. Water splashed on my neck from the sodden ground. What had hit me? As I scrambled to my feet, an unseen hand wrenched one of my axes from my grasp. I glanced in the direction of the attack but saw nothing. Tall silvery stalks lit by starlight swayed, though, as if something had just disturbed them. A hidden brave must've struck me head-on while another waited to twist my weapon away. But how could they see so well on a moonless night?

I switched the remaining axe to my strong hand and drew the shield from my back. I turned slowly, staring into blackness. A breeze licked the meadow into waves and I flinched. The chill crawled up my legs, through my stomach, and rested upon my shoulders. As if a ghost was poised to lean close to my ear and whisper a threat. Heavy, oppressive, the darkness surrounding me held more than night. I was being studied from all sides. Observed and scored. A rat in a maze.

You might not make it to the village, Gabby had said.

Love you too, sister.

I'd prove her wrong. I crouched behind my shield and peered over its rim, weapon drawn back, ready to swing. Once more, an invisible warrior grabbed the handle from behind with the strength of a lion, twisted, and yanked. I gripped it with all my strength. My shoulder popped and the joint seared as ligaments stretched and tore. The weapon slipped, but I managed to hold on. Hands pressed against my back and knives sank through my leather vest. I screamed and turned around, but the assailant yanked and twisted. It was as if playing tug-of-war with a wolf. I swung my shield, trying to bash him with the rim. No one was there. Another yank, and the axe was gone.

I clenched my fists and crouched behind my shield once more. That had been no warrior. No wolf either. Completely silent, not even a curse or a growl. Cold water dripped from my damp hair, and warm blood trickled across my back. Not knives. *Claws.* A cat?

A basso snarl sputtered to life, like the song of a gigantic, angry cicada. I spun in that direction. The growl wandered through the darkness, just out of reach. A minute passed in silence, but the insect returned, closer now. Starlight reflected from a pair of silver orbs the size of marbles among waving flowery stalks. A knife slit of iridescence flickered below them. They moved toward me, into the clearing of trampled grass I'd just produced. No insect. A huge cat, fur black as obsidian, tongue flicking over a shiny wet nose. A full-grown panther.

Arrogant, stupid fool!

The words rang inside my head, but no sound came to my ears. Only the hissing of the wind and the low purr of the cat. Insanity.

Its eyes narrowed, as if it were truly inside me, listening to my thoughts. *Who are you, Vestman?* That long, pink tongue flicked again. A serpent scenting its prey.

With his words, muscles at the nape of my neck cramped, as if pierced by nails. They bulged into a knot and froze, hard as ice on a creek. Even the pain was cold, but without the relief of numbness.

Strong willed, I'll give you that. I like to know who I kill. Whose blood I drink.

A panther that spoke. Was this a trick from Gabby? "You'll never know me."

Its eyes glowed brighter. *Oh, I know more than you realize. You were headed to rescue your sister.*

A cold breeze pressed upon my throat like the rush of ice water.

She'll never make it, of course. Arrogant fools, the lot of you. Strolling into my trap. Your Mi'kmaq whore will be especially relished. I'll have my way with her. Her shaman mother already approved. She no longer had any choice, powerless to protect her rebellious youth. Another tongue flick. *Virgin flesh is a fancy. I'll slice open her stomach and eat her liver as I pleasure myself upon her corpse. Your red-haired sister as well.*

My belly warmed in anger, as if concealing embers. But the cold knot remained between my shoulders. A battle between the two sensations.

The cat swished its tail as it spoke, amused with its own monologue. *But you're more than her brother. No ordinary mortal can converse with spirits. Why haven't I been told of you? Your mother is loyal to Ernick, a worshipper of Malsumis. How did she keep a shaman son hidden all this time?*

The frozen knot twisted again, rolling up my neck. The heat in my belly rose to my chest, then traveled down my arms, burned my wrists, and filled my fists. As if I gripped a flaming branch. If I only had just one of my axes. If Gabby had warned me earlier, maybe I'd have a chance. But now, if I ran, the animal would overtake me in a few strides. My only hope was to keep the shield between us.

The cat sat, tail flicking, staring at me. Studying my face. Why didn't it attack? Was it stalling, waiting for others?

Bitterness filled my mouth as before, during the battle with the Mi'kmaq. The same spirit, imprisoned, longing for freedom, beckoned me to release it.

Very well. It had worked then. I would let it out.

The heat in my chest spilled from my lips in an animalistic growl. I balled my fists. I needed no other weapon.

The cat lifted its head. Proud. Defiant. *Who are you, Vestman?*

The hair at my nape stood on end, and the chill crept over my skull at the panther's questions. Yet my body was hotter than ever before. Sweat rolled down my cheeks and dripped from my lips, the taste of salt spray flung by a boat's prowl in a gale. The cold knot settled at the crown of my head, clawing at my skull.

Then the ice vanished.

The cat's pupils dilated. Its eyelids quivered and nose flared. Fear replaced its smug expression of curiosity. It shot toward the woods, tearing through the tall grass.

I chased after it. We broke into a wide, muddy trail. Yet my feet carried me as if across solid ground, just like my vision. The black feline shadow pulled ahead, gap widening. I dropped my shield and tore after it, but within seconds it disappeared into the dark cover of the forest, streaking next to the same Douglas fir under which I'd hidden all day.

Ducking beneath low branches, tearing through vines, I scrambled after it. But the darkness there was oppressive. Beneath the dense foliage, I could barely make out trunks. I slid to a stop and listened. No way I could catch the panther, fast as it was. Yet I had to ensure it couldn't hurt Astrid and Kiona. He somehow knew of their plan. In what world did panthers speak, much more without moving lips? No animal, but a demon.

Trunks creaked in a stiff breeze like old wooden stairs bearing an oppressive weight. I glanced up at the sound, and leafy branches swayed, dark clouds swimming against a starry backdrop. To one side, a pair of identical, dim lights glowed as they rocked with the breeze.

But stars don't move in the wind.

I ran back to the Douglas fir and grabbed the stick Kiona had tossed there earlier as a signal. It lay in the same spot. A clean, straight branch the length of my arm, with a sharp, splintered tip. It would do for a short spear.

I sprinted to the tree where I'd seen the panther's eyes and placed my hands upon its rough, woven bark. A chestnut. Branches appeared plentiful, but high and spindly. The trunk was narrow enough. I tucked the spear beneath my belt. With both arms encircling its mass, I wedged my boots against the base and ascended like a lumberjack with a tree belt. Halfway, I gripped a sturdier branch and swung my legs over, then stood and grabbed another. The silver orbs no longer glared down. Had the panther jumped to another tree? Perhaps it had only been an owl and had flown away. For a moment, I felt foolish, chasing a big cat in its own habitat. Like fighting a shark in the sea. Yet the animal had run. Something about me scared it.

You're more reckless than I thought.

I glanced up.

The panther stalked down the trunk toward me, as if gravity were of no concern. *Arrogant, always assuming fault lies with your opponent. I tricked you out from behind a shield. Did I not?*

So, not my brightest hour. Yet the heat, the urgency within me, grew to a searing rage as the panther neared. I pulled the stick from my belt.

The cat paused just above and regarded the weapon. It curled its lip, exposing the thin white daggers that were its canines. It snarled and leapt. Its teeth clamped upon the spear, and long, powerful legs wrapped around me. The full force of its body crashed into me and broke the leafy limb I grasped.

Our plummet seemed too slow, a rift in time. The trees, in flashes of gray and black, flew past in a blur as we fell. Relief, though slight, came knowing the cat's mouth was occupied by my weapon. The panther arched its back and I sensed the ground approaching. I hugged arms and legs tight around his body to soften the impending blow.

We struck the earth with a heavy thud. The impact knocked the breath from my lungs, but centuries of piled leaves and pine needles cushioned the impact. The cat snapped at my neck. I still gripped the leafy branch and shoved it into the cat's mouth.

But its claws began their work, tearing through my leather vest, into the flesh of my back. I hugged its body tighter so it couldn't obtain leverage against me. Its hind legs raked my thighs and sliced my trousers. I stabbed blindly with my spear, slicing the air, then felt the drum-tight resistance of flesh. I shoved and twisted the weapon, sinking it in.

The cat's agonized screech echoed from the trees but was quickly lapped up by the breeze. It wrenched the leafy branch from my grip and spread its mouth. I reached in, snatched its tongue, and yanked. A quick reaction, as if my body knew what to do. Its teeth clamped down, but too late. The bite struck only the side of my hand. Still, it severed my little finger and tore it off. I tightened my grip on the tongue, as if my only hope of salvation. The cat bucked and turned away, but I clamped on with both hands and heaved. Its paws sliced my back, but I tugged till the long, slender muscle tore free like a rotten rope. The top of it the rough texture of sharkskin.

The demonic animal fell limp upon me, its slashing stilled. Blood gushed upon my neck. I shoved it away and the body rolled flaccidly. It struggled to its paws, a white bone jutting from one front leg. Must've broken it when we landed. My spear protruded from the soft underbelly. It coughed and convulsed, then collapsed again.

I crawled toward it. The lean, muscled stomach rose and fell in quick pants as I yanked the stick from its side.

Again, its words rang in my head. *Arrogant fool! Death of this form means nothing to one such as I.*

I jammed the spear into its chest. Gripping the shaft with both hands, I drove it through the rib cage and into the earth below till only a short, bloody, splintered grip was visible. Two warm jets of blood splashed my eye, then ceased.

"Empty threat," I mumbled.

I fell upon my belly, wheezing, inhaling pine and earth. Blood flowed from the panther's ruined mouth and sank through the matted forest floor. The crimson fluid disappeared without pooling, the earth drinking it greedily.

I levered myself up to one knee and glanced at my own body. Nine fingers remained, but all seemed to still work. The panther's bite had removed only the last digit on my left hand, though it had perforated and torn the meaty part of it as well. Blood oozed from several long, jagged slices down my buttocks, but the wounds were skin deep most their length. The thick leather of my vest and heavy fabric trousers had done their job and taken the bulk of the damage. I yanked off a narrow slice and tightened a tourniquet near the stump of my little finger.

At last I stood on shaking legs and glanced about, wondering if Gabby would show again. "*Now* what are you going to throw at me?" I taunted.

Nothing stirred.

She could've at least warned her brother of what to expect. Something like, *Hey, right after I blow you a kiss, a huge, talking black panther is going to try and rip your head off.* All I'd gotten was some babbling about a red sea urchin, and the scent of maple sap. If I ever returned to my normal body, I'd never be able to eat pancakes again.

The wind howling through the trees calmed, as if it had risen to merely muffle the ruckus of the fight. A soft breeze remained and wafted mint, blood, and feces. The scents of the earlier battle when Indian and Vestman had fallen alike on the muddy streamside trail. Cicadas moaned, and a barred owl sounded its lonesome call. Its mate returned it, far across the meadow, from the direction of the Mi'kmaq camp.

The skin on my neck crawled, as with ants. Kiona would be leading the escape any minute. *You might not make it to the village,* Gabby had said.

Wrong again, sis.

Chapter 30 – White-Muzzle

Kiona cracked an eye open and peered across glowing coals. Mother lay on the far side of the small fire, but tonight her back was to it. The dim orange glow danced anew upon on her straight, shiny black hair. Her breathing was deep, slow, and even. The exhaustion of smoking and chanting all last night, seeking her spirits' favor for the protection of the tribe, had finally taken its toll. Dreaming was the only time she ever seemed at peace, and even then, her lips quivered restlessly. A leather sleep-wrap covered her hips and legs, but the tall, slender grace of her runner's form was still evident. A beautiful woman, outwardly. But inside...

Kiona stood slowly. She picked her way across the wetuom and slipped outside into the cool night air. The glowing eyes of the Star People winked down at her afresh, no doubt curious to see if her plan would succeed. Huritt's battle wounds had been minor, so he was still able to stand guard over Astrid tonight.

She jogged between wigwams, toward the center of the village, moccasined feet padding silently upon the trail. Passing many huts, she finally reached the expansive grassy common area at the center of the village. Children playing and men bartering in daytime, now it lay empty, eerily silent in the cool dark. The chief's longhouse stretched the entire length of one side. The neighboring wigwam was covered in birch bark, darkened with age, sloughed shingles strewn about it, as if the hut suffered from a wasting disease. Its dome-shaped roof leaned precariously forward, like a tired woman warming herself at the guard's fire smoldering before it. Each spring after migration, braves would splint up each structure's skeletal framing and cover cracks in the skin with fresh bark or grass mats, ensuring all were weathertight. But with so many injured by the recent battle, the huts would likely display winter's wounds for months. Crooked-Eye stood on one side of the door, Huritt the other. Both warriors gripped short spears, the ones carried when among the village.

Kiona ducked into the shadowy doorway of an empty hut and peered out. She pressed the knuckles of her thumbs together, held them to her lips, and, mimicking a mockingbird wooing a mate, blew the slow, rolling call of the bobwhite. Then the cardinal's clipped chirp. It was a grand imitation, but she made sure to hold the notes a bit too long. She needed to sound like a flawed imitation.

Crooked-Eye turned to the song and held his spear in front of him. Huritt glanced about, then smacked Crooked-Eye on the side of the skull with a fist-sized rock. The guard's legs collapsed and he dropped like a deer pierced with a well-placed arrow. Huritt grabbed the brave and quickly dragged him inside.

Kiona followed. "Did you kill him?"

Huritt lay the guard upon a mat, to one side of the door. "No. He will wake soon." He turned to Astrid, now scrambling to her feet, and drew a flint knife from his belt. He smiled, slipped the blade between her wrists, and sawed through her leather bindings. He sliced the tether near her neck, leaving only the strap as a collar.

She placed her forehead against his and stroked his cheek.

Kiona pointed to the door. "We need to go!"

He pulled away and stepped outside. Ambling to one side, displaying an air of boredom, he turned. Then his slow footfalls came from behind the wigwam, but quickened as he suddenly sprinted away.

Astrid squatted next to Crooked-Eye. With trembling hands, she snatched his spear from the ground. "Where's Huritt going?" she whispered.

"Scouting the trail."

A minute later, he stood in the doorway again. "It's clear."

They slipped out of the crumbling hut, past the dying guard fire, toward the eastern trail. Huritt ran ahead, Astrid keeping pace so closely her feet threatened to trip him. Kiona trailed them both, glancing behind to ensure that no one followed. One of Crooked-Eye's feet jutted from the door opening. Huritt hadn't pulled him far enough inside. But no matter. They'd be under the protection of the forest by the time he awoke and figured out what had happened. Trackers would follow in the morning, but by then they'd have escaped.

The field of tall grass surrounding the village stood like a rolling black wave ready to crash ashore. Over its silver starlit blades danced thousands of lightning bugs, swirling and flashing and swooping. As if the Star People had come down from heaven to welcome them.

Huritt ran toward the wide trail through the meadow. Matok would be hiding somewhere in the grass next to it.

Ahead, two tall, dark shapes stepped into their path. One looked female, with thick hair cascading to her knees. The other was a warrior gripping a spear, upright, not aimed in outward threat. Huritt brought their group to a halt three strides away.

"Stop this foolishness," ordered Mother's voice. She shrugged a deerskin from her shoulders and it dropped to the ground. Her bed covering, not hair.

"Take the prisoner back, Huritt," boomed the deep voice of Great Scout, who stood next to her. His words sharp, edged with threat.

Huritt stepped in front of Astrid and leveled his spear. "No. Imprisoning the innocent is evil. We do this for the sake of the tribe."

Mother raised an arm to point a slender finger at Astrid. "I will tell you what is evil, young brave. The way her kind steal and enslave us. It is not evil to protect your tribe. Your family. That's all we've done. She is our peace gift. The spirits told me to take her, and the family elders agreed. The fire-haired demon-girl has placed you under her curse. You've been tricked."

No. Gifts aren't stolen. Imprisoning Astrid would not maintain peace. Mother was trying to twist the Three Truths to her own advantage. To cover a rotten stick with new bark.

The shadow of a man approached, running toward them through the meadow, behind Mother and Great Scout. Dots of light flickered and scattered as he passed. He held a round shield across his chest. Matok! He slipped into the grass at the edge of the meadow, limping.

Mother stepped toward Huritt, within striking distance. A show of trust, meant to engender the same toward her. Kiona was used to such tactics.

"You've been deceived, Huritt," the shaman said. "Which is why you see no braves with us. You and Kiona have been lied to. If you take the prisoner back, no elders will know."

Huritt twisted the spear in his grasp, as if considering his options.

Don't believe her.

Starlight glinted upon Mother's teeth, revealed by her smiling lips. "You're thinking about how you erred. How you struck the other guard. Don't worry. We'll tell him you both were attacked, and you stole the enemy back. You won't be remembered as a traitor, but a hero. For protecting our prisoner."

Huritt rolled his shoulders forward. He growled, "She has a name. *Astrid.* Do not make me do this."

A gentle gust blew Mother's hair, whipping it across her face. The meadow behind them flashed to life as more lightning bugs glowed and flickered in the rising breeze, trying to orient themselves in the turbulent current.

Great Scout lifted his spear but only held it loosely at his hip, pointed toward Astrid. "You're a warrior, my son. Even now, a skilled brave. We all serve a master. Choose whom you serve. The spirits of our ancestors, or the demons of this invader."

The tendons on the back of Huritt's hand stood straight, like the shafts of cattails. Readying for a strike.

Mother stepped between the two. "No need for this. Kiona, see what trouble you've begun? You started this. Only you can end it." She held out both hands. "Come home with me, and all will be forgiven. The prisoner will be cared for. We have done her no harm."

Kiona glanced at Huritt, whose gaze was fixed on his father's spear. Great Scout had often instructed the braves, saying, *Watch your enemy's weapon, not his eyes. His gaze cannot kill you.* If Kiona persisted in her rebellion, Huritt or Great Scout would be injured. Possibly killed. A family torn apart. Was it worth it? Was it right to destroy one life to save another?

She glanced at Astrid, who stood behind Huritt, his knife clutched in one hand. Her eyes were hard and dark, but the reflection of the firefly light burned in them. Her shoulders drooped. She lowered her blade. "It's OK, Huritt," she said. "I'd rather be your tribe's prisoner than have you fight your father."

Such a pure heart. Astrid wished to maintain peace, even at the cost of her own freedom. How was it the prisoner was concerned with keeping the Three Truths and Mother was not? Keeping Astrid captive was no good. The evils faced now would only be delayed. They would return later, stronger. Great Scout had been right. Tonight, they must choose.

Kiona gripped the antler handle and drew her own flint blade from her belt. She pressed her thumb against the nub and pointed the knife toward Mother. "Your spirits tell you to do things that break the Three Truths. They destroy peace. They bring no life. Only darkness, disease, and death."

Mother's shoulders sagged. She stepped back to stand next to Great Scout. Partly behind him, as if shielding herself. Mother, at a loss for words? She would never back down so easily. Surely Kiona's speech hadn't scared her.

Warm fur brushed Kiona's bare leg. She glanced down and gasped. A huge gray wolf with a white muzzle and broad head stood next to her, its shoulders almost to her hips. The hair along its neck and back stood in a ridge, but it didn't growl. Its coat bristled, thick and healthy, as if still anticipating the cold of winter. She jumped back, but the animal didn't attack. It stared balefully at Mother.

"I'm proud of you, daughter," Mother said as she withdrew another pace. "Why didn't you tell me the spirits had begun to visit you? Let me teach you their ways. With my help, you will grow in understanding." She turned in place, arms stretched toward the surrounding huts. "You can help protect our people."

Another wolf, almost as large as the first, trotted from behind a wigwam and came to stand next to Huritt. The warrior slowly inched away. He pointed his spear at the animal, then glanced nervously to Kiona before returning his gaze to the weapon held by his father. He whispered from the side of his mouth, "Kiona, what are you doing?"

She wasn't, as far as she knew. From where were these wolves appearing? No spirits had ever visited her. Were they spirits at all? None of Mother's stories had included these animals. *Wolves have dark souls*, she'd always said. Maybe they were a bold pack on the hunt.

"I'm impressed with your powers, daughter. But do not be foolish." Mother's voice had taken on the grating edge of fear. "You see now this battle is not between our families, but among the spirits. You are being led astray by evil, the demons of the prisoner. Rule your own spirits. Let me help you control them." She held her hands toward her, pleading, all the while inching away.

Another wolf peered out from between two huts. A half dozen more trotted from between the wetuoms and down the various trails. A black pair flanked Astrid, hair along their back erect, like a shark's dorsal fin, teeth bared, but silent. *These* must *be spirits.* There was no other explanation. All of them glared at Mother. But why? She was the shaman. Perhaps their rescue of Astrid had triggered a spiritual war. Yet, it was Mother who had broken the Three Truths. So...these wolf-spirits *were* truth, and Mother was the enemy. Her spirits, demons. Followers of Malsumis. It finally made sense!

White-Muzzle loosed a quiet, low growl. A faint rumble that seemed to drop from the sky upon her shoulders. A slender wolf near Great Scout licked its jowls. Mother laid a hand on the warrior's shoulder. "We must go"—she said, glancing warily at the four-legged army about them—"for the protection of the tribe." As they retreated, she called back, voice thick, as if clogged with tears, "You made your choice, daughter. There can now be no mercy."

Once the pair was out of sight, the wolves bolted toward the eastern trail.

Kiona cried and broke into a sprint after them. "Follow them!"

Huritt and Astrid chased after her, his heavy steps thudding like the gait of a bear. But just past the trailhead, the pack of wolves skidded to a halt. White-Muzzle panted and whimpered.

"Why are they stopping now?" Astrid asked, heaving.

"I don't know," Kiona managed between breaths.

A rustle in the grass. Huritt stepped in front of Astrid again, his bulk shielding her. Matok limped from the dark meadow. In the sudden confusion with the wolves, Kiona had forgotten he was there.

Huritt leveled his spear at him. "We cannot trust this one. He probably told Mother of our escape."

Kiona jumped between them. "Don't be foolish." She pointed down the trail. "We need to go."

"He is not coming with us."

Matok clenched his fist and raised his shield. "Get moving. You have no idea what I just went through to get here. Killing you would be easy as..." He fell silent and his body swayed, as if he was about to pass out.

Astrid peered around her protector. "Brother!" She forced her way past. They hadn't mentioned Matok's involvement, to spare her the anxiety. Astrid wrapped her arms about his waist and squeezed. His face brightened, but he rocked on his feet. He leaned upon her, as if too exhausted to stand.

White-Muzzle licked his nose, whimpered, then the pack bounded down the trail again.

Chapter 31 – Another Must Die

I woke to the scent of warm earth and the stench of old sweat. Stiff fur rubbed one cheek. A fire snapped and crackled nearby. *Again.*

I bolted upright.

I sat inside Spear-Face's wigwam, on the same bushy fur rug. Same tawny mound of skins across from a tiny twig fire. But the green vine climbing the bark wall had grown. It now reached the smoke hole in the ceiling and had budded into a melon-sized clump of white, star-shaped flowers. The angle of the sun through the opening evidenced late afternoon.

Outside, Spear-Face's playful voice sang out. "It's awake!" Leaves crunched near the door. The room darkened as Kiona and Spear-Face struggled through the narrow opening simultaneously. "Let me in," she said, gently pulling the skinny man behind her.

She dropped to her knees next to me, jostling the bison skin, sending a knife of pain through my skull. I winced.

"You're hurting," she said, placing a palm upon my cheek. Her gentle touch almost made me forget the migraine's blade inside my head.

Spear-Face stepped through now, then turned toward the doorway. "It need water!" Heavy footfalls hurried away, Huritt by the weight of their pounding. The medicine man turned back to me, standing below the white flowers, tattooed spears dancing upon his cheeks and forehead as he smiled and blinked. "Where it hurt?"

Kiona scowled. "Stop calling him *it*, Grandfather. Why do you do that?"

The spears stilled. "I found it...found *him* in the woods. I thought he was a spirit. Or a batsolowanagwes."

She snorted. "He is none of those."

The tattooed weapons skipped again. "Where do you hurt?"

When I rolled stiff shoulders, the gashes on my back screamed. A searing burn ran the length of my spine and sharp pain filled the wounds, as if reopening. Thighs and buttocks complained of the same sensations. My body was angry with me.

My vest lay folded near the far wall beneath the shaft of the vine, brown bloodstains where the cat's claws had sliced. A doeskin blanket covered me below my waist. Whoever said that what doesn't kill you makes you stronger had obviously never been mauled by a black panther.

Opening my eyes intensified the headache. Still, I managed to focus on Spear-Face. "A better question would be, where don't I hurt."

He held out a sand-colored wooden bowl to Kiona. She gave it to me. A brown liquid sloshed near the rim. The cup was warm, as if it had been sitting near a fire. Fine wood slivers swirled near the bottom. "What is this?" I asked.

Kiona stared, as if surprised I didn't know. "Willow bark, of course."

"You want me to put it on my cuts?"

Her eyes dimmed. She stroked my cheek. "No, silly. Drink it."

Spear-Face's medicine had certainly helped earlier, so I drank. The earthy taste was both bitter and mildly sweet. Halfway through, I realized how thirsty I was and finished off the cup, even slurping up the wood chips to suck out their moisture. Huritt's bulk filled the doorframe, and he passed a skin-colored sack to me, the same one Spear-Face had given me on my earlier visit. I slugged down the water, and the toothy grip of the migraine began to relax. My stomach soured, presumably from the medicine, but didn't make me nauseous.

Spear-Face smiled and took back the empty waterskin. "Willow bark help with pain from cuts. Water take away headache."

Huritt retreated outside, uncovering a thin, pale-faced girl behind him. A healthy crop of sun freckles spotted the nubs of her cheeks and the bridge of her nose so tightly, they resembled the mask of a racoon. Thick, curly red hair fell in wild locks to her shoulders.

"Gabby?" I threw back the deerskin blanket, jumped to my feet, hopped over the fire, and wrapped arms around her narrow shoulders, my own hair cascading about her face. She hugged me, though timidly, probably not wanting to open the wounds on my back. They burned, and my thighs screamed in protest at the new movements, but I didn't care. True, she wasn't Gabby. But Astrid could've been her twin, and I was just as happy to see her. Unable to enjoy our victory last night, I reveled in it now.

I freed her from my embrace and glanced at Kiona, still kneeling next to where I had lain, straight black hair falling gracefully to curvy hips. A playful smirk on her thin lips I hadn't seen before.

"Yes! A tough badger," Spear-Face exclaimed. "He'll make a fine brave, granddaughter." His head bobbed playfully. He beamed a full, yellow-toothed smile and pointed at me.

I glanced down and my stomach knotted. I stood next to the dim fire, naked. Not wearing a stitch of skins, except my own. I cupped myself and hopped over the small blaze, then snatched up the doeskin and wrapped it back around me. Was that disappointment on Kiona's face? I grabbed my shredded vest, but the trousers weren't hidden below it.

Kiona held them out to me on open palms, the garment folded. Tidy stitches of thin leather mended the slashes the cat had inflicted.

"Thank you." I nodded, accepting her gift. Then I stood in embarrassed silence while everyone stared at me. Privacy apparently wasn't held in esteem by either Vestmen or Indians. So I turned my back, dropped the blanket, and quickly pulled on the stiff pants. They clung to my thighs, heavy with moisture, recently washed.

A chill shot up my back and I spun around. Kiona stood behind me, a fat length of aloe leaf in her hand, squeezing the clear juice from the triangular stem onto one finger.

"Turn back."

I did, and she worked the gel gently into other gouges in my flesh. As she rubbed, she relayed the events of last night, none of which I remembered.

I had been in a trance, she claimed. But I figured it was probably a state of semiconsciousness induced by blood loss and dehydration. Once out of the meadow, the wolves had headed north and we'd followed them all night. Huritt had carried me much of the way. The pack had gradually thinned as wolves ran off. By dawn, they'd all disappeared. As the last one dashed out of sight, we'd been standing before Spear-Face's wigwam.

I flinched at the sting as she rubbed aloe into a painful, deep wound. "So, you met your grandfather?"

She applied the sticky substance into another long cut that ended near my waist. "Yes. He told me everything. The parts you left out. How Mother killed his wife. Her own mother." Her caress stopped. "Thank you for not telling me. It was better it came from him. I wouldn't have believed you." She reached around and pulled at the belt-string of my trousers.

I snatched the waistband before they dropped. "I'll...do my legs myself. Thank you."

Another moment of awkward silence. Finally, everyone got the hint and ducked outside.

Spear-Face stepped under the door flap and his playful voice trailed away. "Yes, a strong badger and fine brave. But Kiona can't even get his trousers off."

"Grandfather!" she scolded, sounding shocked.

I smirked, then let the pants fall. I grabbed another aloe leaf from a neat pile near the fire and glanced over my body. The hole in my thigh from the arrow was healing nicely, but still stung. I rubbed the sore lump that crowned my temple where Kiona had knocked me unconscious. A neat slice ran across my belly where her blade had nearly ended my life. Now, fresh claw wounds raked along my back and thighs, and my mangled hand was missing part of a little finger.

If I ever got home, if the real Matok returned, for the rest of his life the poor soul would wonder what had happened to his body. The thought jolted me. With Astrid freed, would Gabby end this journey now? Was my work here finally complete? The idea of leaving somehow pained my thoughts even more than the slices did my back. This world, though dangerous and violent, allured me nonetheless. Like the vine above my head, climbing toward the smoke hole, sprouting blooms, I had found light in this dark place. Kiona, and friends. A sister, but yet not my sister. Even a schizophrenic medicine man. I'd miss all their company. And here, I was stronger. Confident. Bold. Maybe I could stay...

I tugged on thick leather boots and slipped the vest over my head. My headache had retreated, but the stiff garment irritated the wounds on my back. When I turned, Huritt stood inside the door, club in hand, blocking the way. He hulked even larger than I remembered, his face stern and sharp. His hair hung in a single tight braid down his neck. That was new.

"If you hurt them, I will kill you," he said flatly.

"Who?" I asked, surprised at his turn of favor. His expression had been bright just moments earlier.

He glanced to the side, in the direction the others had retreated. "Any of them. Even the crazy old man."

"They mean a lot to you?"

"They are my only family now."

"And Astrid?"

He reached behind his neck to stroke his braid. "My wife."

"Ah." I smiled and slapped his shoulder. "Then I'd expect nothing less."

He studied the reddening skin where I'd smacked him. The expression of male endearment apparently unfamiliar. I'd have to be clearer. "I'm sorry you lost your family, but happy you have a new one." His tense jaw softened, but his expression quickly regained an edge.

We walked outside and Astrid stepped up next to me, slipping an arm gently around my waist. Her soft, rapid words flew like a flapping bat. "Brother, where are the others? We can't stay here. It's still too close to the Mi'kmaq village. Is Halfdan here, or did Father put you in charge of the raid? How is Mother? I'm certain she's worried to a fever. But we can't go back now—I married Huritt last night. Father would make me marry Halfdan. He's mean as a viper and stinks like a sheep. And the women of the clan say he couldn't produce a child if he ate all the oysters in the ocean. I'm so glad you're feeling better. Who clawed you like that? You slept such a long time, trackers are probably only a few hours away. If they find Kiona's grandfather, they'll kill him. We need to move and bring him along. So, where are you taking us?"

My head ached again. I pinched the bridge of my nose. Astrid *was* Gabby's twin, at least in tongue. God help Huritt...

I cracked an eye to look at her. "Congratulations on your marriage. Did you stop talking long enough to consummate it?"

She flushed, but one corner of her mouth turned up.

I gave her a hug as my back screamed in protest. "I have just as many questions for you." I'd imagined once we'd rescued Astrid, I'd find myself back to my own time, as abruptly as I'd been brought here. So, maybe my mission *was* to return her to the Vestmen. But no. She had a new life now, with Huritt. And we certainly couldn't return to his tribe. And I couldn't make sense of the cryptic guidance Gabby had given about a red sea urchin.

Spear-Face sat on the bare dirt between two towering pines, a mound of cold black coals before him. He pointed to a smooth log, and I gingerly sat in a crook, avoiding resting upon the cuts on my butt.

"Tell us what attacked you," he said.

Astrid sat next to me and leaned in to listen. When I spoke to her, my words came out in Norse. Kiona translated for Spear-Face and Huritt as I related the story of the fight with the demon-cat. When I got to the part about climbing the tree after it, Spear-Face hopped up, covered his ears, and ordered, "Speak no more." He trotted off, only to return a few minutes later and ask me to continue. His schizophrenic antagonist remained mute, perhaps no longer needed with so much real company. Even his speech grew in coherency as he spoke with us.

I ended the tale, repeating the beast's last threats as it died, to kill Kiona and Astrid. And that death meant nothing to him, as if he meant to return.

Huritt puckered his lips and nodded contemplatively. Astrid gazed intently at me, smiling, and now so close she was nearly in my lap. But the tanned skin of both Kiona and Spear-Face had washed pallid.

The medicine man crossed his arms as if hugging himself. He rocked back and forth. "Assassin take form of black panther. The darkest spirit." He glanced at Kiona, whose jaw was tight and eyes wide. "Not even your mother could summon this demon."

She laid a hand on his shoulder. "Mother said a black panther killed you, Grandmother, and Father. That the same animal bit off her hand. Was that a lie too?"

Spear-Face continued rocking, as if soothing a crying baby. "I flee by then. Your mother's spirits too powerful for her to control. Many of them demons." A tear ran down the long shaft of a tattooed spear. "She was a happy child, before spirits spoke to her. Now I am worried for another shaman."

Kiona backed away. "Mother only thinks the spirits speak to me. They don't. Those wolves we told you about, I didn't call them. None of us knows where they came from."

Spear-Face stilled, thoughtful, as if contemplating a revelation. "Your mother right about war between the spirits. But not hers and yours." He turned to stare at me. "Panthers are solitary and selfish. Wolves are noble. Give one's life for the pack. We cannot stay here. Mi'kmaq will come for their prisoner and Kiona. *You* know where we must go."

But, wasn't this where Gabby had led us, even if using wolves? Shouldn't we stay here?

He stretched out an arm toward me, fingers splayed and curved like claws. "White-Muzzle came to protect you, young shaman."

I rubbed a painful slice in my thigh. "Then he showed up a bit late."

He blinked quickly, the spearheads on his forehead danced, and his eyes sparkled in the sunlight. "The fight with the panther was for you alone." He leaned forward and his gaze darkened. "But White-Muzzle not act on his own. He sent by another. The spirits are at war. Do you see any now, young shaman?"

I glanced around, but no wolves. No Gabby. And I was certainly no shaman, but that wasn't worth arguing. "None."

He straightened fingers and thumped them against my chest. "Then *you* must lead us. You bringing sister back from prison. Back from death. If you wish her to live, another must die. It is the law."

Chapter 32 – Second Visit

Cresting a hill, I climbed to a broad boulder and leaned against a thin pine sprouting from a dirt-packed fissure that ran down its center. Rocky ground fell away before me. Cool night air swept up the slope, blowing my hair back from my shoulders. Stony earth below provided little purchase for tree roots, stunting vegetation, and allowed a panoramic view of the broad valley ahead. The dim orange glow of dawn burned from behind a far ridge, like the radiance of a distant wildfire. The same wide creek upon which I'd rowed with the Vestmen in the longboat when we first penetrated this untamed country curved across the landscape. Waning stars and strengthening dawn reflected upon its shimmering surface as it flashed and danced, a silver ribbon through the rugged land.

But the valley and meadow below still lay in darkness, save the red dots of campfires near the river. It was the gentle bend in the stream where the Abenaki village sprawled on a low bank. The scene reminiscent of how the Mi'kmaq camp was situated, the same flowing waters providing nourishment for them both. The hushed rasp of light breathing, gentle crunch of pine needles, and the *thump-thump* of a walking stick approached from behind me. Everyone had maintained a good pace during our trek. Especially Spear-Face, who'd plodded steadily with his long strides, smiling as Astrid chattered beside him incessantly, despite how he understood nothing she said. Embarking yesterday evening from his hut, we'd traveled all night.

Kiona came to stand next to me. She raised her chin to a rush of wind, as if scenting the breeze. Dawn's glow sparkled in her onyx eyes. "We would have made better time if we'd taken the streamside trail."

I glanced toward the water. "Yes. But the Abenaki have lookouts stationed there. I'm hoping to avoid a warrior's welcome."

Her gaze followed the river as well. "They have lookouts stationed many places. We may meet such a fate regardless."

I cinched the leather strap tight that fastened my shield to my back. I gripped a thick maple branch the length of my arm, a knot crowning its end, a makeshift club. It was my only weapon since the demon-cat had wrenched the axes from my grasp in the darkness. Kiona stepped nearer and leaned her head against my chest. Her skin brushed smooth and soft, still warm from the walk. I wrapped an arm around her shoulder.

I hadn't yet told her how I wasn't from this world. But I needed to, and would soon, for if I was called back to my own time, I supposed she'd be left with the real Matok. How sad that would be. He would have no recollection of her. But I certainly could never forget. Who knew. Maybe I would just stay here. For now, I simply enjoyed her warmth.

But uncertainty stalked my mind. Would the Abenaki provide us protection? Even with the family connection to their shaman, Kiona her niece and Spear-Face her father, their acceptance wasn't a certainty. Gabby had said, *You know where to take her*, speaking of Astrid. The Abenaki camp had seemed like the logical choice, but it was also our only option. Still, was this what Gabby had meant? Why couldn't she communicate more clearly? She loved irritating me as much in her afterlife as when she'd still been alive.

For a few minutes, all of us stood together and gazed at the rising sun, its brilliance warming our cheeks. Finally, Spear-Face pointed his long walking stick toward the village and hopped like an excited toddler. "I want to see my daughter."

We picked our way single file down the rocks and through a towering pine forest, finally breaking into the low meadow that surrounded the Abenaki village. The clearing was modest in size compared to that of the Mi'kmaq. But unlike that camp, newer bark and animal hides covered these wigwams. Still, their numbers appeared to be about half. Spear-Face quickened his pace and led our troop, high-stepping like a drum major at a parade.

We traveled down a narrow path through low grass. A hundred yards from the cluster of dwellings there came a grating call from the village, like the shriek of a tortured rooster. Spear-Face froze and held his walking stick over his head. I slipped the shield from my back. Huritt stepped next to me. A dozen warriors with spears and clubs poured out of wigwams from either end of the village. They formed two parties and sprinted toward us, whooping and leaping like deer. Faces were blue, red, and green. And each strained to outrun his brother to reach us first, eager for battle. I turned one way and Huritt the other, creating a barrier between the raiding parties and our own. Spear-Face stood alone, statue-like, fifty feet ahead of us.

The warriors fanned out and closed in as one man, quick and synchronized. No escape. As they neared, they raised spears to strike. My hand closed around the grip of my club, wishing it were an axe. Their angry calls squawked like a flock of startled birds. Faces grimaced in hate. They'd expected us.

A high-pitched whistle rose from behind them and the warriors stopped. Their breathing was labored from the run. Sweat sharpened the already close air. A small one, with two red stripes down his chin, as if to resemble dripping blood, sneered and turned the shaft of his spear in his grasp. He didn't like being halted. The others stared at him, as if he was their leader. If so, then who had called them off?

Another group approached from the village. A pair. A flabby warrior with jiggling flesh rolls dangling from his arms, and their crazy shaman, the one who'd asked me for a blessing earlier, after she'd grabbed my crotch and the creepy sensation of an ice-cold spider had crawled up my windpipe. The same mask of woven brown grass covered her eyes, and wrinkled cheeks smiled from beneath. She stopped in front of me and waved an arm overhead, then laid a flat palm on my shield. She stared at it, as if mesmerized by its pattern. With a black, pointed fingernail, she traced its circular band of blue, recognition creasing her eyes. She reached up and pulled off her woven cover as she had first back in the chief's wigwam. The fat warrior next to her raised a flat-bladed hand, protecting his view from her face.

I lowered my shield.

The wrinkles in her skin seemed deeper than before, each highlighted by tan dust settled into the creases. She smiled, and her eyebrows seemed to dance, like Spear-Face. She stepped closer, slipped her hand between the flaps of my vest, and traced the same finger across my chest, gently scratching my skin, from one shoulder to the other, tattoo of Thor's hammer to the cross.

Her breath was rosemary, as if she'd been chewing the pungent herb. "Have you chosen, young warrior?"

The faint scraping of her nails made my neck crawl. I maneuvered the shield between us, covering my waist, in case she grabbed for my crotch again. "Decided what?"

"Which master you serve?"

Red-Stripe glowered, but it wasn't their intention to kill us or they would have done it. We were woefully outnumbered. And as for this shaman, Gabby's riddles were quite enough for me. I didn't need this creepy lady adding to them. But we also needed her tribe's acceptance, and their protection. It was essential I tread lightly.

I answered, "I serve no master."

All five sharp nails slid down my chest and pressed against my sternum, but they didn't break skin. No ice spider crawled up my throat this time. So...progress. Maybe.

"Then your master has chosen you. We knew of your approach. Do you know how?"

I glanced at Astrid. "I'd guess you were told by the same red-haired spirit that visited you earlier. One that looks a lot like her?"

The shaman tapped the cross on my shoulder. She leaned closer, as if not wanting her guard to overhear. I flinched as her nails began to sink into my skin. "No. Because my spirits left again. They flee when you approach."

I inched back, away from her claws. "Sorry they went away, but I don't have anything to do with that."

She closed the gap between us and stood on her tiptoes, as if to kiss me. Her next words were clipped. "An assassin, a black panther, told me he would quiet my spirits if I kill you. Yet, they flee when you are near. I don't know whether you are a blessing or a curse." Her gaze drifted to my shoulder. She dropped her hand at last, and I drew a breath of relief. She strolled around me, but I stared at the red-striped warrior, spear still cocked. Her finger traced the slice of one of the tears in the back of my vest. "The assassin found you, it seems."

"He killed the panther," Kiona said flatly.

Suddenly, the old woman screamed. When I turned, the two were locked in a struggle, tearing at each other's hair. Kiona spun as the shorter woman crawled upon her back. A spear thudded into my shield. Another landed at my feet. The flabby bodyguard whooped and rushed between us, yanking at Kiona's arm. At a sharp word from the shaman, he dropped his head and backed away.

"Niece!" she shouted. "Your mother's twin!" A single tear wet her wrinkled cheek as the two whirled and hugged. So, they hadn't been fighting. Kiona lowered her aunt and tore herself free. She pointed at Spear-Face, still standing with walking stick raised over his head.

The old woman had been so preoccupied with my shield, she apparently hadn't noticed him or Kiona. She rubbed an eye with a knuckle. "Father?"

He dropped to his knees and opened his arms. Even so, he was still taller than the diminutive shaman. He blinked, playful eyes glistening and spears dancing upon on his forehead.

She charged and bowled him over into the grass. As the long-lost father and daughter hugged and wept, the warriors surrounding us slowly lowered their weapons. Even Red-Stripe's expression softened. The pair stood, giggling. She, short and wrinkled. He, tall. And, though furrowed skin covered his face, she could have passed for his parent instead of the other way around. Shamans must lead a hard life.

Whenever she faced their direction, the warriors glanced away nervously. She said, "Rimlaw insisted you were dead."

He straightened to his full height. "To you, daughter, I had to be dead. So that today I could live again." He stroked her gray-streaked hair. "I could not endanger your family, or your new tribe."

She turned her head and regarded me. Even her cheeks smiled as she stared. When she grinned, the slope of her almond-shaped eyes and sharp set of her jaw evidenced his paternity.

She stepped before me. "I sent you to certain death. But you returned with your life, and mine as well." Her gaze drifted to Huritt and his long ponytail, his body shielding Astrid from the warriors. Then to Kiona and me. Her eyes widened as another flash of recognition shot across her face. She rushed to Kiona and grabbed her hands. "And you are married!" She plucked at the seams of her niece's dress and stretched it tight against her flat belly. "But your hips have born no children." Her voice dropped in low conspiracy. "I will make you a tea that will—"

Kiona brushed the shaman's hands away. "Aunt. We're not married."

The old woman glanced at me and squinted. "Then what is wrong with him?"

"No. He's only...helping us. He led us here. But, no. We aren't married."

The old woman gave another wrinkled smirk. "Then we will seek the chief's approval. The ceremony will be tonight."

With a nod, she turned her back to Kiona and grabbed my arm. "Apprentice, you must meet your other Vestmen. The chief has not killed them yet."

Apprentice? *Why do these Indians always think I want to become a witch doctor?* "There're more of us here?"

She lifted her mask from the ground and set it back upon her head, concealing her expression. "Oh, yes. Several."

My chest tightened. "The leader? The angry man with white hair?"

"No. Rebels. They fled him, or so they claim."

A seagull called from above the river, but when I looked, the sky was empty. My stomach knotted with cold dread. Maybe the bird had merely flown out of sight behind the trees, but it had sounded just like Gabby's laugh. Was she going to take me back now? Just when I wanted to stay? Or was another evil waiting?

The shaman tugged my arm again. The wounds on my back and buttocks burned as I walked next to her. A chill breeze carried the scent of honeysuckle. No, something subtler. Something about my own grandfather. And duck hunting...maple sap!

In the distance, a brave darted from the cover of the woods into the meadow, running down the streamside trail. One arm pumped furiously; the other clutched the shaft of an arrow impaled into his shoulder, it's fletching the same blue as those that had flown at us from the forest during the Mi'kmaq ambush. The enemy hadn't wasted time finding us.

I yanked the spear free from where it had pierced my shield and pointed it toward the approaching lookout. Catching Red-Stripe's eye, I shouted, "Ready every brave. Now!"

Chapter 33 – No Barter

I shoved Kiona toward the Abenaki village. "Go! Take Astrid. Get safe."

Red-Stripe turned to a lanky brave behind him who, cupping hands to mouth, sounded a shrill, warbling whistle. The camp burst like ants escaping rising waters as villagers poured from wigwams. Women slung crying babies onto their backs and tugged the arms of toddlers. Men scrambled, grabbing spears, clubs, tomahawks, and flat-bladed weapons that resembled curved wooden swords. Children twisted among them, crying and dodging in attempts to avoid being trampled. Within seconds, their first warriors sprinted into the meadow.

Red-Stripe pointed his spear toward the river, calling, "Sibo! Sibo!" and two dozen turned in that direction, a lanky one missing an arm leading the pack. Red-Stripe held the spear overhead and called, "Ki kon! Ki kon!" and another group sprinted to us.

Kiona still stood, black eyes flecked with gold in the sun, grasping Astrid's hand, staring at the approaching men. The tiny old shaman shoved them toward the village, into the approaching whoop and thud of running braves. She shouted, "The chief will not surrender your friend."

Kiona pushed past her, grabbed my neck, and touched her forehead to my own. Then she and Astrid raced toward the village, the pair bounding like deer, Astrid hiking up her long dress to her knees, dodging the waves of warriors racing against them. Astrid smacked into one and he lifted her from the ground, thick, pale arms wrapped about her waist. *Tryfing!*

Huritt cocked his spear and charged, biceps knotted.

I chased, glad the man wasn't a swift runner. "He is a friend of Astrid. He won't hurt her."

Huritt slowed when Tryfing gently dropped Astrid to the ground and she shot toward the village again. Tryfing trotted toward us, unaware of the anger he'd stirred. Ten other shields ran beside him. The wild white hair of One-Eye bounced atop the rim of one. Tryfing stopped before me, face flush, beads of sweat forming in the cool morning air. "You're still... Are you..."

"The same," I said.

He grinned and jerked a thumb over his shoulder where Kiona disappeared around a wigwam. His voice conspiratorial. "You're more like Matok than you know. Gone a few days, slinking around the forest by yourself, and you *still* show up with a woman." He gripped my forearm and slapped my shoulder. "Where are your axes?"

I glanced at my empty belt. "There was this panther that—" Forget it. He'd never believe me.

He shook his head. "Same man. You'd lose your walnuts if they weren't strapped between your legs." He pursed his lips and gazed at the forest. "If Halfdan is leading the party, he won't raid right away. He'll give time to make us anxious. If not him, I can only guess."

A heat rose inside my lungs and burned my chest. I twisted the spear shaft within my grip. "Whoever it is, they're not waiting."

* * * *

Kiona and Astrid raced toward the wigwams. Astrid ran quickly, Kiona thought, especially considering Vestmen were so much slower than Mi'kmaq. To keep from being separated, the two grasped each other's hands as they wove between huts. A young boy shoved his way between them, chubby cheeks and stunted gait just like Nabid. But she ignored the ache in her chest. She might be able to see her little brother again, one day. *No*, that was her old family. The spirits would provide a new one. And already had. Grandfather, a wild shaman aunt, Astrid...and Matok. These were hers. Along with the tribe that dashed about them now, all because she had brought Astrid among them. When the Mi'kmaq attacked, many would die. Maybe Mother had been right and she should've left her friend as a prisoner. She glanced at Astrid, skin reddening to match her hair with her exertion. The life of one for the peace of all? *No*. One could not imprison the innocent without inviting evil any more than one could swallow a coal without being burned. The Three Truths: *Peace: Is this preserved? Righteousness: Is it moral? Power: Does it preserve the integrity of the tribe?* The spirits insisted on protecting the blameless.

The gaggle of women and children twisted down a maze of paths headed east, away from the meadow from where the injured lookout had appeared. All tribes had meeting places, where warriors would run after a battle to collect their families. Kiona needed to see where everyone was fleeing and find a family Astrid could follow to safety. Then she would make her way back to the meadow. She could hurl a spear better than many of the younger Mi'kmaq warriors.

A skinny boy with bony legs stumbled in the dust before them. She stopped and lifted him from the ground. Back on his feet, he stared with mouth agape, fear in his eyes, then tore off. Of course the village would be scared of her. She was Mi'kmaq, and Astrid a fire-haired an invader. There was no time for explanations now. Only fighting or fleeing.

"Wait!" she shouted. "You dropped your knife!" But it was too late. The child was already gone, lost in the knot of huts and hurry. She lifted the weapon from the dirt, a short blade of obsidian no longer than an arrowhead, bound with a leather tie to a wooden handle. An expensive knife, even though so small. She padded her leather belt, feeling the lump of her own flint blade beneath it, and held the weapon to Astrid. Huritt's larger knife was strapped in her belt, but small blades were useful. Astrid slipped it into a pocket, invisible along the seam of her dress.

A thick cloud of dust stirred by the tribe's commotion floated over the wetuoms like morning fog. Sunrise set it ablaze in a glare of bright yellow. Inside it, shadows of women and children shot about the murk. Fish swimming in muddy water. A girl ran past them into the haze and disappeared, swallowed whole. An eagle soared above, coldly observing the panic. The entire image surreal. Kiona had to make it through the confusion and get to the far side of the village. Then she could point Astrid in the right direction and return to the meadow. To Matok.

"What do we do?" Astrid asked, panting.

Kiona tightened her grip on her hand and bounded into the glaring dust, toward the rising sun. A scream sounded from ahead. A child. Or maybe a woman? Difficult to hear over the noise. Turning a corner, the pair ran headlong into a brave sprinting in the opposite direction.

"Sorry!" Kiona exclaimed, stunned, then stumbled aside to continue.

The brave matched her step. Kiona yielded again, but the warrior would not let them pass. She glanced up and, *Crooked-Eye!* A corner of his mouth curled devilishly. He grasped her wrists and spun her around, his grip welting her skin. She bucked and kicked, but he held her tight, pinning her arms by wrapping his own about her. He seemed stronger than even Huritt. He leaned to her ear and licked it, breath stinking of a rotting tooth. "No Mother to protect you now, traitorous whore. I told the tall Vestman I'd return and pleasure myself on your corpse. Time to make good on that word." He shoved her toward a wetuom, gripping her throat and pinning her close, locking her arms.

Astrid pounded his shoulder with her fist, but he marched, undaunted, toward the dark opening. *The knife!* she tried to yell, but she couldn't draw a breath.

"Look how the prisoner follows you, even to her death," he purred. "*She* is the prize. I'll enjoy the both of you, and be rewarded for it." Great Scout ran from the cloud and grabbed Astrid, pinning her arms to her body. Crooked-Eye stared at him, tongue flicking like a snake. Another brave, club in his grasp, shoved Crooked-Eye toward the meadow. As they walked, Crooked-Eye lifted Kiona's skirt and groped her thigh. His breath hot and putrid on her neck. "No matter. You will keep. I will have you."

* * * *

I studied the edge of the meadow, low grass disappearing into the forest of towering pines. A flick of white toward one end of the field, and a deer bounded away. Another stood at its edge, motionless, staring. A huge buck with a rack as broad as that of a moose. Its nose pointed our direction, then to the forest, and back again. As if directing the show. Finally, it stared toward the village, dust cloud stirring over it as the tribe scrambled to safety.

The old shaman and her flabby bodyguard trotted next to me. She pointed toward the animal and said, "Gluskabe likes to wear the disguise of a stag. He sends us a good omen."

A line of bright, multicolored, round shields stepped from beneath the shadow of the trees. The rising sun glinted from the polished hub of one in the middle. *Halfdan.* A few steps into the meadow, the line halted. Fifty Mi'kmaq warriors scrambled from the forest and joined them, wielding spears and bows just as they had on the streamside trail. Their faces colored as radiantly as the Vestmen shields. Sweat on shiny brown skin shimmered golden as they stared into the sun behind us and formed a rank extending the Vestmen's neat line. No ash-colored soot this time. The field fell silent. A snort like a bull, and the buck pawed the ground.

If you are Gluskabe, we could use another pack of wolves right about now.

Red-Stripe whooped, and his braves formed a line that extended down to the river. A hundred at least. We outnumbered them two to one. Certainly this wasn't all the Mi'kmaq warriors, even after the battle at the river. Tryfing and the Vestmen lined up on either side of me. Curly stood to my right again. I hadn't had the chance to ask what had driven them to mutiny against our leader. But now it made no difference. Sides had been chosen. Their shields were raised and faces hardened. I needed not doubt their loyalty.

Halfdan stomped toward us and stopped fifty yards from our position, outside the range of arrows. In his attempt to conceal a limp, his gait appeared as if one leg were shorter than the other. The poison arrow from Kiona's little brother would still be very painful without the aid of Spear-Face's medicine.

"You're a traitor, Matok!" He pointed a long sword across our rank. "All of you! Surrender Astrid and I'll consider it an act of loyalty. I'll forget your rebellion. That of your entire band."

The leather-clad Vestmen on either side of me stood silent, shields raised. The tip of Tryfing's long gray sword shook, as if eager for blood. The man next to him dug the toe of his boot into the earth, like a runner positioning his feet in the chocks. The heat in my chest began to spread down my arms. The buck snorted and swung its rack. Ranks had been drawn, in this world and, it seemed, in the realm of spirit.

Decisions had been made.

"I can't do that," I shouted back.

His tone hardened. "We will bring her back together. We will both be heroes!"

Why was he negotiating? His speech was stern, but the Mi'kmaq hadn't committed all their warriors. This was a bluff. They had left many of their number to guard the village, no doubt. Halfdan and his troop couldn't attack. "She is wed now. Her family is among the Indians. Go home and tell my father."

He spit the words. "She wed no Skræling! They are ignorant, skin-wearing beasts."

I glanced at Tryfing. He shook his head. "There is no way of avoiding this."

"They aren't going to attack," I murmured. "They're outnumbered."

Red-Stripe stood next to me, club in hand, spear cocked. The tiny shaman sniffed the air beside him, beaming, as if enjoying a fragrant rose. Spear-Face held his walking stick before him like a knight's lance, pointed tip carving small arcs in the breeze. His nose wrinkled, but a playful expression remained in his gaze. Smiles must've meant something different in this culture. Or he was perpetually happy, even in life-or-death battles.

I turned to Red-Stripe. "He will not negotiate. He demands my sister, the red-haired girl. Are you certain your braves want to defend her?"

Red-Stripe curled his lip and growled, "Our chief protects her. So do we. Why are we talking? There is no bartering with the enemy."

The old woman held out her hand, and the fat guard standing before her passed her a club. She gripped it like a bat. "Do not be double-minded, Vestman."

Somehow I'd become the spokesman for a tribe to which I didn't belong. The same tribe now standing beside me in battle line. One protecting us as if their own. The breeze lifted the hair from my shoulders and cooled my cheeks. The old woman was right. There was no avoiding this battle. No negotiating with such an enemy. I shouted into the rising wind, "Astrid has made her choice. And we stand beside her."

* * * *

Kiona kicked and bucked as Crooked-Eye hauled her toward the meadow. Her throat burned, and she choked on dust as she strained and pulled. Her minder slapped her on the side of the head, only the most recent of many such blows. The screams of women and children faded, their ruckus drown by the rising ring in her ears. The pain between her temples ebbed and her legs buckled, refusing her commands to resist.

Crooked-Eye tightened his hold and leaned forward, straining to keep her moving.

She stumbled, but managed to stay upright. Dust settled upon her sweating legs, making them ashen. Like the dream she'd had before the migration where she'd smeared soot over her body and joined the braves preparing for an attack. But this was real, no nightmare, she assured herself, struggling to maintain consciousness.

The air cooled as a breeze picked up, and the pain in her head began to rise again. An unfortunate effect of her awareness returning. Her ear throbbed, full of fluid. Blood dripped from the corner of her mouth. She hadn't passed out, but almost, she suspected. Astrid knelt in the grass next to her, face flush, lips bloodied. Matok stood in the middle of the meadow, gripping Huritt's arm. Why weren't they trying to rescue them?

She glanced about and Crooked-Eye jammed an elbow into her temple. But not before she saw the reason for Matok's hesitation.

More than a hundred Mi'kmaq warriors stood behind them. They must've divided their forces, snuck around the meadow last night, and attacked the village from both directions. Now, Matok and the Abenaki stood in the middle of the field, surrounded. She and Astrid would be used as a trade, to force Matok to surrender. Her tongue soured, glancing the horrible white-bearded Vestman on the far side. He laughed. "You had your chance, Matok. I admire your courage. Too bad your death will bring shame to your father. But his wheat has dropped its seed. He stands now, nothing but straw. He will yield."

The near line of Mi'kmaq warriors stepped into the meadow until they stood in front of Kiona and Astrid. Crooked-Eye's grasp loosened as he held her wrists with one hand and grasped his spear in the other. He was preparing in case he needed to defend himself during the coming battle. Great Scout gripped Astrid by only one arm. Her head drooped, as if in surrender to fate, but her eyes flashed scorn. Huritt's knife was no longer tucked in her belt. Great Scout must've taken it. But slowly, almost imperceptibly, her arm moved toward the hem of her dress where she'd stashed the child's obsidian blade.

Kiona's eyes throbbed as she glanced to her own belt, where a compact bulge hid her own flint knife. She locked gaze with Astrid and gave a slight nod.

No one would use them as barter.

Chapter 34 – A Choice Made

Red-Stripe shouted to me over the din of whoops and battle cries. I would lead our Vestmen and three dozen Abenaki warriors in an attack against Halfdan. He would take the rest and rush the enemy at the village. With them occupied, the women and children might have a chance of escape. Both our assaults would now be against superior numbers, but whichever side began to falter, the other would come to its aid.

A dozen warriors on either side of our rank crowded close. "Don't get near their shield wall!" I yelled. "Defeat the Mi'kmaq braves, then attack the Vestmen from behind."

The wrinkled shaman nudged me with her club. "To free your sister, one more must die."

Yeah. Heard that a few times already. And something about a red sea urchin, probably. "I'm not concerned with meeting that quota today. Just do your part by getting whatever spirits you can on our side."

She faced the stag at the edge of the forest. "These spirits lined up for battle long ago. This is an ancient fight."

It had been a while since I'd seen Gabby. Now, I'd welcome her advice, no matter how vague.

The shaman nudged Huritt, his gaze daggers sinking into his father who now gripped Astrid's arm. "You have chosen, young warrior?"

He nodded. "I have." A tear streaked his cheek, though his face flushed with anger.

Red-Stripe raised his spear, and a cry as from angry gulls rose among his braves. Apparently, he wasn't going to let the morning wear on.

The old woman gripped my arm. "Wait for your bride. She will show you when to strike."

* * * *

Kiona chanced another glance at Astrid. The girl's hand had made it to her dress seam. Fingers probed inside the hidden pocket. They stilled, and she smiled.

Kiona spun away from Crooked-Eye. His grip tightened instinctively, but she wrenched an arm free. She continued her turn, twisting toward him, yanked the knife from her belt, and plunged it into his neck. Blood spewed from the deep gash. Still, he raised his spear and cocked his arm. But his eyes rolled and the javelin dropped, gouging the ground at her feet.

She turned just as Astrid wrenched her arm free of Great Scout's grasp. He gripped his side, blood oozing between fingers. Several braves turned at the sound of the scuffle behind them. Kiona yanked the spear from the ground, grabbed Astrid's hand, and the two shot away.

* * * *

I stared with wild amazement as Kiona stabbed her guard through the neck. Before I could raise an arm to point at the scene, Astrid wounded her minder as well and the two disappeared between huts. A whistle sounded, a great shout arose from our rank, and our lines dashed apart.

Tryfing bolted, surprisingly quick on his feet. He wielded the same wild-eyed rage I'd seen on the streamside trail. He led our advance, and even I strained to keep up. The ground thudded beneath our feet. Firm. Not watery as the Mi'kmaq meadow had been.

Halfdan turned and sprinted back to his line when we broke from the center of the meadow. They overlapped shields, hunched low, and raised a growl like a caged animal. The same impenetrable wall that had saved us from the earlier Indian attack. The same tribe with whom they were now allied.

The rising sun burned the back of my neck as I sprinted toward him. How was I going to fight such a man? I held no sword or axe. Only a spear and a club on my belt. I was taller, but he stronger. His only weakness his wild rage. How could I use that against him? Taunt him, a seasoned fighter, into making a foolish move?

As we neared, Tryfing leaned against his shield and slammed into his waiting opponent, sending him sprawling onto the ground. The air thundered with grunts and wooden crashes as our lines collided. Yet, instead of shooting through their line and pouncing upon his disabled opponent, he turned and doubled up against another.

I leaned into my shield as well, scenting the leathery balm of its strap, and continued toward Halfdan. Our shields met, my neck snapped, and I crumpled to a knee, dazed. As if I'd struck an oak.

Halfdan stepped forward and thrust his blade over my shield, but Curly jabbed at his side, persuading him back into his rank.

The integrity of our own line. *That's* why Tryfing hadn't pursued his victim. He wouldn't leave other men exposed.

I stepped out of Halfdan's reach and gripped the spear near its end. He turned to strike Curly, but a jab at his shoulder sent his arm back behind the safety of his shield. I thrust at his feet, but he danced away. Attacks over his rim gained nothing. If only I had someone behind me, to strike low while I went high.

He growled. "What is this coward's method you use? Fight me at the line, like a Vestman, so you can die with honor!"

If I could just wound his leg, he'd be slower, easier to take. I inched forward, low, and thrust at his feet again. He stretched his weapon overtop. I ducked the strike and backed away.

"You fight like a deserter! Valkyries will sneer at your cold corpse as they fly over this field."

Whoops and shouts of Indians neared as our flanks began to curl toward us. Not good. One of our braves crawled away, arrow in his belly. Only a few others lay fallen, however. Still, the Mi'kmaq were driving the Abenaki back. If they collapsed upon us, we'd be surrounded. The enemy's center needed to yield, and Halfdan held that ground.

His white beard twisted in the rising breeze below the thong that bound it. The now-familiar heat in my arms spread to my hands. Time to see what the real Matok was capable of. To let him out again. I stepped forward, shield high, and feigned another low strike. He dropped his shield and danced away from the thrust. I reached long arms over their ranks and plunged the spear down. It sank into something soft then snapped. Pulling it back, I noted a foot had been broken from the weapon. A flash of steel near my feet and I jumped back. But his blade caught my calf, slicing through my trousers where Kiona had stitched. Warm blood dripped down my ankle.

A hollow *Crack-thunk!* and Tryfing split the skull of his opponent as he scrambled to mend their line. One-Eye whooped like an Indian at the sound. Spear-Face scrambled about behind the Abenaki lines like a taunting jackal, jabbing his long walking stick at the tender belly of Mi'kmaq warriors as they were otherwise occupied.

Halfdan gazed down his rank. Had I wounded him at all, or had he just grabbed and snapped my weapon? Ignoring the pain in my leg, I hopped up and pressed against his shield again, but he smacked mine like a battering ram and sent me flying, though I managed to maintain my footing. His thrusts and slashes were compact, fluid, and powerful. If he weren't trying to kill me, I might have been impressed. I couldn't win at his game. And his only weakness was anger...

I stepped back and danced about, jabbing at his head and feet. I'd never wound him this way, but he cursed and screamed. Slowly, he inched forward.

That's it. I'm weak. Come to me.

The clang of steel and grunts of men swelled from our line like the churn of a hailstorm, while hoots of Indians and thuds of wood sounded behind us. Our flanks had curled. The middle had to yield. I hadn't much time.

"You know why Astrid doesn't want to marry you, Halfdan?" I shouted so all could hear.

He snarled.

"The women of the clan warned her of you. They'd rather wed a goat instead of enduring your disappoints."

"Fight me like a man, Matok!"

"Impotent pig! Fight is the only thing you can do as a man. What Vestman would have a chieftain that can't pleasure a woman?"

His face flamed crimson. He raised his weapon and charged, roaring. His blow sprawled me to the ground. His sword sliced down, but I rolled and it sunk into the dry earth. I hopped to my feet. In a blur, a warrior rushed him from his flank, his spear sinking into Halfdan's ribs. He spun and yanked out the weapon. Too close for his long sword, he swung at the new attacker, crashing his massive fist into his head. The Indian fell to his feet and...it was Kiona!

I jabbed at Halfdan's other side with my blunted spear, but he deflected the strike. He withdrew a step and slashed at Kiona. It would mean my death, but I knelt beside her and raised my shield. The blow tore off my handle and sent the round disc rolling across the grass. The edge of his blade sank into my arm and crunched bone. He raised the weapon for another strike. Kiona rolled forward as the blow sliced down. Steel sank through my chest and shattered my shoulder as he thrust his blade through my body, pinning me to the earth. Pain shot through my spine, down to my toes, then disappeared in a flash. Halfdan leaned over me and gazed into my eyes, his veins on his neck like roots of a tree. Spittle flew from his lips as he shouted, "Die, coward! Without sword or shield in your hand."

His eyes closed and his face twisted, but not from rage. Pain. He dropped his shield and stared beneath his legs. Kiona crouched there, arm raised into his crotch, blood flowing down her arm, dripping from the antler horn of her knife. The old shaman flashed into view, cracked him on the skull with a club, and he fell back. In a rush, Spear-Face plunged his walking stick into his belly. The opposing Vestmen behind him stared in awe and stepped back. Tryfing felled another with a quick thrust. A whistle floated from the woods, ending in a low note, and the Mi'kmaq line began to disintegrate into retreat.

I tried to sit, but the steel wouldn't allow it. Kiona knelt over me, black hair falling upon my face, scented of mint and honeysuckle. The rising sun still flecked her dark eyes in gold. I raised an arm, the only one that still worked, and brushed her soft, high cheeks, streaking them with blood. She grasped the handle off the sword to yank it out, but her aunt steadied her hand. Kiona placed her lips to my ear. Her breath was hot upon my skin. "I'm sorry, Matok. I'm so sorry."

Her words floated in the rising breeze. It was a chill wind, so cold it promised snow. "Don't be," I managed, my hand falling to her neck, stroking her soft skin. "I made my choice, and it was you."

Chapter 35 – Maple Sap

Cold air gripped my throat and I coughed. I closed my eyes, but still a blinding whiteness filled them.

I was dying.

The pain in my shoulder had already fled, and now even the pricking of the grass against my neck disappeared. My senses were slipping away, one by one. Still, the mint and honeysuckle of Kiona's hair filled me.

One last glance. I could manage that. I cracked an eye. An afternoon sunset blazed over the sea through dock pilings.

What?

I blinked open the other. Gray-blue water disappeared into a horizon of the same color. The transition was so seamless, it was impossible to distinguish where one stopped and the other began. I leaned against a pole, panting, short of breath. I pulled my hand away, palm coated with sticky black creosote from the ancient wood. I stood below our cottage dock near shoreline, in a frosty slurry of white-and-ice-blue hailstones that covered the entire beach. My feet ached with the cold. I stumbled from below the wharf. A clear, virgin sky to the north blazed warm and bright, while the flashing fury of a retreating storm masked the south.

A fat, inch-long splinter stuck from my thumb. Must've gotten it from leaning on the rough piling. I yanked it out and squeezed to ensure that the wound bled well, cleansing it. Satisfied, I shook my hand, spraying crimson droplets at my feet. A large one splattered a green sea urchin, floating in the white soup. It must've been killed by the hail. Several more drops fell from my thumb, oozing between the creature's needles until it was stained with the warm liquid. Then I stared. *Don't stop until you've found the red sea urchin,* Gabby had said.

Red, from my own blood.

I patted my shoulder, where Halfdan's sword had just pierced me. No wound. And my hand was no longer mangled. My little finger held all its joints. I gingerly placed a palm down the back of my cargo shorts, and even the gouges from the demon-cat had disappeared.

Could it have all been... *No!* There was no way I imagined it. I must still be there, dying on the battlefield, and *this* hail-churned beach my final dream. I closed my eyes, willing to return, for one last glimpse.

I sneezed and my eyes peeked open. Still in Maine, feet numb in ice water.

Oh well.

I lifted the hem of my blue T-shirt to wipe my running nose, and my eyes ached as I studied a neat red ridge that ran from belly button down my side, disappearing near the top of my hip. Kiona's blade. But then I smiled. The only scar that remained was from her.

I picked my way through the ice toward a sea ladder nailed to the top of the weathered structure. The wet wood was slick, but I shot up its length, my feet solid beneath me. Three inches of hail coated the deck. I stared at the horizon, hoping for a distant sail. None appeared. An offshore breeze picked up, and I shivered in the cold.

I made my way back toward the dune, its green-and-brown salt grasses beaten down, but tufts still waving in the breeze. Like the Abenaki meadow. The weathered-gray cedar roof on the cottage was pocked and scarred black from the storm. I picked my way up the trail, carefully placing each step, as if the ground might disappear.

Wait, Nikki had been outside with me at the approach of the storm. I needed to make sure she was OK.

"Michael?" A soft, familiar voice called from the south, the direction of the storm. But not Nikki. Who?

I turned and headed back to the dock. A girl trotted up the beach on long legs, tight calves. A runner. She wore denim shorts and a fire-red spaghetti-strapped swim top. "Christine!" I called and waved.

She slipped, but managed to stay on her feet. Her every step seemed precarious, as if she was unable to see her footing beneath the hailstones. Her arms circled as she struggled to maintain balance.

I grabbed the railing and jumped over the side, landing in the shallow slurry with a splash. I stayed upright, but my ankles stung. I was going to have to remember I was no longer in Matok's body.

I jogged to her and steadied her elbow.

She held her hand over her mouth. "You just jumped off that dock."

I glanced back at it. "Yeah. I didn't want you to fall."

212

"Michael, that's fifteen feet in the air. At least."

I waved a hand. "You OK, though?"

"Me? I came out here to see if *you* were still alive. You were sitting on the end of your pier when the storm came. I saw you take shelter below it, so I didn't worry too much. But then I couldn't see you with all that hail dropping. And afterward, you weren't there anymore. I thought I was going to find you unconscious or drowned in this ice water." She shoved my chest. "You shouldn't scare people like that! I was worried you were dead."

So, all those days with the Vikings, with Kiona, had been mere minutes here.

The sun glinted off Christine's brown eyes, flecking them with gold. *Really?* I reached a hand to brush her high cheeks, but pulled back. "I'm sorry, I'm not trying to be creepy, but you've got some Mi'kmaq, or maybe Abenaki in your family, don't you?"

She raised an eyebrow. "How can you tell? Most people down here don't even know about those tribes anymore."

Why not try? I reached and gently brushed her cheek with the back of my fingers. She didn't recoil. "Some of your facial features. Stunning, really, now that I see you. Up close, I mean."

She flushed. "Most look at my blonde hair and say, *Scandinavian.* I may be pale skinned, but we've got Odawa, Penobscot, Abenaki, and even Mi'kmaq in the woodpile." She covered her mouth and chuckled. "And my grandmother is crazy. She came down with us again this year. You remember her at all? As the storm rose, she started chanting. She thinks she's a witch doctor."

I tried, but only distantly recalled seeing a small, old woman with them one year a long time ago. "Really? A shaman?"

She straightened her back. "Crazy as a loon, but still kicking. Almost a hundred years old. She's scary. How do you know about Algonquian tribes?"

I shrugged. "I don't, really." My fingers rubbed the scar on my belly. "But I've spoken with a few Native Americans before. I'd love to talk with your grandmother. I'll bet I wouldn't think she was crazy at all."

Nikki called from behind us, high on the dune. "Hey brother, you OK down there?" Sun shone on her black curly hair as it danced along with the grass stalks around her.

I blew a sigh. Thank goodness she was OK. "Yeah. OK sis! What about up there?"

213

A coy smile creased her lips. The look she gave before she'd say something crude, like she had back before the storm when Christine had waved to me. "We're all OK. Looks like you might find something in that barrel after all. Let me know if you need help figuring it out."

Christine scrunched her nose. "What barrel?"

I stared at her, careful not to let my eyes wander. But her swimsuit didn't make it easy. "An inside joke. But only *she* thinks it's funny."

Nikki pointed toward the cottage and flicked her curly mop to one side of her head. A gesture Gabby used to do. "Love you, brother. I'm headed back up."

Christine gripped my arm. "She's so cute. You're lucky she still likes you. Most girls think older brothers are creepy."

I smirked. "Yeah. Well, sisters can be difficult."

Gabby certainly had been. Had she called me back to the Vestmen's world, toying with me, or had she been its prisoner as well? Would she show up as a spirit in this one?

To free your sister, one more must die.

And I had perished back there. Right on the battlefield. I'd freed my Vestman sister, Astrid, from the Mi'kmaq. So, the crazy Abenaki shaman's prophecy had been fulfilled. Just not in the way I'd thought it would. And Astrid would have a new home and family among them. Even Kiona had escaped her mother's evil chains and been reunited with the other side of her family, along with Spear-Face. What had Gabby said beneath that huge chestnut when I'd asked her why all this was happening to me?

Life isn't about you. Maybe none of this is about you at all.

Maybe it had been for them. My cheeks warmed at the thought. But I'd benefited as well. I'd left this world, chained by my past, as if it defined me. Fearful. Now, I'd fought in a shield wall, spilled the blood of warriors, and even killed a demon with my bare hands. Plenty of my own blood had been shed as well. Sure, I'd lost that life, but gained another. *Fear is so illogical,* I thought. *It's selfish. Narcissistic, even. Self-defeating.*

Christine lifted a foot and shook the slush from the laces of blue Nike running shoes. She slipped, but her fingers dug into my arm and she pulled herself back up. She smiled, and for a second, her eyebrows seemed to dance on her forehead. But then the expression was gone.

To free your sister, one more must die.

I'd died for Kiona. And Astrid. For family, and friends. And now, standing on a crystal-white beach, sun warming my neck, crisp salt air rolling from the ocean, with Christine clutching my arm, I was reborn. Fearless. Ironic, how giving my life in one world meant gaining it in another.

High on the dune, Nikki puckered, blew me a kiss, and then turned up the trail toward our cottage. I stared after her. It had been Gabby's exact gesture before the attack of the demon-cat. The wind shifted, and a warm breeze traveled down the bank, scented of mint and honeysuckle. No, not honeysuckle. Milder than that. *Maple sap!*

My feet ached, the chill of the water suddenly gripping them. My eyes watered as a sharp pain stabbed into my forehead. The scar across my belly burned, as if reopening. A seagull called from above us. Or had it been Gabby's laugh?

Christine placed fingers under my chin and turned my head toward her. "What's wrong? You look worried all of a sudden."

My gaze flitted across the dunes, down the twinkling icy beach, and out to the frothy sea. The sweet maple perfume filled me. "Let's get you inside. It's cold now, out here in the open."

Author's Note

Much research was conducted in the scripting of this novel, and I made every attempt at a plausible story that honored both the Vikings and the Algonquin peoples within the confines of historical context.

The Vikings of these regions were called Vestmen (West-men) by their Norse-Gael counterparts, though most spellings use Vestmenn. These Vikings did, in fact, land upon North America. Their encounters with the native peoples are documented in the *Saga of Erik the Red* and the *Saga of the Greenlanders*. According to NPR.org, "The Vikings' early expeditions to North America are well documented and accepted as historical fact by most scholars. Around the year 1000 A.D., the Viking explorer Leif Erikson, son of Erik the Red, sailed to a place he called 'Vinland,' in what is now the Canadian province of Newfoundland. Erikson and his crew didn't stay long — only a few years — before returning to Greenland. Relations with native North Americans were described as hostile." This backdrop made the capture of Astrid conceivable, as was their venture south to Maine for her rescue. Tryfing's explanation of Matok's family tree in chapter 6 includes Thorvald Asvaldsson, Erik the Red, and Leif Erikson in our hero's lineage.

Christianity had reached the Vikings by this time. In fact, Leif Erikson is purported to have landed upon Vineland when blown off course while bringing Christianity to Greenland. Old ways don't die easily, hence the description of both Christian and pagan themes within the local Viking culture.

Much about the Algonquin tribes of these regions has been lost to history and I took liberty expounding upon what is known. The Abenaki and the Mi'kmaq are two tribes that lived in the area between Newfoundland and Maine. Most accounts paint the Mi'kmaq as a more warlike tribe, so they became the adversary in this story. All purportedly believed in The Three Truths as presented. Gluskabe and Malsumis are characters in their stories and belief systems, along with Tabaldak as creator. Many other myths and characters were used in this work and I hope to have honored them. The story of Gluskabe told to Astrid by Kiona, however, was purely from my imagination.

Shamanism is believed to have been practiced by these Algonquin tribes. When developing both shamans, I borrowed heavily from an interview with a South American shaman from a previously unreached tribe. Missionaries had visited his area and this dear man had become a Christian. His interview provided invaluable insight into the life and mind of a shaman and I wove many of his experiences into this work.

I hope this novel enabled you to see beyond the first story and enjoy the second, the one the book is truly about. If so, it will come as no surprise that I am a Christian myself, hence the heavy use of Christian themes and metaphor. Missed them? They are everywhere, blooming just beneath the surface. If you want to learn more about Christianity, pick up a Bible and begin. It is the most fantastic literature ever written and can introduce you to a personal relationship with God himself. I suggest starting in the book of John, about three quarters of the way through, and attending a local church that teaches from the Bible.

The cover image of the ship *Islendingur* is particularly fitting for this novel since that vessel voyaged from Iceland to North America, following much the same route as the Vestmen in our story. Detail on the *Islendingur* and its story is available on Wikipedia.

Thanks again for reading. God bless!

We hope you enjoyed *Vestmen's Gale*. Don't miss the next exciting thriller by David McCaleb:

Son of Blackbeard

Read on to enjoy an exciting preview...

Son of Blackbeard

DAVID McCALEB

Chapter 1 – Right Hand

"Maybe it's an old coffin," I said, kicking a busted conch down the beach before of us. The hard sand chirped beneath our heels with each step. My gaze followed the white shell as it skipped across the crusty surface. It traveled straight, exactly where I'd aimed, pointed to the grassy marsh a hundred yards ahead.

Maddi jogged to catch up. "You never answered my question. What were you doing out here last night?"

I'd tell her soon enough, but for now the whole experience was still dreamlike. *Huh, I hadn't thought of that.* Could it have been a dream? No, my jean legs were still damp this morning from landing the skiff on the beach. The experience had been real.

"If it's a coffin, it could've floated out," she continued, never one to let silence linger. "Granddad told me they found lots of them drifting on the water downtown after the Ash Wednesday Storm decades ago." She tucked her hands into pockets on the front of her pink sweatshirt, the same designer brand all the sophomores wore. The hood was pulled up so it shielded her from the stiff wind at our backs. Fine brown hair blew in the breeze and whipped her cheek. She brushed the tangle behind her ear and the tip flapped against thin lips. She squinted at the low morning sun and a paint of freckles shimmered below her eyes, bridging her nose. And it wasn't even summer yet. Each year, by the time school started, the specks would grow so densely her complexion appeared bronze, her only natural color remaining as flecks of white.

Dwayne replied softly, as if afraid she'd take offense. "A floating coffin wouldn't burry itself again. Someone would've found it by now." He took a few steps and kicked the same conch with a *chirp!*, his feet shod in black waterman's boots, original Muckers. Expensive. Not the Chinese-made knockoffs. But Dwayne was a come-here. His family had just sold their apartment in Manhattan and bought a real house on the west side of Chincoteague. His dad was the new doctor at the Health Center, so that's how he could afford the premium treads. Though until last month if you'd asked him what muckers were, he'd probably have told you they were small, furry, and in the rodent family. Now he'd grown a curly blond beard, a camo jacket covered his thin frame, white paint dotted his jeans, and as soon as he got his license he'd purchased an old F150, pretending like he'd been born here. But he lacked the mightier-than-thou attitude of most northerners, so he wasn't as annoying as some made him to be.

Dwayne kicked the conch again, busting it in two. "And we're a couple miles from downtown. It would've had to be a hurricane to move a coffin all the way out here."

Half the shell crunched under my heel, my own feet shod in white no-name waterman's boots from Walmart. But mine knew what work meant. As young as I could remember, my father had me on a boat all summer till my short black hair bleached to brown and my skin tanned to walnut. We clammed or crabbed or whatever other hustle dad had going to make ends meet. When his carpentry business finally demanded all his time, I couldn't tear myself from the draw of the ocean and continued with other watermen. I spent most of the hottest months standing in marsh and tide, up to my shoulders sometimes, lifting fifty-pound oyster cages over my head to others on a barge. My football coach certainly liked the results. I was the strongest senior on the team. But now I'd just turned down a full-ride scholarship to Virginia Tech because Mom needed help with the bills since Dad had been killed.

My gut knotted when I thought back to the final days of last summer. I'd trudged into Dad's workshop around lunchtime and found him bled out on the floor. He'd cut off his right hand with the radial arm saw. A leather belt loosely encircled his wrist where he'd tried to cinch a tourniquet. Blood still dripped from the nub like the neck of a dear when hung for skinning. I searched my mind, but still couldn't see his face as he lay there. Yet I recalled vividly the omnipresent crimson spray, sprinkling all his tools, and the mobile phone on the floor next to his head. They never found his hand. Chief said a stray dog must've carried it off, though I swore the door had been shut.

"What you thinking about?" Maddi asked, her raised eyebrow indicating she knew exactly where my mind had wandered.

What had Dwayne been talking about? Oh, the storm. "Yeah. My grandad told me it was the worst nor-easter ever, back in 1962. Lasted days. All downtown was under water. Coffins are sealed, so they're like skiffs. Lots of them popped out of the ground and were floating around. Old timers still get scared talking about it."

Grandma says we had a foot of water in the living room, and cats floating in the crab steamer."

Dwayne pulled off his black knit cap and ran fingers through neck-length, coarse blond hair. "Still, probably just a piece of a dock."

Dwayne didn't know a dock from a bulkhead. I turned my head and spit into the white surf washing beside us. A gust lifted sand, stinging my cheek, but sunglasses shielded my eyes. "No. The wood is thinner than that. And tight-grained. Plus, piers don't use copper straps. This thing has hammered metal around the edge."

Maddi jogged again, her short legs struggling to maintain pace with my long strides. "I thought you said you didn't dig it up."

"I only dug a little. Just the corner was sticking out. I tried to lift it, but it didn't budge."

"So, you made us come out here to help you salvage some old, washed-up crate?" she asked.

I stopped at the edge of the surf and white foam swirled around my feet. "I didn't *make* you guys do anything. Dwayne messaged me early this morning, asking me what I was doing. So I told him. A few minutes later, he's on my doorstep, then sitting across from me at breakfast. You were in your pajamas picking up the paper when we were walking down to the marina. Next thing I know, you hopped on the bow as I was priming the motor. So, I didn't *make* you do anything." I shoved her shoulder playfully, but she stepped back into a rut and fell to her butt on the sand.

Her eyes squinted to slits and she pursed her lips. In a flash, she was on her feet and swinging. Still couldn't hold her temper. I backed away and raised my hands in surrender. "I'm sorry. I didn't mean to." But her punches came fast and strong. She'd landed several when Dwayne grabbed her from behind.

"Let me go!" Her legs kicked as he lifted her from the sand.

I leaned on my knees and panted, air seemingly in short supply despite the strong breeze.

Dwayne struggled to maintain control. "I'll let you go if you calm down!"

Her legs ceased flailing and he spread his arms, dropping her. She stood next to me and bent over. Her eyes were wet. "I'm...I'm sorry. You OK?"

I could never get angry at Maddi, much less strike her. I drew in a timid breath, my gut aching as if it had forgotten how. "Yeah, but only cuz you hit like a girl."

The corner of her mouth curled. A punch came from her hip, no telegraph, and caught me just below the bellybutton. But I knew it'd be coming. Dwayne grabbed her arm and she spun. Glancing her expression, he backed away like a puppy from a tomcat.

I lifted a palm toward him, the other covering my gut. "It's OK. Just an inside joke." Maddi stepped next to me and slipped an arm around my waist. I leaned on her shoulder and we continued toward the marsh.

Dwayne followed a few steps behind, then another conch shot past us with a *chirp!* "You guys are weird."

I stepped gingerly, my toes tingling. "Maddi's the sister I'm glad I never had."

She sniggered but I resisted the urge, my gut still burning. The joke had been on me, a few years ago now. Maddi's mom had run off with a farm equipment salesman down the county. Maddi had just gotten back from visiting her "new family" over Christmas and she'd been saying how she was so betrayed and just wanted to hit someone. At the time, she was only twelve and thin as a cattail, so I'd said she could get it out of her system and hit me. She'd thrown a half-hearted punch to which I'd commented, "You hit like a girl." Since then, she'd gotten much better.

Maddi squinted up. "It could be a piece of an old boat. There were lots of wrecks here, and the islands are always shifting. There was a sloop from the 1800's just uncovered by a storm down in the Outer Banks."

I peered along the tan strip of beach ahead, dotted with brown seaweed clumps flapping in the breeze. It was a sandy peninsula a few hundred yards wide, forming Tom's cove behind it. At its tip was Assateague Island Hook, a small, marshy flat, the far side of which was our destination. Now recovered, I stood upright as we walked three abreast past the old Coast Guard Station sentried near the middle of the flat. It was a proud two-story whitewashed home, still standing plumb despite the fact it was retired before I was even born, with a small, enclosed watch tower closer to the beach. I stepped into a wide tire rut and followed its track. The bottom was packed firm, so it must've only been from early yesterday. Lots of anglers enjoyed this spot, though none were out this hour of the morning. Which is why I'd left at working-man's hours to get here. I didn't want anyone else to see what I'd begun to uncover.

We marched on, following tire tracks when we could, stammering across ridges like drunks when they ended.

On the far side of the Hook, Madi lifted her head, freed her hands from pockets, and started to run. She called back, waving an arm. "I see it! I'll race you there."

I glanced at Dwayne and we took off in a sprint, though our boots checked our pace to a lethargic slog. Maddi beat us.

We stopped next to the hole, which opened a yard across and shallow. The anxious stab in my side receded at this further confirmation that I hadn't been dreaming. The sand below the surface had been coarse, wet, and packed hard, so last night I couldn't dig deeper without tools. Still, I'd built up a mound around the site, like a large berm encircling a sandcastle. From the center protruded the wooden corner. It was lighter in color than I remembered, though the sun had been well set when I'd tripped upon it in the dark.

"You did all this by yourself?" Maddi asked. She pointed to ragged cuts in the bottom of the hole. "What are those?"

I grabbed a yard-long driftwood branch from the mound, the shaft straight as a spear. "I tried to loosen it up this. Didn't work. So after a bit I came home."

What I thought had been copper straps now seemed brown with corrosion instead of green. I flicked open my Spyderco and, using the point, scraped the bands. Fresh gold-colored metal shone back. "Brass," I said, and pondered whether that meant it wasn't as old as I thought it was. I slid the blade across the wood, but it barely scratched it. "Locust," I murmured.

Dwayne hopped down into the other side of the shallow pit. His lip curled again. If he was going to try to look like a native, he needed to lose his perpetual *I don't get it* expression. "Locust?"

I snapped the knife shut. "Yeah. Difficult to work, but it doesn't rot. Only gets harder with age. You know those fence posts leading down to the water on the west side of the marina? They're left over from when Big Timmy Thornton grazed his ponies out there."

Dwayne shrugged.

Maddi squatted and scraped the sand with fingernails. "Grandpa says Big Timmy was a famous preacher during prohibition. All the locals know stories about him. Michael's just saying those posts have been there a while."

A gust blasted across the Hook and the old Coast Guard watch tower gave a metallic shudder. Though it was almost a thousand yards away, it still seemed to peer down at us. I glanced across the mouth of the creek to the launch pad at Wallops Island. The water tower there soared twice as tall as any rocket that had ever stood next to it. And though it was at least three miles away, it too seemed to study us. I shrugged off a chill, pulled two garden trowels from my back pocket, and passed one to Maddi.

As we scraped away the moist, brown sand, a box took shape, smaller than I'd suspected. Once I found the bottom edge, the chest pried loose with little effort. It was the size of a backpack, but weighted as if filled with water. A few of the boards were cracked, but the brass banding seemed to hold. A lid secured the top with a latch and, instead of a lock, a pocked and rusted iron loop hung like an earring, leaving a blood-red stain on the container's surface. The wood of the rim below the lid was dark, as if rot had finally started to set in where most vulnerable. Maddi grabbed the other side and we hoisted it atop one of the berms. Scarlet water bled from one corner, spilling onto the sand.

"I was secretly hoping it'd be a treasure chest, but it don't look like one," Dwayne offered.

I inserted the driftwood shaft into the metal ring. "Who knows what one of those look like. This is heavy, but not enough to be holding gold. Plus, people have shot holes in all those ancient treasure stories. This is just a bait chest from an old wreck." With a yank, I pried off the ring. Maddi cracked open the lid and the hinges broke loose as if affixed to a sponge. A few blood worms wriggled inside atop packed, wet sand.

Dwayne grasped a grass stalk and flicked the creatures off, then began to dig with his fingers. "Maybe it's just a few coins, buried."

I grabbed the chest and flipped it upside down, spilling sand, dirt, and scallop shells the size of pennies onto the beach. "Told you. Nothing. Just an old box packed by the wash of the tide." I examined the banding. "Wonder who could tell us how old this thing is."

Dwayne reached down and plucked timidly at a wood shard amongst the refuse, but it didn't move. He tweezed it between fingers and lifted, as if picking up trash from a ditch. Sand fell away. "Crap!" he shouted, threw it down, and jumped back as if it were alive.

I chuckled. "It's just the underside of a horseshoe crab." But, how would one of those have gotten in the box? And where was the rest of it, the shell the size of a dinner plate? I leaned over and stared, but before I could reach for it, Maddi snatched it up.

"It's no horseshoe crab. It's a hand, like the skeleton in bio class." She moved a joint between her fingers. "But, it's not real, or it would fall apart. It feels like plastic. Probably just a Halloween decoration. How'd it get inside an old box?"

The digits were too flat to resemble a piece of a skeleton. If it *was* a plastic prop, it was a poor reproduction. Yet, the scale was correct. Each ribbon-like finger extended several inches but hooked down at the end. A short, fat one must've been the thumb. The wrist piece was thin, fat, and C-shaped, like a bracelet.

Maddi placed it atop her hand. "Maybe it's supposed to fit like a glove." But the fingers were at least a half-inch longer than her own. She tried to bend the bracelet closed to snug her wrist, but it didn't budge. "The plastic is stiff. It's too big for me."

"Try mine." I dropped the driftwood and stretched out my arm, palm up. As soon as it touched my skin, a searing pain shot through my funny bone to my fingertip, like someone had smacked my elbow with a hammer. I screamed and Maddi startled, eyes wide. She tugged on the glove, but it held fast.

In a panic I reached over, shoved fingers below the wrist piece, and pulled. "Get it off!" Liquid pain burned where the device stretched across the pads of my fingers. Slowly, we peeled it back, the effort as if removing the very bones of my hand, but it yielded. Sweat dripped from my lip and I panted in fright and exhaustion.

Maddi slipped an arm about my waist. "You OK?"

"Yeah," I sighed.

She gripped my palm and studied ribbons of red, swollen scar tissue where the glove had been lain, like those left when healed from a surgery. A shot of fear and I glanced at my other hand, still gripping the glove we'd just torn off. Its skin was completely unaffected.

Acknowledgements

As always, my debt of gratitude is immense. Should I name everyone who helped me in some manner with this novel, the list would begin with the Blessed Mother and end with my spouse. Should I fail to mention anyone, please forgive me. My only excuse is that I tend to be a self-absorbed idiot.

Thanks to all the members of the AA writing group, *Author's Anonymous* as I like to refer to us. Your candid and painful critiques are immensely welcome. Thank you to Lenore Hart and David Poyer for leading our motley crew, and your tireless application of writing wisdom. I apologize for my recent absence but look forward to returning to your ranks soon.

Thank you to my wife for not divorcing me. For real. Like most authors, I'd deserve it. Thank you for putting up with my hyper-focused, all consuming, world-will-come-to-an-end-if-I-don't-get-this-finished style of writing. I am aware that often my body is present while my mind is chasing characters through distant forests, often with knives. I'm getting better though. More present. No? Well, thank you all the same. I love you dearly!

Thanks to my daughter, Abigail, for simply being interested. You have no idea how encouraging your questions are. "How is the novel coming?" "Did you figure out how you're going to tie up the loose end about the shaman?" "What's the next chapter about?" Thank you for playing such a huge role in this novel, from brainstorming plot ideas to book cover design. You are an immensely talented young lady. If you ever want to live as a poor, frustrated, hungry artist, you would make an awesome author!

Thanks to Heather Graham. I don't know if you even remember me pulling you aside a year or two ago at Thrillerfest, but I had just finished the Red Ops series, was contemplating starting *Vestmen's Gale*, and changing genres was scarry. "You should write it," you told me. I did. Thank you.

Thanks to April LeHoullier for catching all those sppelling, cApitalization, punctuation. and myriad of other inconsistencies with your copyedit talents.

227

Thank you to Antonio Otto Rabasca for his gracious provision of the photo of the *Islendingur* used in the cover art. A more fitting image could not have been possible.

To my readers, thank you for enjoying this work! Your comments and feedback are incredibly encouraging. Please reach out to me on social media. I'd love to connect. But I warn you ahead of time, I'm really boring in person.

To all, God bless!

David McCaleb
davidmccaleb.com

About the Author

David McCaleb is aging, but in the tradition of all writers he stubbornly sticks with his original author photo in a vain attempt to maintain his youth. This shot shows a less jaded, younger version of the novelist, much easier on the eyes. You should thank him.

He was born on the Eastern Shore of Virginia. Growing up on a farm, he studied the teachings of nature, enjoying hunting and fishing, intermingled with hard labor. One of the last green belts on the East Coast, the Eastern Shore is steeped in creative culture, with which he credits much of his inspiration.

He attended Valley Forge Military College and then was accepted into the United States Air Force Academy. He served in the Air Force as a finance officer, receiving multiple awards acknowledging his skill in helping the government ~~waste money~~ track expenditures. After his military service, he spent time in the corporate world, then started an internet retail business and almost starved, but somehow managed to grow it into a successful enterprise.

He returned to the Eastern Shore where he currently resides with his wife and two children. Though he enjoys drawing, painting, and any project involving the work of hands, his chosen tool is the pen.

davidmccaleb.com

Made in the USA
Middletown, DE
08 March 2021